TINSEL

"You'll be able to watch any movie whenever you want now," she said out of the blue. "There are certain advantages to your new situation. And I think you'll adapt pretty well."

"Huh?"

"I'm not very good at breaking bad news," she commented weirdly, finishing off the last of her drink. Whatever she was driving at, I only cared that she was setting a good example with the martinis. I finished my drink and signaled for the waiter.

"He won't be able to see you," she said.

Now I was becoming irritated. "Look, babe, I put him in *Scream Bunnies on Mystery Island* and used him on the day of the big topless scene. He sure as hell is going to take my order."

If I'd been thinking clearly I would have noticed the unusual touch of her reaching over and taking my arm. Her fingers burned as if they were small bands of hot metal. I yanked my arm away just as she stared into my soul with those big, bright eyes of hers and intoned, "You're dead, Kent . . ."

—from "A Real Babe" by Brad Linaweaver

The Horror Writers Association Presents

Under the Fang (edited by Robert R. McCammon)
Freak Show (edited by F. Paul Wilson)
Deathport (edited by Ramsey Campbell)
Ghosts (edited by Peter Straub)

Published by POCKET BOOKS

The Horror Writers Association Presents

PETER STRAUB'S GHOSTS

Edited by Peter Straub

POCKET **STAR** BOOKS
New York London Toronto Sydney Tokyo Singapore

An *Original* Publication of POCKET BOOKS

A Pocket Star Book published by
POCKET BOOKS, a division of Simon & Schuster Inc.
1230 Avenue of the Americas, New York, NY 10020

ISBN: 0-671-88599-5

First Pocket Books printing April 1995

10 9 8 7 6 5 4 3 2 1

POCKET STAR BOOKS and colophon are registered trademarks of Simon & Schuster Inc.

Cover art by Kirk Reinert

Printed in the U.S.A.

Copyright Notices

Contents

CONTENTS

MOM AND DAD

COLD

OUR WORK

HUNGER: AN INTRODUCTION

Peter Straub

On the bare, sunlit stage the hungers could begin.

—John Ashbery, "Faust"

I HAVE A STURDY FIRST SENTENCE ALL PREPARED, AND AS SOON as I settle down and get used to this reversal of our usual roles I'm going to give you the pleasure. Okay. Here goes. *Considering that sooner or later everybody is going to die, people know surprisingly little about ghosts.* Is that clear? Every person on earth, saint and turd, is going to wind up as a ghost, but not one of them, I mean, of *you,* people, knows the first thing about them. Almost everything written or spoken about the subject is, I'm sorry, absolute junk. It's *disgusting.* I'm speaking from the heart here, I'm laying it on the line—*disgusting.* All it would take to get things right is a little bit of common, everyday, sensible thinking, but sensible thinking is easier to ask for than to get, believe you me.

Now I see that I have already jumped my own gun, because the second sentence I intended to deliver was: *In fact, nothing ever said about ghosts even comes close to the truth.* And the third sentence, after which I am going to scrap my prepared text completely and speak from the heart, is: *A lot of us are really steamed about that.*

For! The most commonly held notion about ghosts, the granddaddy, the notion that parades as grown-up reason cutting right to the heart of things, shakes its head, grins, fixes you in the eye with a steely little glint that asks if you're kidding, and says—Ghosts don't exist.

Wrong.

Sorry, wrong.

Sorry, I know, you'd feel better if you could finally persuade yourself that every account of encounters with beings previously but not presently alive are fictional. Doesn't matter how many people say they've seen the same woman in black walking back and forth in front of the window from which in 1892 the chambermaid Ethel Carroway defenestrated a newborn infant fathered by a seagoing rogue named Captain Starbuck, thousands of people might swear to having personally seen poor Ethel's shade drag itself past that window, it don't, sorry, it doesn't matter, they're all suffering from mass hysteria. They saw the curtain move in a breeze and imagined the rest. *They want you to think they're interesting.* You're too clever to fall for that one. You know what happens to people after they die, and one thing you know for sure is that they don't turn into ghosts. At the moment of death, people either (1) depart this and all other possible spheres, leaving their bodies to depart in a messier, more time-consuming fashion; or (2) leave behind the poor old skinbag as their immortal part flies heavenward, rejoicing, or plummets wailing to eternal torture; or (3) shuffle out of one skinbag, take a few turns around the celestial block, and reincarnate in another but fresher skinbag, thereupon starting all over again. Isn't that more or less the menu? Extinction, moral payback, or rebirth. During my own life, for example, I favored (1), a good clean departure.

Now we come to one of my personal bugaboos, or I could say, anathemas, in memory of someone I am going to have to bring in here sooner or later anyhow, my former employer, Harold McNair, a man with an autodidact's fondness for big words. Mr. McNair once said to me, *Dishonesty is my anathema.* One other time, he used the word *peculation.* Peculation was his anathema, too. Mr. Harold McNair was confident of his personal relationship to his saviour, and as a result he was also pretty sure that what lay ahead of him, after a dignified and painless leavetaking in the big bed on the third floor, was a one-way excursion to paradise. He was, as I say, pretty sure about that. Maybe every now and then the thought came to him that a depraved, greedy, mean-spirited weasel like himself might have some trouble squeaking through the pearly gates, no matter how many Sundays he put on his best suit and strutted over to the church on Abercrombie Road to lip-synch to the hymns and nod over the sermon—yes, maybe Harold McNair had more doubts than he let on. When it came to the biggie, when it came down to what you really have to call the crunch, he did not go peacefully, not at all. How he went was screeching and sweating and cursing, trying to shield his head from the hammer, struggling to get back on his feet, for all the world as though he feared spending eternity as a piece of bacon. And if asked his opinion on the existence of ghosts, this big-shot retail magnate would probably have nodded slowly, sucked his lower lip, pondered mightily, and opined that—

Okay, I never actually *heard* the position of my former employer in re ghosts despite our many, ofttimes tediously lengthy colloquies. Harold McNair spoke to me of many things, of his anathemas, dishonesty, and peculation, of yet more anathemas including the fair sex, any human being under the age of nineteen or twenty, folk of the Hebraic, Afric, or Catholic persuasions, bowel irregularities, customers who take up fifteen minutes of a salesperson's time and then just sashay out without making a purchase, customers—*female* customers—who return undergarments already worn, tight shoes, lumpy potatoes, dogs of any kind, loud music, people from California or New York City, small print, warts and wens, cysts and pustules, longhairs, eggheads, perfessers, pinkos, and people who hold hands in public. He had so much to say on these and the many other topics that excited his disapproval, even indignation, that he never got around to describing his conception of the afterlife, even while sputtering and screeching and rolling his eyes as the hammer sought out the tender places on his tough little noggin. Yet I know what Mr. McNair would have said.

Though ghosts may fail to be nonexistent, they are at least very few in number.

Wrong! This way of thinking disregards the difference between Ghosts Visible, like poor Ethel Carroway, who dropped that baby from a fourth-floor window of the Oliphant Hotel, and Invisible, and disregarding that difference is just exactly like pretending there's no difference between Living People Visible, like Mr. Harold McNair, and Living People Invisible, like myself, in spite of everything the way I was way back when, not to mention most everybody else, when you get right down to it. Most people are about as visible to other people as the headlines on last Monday's newspaper.

I desire with my entire heart to tell you what I'm looking at, I yearn to describe the whole of the visible world as seen from my vantage point beside the big azalea bush on my old enemy's front lawn on Tulip Lane, the spot I head for every day right about this particular time. That would clear up this whole thing about *numbers* right away. But before I get into describing what I can see, I have to get around to introducing myself, since that's the whole point of my being here today.

Francis T. Wardwell is my handle, Frank Wardwell as I was known, and old Frank can feel himself getting all heated up already about the third numbskull idea the run of people have about ghosts, so he better take care of that one right away before he goes any further. The third idea is—Ghosts are ghosts because they're unhappy. Far too many people believe that every wandering spirit out there is atoning for some old heart-stuffed misery, which is why they suppose Ethel drifts past that window now and again.

Ask yourself if anything is ever that simple, even in what *you* call experience. Are all the criminals in jail? Are all the innocent free? And if the price of misery is misery, what is the price of joy? In what coin do you pay for that, laddy, shekels, sweat, or sleepless nights?

Though in every moment of my youthful existence I was sustained by a most glorious secret that was mine alone, I too was acquainted with shekels, sweat, and what the poets call White Nights. No child of luxury, I. Francis Wardwell, Frank to his chums, born to parents on the ragged-most fringe of the lower middle class, was catapulted into corporeality a great distance from the nearest silver spoon. We were urban poor (lower-middle-class-poor, that is), not rural poor, and I feel deeply within myself that a country landscape such as that of which I was deprived would have yielded to my infant self a fund of riches sorely needed. (Mark the first sounding of the hunger-theme, to which we will return betimes.) Is not Nature a friend and tutor to the observant child? Does it not offer a steady flow of stuff like psychic nutrient to the developing boy? Experts say it does, or so I hear, and also that much do I recall from my reading, which was always far, far in advance of my grade level. (I was reading on the *college level* before I was out of short pants.) Old-time poets all said Nature is a better teacher than any other. In my case, blocked off by city walls from the wise friend Nature, I was forced to feed my infant mind on the harsher realities of brick, barbed wire, and peacock-feather oil slicks. That I went as far as I did is testimony to my resilient soul-strength. Forbidden was I to wander 'mongst the heather and cowslips, the foxgloves, purple vetch, tiger lilies, loosestrife, and hawkweed on country lanes; no larks or thrushes had I for company, and we never even heard of nightingales where I came from.

I wandered, when I had that luxury, that is when I wasn't running my guts out to get away from a long-nosed, red-eyed, smirking Boy Teuteburg, through unclean city streets past taverns and boarding houses, and for streaky gold-red sunsets I had neon signs. The air was not, to put it good and plain, fresh. The animals, when not domestic, were rodentine. And from the seventh grade on, at a time when I suffered under the tyranny of a termaganty black-haired witch-thing named Missus Barksdale who hated me because I knew more than she did, I was forced to endure the further injustice of after-school employment. Daily had I to trudge from the humiliations delivered upon my head by the witch-thing, Missus Barfsbottom, humiliations earned only through an inability to conceal entirely the mirth her errors caused in me, from sadistic, unwarranted humiliations delivered upon the head of one of the topmost students ever seen at that crummy school, then to trudge through sordiosities to the place of my employment, Dockweder's Hardware, where I took up my broom and swept, swept, swept.

For shekels! In the sense of measly, greasy coins of low denomination in little number! Earned by my childish sweat, the honest sorrowful perspiration, each salty drop nonaccidentally just exactly like a tear (and that, Missus Doggybreath, is what you call a metaphor, not a methapor, as your warty mustachy mouth misinformed the massed seventh grade of the Daniel Webster State Graded School in the winter of 1928), of a promising, I mean really and truly *promising* lad, an intelligent lad, a lad deserving of the finest this world had to offer in the way of breaks and opportunities, what you might want to call, and I looking back am virtually forced to call, A Shining Boy!

Who day and night had to check over his shoulder for the approach of, who had to strain his innocent ears in case he could hear the footfalls of, who was made to quench his glorious shining spirit because he had to live in total awful fear of, the subhuman, soulless, snakelike figure of, Boy Teuteburg. Who would crouch behind garbage cans and conceal himself in doorways, was a lurker in alleys, would drag at his narrow cigarette with his narrow shoulders against the bricks and squint out from under the narrow brim of the cap on his narrow head, was a low being of no conscience or intelligence or any other merits altogether. A Boy Teuteburg is not a fellow for your flowery fields and rending sunsets. He is a creature of the streets and knows no better. And such as this, a lowly brutal creature with no promise to him at all except the promise to wind up in jail, became yet another, perhaps the most severe, bane of the Shining Boy's existence.

Between Daniel Webster State Graded School and Dockweder's Hardware Emporium would this young terrorist lurk of an afternoon, stealing some worthless titbit here, hawking on the sidewalk there, blowing his nose by pressing two fingers against one nostril, leaning over and firing, then repeating the gesture on the opposite side, all the while skulking along, flicking his puny red eyes over the passing throng (as *Dickens* had it) in search of children younger than he, any children in actual fact, but in most especial one certain child. This, you may have divined it, was yours truly. I know for a fact that Boy Teuteburg had a singular hatred for the child-me because of what befell me when I was able to convoy myself from one place to another amidst the kidlings of my age—other little sparrows of the street (as *Blake* might put it)—to subsume myself in the shelter of a nattering throng of classmates. We all feared Boy, having suffered under his psychotic despotism for years of grade school. Our collective relief at his eventual graduation (he was sixteen!) chilled to dread when we discovered that his release from the eighth grade meant only that Boy had been freed to prowl eternally about Daniel Webster, a shark awaiting shoals of smaller fishes. (A *simile,* Missus Doggybark, a *simile.*) There he was, smirking as he tightened his skinny lips to draw on his skinny cigarette—circling. Let us say our convoy of joking lads rounds the corner on Erie Street by the Oliphant Hotel and spreads across the sidewalk as we carry on toward Third Street, home for some, Dockweder's and the broom for me. Then a stoaty shadow separates from the entrance of Candies & Newsagent, a thrill of fear passes through us, red eyes ignite and blaze, some dreary brat begins to weep, and the rest of us scatter as Boy charges, already raising his sharp and pointy fists. And of all these larking children, which particular boy was his intended target? That child least like himself—the one he hated most—myself—and I knew 'mongst my peers, rushing first to this one then to that, my friends, their morality stunted by the same brutal landscape that had shaped our tormentor, would'st push me away, abandon me, sacrifice me for their own ends. It was me, I mean I, he searched out, and we all knew it. Soon the others refused to leave the school in my presence, and I walked alone once more. Oft were the days when the body that wielded the broom ached with bruises, when the eyes within the body were dimmed with tears of pain and sorrow, and the nose of the body contained screws of tissue paper within each nostril, purpose of, to staunch the flow of blood.

And oft, too, were the nights when from a multiplicity of causes young Frank Wardwell lay sleepless a-bed. His concave boyish tummy begged for sustenance, for the evening repast may have been but bread and sop, and the day's beating meant that certain favored positions brought him pain. Yet hunger and pain were as nothing when compared to the true reason sleep refused to grant its healing balm. This was terror. Day came when night was done, and day brought Boy Teuteburg. So fearsome was my tormentor that I lay paralyzed with fear 'neath my blankets, hoping without hope that I might the next day evade my nemesis. Desperate hours I spent mapping devious alternate routes from school to store while still knowing well that however mazy the streets I took, they would deliver me unto Boy. And many times I sensed that he had glided into our yard and stood smoking beneath our tree, staring red-eyed at my unlighted window—other times I heard him open our back door and float through the kitchen and hover motionless outside my door. What good now was my intellectual and spiritual superiority to Boy Teuteburg? What good were my yearnings? Ice-cold fear was all I knew. Mornings, I dragged myself from bed, quaking opened my door to find Boy of course nowhere in sight, fed my ice-cold stomach a piece of bread and a glass of water, and dragged myself to school, hopeless as the junkman's horse.

Had I but known of the thousand eyes upon me. . . .

Why does Ethel Carroway report to her window on the fourth floor of the Oliphant Hotel at the full of the moon? Guilt? Remorse? Grief? You shall hear of Ethel Carroway.

In life, this was a thoughtless girl, vibrant but shallow, lively and loud, the epitome of a Visible, who felt no more guilt than does a cast-iron pump. For months Ethel had gone about her maid's duties in loose overblouses to conceal her condition, of which even her slatternly friends were ignorant. The infant signified no more than a serious threat to her employment. She never gave it a name or fantasied about its life or thought of it with ought but distaste. Captain Starbuck had departed the day following conception, in any case a hasty, rather *scuffling* matter, no doubt to sow his seed in foreign ports. Delivery took place behind the locked door of Ethel's basement room and lasted approximately twelve hours, during which she twice had to shout from her bed that she was violently ill and could not work. (Her exact words were, "Sick! Pukin'! Leemee 'lone!") During the process, she consumed much of a bottle of bourbon whiskey given her by another priapic guest of the Oliphant. When at last the child triumphantly bullied its way out between her legs, Ethel bit the umbilicus in two and observed that she had delivered a boy. Its swollen purple genitals were a vivid reminder of Captain Starbuck. Then she passed out. An hour later, consciousness returned on a tide of pain. Despite it all, Ethel felt a curious new pride in herself—in what she had done. Her baby lay on her chest, uttering little kittenish cries. It resembled a monkey, or a bald old man. She found herself almost regretting that she had to dispose of this creature, who had caused her so much pain. They had been through the day together, they had shared an experience that now seemed almost hallucinatory in its intensity. She wished the baby were the kitten it sounded like, that she might keep it. She and the baby were companions of a sort. And she realized that it was hers—she had made this little being.

Yet her unanticipated affection for the infant did not alter the facts. Ethel needed her job, and that was that. She had to kill the little thing. She tried to move her legs to the side of the bed, and a fresh wave of pain made her gasp. Her legs, her middle, her arms, the bed, all were soaked in blood. Her sheets would have to be burned. The baby mewed again, and more to comfort herself than it, she slid the squeaking child upward toward her right breast and bumped the nipple against his lips until he opened his mouth and began to suck. The baby, like Ethel, was covered with blood, as well as with something that looked like dark grease. More than anything else at that moment, she wanted to wash herself off—she wanted to wash the baby, too. At least he could die clean. She moved the baby to her other breast, which had no more milk than the first. She stroked his back, and some of the blood and grease came off on her hand, so she wiped his back with a clean part of the sheet.

Some time later, she swung her feet off the bed, ignored the bolts of pain, and stood up with the baby clamped one-handed against her chest. She would give him a gift. Grimacing, she limped to the sink against the wall, turned on the hot water, put in the stopper, mixed in cold until tepid water half-filled the sink, and shut off both taps. Then she lowered the baby into the sink. As soon as his skin touched the water, his eyes flew open and appeared to search her face. For the first time, she saw their color—a violent purple-blue, like no other eyes she had ever seen. The baby was frowning magisterially. His legs contracted under him like a frog's. The violent eyes glowered up at her, as if the baby knew what Ethel was ultimately going to do, did not at all like what she was going to do, but accepted it. She wiped him with her washcloth until he was pretty much clean, and he kept frowning up at her, scanning her face with his astonishing eyes.

She considered drowning him. Then she would have to carry his body out of the hotel, and she didn't even have a suitcase. Besides, she didn't like the idea of holding him under the water while he looked up at her with that funny old-king frown on his face. Ethel let the red-brown water drain from the sink and wrapped the baby in a towel. She set him on the floor while she refilled the sink and rubbed the washcloth over her body, wincing and gasping. When she picked him up his eyes flew open again, then closed as his mouth gaped in an enormous yawn. She limped back to bed, tore the sheets off one-handed, cast a blanket over the mattress, and lay down and fell asleep with the baby's head at the base of her neck.

It was still dark when Ethel came awake. She had no idea of the time, indeed if it were still the same night, but the quality of the darkness told her that it would soon be morning. The baby stirred on her chest, and its arms, which had worked free of the towel, jerked up and paused in the air before drifting back down. This was the hour when, except for the furnace man, the hotel was still. All the halls were empty, and a single sleepy clerk manned the desk. In an hour, the bootboys would be setting out the night's polished shoes, and a few early-bird guests would be calling down their room service orders. In two hours, Ethel Carroway was supposed to be in uniform, reporting for hall duty. She intended to do this. When it was noticed that she was in pain, she would be allowed another day off, but she had to report. So she had about an hour in which to decide what to do with the baby and then to do it.

If she smothered it in her room, she would have to transport the dead body through the basement to get it outside. The furnace man would be sure to ask her what she was doing. What you got all wrapped up there, Ethel? Some food? Lemme see. Ethel wished she had thought far enough ahead to borrow a valise from one of the other girls, but when in her life had she thought more than an hour or two ahead? She pressed the baby to her chest and stroked its head. She could not keep the body in her room. There wasn't an inch to spare and anyhow the supervisor would be sure to find it on a room check. Poor baby, she thought, it wasn't even his fault he had to die. He was a sweet baby. She rocked him in her arms, thinking how nice it would be to keep him with her and play doll-games with him when she was off-duty.

Then she saw her plan, whole. If she went toward the service stairs after leaving her room, she would avoid the realm of the furnace man. Once on the service stairs, she could go anywhere in the hotel without being seen. The halls were almost certainly empty. She could quietly reach one of the upper floors, open a window, and . . . let the baby fall. That would be that. Her part would be over in an instant. And the baby's death would be a matter of a second, less than that, a moment too brief for pain. Afterward, no one would be able to connect Ethel Carroway to the little body on the sidewalk. It would look as though a guest had dropped the baby, or even better, as though an outsider had entered the hotel to rid herself of an unwanted child. It would just be a mystery—a baby from nowhere, belonging to nobody, fallen from the Oliphant Hotel. Police Are Baffled. Ethel saw no flaws in this plan—as long as she could leave and return to her room unseen. And to be as certain as possible of being unseen, she had to act now.

She pulled on a nightdress and wrapped herself in an old hotel bathrobe. Then she swaddled her child in the towel, hugged him to her chest, and silently left her room. On the other side of the vast, dark basement, the furnace man snored on his pallet. Gritting her teeth and cradling the dozing infant, Ethel limped toward the stairs.

The second floor was much too low, and the third seemed uncertain. To be safe, she would have to get up to the fourth floor. Her legs trembled, and spears of pain shot up from the center of her body, and she was weeping and sweating before she made it to the second floor, but for the sake of the baby she forced herself to keep climbing. When at last she reached the fourth floor, she opened the door into the corridor and leaned against it for what was no more than a minute in real time but seemed dangerously long. A cocoon of pain surrounded her entire body, and sweat stung in her eyes. Beneath the flicker of the gas lamps, the corridor was empty. Ethel carried her baby down between two rows of diminishingly numbered doors and reached the alcove that contained the guest elevators. On the far side of the alcove, two large casement windows at the front of the Oliphant looked out onto Erie Street. She hugged the baby close with one hand and struggled with a window catch for a moment before sliding it out of its latch and pushing the heavy window open. The baby's head lolled back.

Cold air streamed in through the window, and the baby tugged his brows together and scowled as if he had been surprised by an unforeseen philosophical dilemma. Impulsively, she kissed the top of his head and then hitched herself closer to the window. The metal ridge at the bottom of the casement pressed into her hip. She moved her hands to grip the baby beneath his armpits, and the towel came loose and dropped onto her bare feet. The baby drew up his legs, kicked out convulsively, drew them up again, kicked out, as if trying to reject the cold. A bright, mottled pink rose up into his cheeks and covered his face like a rash. His mouth was a tiny red beak. Freezing air rolled over them both. One of the baby's eyes shuttered itself behind a wrinkled lid in an involuntary parody of a wink. The other slid sideways and focused upon her a gaze that seemed both reproachful and distressed.

Gripping his sides, Ethel turned to face the window, extended her arms, and moved his kicking body through the casement to hold him out above the street. She could feel the thin, sturdy little ribs beneath his skin. The metal frame pressed against her belly. Ethel took a sharp inward breath and prepared to let go of the baby by loosening her grip on his sides. Instantly, unexpectedly, he slipped through her hands and dropped away into the darkness. For an instant, no more, she leaned forward openmouthed.

What happened in that instant, people, what happened to her as she watched her baby fall away toward the Erie Street sidewalk, is the reason Ethel Carroway returns to the window on the fourth floor of the Oliphant Hotel.

The remainder of her story can be quickly told. An Oliphant doorman found the dead infant half an hour after it had slipped from Ethel's hands, and as soon as the morning shift began, the entire staff knew that someone had thrown a baby from an upper-floor window. Two policemen went from room to room, and in a maid's basement chamber came upon an exhausted young woman stuffing bloody sheets into a pillowcase. She refused to answer their questions, but denied having given birth recently or at any time. A medical examination proved her denial inaccurate, and she was arrested, tried, and condemned to death. In April 1893, Ethel Carroway departed from her earthly state at the end of the hangman's rope. During the next few years, several fourth-floor guests at the Oliphant remarked upon a peculiar atmosphere in the area of the elevators. Some found it unpleasantly chilly even on summer days, some found it suffocatingly overheated in winter, and a European recitalist (the mezzo-soprano Nelly Tetrazetti, "The Golden Bird," touring the northern states with a program of songs related to faery legend) complained that what she called a "nasty, nasty porridge" in the elevator alcove was constricting her voice. In 1910, the Oliphant was sold to a man who reduced services and raised prices, and in 1916 it went out of business. It stayed empty, deteriorating steadily, until 1922, when new owners renewed it and ran it as a residential hotel until 1931, when they too went broke and sold it for use as a girl's boarding school. Students of Erie Academy for Girls first reported seeing a figure in black on the fourth floor; by 1961, when the bankrupt Academy closed its doors, local lore had supplied the spectral figure with Ethel Carroway's name, and when the Oliphant reopened yet again two years later, she began putting in her continuing regular appearances, not unlike Nelly Tetrazetti, "The Golden Bird." Over the decades, Ethel acquired a certain modest, though significant fame. The Oliphant devotes a long paragraph of its brochure to her, an undoubtedly idealized portrait hangs over the lobby fireplace, and a bronze plaque decorates the site of the crime. Guests with amateur or professional interests in the paranormal frequently spend whole weeks in the hotel, waiting for a glimpse of her. (Unfortunately, none of these guests have ever been granted their wish.)

But Ethel Carroway does not reappear to linger before her window (her window's replacement's replacement's replacement's replacement) to increase or encourage her fame. She does it for one reason only.

She's hungry.

* * *

I have told you of bad Boy and the thousand eyes, nay the thousand thousand eyes, fixed upon the unknowing Shining Boy, myself, and alluded to a secret. As I have introduced myself, at this point now I shall in the same forthright manner introduce the matter of the wondrous secret by laying it out on the methaporical table. All through my life I possessed a crystalline but often painful awareness of my superiority to nearly all other people. To put it squarely: I almost always understood that I was better than the others. Just about *all* the others.

A fool may say this and be ridiculed. A madman may say it and be Bedlamized. What fate befalls the ordinary-seeming mortal whose extraordinary gifts, not displayed by any outward show, he dares to proclaim? He risks the ire, disbelief, and growing irritation of his peers, in humbler words, spitballs, furtive kicks and knocks, whispered obscenities, and shoves into muddy ditches. Yet—and this must be allowed—*that the mortal in question is superior has already aroused ire, irritation, and even hatred amongst those who have so perceived him.* Why was I immediately the focus of Boy Teuteburg's sadistic and psychopathic rage? And why did my fellow-kidlings not defend me from the depredations of our common enemy? It was not only mingled relief and fear that made them cast me out, no. *What inflamed our enemy, Boy, chilled them.* It would have been the same had I never taken the generous pains of illuminating their little errors, the same had I never pressed home the point by adding, *and I know this because I am more intelligent than you.* For they already knew of my superiority. They had seen me struggle to suppress my smiles as I instructed our teacher in her numerous errors, and surely they had likewise noted the bright inner soul-light within their precocious classmate.

Now I know not to speak of these matters (except in privileged conditions such as these). In my midtwenties I gave all of that up, realizing that my life had become a catastrophe, and that the gifts which so elevated me above the run of mankind (as the protagonists of the great *Poe* know themselves raised up) had not as it were elevated the outward circumstances of my life in the same fashion. I was condemned to the prison-house (what I thought was the prison-house) of ordinary mortal existence, the life given over to a meaningless job, dull pleasures, despairing dreams. The inward soul-light had guttered and dimmed, and would no longer draw the attacks of the envious. Life had circled me 'round and stolen what was most essentially mine.

Not all ghosts are dead, but only the dead can be counted on for twenty-twenty vision. You only get to see what's in front of your nose when it's too late to do you any good.

At that point, enter hunger.

My life had already lost its luster before I truly understood that the process of diminishment had begun. Grade school went by in the manner described. My high school career, which should have been a four-year span of ever-increasing glories culminating in a 4.0 average and a full scholarship to a Harvard or even a College of William and Mary, ground itself into a weary repetitive pattern of Cs and Ds hurled at me by indifferent fools long incapable of distinguishing the true creative spirit from the glib, mendacious copycat. In his freshman year, under the pen name "Orion," young Frank Wardwell submitted three meritorious poems to the school literary magazine, all of which were summarily rejected, one on the grounds that several of its noblest phrases had been copied down from poets of the Romantic movement. Did the poets own these phrases, then? And would then a young chap like Frank Wardwell be forbidden to utter these phrases in the course of literary conversations such as he never had due to the absence of like-minded souls? Yes, one gathers, to the editors of a high-school literary magazine. The doctrine that poetic utterance becomes the common property of man was alien to them.

I turned to the creation of a private journal, in which to inscribe my deepest thoughts and record my exalted and far-reaching imaginings. But the poison had already begun its work. Brutal surroundings, moral isolation, inferior teachers, these had robbed my pen of its freshness, and much of what I set down was only lamentation over my misunderstood and friendless state. In coming from the deeps to seek expression, my high-arching thoughts met the deadly ignorance that surrounded me and shriveled from gleaming heroes with cascading blond hair into gat-toothed dwarves. And my imaginings, the tales with which I had vowed to storm this world's castles, refused to take wing. I blush to remember how, when stalled in the midst of what was to be a furious tale of awe and terror, my talent, struck down early by a vision-denying world, turned not to Great Imagination for its forms but to popular serials broadcast at the time over the radio waves. "The Green Hornet" and "Jack Armstrong, the All-American Boy," my personal favorites among these, supplied many of my plots and even, I grant, some of my less pungent dialogue.

All my endeavors went the way of the private journal. A young person losing his life by the gradual draining away of his spirit cannot be fully aware of the damage daily done to his being. Some vestige of the inborn wonder will beat its wings and trust that flight will come, and I saw with sad and weary regularity the evidence that I was as far above my teachers and fellow students at Edna Ferber High as I had been at Daniel Webster State Graded School. Yet my well-intentioned and instructive exposures of their intellectual errors earned me no gratitude. (Did you really imagine, Tubby Shanks, you of the quill-like red hair and carbuncled neck who sat before me in sophomore English, that Joyce Kilmer, immortal author of "Trees," was necessarily of the female gender, for the sole reason that both your mother and sister shared his Christian name? My remark that

Irish scribe James Joyce then must be a sideshow morphadite did not deserve the blow you addressed to my sternum, nor the wad of phlegm your acolyte, Stewart Siddley, deposited on my desk at close of day.) True, I had no more to fear the raids of Boy Teuteburg, who had metamorphosed into a sleek ratty fellow in a tight black overcoat and pearl gray snapbrim hat and who, due to a busy round of appointments in pool halls, the back rooms of taverns, and the basements of garages, had no time for childish pursuits. Dare I say I almost missed the attentions of Boy Teuteberg? That I almost longed for the terror he had caused in me? And that his indifference, what might have even been his lack of recognition, aroused within me nameless but unhappy feelings on the few occasions when we ancient enemies caught sight of one another, me, sorry, I mean I, dragging through our native streets at the end of another hopeless day at Edna Ferber, he emerging from an Erie Street establishment known as Jerry's *Hotcha!* Lounge, then his narrow still-red eye falling on mine but failing to blaze (though the old terror did kindle in me, that time), and then my immemorial foe sliding past me without a word or gesture to mark the momentous event? At such times even the dull being I had become felt the passing of a never-to-be-recovered earlier soul-state. Then I had known of my superiority and nurtured myself upon it; now, knowing of it still, I knew it did not make an ounce of difference. Boy Teuteburg had become a more consequential person than Francis T. Wardwell. I had seen the shades of the prison-house pulled down till nearly all the light was blocked.

Soon after the unmarked momentous event, two other such pulled them fully down.

After an unfortunate incident at school involving the loss of a petty sum on the order of six or seven dollars from a handbag left hanging on a lunchroom chair, an incident admittedly not the first of its kind, the meaningless coincidence that I had been seated adjacent to the chair from which hung the forgotten reticule somehow led to my being blamed for the loss of the insignificant sum. It was felt, quite falsely, that I had been responsible for the earlier incidents. I defended myself as any innocent party does, by declining to respond to the ridiculous accusations. I did possess a small, secret store of money, and when ordered to repay the careless girl who had been the real source of the crime, I paid her the wretched seven dollars from this source.

Unbearably humiliated, I chose not to subject myself to the hostile stares and cruel whispers I would meet in the school's halls, so for some wretched days I wandered our streets, spending far too many quarters from my precious cache in coffee shops and movie theaters when supposed to be in class, and then reporting as ever to Dockweder's Hardware, where having passed down my broom to a shifty urchin of unclean habits, I was entrusted with the stocking of shelves, the fetching of merchandise to the counter, and during the generally inactive hour between four-thirty and five-thirty, the manipulation of the cash register. On the fifth day after my self-imposed suspension from school, Mr. Dockweder kept me after work as he ostentatiously balanced out the day's receipts, the first time I had ever seen him do so, found the *awesome,* the *majestic* sum of $1.65 missing from the cash tray, and promptly accused me of the theft. Not the ordinary boyish mistake of returning too much change to an impatient customer or hitting a wrong button when ringing up a sale, but the theft. I protested, I denied, alas in vain. Then look to the boy, I advised, I think he steals from the stockroom, too, fire him and the pilfering will cease. As if he had forgotten my seven years of unstinting service, Mr. Dockweder coldly informed me that sums of varying amounts had been missing from the register many nights during the period when I had been entrusted with its manipulation between the hours of four-thirty and five-thirty. He demanded I turn out my pockets. When I did so, he smoothed out one of the three bills in my possession and indicated to me on its face the check mark he had placed on every one of the register's bills before leaving the counter in my charge.

Now, in all honesty, a check mark might be made on a dollar bill in a hundred different ways. I have seen every possible sort of symbol used to deface our nation's currency. Mr. Dockweder, however, would accept none of my sensible suggestions—his mind and heart were closed alike. He insisted on bringing me home, and as we took to the streets gripped my shoulder in an iron clamp. Once in our dwelling, he stood in the shabby parlor and denounced me. My hottest denials went unheard. In fact, I was trembling and sweating, undergoing a thousand torments, for once or twice I had dipped into the register and extracted a few coins, a quarter, a dime, a penny or two, coins I assumed would never be missed and with which I could sustain myself throughout the long day. I even *confessed* these minor lapses, thinking to improve my situation with a fine show of honest remorse, but this fearless candor did me harm. My father repaid to Mr. Dockweder from his own skimpy reserve of cash the inflated sum claimed to be missing, vowed that I personally would make the amount good to him, and informed me that I would henceforth clear my head of nonsensical ideas and learn the ways of the real world. He was sick of my airs and highfalutin manners, sick of my books, my affected mode of speech, my uselessness—sick of me. From that day I should work. Work, I mean, as a dumb beast works (my father, an alcoholic welder, being one such), without hope, without education, without letup, without meaning, and with no reward save an inadequate weekly pay packet.

That evening, still reeling from the depth and swiftness of my fall, I let myself out of our house after the welder and his weeping wife had collapsed into bed and went staggering through our streets. What I had been, I scarcely knew; what I now was, I could not bear to see;

what I was to become, I could not imagine. Life's prison-house rose up about me on all sides. In that prison-house lay a grave, and within that grave lay I. The streets took me, where I did not know or care, and at careless intervals I looked up to see before me a featureless wall, a urine stain belt-high beneath broken windows in an abandoned warehouse, heaped-up tires in a vacant lot. These things were *emblems.* Once I caught sight of a leering moon, and once I heard the shuffle of feet close by and stopped in terror, sensing mortal danger on all sides, and glanced all round at empty Erie Street.

Bitterly, the stillborn fantasies of childhood returned to me, their former glow now corpse-gray. Never would I kneel down in fields and woods 'midst bird's-foot trefoil, daisy fleabane, devil's pulpit, Johnny-jump-up, jewelweed, the foxglove, and the small sundrop. Never would I hear the lowing of the kine, the tolling of bells in a country church, the far-off call of the shepherd, the chant of the lark. Mountain lakes and mountain rivers would never take me in their chilly, breath-giving grasp. The things I was to know were all but *emblems* of the death-in-life ranged 'round me now.

I raised my all-but-unseeing eyes to the facade, six stories high, of the Oliphant Hotel, dark dark dark. Above the lobby, dimly visible behind the great glass doors, the windows hung dark and empty in the darker brick. Behind those windows slept men and women endowed with college degrees and commercial or artistic skills, owners of property, travelers in foreign lands, men and women on the inside of life. They would never know my name, and I would never be of their Visible number. All radiantly Visible themselves, they would look at me no more in daylight than at present—and if they happened to look, would see nothing!

A figure moved past an upper window, moved back, and then reappeared behind the window. Dark dark dark. A guest, I thought, wandering sleepless in the halls, and thought to turn away for my long journey home.

Some small awareness held me, looking up. High above behind a casement window hovered a figure in black garb, that figure, I now observed, unmistakably a woman's. What was she doing, why was she there? Some trouble had sent one of the gilded travelers roaming the Oliphant, and on that trouble she brooded now, pausing at the window. Recognizing a fellow-being in misery akin to my own, I brazenly stepped forward and stared up, silently demanding this woman to acknowledge that, despite all that separated and divided us, we were essentially the same. White hands twisted within her black garment. We were the same, our world was the same, being dark dark dark. Perhaps the woman would beckon to me, that we could each soothe the shame of the other. For streaming from the woman was shame—so I thought. An oval face emerged from shadow or from beneath a hood and neared the glass.

You shall see me, you shall, I vowed, and stepped forward once again. The alabaster face gazed at a point some five feet nearer the hotel than myself. I moved to meet her gaze, and just before I did so, experienced a hopeless terror far worse than anything Boy Teuteburg had ever raised in me. Yet my body had begun to move and would not stop when the mind could not command it. Two mental events had birthed this sick dread: I had seen enough of the alabaster face to know that what I had sensed streaming out was something far, far worse than shame; and I had suddenly remembered what the first sight of this figure at this window of this hotel would have recalled to me had I been in my normal mind—the legend of the ghost in the Oliphant. Ethel Carroway's eyes locked on mine. They scorched my innards. I could not cry out through my constricted throat; I could not weep from my singed eyes. For a tremendous moment I could not move at all, but stood where her infant had fallen to the pavement and met her ravishing, her *self-ravishing,* glance with my own helpless glance. When it was over—when she released me—I turned and ran like a dog whom wanton boys have set on fire.

The following day my father commanded me to go to Mr. Harold McNair at McNair's Fine Clothing & Draperies and enquire after a full-time position. He had recently done some work for Mr. McNair, who had spoken of a job opening available to an eager and hardworking lad. Now that my circumstances had changed, I must try to claim this position and be grateful for the opportunity, if offered. I did as my father commanded. Mr. Harold McNair had indeed a position available, the position being assistant stock boy, hours 7:30 A.M.–6:00 P.M., Monday–Saturday, wages @ $0.45/hr, meals not supplied. He had thought the welder's boy might be responsive to his generosity, and the welder's boy, all that remained of me, was responsive, yes sir, Mr. McNair, sir. And so my endless drudgery began.

At first I worked to purchase, at the employee rate, the shirts and trousers with which an assistant stock boy must be outfitted; and at intervals for the next twenty-nine years I spun long hours into dress shirts and neckties and worsted suits, as Rumpelstiltskin spun straw into gold, for a McNair's representative must advertise by wearing the very same clothing to be sold to McNair's beloved customers. I had no friends. The only company I knew was that of my fellow employees, a cringing half-brained lot devoted to sexual innuendo, sporting events, and the moving pictures featuring Miss Jean Harlow. Later on, Wallace Beery and James Cagney were a big hit. Even later, one heard entirely too much of John Wayne. This, not forgetting the pages of our Sunday newspaper wasted upon the "funny papers," was their culture, and it formed the whole of their conversation. Of course I held myself apart. It was the old story repeated once again, as all stories are repeated again and again, eternally, just look around you. You are myself, and I myself am you. What we did last week, last year, what we did in our infancy, shall we do again tomorrow. I could take no delight in the gulf that lay between my intellect and theirs, nor could my fellow workers. Doubtless all of them, men and women, secretly held the opinion of me expressed near the end of our Christmas party in 1959 by Austin Hartlepoole, an accounting junior who had imbibed too freely of the fish-house punch: "Mr. Wardwell, have you always been a stuck-up jerk?"

"No," I might have said but did not, "once I was a Shining Boy." (What I did say is of no consequence.) By then I was Mr. Wardwell, note. The same superior qualities that condemned me to social and intellectual isolation had seen me through a series of promotions from assistant stock boy to stock boy then head stock boy, thence laterally to manager, shipping department, then upward again to counter staff, Shirts and Ties, followed by a promotion upstairs to second floor, counter staff, Better Shirts and Neckwear, then Assistant Manager, Menswear; in time, Manager, Menswear, and ultimately, in 1959, the year soon-to-be-sacked Hartlepoole called me a stuck-up jerk, Vice-President and Buyer, Clothing Divisions. The welder's boy had done well for himself. Just outside town, I maintained a large residence, never seen by my coworkers, for myself and a companion who shall remain nameless. I dressed in excellent clothing, as was to be expected. A gray Bentley, which I pretended to have obtained at a "price," represented my single visible indulgence. Accompanied by Nameless Companion, I regularly visited the Caribbean on my annual two-week vacation to take up comfortable rooms in the same luxurious "resort" hotel. By the end of the nineteen-fifties, my salary had risen to thirty-five thousand dollars a year, and in my regular banking and savings accounts I had accumulated the respectable sum of fifty thousand dollars. In another, secret account, I had amassed the even more respectable sum of five hundred and sixty-eight thousand dollars, every cent of it winkled away a little at a time from one of the worst people, in fact by a considerable degree actually the worst person, it has ever been my misfortune to know, my employer, Mr. Harold McNair.

All was well until my transfer upstairs into Better Shirts and Neckwear, my "Ascension," we called it, to the vaulted splendors of the second floor, where affluent customers did not have to mingle with the commoners examining cheaper goods below, and where Mr. McNair himself, my jailor-benefactor of years before, was wont to appear from the depths of his walnut-paneled office, wandering between the counters, adjusting the display cravats, remarking upon the quality of a freshly purchased tweed jacket or fox stole (Ladies' was sited across the floor), taking in the state of his minions' fingernails and shoes. Mr. McNair, a smallish, weaselish, darkish, baldish figure in a navy suit, his solid red tie anchored to his white shirt with a visible metal bar, demanded courteous smiles, upright postures, hygienic habits. Scuffed shoes earned an errant clerk a sharply worded rebuke, unclean nails an immediate trip to the employee washroom. The dead thing I was did not object to these simple, well-intentioned codes. Neither did I object to my employer—he was but a fixed point in the universe, like his own God enthroned in his heavens. I did not take him *personally.* Not until my Ascension, when we each fell under the other's gaze.

Living Visibles like Harold McNair do not merely expect to be seen. Though they be discreetly attired, quietly spoken, and well-mannered, within they starve, they slaver for attention, and exact it however they must. In Mr. McNair's case, this took the form of divisiveness, capriciousness, sanctimoniousness, and for lack of a better word, tyranny. He would favor one counter clerk, then another, therein creating enmity and rivalry and an ardent wish in two hearts to comprehend his own heart. He would elect one obscure employee for weeks of special treatment, jokes, confidences, consultations, and then without explanation drop the elected one back into obscurity, to be pecked to death by his peers. He drew certain employees aside and whispered subtle criticisms of their dearest friends. During all this, he searched for his true, secret favorites, those whose contempt for themselves, masked behind a smooth retailer's manner, matched his own contempt for them, masked behind the same. In time I began to think of Harold McNair as a vast architectural structure something like his store, a great building charmingly appointed with fine though not ostentatious things, where a smiling but observant guide leads you ever deeper in, deciding room by room if you have earned the right to see the next, by stages conducting you into chambers which grow successively smaller, uglier, eventually even odorous, finally through foul, reeking stys, and at last opens the final door to the central, inmost room, the little room at the heart of the building, the most terrible of all, and admits you to—the real Mr. Harold McNair.

He knew I was his the first time he saw me behind the Better Shirts counter on the second floor. He may even have known it on the day he hired me, long years previous. In fact, he might even have considered the alcoholic welder laboring in his basement and seen that this man's son, if he had one, would be his as if by Natural Law. His in the sense of easily flattered, thus easily dominated. Ready to be plucked up by a kind word and downcast by a harsh one. Willing to please. Able to sustain attentive silences during the Great Man's monologues. Liable to be supine before power, abject before insult. A thorough and spineless subordinate. A kind of slave. Or, a slave. Long before my final promotion, I had been shown into the final room and met the true Harold McNair. I knew what he was and what I was. In many ways, I had fallen under the sway of a smoother, more corrupt Boy Teuteburg, a Boy who thought himself a noble being and wore the mask of a dignified, modest, successful retailer.

I accepted this. But I had determined to be paid well for the role.

My thefts began with an impulsive act of revenge. I had just departed Mr. McNair's office after a session in which the whip lashed out more forcefully from within the velvet bag than was customary, both before and after my employer had expressed his apocalyptic disgust for all women, those sly scented obscenities, those temples of lust, etc., etc.. Making my way granite-faced through Better Gowns, I noticed an elderly temple of lust depositing her alligator bag upon the counter as she turned to scrutinize a bottle green silk Better Gown with Regency sleeves. A wallet protruded slightly from the unclasped bag. Customer and saleslady conferred in re the wisdom of Regency sleeves. My legs took me past the counter, my hand closed on the wallet, the wallet dropped into my pocket, and I was gone.

Heart a-thud, I betook myself to a stall in the male employee's washroom, opened the wallet, and discovered there sixty-eight dollars, now mine. I had been rash, that I knew, but I was electric with life. All I regretted was that the money had been the temple's, not Mr. McNair's. I left the stall and by reflex went to the sinks and the mirrors. As I washed my already spotless hands I caught my face in the mirror and froze—a vibrant rogueish Visible a decade younger than I looked back at me with blazing eyes, my own.

Anyone in a business that receives and disburses large amounts of cash will eventually work out a method for deflecting some of the cash out of its normal course. Some few will test their method, and most of those will be found out. A dim-witted snatch and grab like mine, unobserved, is a method as good as any. During my tenure in the store, many employees located the imperfections in their methods only when the handcuffs closed around their wrists. (Mr. McNair never showed mercy or granted a second chance, never.) From the moment my living eyes met mine in the washroom mirror, I was already withdrawing from the cash available an amount appropriate to my degraded role, *stealing my real salary.* All that remained was to work out a method that could never be detected.

Many, many such methods exist, though sometimes even these are detected. I will not burden you with the details of mine, save to reveal that it involved a secret set of books. It worked successfully for better than two decades and yielded a sum nearly appropriate to my continuous humiliation. Mr. McNair knew that significant amounts of money were escaping his miserly grasp, but despite feverish plotting followed by the construction of elaborate rattraps, could not discover how or where. The traps snapped down upon the necks of minor-league peculators, till-tappers, short-change artists, bill-padders, invoice-forgers, but never did it come down upon his greatest enemy's.

On the night I placed my hundred thousandth unofficial dollar in my secret account, I celebrated with a lobster dinner and a bottle of French champagne in our finest seafood restaurant (alone, this being previous to the arrival of Nameless Friend) and, once filled with alcohol and rich food, remembered that the moon was full that night, recalled also my night of misery so long ago, and resolved to return to the Oliphant Hotel. Then, I had been lost, a corpse within a grave within a prison; now, I was achieved, a walking secret who had worked his own way to the inside of life. An invisible Visible. I would stand before Ethel Carroway and be seen—I thought I knew within me what had been written upon her face.

I walked (in those pre-Bentley days) to Erie Street and posted myself against an opposite wall to await the arrival of the shade. She would show herself to me again and acknowledge that like her I stood above the common run, distinguished by the intensity of my needs. Mine was the confidence of a lover who, knowing that this night his beloved will yield, anticipates and savors each blissful, earthy pleasure to come. Each moment she did not appear was made delicious by being the moment before the moment when she would. When my neck began to ache, I lowered my chin to regard through the enormous glass doors the Oliphant's lobby, once a place of unattainable luxury. Now if I liked I could take a fourth-floor suite and present myself to Ethel Carroway on home ground. But it was right to stand where I had before, the better to mark the distance I had come. An hour I waited, another, cold and thirsty.

My head began to ache from the champagne I had taken. My feet complained, and my faith wavered. Yet I could not leave—Ethel Carroway had put me to a test which grew the more demanding as the minutes passed. Determined not to fail, I turned up the collar of my coat, thrust my hands into its pockets, and kept my eyes upon a dark window.

Sometimes I heard people move behind, then beside me, but looking toward the sound, saw no one. The champagne worked, I thought, like a drug in my bloodstream, falsifying and deceiving, and so I focused all the harder on the blank window. Yet she would not show herself and acknowledge, by meeting my eyes with her own, my right to *be* acknowledged. Mysterious footfalls came teasingly out of the darkness on Erie Street, as if Ethel Carroway had descended to meet me, but the footfalls were many and varied, and no pale figure in black appeared to meet my consummating gaze.

I had not understood—I knew nothing of Visibles and those not, and what I took to be confidence was but its misshapen nephew, arrogance. The cynosure and focus of myriad pairs of eyes, all of which stared unseen at me, I at last surrendered after three in the morning and wandered sore-foot home through the invisible crowd of those who, unlike myself, understood exactly what had happened there and why. In the morn, I rose from my rumpled bed to steal again.

* * *

Understanding, ephemeral as a transcendent insight granted in a dream, ephemeral as *dew*, came only with exposure, which is to say, with loss of fortune and large residence, loss of Nameless Companion, of super-duper Bentley, of elegant sobersides garb, of gay Caribbean holidays on the American Plan, loss of reputation, occupation (both occupations, retailer and thief), privacy, freedom, many Constitutionally-guaranteed civil rights, and ultimately, of life. As with all of you, I would have chosen these forfeited possessions, persons, states, and conditions over any mere act of understanding, yet I cannot deny the sudden startling consciousness of a certain piquant, indeterminate pleasure-state, unforeseen in the grunting violence of my last act as a free man, which surfaced hand in hand with my brief illumination. This sense of a deep but mysterious pleasure linked to my odd flash of comprehension was often the subject of my thoughts during the long months of trial and incarceration.

I had long since ceased to fear or anticipate exposure, and the incarnadine (see *Shakespeare*) excess of exposure's aftermath would have seemed a nightmarish impossibility to the managerial Mr. Wardwell, stoutly serious and seriously stout, of 1960. Weekly, a handsome sum wafted from Mr. McNair's gnarled, liver-spotted grip into my welcoming hands, and upon my retirement some ten stony years hence I expected at last to float free in possession of approximately two million dollars, maybe three. My employer's rattraps continued to snap down on employees of the anathema stripe, of late less frequently due to widespread awareness of the Byzantinely complex modes of surveillance and inspection which universally "kicked in" at the stage beneath the introduction of my invented figures, on account of their having been devised by the very same anathema they were designed to entrap. Had not the odious McNair decided upon a store-wide renovation to mark the new decade, I should after thirty, with luck forty, years of pampered existence in some tropic port, after sustained experience of every luxury from highestly refined to basestly, piggishestly sensual, have attained upon my death from corrupt old age an entire understanding of my frustrated vigil before the Oliphant, of the walkers and shufflers I had heard but were not there, also of Ethel Carroway and her refusal to recognize one who wrongly thought himself her spiritual equal. But he proceeded on his dubious brainstorm, and I induced a premature understanding by smashing his brains into porridge—"nasty, nasty porridge"—with a workman's conveniently disposed ball peen hammer.

The actual circumstances of my undoing were banal. Perhaps they always are. A groom neglects to shoe a horse, and a king is killed. A stranger hears a whisper in an alehouse, and—a king is killed. That kind of thing. In my case, coincidence of an otherwise harmless sort played a crucial role. The dread renovation had reached the rear of the second floor, lapping day by day nearer the Accounts Room, the Art Department, and the offices, one mine, one Mr. McNair's. The tide of workmen, ladders, dropcloths, yardsticks, plumblines, sawhorses, and so forth, inevitably reached our doors and then swept in. As my employer lived above the store in a velvety lair only his inmost courtiers had seen, he had directed that the repaneling and recarpeting, the virtual *regilding,* of his office be done during normal working hours, he then enduring only the minor inconvenience of descending one flight to be about his normal business of oozing from customer to customer, sniffing, adjusting, prying, flattering. As I owned no such convenient lair and could not be permitted access to his, not even to one corner for business purposes, my own office received its less dramatic facelift during the hour between the closing of the store, six, and the beginning of overtime, seven. A task that should have taken two days thus filled ten, at the close of every which, concurrent with my official duties, I must manage the unofficial duties centered on the fictive set of books and the disposition of the day's harvest of cash. All this under the indifferent eyes of laborers setting up their instruments of torture.

Callous, adamantine men shifted my desk from port to starboard, from bow to stern, and on the night of my downfall informed me that I must immediately jump ship that they might finish, our boss having lost patience with this stage of affairs. I jumped ship and bade farewells to departing employees from a position near the front doors. By six forty-five the store was dark, save for the rear portion of the second floor. At six fifty-five I made my way through the familiar aisles to my office door, through which I observed Harold McNair, on a busybody's journey from the sultan's quarters above, standing alone before my exposed desk alone in my newly thised-and-thatted office and contemplating the undeniable evidence of my various anathematic peculations.

The artisans should have been packing up, but had finished early; McNair should have been consulting his genius for depravity upstairs in the velvety bower, but had slithered down to ensure their obedience. Finished early, the workmen had left, unseen by me, by the back doors. We were alone in the building. As Mr. McNair whirled to confront me, a combination of joy and rage distorted his unpleasant features into a demonic mask. I could not save myself—he knew exactly what he had seen. He advanced toward me, spitting incoherent obscenities. From long, weary habit, I resigned myself to what would come.

Mr. McNair arrived at a point a foot from my person and continued to berate me, jabbing a knobby forefinger at my chest as he did so. Unevenly, his face turned a dangerous shade of pink, hot pink I believe it is called. The forefinger hooked my lapel, and he tugged me deskward. His color grew higher as he ranted on. Finally he hurled at my bowed head a series of questions, perhaps one question repeated many times, I don't know, I could not distinguish the words. My being quailed beneath the onslaught; I was transported back to Dockweder's. Here again were a marked bill, an irate employer, a shamed Frank Wardwell—the wretched boy blazed forth within the settled, secretive, ample man.

And it came to the wretched boy that the ranter before him resembled two old tormentors, Missus Barksdale and Boy Teuteburg, especially the latter, not the smooth rodent in a pearl gray hat but the red-eyed bane of childhood who came hurtling out of shop doors to pummel head and body with sharp, accurate, knifelike fists. I experienced a moment of pure psychic sensation so foreign I could not at first affix a name to it. I knew only that an explosion had taken place within. Then I recognized that what I felt was pain, everlasting, eternal pain long self-concealed. It was as though I had stepped outside my own body. Or *into* it.

Before me on my oaken chair lay a ball peen hammer forgotten by its departing owner. The instant I beheld it, I knew what I would do. My hand found the hammer, the hammer found McNair's head. Startled, amazed, not yet terrified, Mr. McNair jumped back, clamoring. I moved in. He reached for the weapon, and I captured his wizened arm in my hand. The head of the hammer tapped his tough little skull, twice. A wondrous, bright red feeling bloomed in me, and the name of that wondrous feeling was Great Anger. Mr. McNair wobbled to his knees, and I rapped his forehead and set him on his back. He squirmed and shouted, and I tattooed his noggin another half-dozen times. Finally blood began to drizzle from his ears, also from the small abrasions to his knotty head, and I struck him well and truly above the right eye. At that, his body twitched and jittered, and I leaned into my work and now delivered blow after blow while the head became a shapeless bloody brain-spattered . . . *mess.* As the blows landed, it seemed that each released a new explosion of blessed pain and anger within Frank Wardwell, it seemed too that these blessings took place in a realm once known but long forgotten, a realm in which emotion stood forth as a separate entity, neither without nor within, observable, breathtaking, utterly alive, like Frank Wardwell, this entranced man swinging a dripping hammer at the corpse of his detested and worshipped enemy. And there arose in a separate portion of my mind the remembered face of Ethel Carroway gazing down at, but not in fact seeing, the disgraced boy-me on Erie Street, and finally, like a reward, my brief, exalted moment of comprehension arrived, with it that surge of inexplicable, almost intellectual pleasure on the memory of which I chewed so often in the months ahead. Ethel Carroway, I thought, had known this—this shock—this *gasp*—

Then into the office in search of a forgotten hammer came a burly tough in a donkey jacket and a flat cap, accompanied by an even burlier same, and whatever I had understood blew away in the brief cyclone that followed. Fourteen months later, approximately dogging the footsteps of Ethel Carroway, I moved like a wondering cloud out of a sizzling, still-jerking body strapped into our state's electric chair.

The first thing I noticed, apart from a sudden cessation of pain and a sensation of generalized lightness that seemed more the product of a new relationship to gravity than any actual weight loss, was the presence in the serious room of many more people than I remembered in attendance at the great event. Surely there had been no more than a dozen witnesses, surely all of them male, all reporters save but two, in there with me? During the interesting period between the assumption of the blindfold and the emergence of the wondering cloud, forty or fifty people, many of them women, some even children, had somehow crowded into the serious little room. Despite the miraculous nature of my exit from my corporal self, these new arrivals paid me no mind at all. They parted for me without moving, that I might stay or go, as I wished. Neither did they dwell upon the enthroned corpse of the fiend, Francis T. Wardwell, from which steadily rose curls and twists of white smoke as well as the mingled odors of urine and burned meat, though this object was the undoubted focus of the original twelve, one nervously caressing a shabby Bible, one locking his hands over a ponderous gaberdine-enclosed gut, the rest scratching their "observations" into their notebooks with chewed-looking pencils. The new arrivals stared at *them*—the Bible-thumper and the warden and the scribbling reporters. I mean, they were *staring* at these unremarkable people, *lapping them up* with their eyes, visually *devouring* them.

The second thing I noticed was that except for the forty or fifty male and female shades who it had just occurred to me shared my new state, everything in the serious room, including the unevenly applied green paint on the walls, including the calibrated dials and the giant switch, including the blackened leather straps and the vanishing twists of smoke, including even the gritty layer of road dust tramped over the newly washed and dazzling black-and-white mosaic floor, also including even the bitten pencils of the scribes, but most of all including those twelve mortal beings who had assembled to witness the execution of Francis T. Wardwell, mortal beings of deep, that is to say, radiant ordinariness, expansive overflowing heartbreaking light-shedding meaning-steeped—

The second thing I noticed was that everything—

At that moment, my own hunger slammed into me, stronger, more forceful, and far more enduring than the river of volts which had separated me from my living self. As avid as the others, as raptly appreciative of all you still living could not see, I turned ravening to gaze upon the nearest mortal man.

Posted beside the blazing azalea bush on Boy Teuteburg's front lawn, I observe, mild word, what is disposed so generously to be observed. After all that has been said, there is no need to describe, as I had intended at the beginning of our journey, all I see before me. Of course the street before me is thronged with my fellow invisibles, wandering this way and that on their self-appointed rounds; of course some six or seven fellow-invisibles are at this moment aimlessly stretched out upon Boy Teuteburg's high-grade lawn of imported Kentucky bluegrass, enjoying the particularly nice skies we have at this time of year while awaiting the all-important, significance-drenched arrival upon the trembling stage of a sweet mortal being, Tulip Lane resident or service personage. These waiting ones in particular, like myself, resemble those eager ticket buyers who, returning to a favorite play for the umpty-umpth time, clutch their handbags or opera glasses in the dark and lean forward toward the rising curtain, breath suspended, eyes wide, hearts already trilling, as the actors begin to appear in their accustomed places, their dear, familiar words to be spoken, the old dilemmas faced once again, and the plot to spin, this time perhaps toward a conclusion equal to the intensity of our attention. Will they get it right, this time? Will they see? No, of course not, *they* will never see, but we lean forward in passionate concentration as their aching voices lift again and enthrall us with everything they do not know.

Boy is an old Boy now, in his eighties I believe, though it may be his nineties—distinctions of this sort no longer compel—and wonderfully, an honored personage. He ascended, needless to say without my vote, into public life as a city councilman near the time of my own "Ascension" to the second floor, and continued to rise until a convenient majority elected him Mayor shortly before my demise, and upon that plateau he resided through four terms, or sixteen years, after which ill health (emphysema) restrained him from further elevation. His mansion on Tulip Lane contains, I am told, many rooms—seventeen, not counting two kitchens and ten bathrooms. But I do not bring myself here to admire the mansion of my old adversary, now confined, I gather, to an upper floor and dependent on a wheelchair and a ready supply of oxygen. I certainly do not report to Tulip Lane at this time of the day to gloat. (Even Boy Teuteburg is a splendid presence now, a figure who plants his feet on the stage and raises his brave and frail voice.) I come here to witness a certain moment.

At this time of the day, a little girl opens the door of the room beyond the window next to the azalea. She is Boy Teuteburg's youngest grandchild, the only offspring of the failed second marriage of his youngest child, Sherrie-Lynn, daughter of his own failed second and final marriage. Her name is Amber, Jasmine, Opal, something like that—Tiffany! Her name is Tiffany! Tiffany is five or six, a solemn, dark-haired, rather smudge-eyed child generally attired in a practical one-piece denim garment with bib and shoulder straps, like a farmer's overall, but white, and printed with a tiny, repeated pattern, flower, puppy, or kitten. Food stains, small explosions of catsup and the like, provide a secondary layer of decoration. Beneath this winning garment Tiffany most often wears a long-sleeved cotton turtleneck, blue or white, or a white cotton T-shirt, as appropriate to the season; on her feet are clumsy but informal shoes of a sort that first appeared about a decade ago, somewhat resembling space boots, somewhat resembling basketball sneakers; in Tiffany's case, the sides of these swollen-looking objects sport pink check marks. Tiffany is a sallow, almost olive-skinned child in whom almost none of her grandfather's genetic inheritance is visible. Whitish gray streaks of dust (housekeeping has slacked off considerably since Mayor Teuteburg's retirement to the upper floor) can often be seen on her round, inward-looking little face, as well as upon the wrinkled sleeves of her turtleneck and the ironic pastoral of the white overall.

Smudgy of eye; streaky with white-gray dust; sallow of skin; dark hair depending in wisps and floaters from where it had been carelessly gathered at the back, and her wispy bangs unevenly cut; each pudgy hand dirt-crusted in a different fashion, one likely to be trailing a single foot-long blond hair, formerly her mother's; introspective without notable intelligence, thus liable to fits of selfishness and brooding; round of face, arm, wrist, hand, and belly, thus liable for obesity in adulthood; yet withal surpassingly charming; yet gloriously, wholly beautiful.

This smudgy little miracle enters the room at the usual hour and, as is her habit, marches straight to the television set located immediately beneath our window, tucks her lower lip between her teeth—pearly white, straight as a Roman road—and snaps the set on. Blaring music erupts from the speakers. It is time for the adventures of Tom and Jerry. By now, most of those invisibles who had been sprawled out on the Kentucky bluegrass have joined me at the window, and as matters proceed, some of those who have found themselves out on Tulip Lane will wander up, too. Tiffany backpedals to a point on the floor well in advance of the nearest chair. The chairs have been positioned for adults, who do not understand television as Tiffany does and in any case do not ever watch in wondering awe the multiform adventures of Tom and Jerry. She slumps over her crossed ankles, back bent, clumsy shoes with pink check marks nearly in her lap, hands at her sides, sallow face beneath the uneven bangs dowsing the screen. Tiffany does not laugh and only rarely smiles. She is engaged in serious business.

Generally, her none-too-clean hands rest on her flowered denim knees, on her pink-checked feet, or in the little well between the feet and the rest of her body. At other times, Tiffany's hands explore unregarded on the floor about her. These forays deposit another fine, mouse-gray layer of dust or grime on whatever parts of the little probing hands come in contact with the hardwood floor.

During the forays, the small person's face maintains a soft immobility, the soft unconscious composure of a deep-diving rapture; and the conjunction of softness and immobility renders each inner delight, each moment of identification or elation, each collusion between drama and witness, in short, you people, each emotion that would cause another child to roll giggling on the floor or draw her smeary fists up to her cheeks, each emotion is rendered *instantly visible*—written in subtle but powerful runes on the blank page that is Tiffany's face. As the eerie tube light washes over this enchanted child's features, her lips tighten or loosen; an adult frown redraws her forehead; mysterious pouches 'neath her eyes swell with horror or with tears; a hidden smile tucks the corners of her mouth; joy leaps candlelike into her eyes; the whole face irradiates with soul-pleasure. I have not even mentioned the dreamy play brought over the wide cheeks and the area beneath the eyes by thousands of tiny muscle movements, each invoking the separate character, character as in fictional character, of a piquant, momentary shadow.

And from time to time, a probing hand returns to base and alights on a knee, a space shoe, wanders for a second through the dangling wisps, hesitates, and then, with excruciating patience, approaches the opening mouth and, finger by finger, enters to be sucked, tongued, warmed, above all cleaned of its layers of debris. Tiffany is eating. She will eat anything she finds, anything she picks up. It all goes into her mouth and is absorbed into Tiffany. Cookie crumbs, maybe; mostly dust; loose threads from who knows what fabric; now and then a button or a coin. When she is through with her fingers she might graze over the palm. More often, she will extend a newly washed forefinger and push it into a nostril, there to probe and tease until the glistening morsel is extracted, this morsel to be brought unhesitatingly to the portals of the mouth and slipped within, then munched reflectively until it too has been absorbed into the Tiffany from whence it came.

We watch so intently, we crowd so close, thrusting into the azalea, breasting the window, that from time to time she yanks her eyes from the screen, having heard some dim version of what I twice heard on Erie Street, and glances at our window. She sees but a window, a bush. Instantly, she returns to the screen and her ceaseless meal. I have given you Ethel Carroway letting fall her child, and I have given you myself, Frank Wardwell, battering in a tyrant's brains; but no riper spectacle have I summoned to this stage than Tiffany. She embraces and encompasses living Ethel and living Frank, and exactly so, my dear ones, does Tiffany embrace and encompass you.

DARK

STYX

Norman Partridge

THERE HAD TO BE A PLACE WHERE THEY COULD BE ALONE, A quiet place where they could find an ending. A place empty of everything but shadow, where they could be together. The man behind the shuddering steering wheel of the old Dodge van, the broken doll of a woman hunched in the rear, the ghost of Buddy Holly whispering haunting promises of sweet kisses he'd miss.

Buddy's promises were cold and dead, but they kept coming, verse after verse, traveling from the afterlife via completely unsupernatural means—a Maxell cassette, a Panasonic boom box, and six fat Duracell batteries. The man behind the shuddering wheel drove on, his knuckles as large as mushrooms, as red as rare beef. The steering wheel was his tiller on this black Styx of a highway and the big Dodge van was his ferry. He held on, his grip vise-tight, his jaw clenched, his lips drawn back in the hideous grin of a man chewing his own heart.

Buddy Holly's song rode the icy wave of a big Hammond organ, a horribly steady drumbeat, a guitar line as pure and frightening as the night. Frightening. Because things waited for the man just beyond the Highway Styx. Exits. Service stations. Telephones. Desert casinos offering one last chance to those with no chance at all.

Most of all, other people waited beyond the road. People who would ask questions about a man driving too fast, a woman broken and battered.

Still, he had to take the chance. After all, the van required gas. The man required food. To obtain these things, he required money. The woman required . . . What? The man thought he knew the answer to that question, though he could not translate that answer into words, and that was why each stop was made quickly.

The woman remained in the van. Desperately injured, still unconscious. In the casino, thc man focused on the ATM as if it were the most beautiful thing in the world. He didn't spare a glance for the slots or the thin-shadowed cocktail waitresses or the bullet-ridden car which rotated with macabre slowness in the center of the gambling pit, its shadow as heavy as Detroit steel. The man ignored these things because he knew that this was not a time to examine irony, which was a habit that had powered him forward for twenty years. His vision, his mission, was monastic in its purity. He hid his hands from the view of others and kept his eyes off the shadows that pooled at the ankles of the living. It wasn't hard. The people around him were either in a hurry to get to Vegas, or glad to be free of it, and they weren't exactly observant.

Outside the casino, the man tossed the ATM card into the night, his right front pocket thick with twenties. He pulled into a service station, topped off twin tanks and attended to a parched radiator, gobbling a cheeseburger while he worked.

He returned to the safety of the Highway Styx. But even the safety of the highway was relative, for the night was so much more than one big shadow. In the heart of night, engines growled like hungry beasts and inquisitive high beams severed the fiber of midnight anonymity. A

Highway Patrol cruiser hugged the shoulder just ahead. A black sedan with smoked windows passed on the right, then slowed. The man drove on, passing the cop, passing the sedan, passing other drivers lost in faint green rivers of dashboard light.

Vegas was still so close, just a U-turn and a couple hundred verses away (as the dead rockin' boppin' Texan sings). . . . An empty house stood in Vegas. And in that empty house, a man waited. Or what once had been a man. He waited in the dark, without a shadow. Soon daylight would come, and men would return to the empty house like vampires seeking shelter. They would find the man who had no shadow. And then others would travel the Highway Styx.

The driver palmed shadows from his raw knuckles, his face. Wiped his palms on his jeans, leaving dark stains, immediately regretting his stupidity. He could get rid of bloodstains—that was as simple as changing his clothes, which he'd done shortly after leaving the house in Vegas, but these were stains of another kind.

Buddy Holly sang about people who took things for a game, and people who didn't understand, and sweet lovin' that was better than a kiss, and the driver's eyes were no longer fixed on the highway with its hungry, growling cars or the things that waited beyond it.

The rearview mirror trapped his gaze—a slab of silver nailed to the night sky, containing the woman. And that was as sweet an illusion as could be imagined, because for the last twenty years the man had known that such a thing was impossible.

He had to be careful. The mirror was no more a cage than the van, or the highway. That was why he had to hurry. Get off it. Find a place where others wouldn't interfere.

The man reached for the mirror, but he couldn't change its angle, not when it held her reflection. He could only touch it, touch her. . . . He could only listen.

Buddy Holly had changed his tune.

Just you know why . . . The man thought it, but he didn't dare say it, because the woman in the mirror was staring at him from behind a mask of bruises and blood, her lips puffy with a tortured smile that ran deeper than simple wounds of the flesh, and all the man could think of was that he had to drive faster because this road was so damn long, and he had to find the place where it came to an end, where there were no other cars or exits or *people,* where the van would be free of harsh white boundaries and tempting detours, where they could be *alone.*

An empty place.

He drove, faster now, the music his fuel.

The van's headlights washed a sign: NO SERVICES THIS EXIT.

"We've crossed the river," the man said, downshifting, hugging the off ramp.

The steering wheel shuddered. Much worse, the steering column rattling now, because the smooth black highway was gone.

But the man kept driving.

Into the night. Across the earth, the sand, the shadows.

To the place that waited for them.

It was obvious that the big Italian couldn't quite believe what he'd heard. "You expect me to pay him for *what?"*

The doctor, a florid-cheeked Irishman, blanched. "It's strictly legitimate, Carmine. The cops pay for Mr. Bramble's services. So do the feds, though you never read about it in the papers. That's a sizable plus." The doctor turned to Bramble. "That's correct, isn't it?"

Bramble smiled. "I'm discreet, if that's what you're trying to say."

Carmine Tonelli muttered a few words which were very indiscreet, eyeing the black man suspiciously. "Let me get this straight—you're telling us that you can find out who killed my brother by talking to his ghost?"

Bramble sighed. "It's not quite that simple, but—"

"Lew might buy this shit," Carmine said, thumbing the doctor's sunken chest, glaring at the little man. "But I didn't grow up in the Hamptons with a silver spoon and an antique Ouija board. Look, I got a dead brother upstairs. I need someone who can give me some real answers. I don't mean the cops . . . we don't handle things that way. We're—"

"Discreet?" Bramble offered.

And now Carmine's glare was all for him. "Don't get smart with me. You're not smart, you see? I been around. I heard some of this spookshow boogieman shit before. Maybe not your particular line, but my mama spent a goddamn fortune on palm readers. My idiot sister, too. I got a few gypsy pelts on my wall. I know the look of a bloodhound that's got the money scent. So don't try—"

Bramble held up a hand. "The price just doubled."

Lew gasped. "What?"

"I can ignore the canine reference, which might be purely coincidental, but the other . . ." Bramble shook his head. "*Spook*show . . . *boogie*man. You want to talk like that, Mr. Tonelli, it's going to cost you."

Carmine's eyes narrowed. "What's this golden-tongued asshole doing in my house, Lew? Get this nig—"

"Tripled," Bramble said.

"—out of here!" Tonelli turned and started for the staircase.

Bramble watched the big man traverse a patch of morning sunlight that spilled from an upstairs window. Carmine's shade played out behind him. Thin for a fat man, dull and nearly brown—an ugly stain on the white carpet. The sunlight ate at the edges of the thing as if trying to eliminate it, until the mobster's shade trailed behind him like the tattered train of a whore's wedding dress.

Dreadful. Bramble had to look away. "Colon cancer, wasn't it?"

Carmine Tonelli stopped cold, but he didn't turn.

"That was three years ago," he said. "The doctors got it. All of it. And you read about it in the *National Enquirer.*"

"Don't be so sure." Bramble paused before continuing. "You don't sleep much anymore, do you, Mr. Tonelli? You see things in your dreams. Dead things, dead people. They aren't pretty and they never shut up, do they? You close your eyes and you go to sleep, and you find yourself among the long shadows, and there are nasty whispers under your pillow."

Carmine whirled. Now there was a gun in his hand, but Bramble's eyes stopped him cold. Something dangerous lurked in those brown-black pools . . . something that knew too much.

"It's a funny thing," Bramble said. "Some people are more dead than alive. They've got one foot planted in another world, and they could step over at any moment."

Carmine turned toward the bedroom at the top of the stairs. "Okay," he said. "Triple my original offer. Consider your pound of flesh extracted; consider my *Eye-tie* ass scared good and proper. Now get your *African-American* ass up here. I ain't leavin' my brother lookin' like this for long."

The abandoned motel fought the morning light. Peeling white paint caught the sunrise and sent it tumbling away in rippling heat waves that worried the net of yucca trees surrounding the property.

Dead leaves rattled and stuttered like wild castanets in the yucca forest. The man smiled. The trees didn't like the sunlight any better than he did.

He sat under a slight overhang that ran the length of the motel. The sunlight could not find him. He closed his eyes and tried to catch the yucca beat, strumming his guitar, picking out the heart of one Buddy Holly song or another with aching, swollen fingers.

"Peggy Sue" worked pretty well. The rattling leaves provided a driving, if erratic, beat.

"If you knew . . ." the guitar player said, and then he

laughed as the memory of the man in the house in Vegas played through his head like a familiar riff.

That man hadn't known anything at all.

Vince was the man's name. The guitar player didn't know much about him, apart from the fact that Vince was connected to the woman and Vince was afraid of guns. Too bad on both counts, especially the latter. If Vince hadn't panicked at the sight of the gun, he might be okay right now, and the man with the guitar might still have some bullets in the pistol tucked beneath his waistband.

He might never have felt the warm flecks of blood spraying his face as the pistol bucked in his hand and Vince's chest erupted in a half-dozen wounds. But Vince had mistaken the guitar player for a jealous husband, or a knight in shining armor, and the man wasn't either of those things. Not at all. Hell, he was only a guitar player.

Dry heat killed the breeze and quieted the yucca trees. Tangled shadows stretched from countless trunks, shimmering, dancing on the sunbaked desert sand.

Scratch one rhythm section. The man's fingers traveled cool steel strings, all alone.

There were no shadows in music.

Not even when you played a dead man's songs.

"Is something wrong?" the doctor wanted to know.

Bramble ignored the question. "Tonelli, do you know who was with your brother last night?"

Carmine didn't take his eyes off the bullet-ridden corpse. "What's the matter?" he asked. "Vince not talkative, or what?"

Bramble knew the time had come to ignore sarcasm. "The more you can tell me, the more I'll know."

Carmine sighed heavily. "Like the old saw goes: I am not my baby brother's keeper. Get that straight. I can tell you that Vince wasn't particular about his women. Picked 'em up like most guys pick up a six-pack. Drained 'em and tossed 'em. That was Vince."

Drained 'em and tossed 'em. The words sent an unfamiliar shiver up Bramble's spine. He bent low, close to the corpse. Oyster white flesh. Lips gone blue, going black. Bramble ignored these things, looking for shadows that most people couldn't see. Some called them ghosts, but Bramble didn't use that word. It wasn't quite accurate—after all, he could glance at Carmine Tonelli and see his "ghost," and Tonelli wasn't even dead. Not yet, anyway.

No. What Bramble could see was the essence that often remained even in the wake of death—the human soul, the human spirit. Or, as his mother had called it: *the shade.*

Some people took a long time to die. Like Carmine Tonelli, they lost their shades bit by bit, piece by piece. And if they lived an especially long time, they might leave behind nothing more than a few tatters, like pieces of a crazy quilt.

But this . . .

Vince Tonelli was much younger than Carmine. But on the floor, next to his corpse, Bramble saw nothing more than a narrow crescent moon of oily blackness—rich and heavy, but painfully thin.

The edges of the crescent moon were ragged.

Torn.

As if something had ripped the biggest part of Vince Tonelli's shade free.

Stolen it.

Bramble had never seen anything like it. Generally, it took hours, days, for a shade to overcome the trauma of death and move on, if indeed it moved on at all. To heaven, to hell . . . to somewhere, Bramble had no idea and cared less. Money over metaphysics any day, as far as he was concerned. But with so little of Vince Tonelli's shade remaining, Bramble didn't know how much he could learn.

"So," Carmine said, "who did it? Tell me, so I can kill the bastard."

"Give me a minute." Gingerly, Bramble stretched out a hand.

He touched Vincent Michael Tonelli's shade, expecting the familiar icy ripple to travel from his fingers to his brain, expecting the connection.

But the shade rippled, pulled away, up the corpse's arm.

And it was *warm!* Bramble stumbled back, wiping his fingers on his slacks, whimpering.

The corpse's eyes flashed open.

"Help me!" Vincent Michael Tonelli screeched. "Jesus God, help me!"

In this case, music didn't exactly soothe the savage beast. The man's fingers knotted in pain; even three chords could be hell when your knuckles were hamburger meat. And the desert air didn't help any. It was too dry—like sandpaper on his voice.

The man set the guitar aside. He rose and stepped away from the overhang, into the light.

The sunshine felt good on his knuckles. He opened the back of the van and took a cold cheeseburger and a can of beer from the ice chest. Funny, dipping his hands in the half-melted ice felt good, too.

He drank first, and his throat felt a little better. He figured he could make it feel better still. He drained the first beer, and then he got another. After his fourth beer, he remembered to eat the cheeseburger, even though he wasn't really hungry anymore.

Something to wash it down. That was what he needed. Another beer. A can crumpled in his powerful fist, which didn't hurt so much anymore. He stared down at his cowboy boots, wondering if Buddy Holly would have liked them. That made him giggle. He looked at his boots and the ground that surrounded him, twisting his neck this way and that like some crazy long-necked bird, and all he could see was sand bleached white by the unrelenting sunlight.

That made him laugh.

"Shadow-free, that's me." He hadn't cast a shadow in twenty years, since the night he first met the woman in a Lubbock honky-tonk. Back then he was a guitar player ripping through one Buddy Holly request after another for a drunken, sentimental crowd. Twenty years since she'd torn his living shade from his backside. And hardly anyone ever noticed, because guitar players, good ones, moved in the night.

He wasn't all that good, but he sure as hell had learned how to move.

Twenty years, and now he'd finally tracked her down.

He figured another beer would be pretty good about right now, but he didn't get one. Instead he wondered how many men she'd been with. Hey, scratch that, this was the nineties—how many *people* had she—SCRATCH THAT, TOO—had *it* been with?

He wouldn't think of the battered thing in the motel room as a woman, because that was what had gotten him into trouble in the first place. Still, he wondered about other people who had crossed paths with that thing. He wondered how many—who couldn't see shadows the way he could—didn't even know that something was missing.

How many how many I wonder . . . but I really don't want to know.

Buddy Holly didn't do that one.

Singing it anyway, he stumbled to the door of room number 12.

He got it open. Spilled into the room with the morning light.

There she was, all bruised smirk, lips buttoned tight.

"Give it back," he said.

She didn't say anything.

He hit her again, flush, just the way he'd hit her—SCRATCH THAT, hit *it*—at the house in Vegas before the guy with the torn shade got all stupid-brave and tried to attack him.

Her nose started bleeding.

"Don't pretend with me," he said. "Just you know why."

A wave of cold laughter shivered over him. "It's funny." A girlish voice just above a whisper. "I *almost* remember you."

He hit her and hit her, until she was gone and both eyes rolled up in the thing's head and thick shadows spilled from its lips.

Carmine was gasping for breath. "You think he's *here?"*

Bramble didn't spare Tonelli a glance. There were too many people in the casino, too many shades to watch. "I don't know," he said. "Your brother . . . the way he is . . . This *isn't* the way I usually work. Let's just say that I've picked up a scent. Someone connected with your brother's murder was here."

Tonelli's doctor hurried along behind the two men. "I still don't understand," he said. "About Vince, I mean. I examined him. Six bullets in his chest. He doesn't breathe. No heartbeat. He's *dead."*

"No he's not," Bramble said. "He can't die. Someone stole the part of him that would allow that to happen. And unless we can find a way to get it back, you're going to have to keep him locked in that basement for a long, long time."

The scent grew stronger. Close now. Bramble hurried past a thin-shadowed cocktail waitress, pushed through a tight knot of people.

He stopped short, a heavy shadow pooling at the tips of his shoes. A big car loomed before him, a relic from the days of the Depression-era bandits.

"Shit," Carmine said. "It's the car Bonnie and Clyde were killed in. A hook to attract the tourists. If *this* is what your nose has found us, you've screwed up bad, Bramble."

Bramble turned away from the car, as if drawn by a

magnet. He saw a bank of ATM machines along the far wall.

"Look at him," the doctor said. "He really sees something!"

Carmine didn't say a word.

Bramble grabbed the big man's elbow and hurried toward the ATM machines. "You had it right all along, Carmine. I *am* a bloodhound, and I'm about to pick up the scent of money."

Screaming shadows spilled from the thing's lips, and the man was awash in a flood of midnight.

The torrent pushed him backward, away from the thing with the girlish voice, and he grabbed at the casing of the door, but the flood was too strong. He couldn't hold it back.

The black stream boiled from the room, screaming still, and the man lost hold and swam in it, his head above the tide, washed in sunlight now, blinking tattered shadows from his eyes as the great black wave washed across the dry white sand. The man grabbed tight to the base of a Yucca tree and the shadows washed over his head and dunked him once again, each shadow with a different voice, a different scream that could only be heard within the black grip of the onrushing tide, but none of the screams fit him, and he was once more sucked into the dead, swirling chorus.

How many how many I wonder . . .

He broke surface, gasping, thankful for nothing so much as the pure silence of the desert, and he fought the torrid stream, arms flailing, battered fingers grasping a branch, grasping handfuls of dry, prickly leaves, his palms pierced by them, his hands closing vise-tight around the tree as they had once closed around the steering wheel of a van that traveled a highway, a highway that was nothing out of mythology at all, nothing more than a ribbon of asphalt contained by painted threads.

But nothing could contain the shadows. Not the sun, not the earth. They spilled from the abandoned motel, an obsidian cascade a hundred times darker than any highway, cutting a path through the dry desert, *shoveling trenching tearing* into the earth, washing rock and sand and snake and lizard and yucca into the wide emptiness beyond.

They pulled to a stop behind the van, and Carmine Tonelli burst from the rear of the car with a gun in his hand, but the man didn't even move. He just sat there on the van's rear bumper, a beer can in his hand, shade dripping from his body in fat droplets.

Bramble blinked. Blinked again.

Carmine didn't pause. He moved forward, all business, and pressed the barrel of his pistol to the man's temple, sparing a short glance for Bramble. "This the guy?" he asked.

The man wiped his lips, flicked shadedrops off his fingers. He smiled at Carmine, and then at Bramble. An old rock 'n' roll song bounced around inside the van, trapped there. For the first time, Bramble noticed the van's personalized license plate: CHARON.

"Well?" Carmine prodded. "Give me an answer!"

"Wait a minute," Bramble said.

The man studied Bramble. More properly, he studied Bramble's shade. "You're one up on me," he said, chuckling.

"Shut up," Carmine said. "You don't talk."

The man stood up. Carmine's hand started to shake. The man stepped away from the gun, toward Bramble, and Bramble saw nothing but the pure white sand around the man's cowboy boots, no shade at all . . .

"I've wasted twenty years," the man said. "There's no finding it, because there are millions of 'em out there, all flowing God knows where. But let's go down to the river just the same, you and me. . . . We can go swimmin'. Maybe we'll get—"

If he said anything else, the words were lost in the thunder of Carmine Tonelli's pistol.

The man fell. White dust puffed up around him.

And then, in the quiet of the desert, the men from Vegas heard the cool rushing of a river.

"It can't be," the doctor said.

Carmine dropped his pistol. Tatters of shade slipped away from his heels, trickling in weak rivulets across the sand.

Carmine slumped forward, into the doctor's arms.

"We've got to get out of here!" the doctor said. "Now!"

Bramble didn't move. He closed his eyes and listened. "Don't panic," he said. "It's only the wind . . . only the wind."

But Bramble knew these words were lies. Even as he spoke them, he heard the cool rush of shadows . . . the old music trapped in the van. Eyes closed, he heard the quiet movement of a man without a shadow rising from the hot sand . . . and the scream of a doctor who knew nothing . . . and the solitary footfalls of the man . . . cowboy boots digging tired ditches in the white sand . . .

Shadowstained fingers brushed Bramble's shoulder.

The man said, "Just you know why . . ."

JUBILEE

Kathe Koja

ONCE HEARD IT SEEMED AS IF SHE HAD KNOWN THE VOICE forever: exhalation, the sigh of blood through the body, breath's tickle across bare skin; once present, omnipresent since that first time: morning flurry, too-hot bathroom and she brushing her teeth, brushing her hair and as if from the steam in the air itself, the sound of her own name.

I can see you, the voice said.

The tremble of the brush, blunt black bristles and she rigid in panty hose and high-collared blouse, expensive brown silk blouse wet now at the armpits; no one else in the house, no one there to speak to her and the voice again, soft to her ear: *I can see you* once more but without threat or even insistence, as if sharing a fact meant to bring pleasure to both. The feeling in the air not of presence but of—what? Imminence? Shifting like steam, clouding and dissipating and gone and she now there alone, the brush absurd in one hand as the other braced her upright, the silver molding of the sink digging slightly but painfully into her palm.

I can see you, the voice had said.

No memory, no voice from the grave, from the past to force identity: nothing she had ever heard before. Trembling at the sink, the echo heard somehow in her flesh, the pit of her stomach: staring not into the mirror but at the back of the brush, her hand gripping plastic and: Stop it, she thought, just stop it; and hurrying upstairs to change her stained blouse, fingers forced to competence button by button by will. The thing to do with a thing like this, whatever it was, was to ignore it. Just ignore it: like a bad dream, a bad decision, a bad idea: and it will disappear and go away.

She was thirty-six years old. She had been married for eight years, nine in October, to an art director at a moderately successful publisher of self-help books. Sometimes she wept without knowing precisely why. She had never before heard voices, been visited by the divine, the infernal, the otherworldly; she did not believe in the afterlife or the supernatural; she had not wept nor experienced an orgasm for three months before the voice came to her that first time, came to her as if it had been part of her life forever, came to her as if now inside her would never cease or leave.

She did not tell anyone. She would not have known what to say, how to begin. He talks to me, she could have said, he knows my name. There was no threat in the voice, no reason to fear beyond the fact of its existence; perhaps it was her own response that troubled her. She kept her resolve to do nothing; her husband did not seem to notice her decision nor the inner turbulence prompting it. Her husband did not believe in the supernatural, the hidden vagaries of emotion, the sink and drift of the blood, the echo of one's heart found beating in the breast of another. She was having trouble lubricating when they had sex but he did not seem to notice that either.

Long day, empty day, long wasted lunch with a woman from her department, their talk all triviality: the petty, the brief, job and home, work and love, nothing divided by nothing is what? Silence. Exhausted, straining to see through the rain and the path of faulty wipers, mind empty as an empty cup and: immediate, kiss-moist against her ear, sensation intimate as a hand in an intimate place and *Yours,* the voice said, *oh yours* and her head turning instinctively toward and into the voice, hands on the wheel following the motion and the sound of a horn, loud and she swerved back too far like a drunk, like a woman blind, all of it too close: the voice, the car in the next lane, her purse and the big black tote bag and all past momentum on the floor, papers, checkbook, notes a gray stew in the spatter of slush, her wet overshoes lying like the fruit of amputation, cut off in the act of escape.

Escape: the voice: was that what it was? He talks to me, to whom could she have said that? Not her husband, not the woman at lunch; why bring it up? to that silent inner stare, why bring it up when you know you don't want to talk about it? But I do want to talk about it, I have to talk about it, I'm going crazy. Crazy people hear voices: the voice of God, the mutterings of angels, the creeping shriek of devils in the dark house of the brain but this was *different,* she had known that from the first, knew it each time: four times, distinct the memory of each occasion, distinct the sound, the feel of the voice: first her name, then the words *I see you;* then *yes,* the voice had said, *yes, oh yes.* And each time—once more in the bathroom, twice in the kitchen, every time alone—the voice accompanied by that feeling of compounding imminence, a certainty so enormous that it was itself impossible, nothing could be so sure. And afterward hands to face, eyes squeezed shut, reinforcing her corporeality, you are here in this room, you are here in this body in this room. That other is not real. It is not real and not happening . . . and the afternoon light gone to early darkness, the car around her as real as her own body, to try to speak these things aloud to another human creature was less ultimately possible than the existence of the voice itself. Maybe she should invent an imaginary friend, someone to whom she could tell her troubles; perhaps the voice was the imaginary friend.

Perhaps she was the imaginary friend.

Now her hands, her arms shaking so terribly from reaction that she must at once pull over, settle the car by jerks and choppy braking in the larger puddles at the side of the highway, water down the windshield, her hands loose and trembling in her lap and *oh yes,* the voice again and with great tenderness, *that's the way it is for you and for me. It's all real; all of it is real.*

"No," in her own anguish, "what do you *want,"* and she lowered her head against the steering wheel, against the knuckled arch of her shaking hands to feel

breath against her cheek and

Real and present, the voice said. *You; and me.*

"Why are you doing this," whispering, eyes closed. Traffic blurring past. Adrenaline for the accident averted, the conflagration still to come and *I speak to you because you can hear me,* said the voice, *you can hear because I speak* and oh that wave of imminence, as if something was not only going to happen but happen now, this minute, an apparition, a hand to reach from empty air to touch her, touch her bent head, stroke her hair: and in silence, tears, the bridge past expectancy arcing at last into desire: yes, she thought, pain in her head, pain yoked in her bowstring shoulders like a burden too heavy to bear, *yes* and

the touch

did not happen: the imminence gone in the white noise of traffic, roostertail slush and raising her pounding head, opening her eyes: to the end of rush hour and the rain, alone in the driver's seat, arms braced against the steering wheel as if to find purchase in the eye of some deep unknown velocity.

None of it is real. All of it is real.

Wearily hauling the floorboard mess back onto the seat, drip and spatter and pulling back into traffic, confused all at once as to direction—which way? and a line from a song in blunter echo, not the voice but the simpler tones of memory: *It all depends on where you want to go, baby.* Where do you want to go, baby? which way is home?

Clumsy circle at last into the driveway, kitchen light and her husband nodding up as she came in, looking closer and "What's the matter?" pushing back the chair, high back, solid and real: present like the cars on the highway, as a puddle of water, a circle of blood. "What happened? You—"

"I almost had an accident," lying, not-lying, trying to smile back: anything to get out of the kitchen, upstairs to collapse in warmth and cluttered darkness fully clothed across the bed, the muscles in her shoulders aching, present, real. Her body was real.

Yours, oh yours.

What kind of person hears voices? or wants to?

You can hear because I speak.

Sleep was unthinkable but she slept at once, woke when her husband's body touched the bed, his hands touched her body, cool and pleasant, nothing she wanted, nothing real enough to feel and then he was done and she lay naked and chilled and dreaming, landscapes unremembered, the country of the bodiless and the lost to wake all at once with eyes wide open, cloaked again in imminence stringent as orgasm, unmistakable and *jubilee,* the voice said and so close she knew for the first time the feel of the breath, its taste absolute against her lips parted to receive it: and said the word back, "Jubilee."

Yes, with such pleasure it bloomed as a smile, her smile brief and dazzled in the dark: *oh yes. Jubilee, your jubilance: you can see it now, can't you.*

"What are you," mouthing the words, her husband indistinct beside her as if unpresent, outside the room and its reality. "What—"

Yours, the voice said; the curve of her jaw as if stroked by a lover's touch; one deep shiver through her skin, grounding throughout her body like a stone thrown in deep water: layers and ripples, circles of response. *Yours, yours.* Her nipples were hard beneath the covers; jubilance: she parted her legs. Breath on her cheek again, her open mouth.

"Touch me," like breath herself.

Yes as if muffled by flesh, the feel of the word against her and the impending touch so charged and so intense that when it happened—light, lighter than breath, each pale and tiny hair rising equally on thigh and nape—she made a little sound, a sound from depths of throat, body, heart, a sound echoed by the whispers, the susurrations of that voice, no words, nothing but sound now in tandem with the touch again: and again, swept without haste or hesitation, boldly up and down her body, belly, legs, breasts, neck, face with closed eyes and open mouth and back down again: and again: and between her legs, open legs, thighs rigid and knees locked and that penetration light and firm and exact, once in in forever, dissolving like sugar in water, disseminating through her body as if it were a drug whose action she could feel, pinpoint through muscle and blood and *Mine,* said the voice in her ear, *mine now*

and her orgasm like a sound, a bell in the body, deep dwelling ring felt everywhere, breasts, heart, arching thighs, in the heels of her hands dug silent against the mattress, the attenuated line of her jaw, her open mouth into which, exquisitely, excruciatingly, the smallest touch of moisture, a true kiss on the tip of her tongue

and beside her that other body, moving in sleep, muffled in the sheets and blankets and her own heart beating and beating, inner echo like a seashell held to the waiting ear: the sound of the ocean: sea of salt and blood and motion, waves like circles to bring the jubilee.

She woke once more in the night, the dark clear hours of earliest morning to find that she could see through her own body, see down through the sheets and the mattress beneath and the floor beneath that and down and down into dirt and crushed rock and tiny bones: she could see down and up in all directions: she could see many things. Her own testing voice loud as music in her ears, her sigh like a wind from the sea. She could see through the house, every wall a window; she could see patterns of heat and the flickering rise of dust: she could see everything, everything, everything but herself: perceived as warmth and silence, perceived in clarity and loss.

She thought she might never close her eyes again.

True morning now and her husband's small coughs and gruntings, rolling over: to emptiness: undisturbed, not sure where she was and he called her name, not loud, called it again. She was not in the bathroom. She was not in the hall. She was not in the kitchen making coffee, she was not on the porch to get the newspaper, her purse like an artifact on the floor beside the sofa and so she had not left the house. He called her name again, not angry, not annoyed, only wondering.

"Anne?"

I'm here, she said. *I'm right here, see? I'm real.*

"Anne?"

Breathing. Her voice in his ear: *I'm here* but he did not seem to hear her although she could hear everything he said, all the words he knew, all the feelings he had ever felt or dreamed of feeling; she saw his dreams like a frieze unrolling, she saw tiny pains and crevices of loss behind his eyes. *I'm right here,* she said again but without urgency; standing quiet and calm and naked in the corner of the room, sunlight across her bare feet, her small sloping breasts, sunlight on and through her, warm and everlasting, no voice but her own in her ears.

"Anne?" in circles, in circling unease growing deeper, she saw, with each revolution, "Anne?" in dishevelment and dismay and then he stopped, stopped where he was, stopped in the light and the morning silence as if he could see, something, see her, see himself and through himself: as if he heard a voice, its own circles deep and rippling deeper in his mind. Unconsciously he touched himself through his pajamas, held his genitals in one considering hand.

"No," he said.

I'm real, she said, and saw both their voices, open as windows above their heads, open as an open mouth, a spread vagina, ready and waiting as a listening ear.

NOT FAR FROM HERE

Tim Smith

"WANNA SEE A GHOST?" SAID THE AGING, DISFIGURED DERElict. He was twiddling his thumbs—his face dirty, unshaven, the brow over his left eye appeared to be melting over the eyeball itself, like Silly Putty. He was sitting across the aisle of the nearly empty Marta transport bus and, except for the facial handicap, he strongly resembled Thomas Mitchell in *It's a Wonderful Life.*

"Excuse me," Chuck replied, bewildered and repulsed by the sight of the man.

"Wanna see a *real* ghost? Not like all that crap you're reading in that book."

Chuck closed *Strangers Among Us* by Ruth Montgomery and let it rest like a Bible on his lap. He removed his glasses, rubbed his eyes, and lit a cigarette. "I suppose you're going to tell me where to find one. Is that it?" he asked, exhaling smoke.

"Maybe . . ." the man replied, matter-of-factly. "Maybe not so far from here."

Chuck hesitated before telling the old man to disappear. The words echoed in his mind: *Not far from here.* Despite the source, the words had almost a mesmerizing effect on Chuck. For the past year he had been religiously studying the works of Montgomery, Stern, and even the laughable Time-Life books in hopes of being accepted into the Atlanta Research Center for the Investigation of Psychic Phenomena. If the old bum was on the level and the report turned out to be factual, it might be his skeleton key to the multilocked research center door. Although itching to see the supposed ghosts, Chuck masked his anticipation with mock skepticism. "Are they malevolent spirits or poltergeists?" he asked.

"I don't know what the fuck you're talking about," the old man replied, his grin revealing teeth the color of shower stall sludge.

"Okay, I give. What's in it for you?" Chuck asked, approaching from a different angle. The man seemed puzzled. "I mean, how much is this little escapade going to cost me?"

This time the derelict paused. With his good eye scaling up and down, he seemed to be sizing Chuck up for what he was worth. Then, much to Chuck's surprise, the man said, "Nothin'."

"Nothing? I don't get it."

"There ain't nothin' to get, just somethin' to see," the man said, his smile faltering. "Let me tell you somethin', friend. I've been going to this place for a long time, and what I'm goin' to show you has happened *every* time I've been there. I guess what I'm tryin' to say is—I *need* someone else to see it. Make sure I'm not goin' off my rocker. Besides, I like you." The smile returned.

Something is screwy here, Chuck thought. *This old guy's hiding something.* But maybe he was wrong. The man's appearance left much to be desired but Chuck sensed that the man was telling the truth. This *could* possibly turn out to be a legit sighting and, if that was the case, he really couldn't afford to pass up such an opportunity. What harm could it do? The old man was too decrepit to do any damage, so mugging was out of the question. And who knows, this just might be his big break. "Okay, you win. Where are we going?" he asked.

"Next stop. Old Roswell Road," the man replied. "By the way, my name is James. James Henry."

They stood on the corner of Old Roswell and Johnson's Ferry Road as the bus hissed away silently in the night.

"How far?" Chuck asked.

"Couple of blocks, on the right," James replied, and began walking briskly, with a slight limp. Chuck followed.

As the two were walking, it occurred to Chuck that, if this was a scam, James might have some friends waiting to ambush him. But that was ludicrous. How the hell could anybody predict that there would be an aspiring psychic investigator on that particular bus? He kept his eyes peeled anyway as they approached an old dirt drive. James stopped. The name on the mailbox was illegible, worn away with weather and time. The hedges along the sidewalk were in dire need of a manicure, their branches spiderlike, clutching. A lone streetlight illuminated the spot where they stood. Old spiderwebs clung to the pole and floated in the warm August breeze like banners from a forgotten war. The house was not visible from the road.

"Follow me," said James, and led the way down the dirt path.

The walk was dark, except for the occasional glow of Chuck's cigarette. It was a relatively clear night, but the moon was not visible because of the trees. From each side of the driveway, overgrown trees draped with kudzu met above their heads, creating a tunnellike effect that made Chuck feel extremely claustrophobic.

When they emerged from the trees, the moon shone bright, revealing the house. It was monstrous in size; antebellum, Chuck guessed. The front steps led up to four enormous columns supporting a portico, which also doubled as a balcony for the second floor. Parasitic ivy climbed the walls and columns of the house, greedily defending their prize. Dark, empty windows stared accusingly.

The house was centered in the middle of a long unkempt yard, where tall grass and shrubs swayed in the growing breeze. Jasmine and honeysuckle scent mingled, creating a nauseating perfume that was almost physically overpowering. The combined elements made Chuck feel dizzy . . . and scared.

"You're not goin' yellow on me, are you?"

"What?" Chuck replied, trying to muster up his courage. His career stood before him, mocking. Of course, he was scared. Who wouldn't be? It was expected. But he didn't want James to know, so he rationalized his fear with the overall excitement of approaching his first haunting, thereby forcing his negative energy to positive. "No," he said, "let's go."

Chuck immediately marched across the yard toward the front door. His palms were sweating. He was the authority here, *wasn't he?* he thought, desperately trying to assume control of the situation.

"Where are you goin'?" James asked, following. "We can't go in that way."

"Why not?" Chuck replied, stopping.

James paused. "Because it's *locked,* dumb ass. We have to go around back." He moved toward the right side of the house, shaking his head, comically. Chuck hesitated, flicked his cigarette, then followed.

Rounding the back corner, Chuck was surprised to find a glow in one of the second floor windows.

"That's it. We can climb up the trellis and watch them from outside the window," James said, and before Chuck could protest, James began scaling the wall. He was surprisingly agile for an old man, Chuck thought, but was secretly relieved to know that he didn't actually have to go inside the house. He followed James up the trellis and over onto the balcony.

Once there, James walked toward the window and said, rather loudly, "Over here."

Chuck held a finger to his lips and shushed the old man, another futile attempt to assume command of the investigation.

"Don't worry 'bout it," James replied. "They can't hear us."

Chuck shrugged nervously, moved toward the window, and looked in. In the center of the room was an antique, canopied bed. On the bed lay a naked man, blindfolded, motionless, his arms and legs bound, separately, to the four corner bedposts. On the right side of the room a fire burned softly in the fireplace, casting sporadic shadows and making the room appear as if changing shapes. On the far left of the room stood an ancient looking bureau with a silver-handled hand mirror and some old hair combs lying on it. In the corner, next to the bureau, a man sat on the floor, head bowed, face hidden. Scattered throughout the room was an abundance of candles, glowing, beaconlike in the room's vast sea of dimness.

"What *is* this?" Chuck asked, angrily.

"Just wait a minute," James replied. "Those guys are part of it."

"That's not what I'm talking about. The fire, the candles. *Ghosts don't use matches.*"

"It's part of the illusion. Trust me. It's not real. Feel the window."

Chuck did. It was cold.

"Okay. So now what?" Chuck asked, lighting another cigarette. His hands were trembling. He had assumed that when he conducted his first psychic investigation he would be surrounded by people with cameras and tape recorders and such, and here he was on a stakeout, searching for verification of the existence of a spiritual world with some two-bit bum he met on a bus in Buckhead. He felt humiliated. But worse than that, he felt alone and vulnerable.

"Just wait," James said, sliding soundlessly down the wall into a sitting position. "Just wait."

Twenty minutes later the door to the room opened and in walked a man and woman, dressed in what appeared to be clothing from around the time of the Civil War. The man was dashing in his Confederate uniform, a general perhaps. He looked remarkably like Clark Gable in *Gone With the Wind,* down to the pencil thin mustache above his lip. The girl, however, was no Vivian Leigh. She had long blonde hair cascading down her back in tiny ringlets. She was clad in a large hoop skirt, complete with corset. A red bow was centered delicately on the back of her head. She even had a fan.

Chuck was completely absorbed in the illusion. Everything looked so real. No transparent figures hovering in the darkness. These apparitions were the most well defined he had ever seen, at least from the pictures in the Time-Life books. He wished he had his camera.

"What next?" he asked.

"You don't wanna know," James replied, still sitting, facing away from the window.

The "belle" unclasped her dress and the hoop skirt fell to the floor. The man helped her undo her corset and soon she was completely naked except for the bow in her hair. Chuck could see the sweat between her breasts glistening in the firelight with remarkable clarity. The man removed his clothes as well.

"This is unbelievable," Chuck said, his excitement far from hidden. "Who are they?"

"The woman's name is Anna; the man, Richard." James sighed. "They do this every night at exactly the same time. Ten-twenty."

Chuck checked his watch to confirm the statement. "How did you find out about them?" he asked.

"Later, just watch."

Richard withdrew a long feather plume from a vase in the corner. He began stroking the man on the bed with it.

The man writhed in ecstasy. Soon he was erect. Richard then removed a small piece of twine from the night table drawer. He wrapped the twine underneath the man's scrotum and around the base of his penis, tying it tightly.

Anna mounted the man. She squealed delightfully as he entered her. The bed began to rock rhythmically with their thrusts and more rapidly as their hunger increased. Anna remained upright, as the man slid in and out of her. Richard stood in front of the fire, watching.

Chuck watched, too, completely absorbed in the act. He felt himself stiffen.

As the couple approached nirvana, their moans increased. Anna looked at Richard and he nodded. He withdrew a branding iron from the hot coals of the fire and handed it to her.

"Oh, no," Chuck gasped.

The man shuddered with climax and Anna brought the scorching iron down on his chest. He screamed as the pain penetrated him and his seed spilled into her. His body continued to spasm with orgasm despite the pain. Anna quivered and moaned with her own climax. She dropped the branding iron to the floor and leaned down to the man's chest, licking the fresh wound. The man continued screaming and swearing.

"Jesus, we've got to help him," Chuck said, grabbing James by the coat.

"There's nothing you can do," James replied.

Chuck started to say more but was startled to find that Anna had left the man and was approaching the window. Her pubis was wet, the blonde hair dark and slick with her juices. Once there, she pressed her face against the glass. Chuck fell back on his rear with a muffled "oomph" and slid toward the darkness of the ivy-woven trellis. Anna stared through the shadows and into the night. She smiled, the pale moonlight illuminating her ghostly features.

After a moment she turned and motioned for Richard to follow. They left the room, closing the door behind them. The man on the bed continued to whimper. The huddled figure had not moved, oblivious to the events surrounding him.

"Do you think she saw me?" Chuck asked James, who now seemed shrunken as he sat with his back to the wall.

"Anna sees what she wants," the old man answered with a strange choking sound in his voice. In the shadows he seemed to be rubbing his bad eye.

"Tell me everything you know," Chuck whispered angrily. "The man on the bed and the guy in the corner, who are they?"

"I don't know the man on the bed. It's a different one every night. The man in the corner . . ." James paused, appearing ill. "The man in the corner is . . . their father."

"Oh, my God. They're *brother and sister?*" Chuck exclaimed. "How could he let them get away with this? This is sick! Is he unconscious? They must have drugged him." Chuck lit a cigarette. James just looked at him, saying nothing.

The door opened and Anna entered, followed by Richard who was wheeling in a small gurney. Atop the gurney, hemostats and a small variety of other medical instruments gleamed in the candlelight. The man started screaming again. Richard shut the door.

Chuck felt dizzy and sickened by the cruelty of the situation. Here he stood, watching an act of violence that had probably happened over a hundred years ago. Powerless to intervene, yet fascinated by the morbid *decadence*—from a psychic investigator's point of view, that is.

The man was still hard. The tourniquet Richard had applied was doing its job, cutting the circulation yet keeping what blood there was in the organ. Anna stroked him but his screams were nonstop. She looked at Richard lovingly, and he handed her the hemostats. During midscream, Richard used both of his hands to force the man's mouth to stay open. After fishing for a moment,

Anna grasped the stranger's tongue tightly with the hemostats and the screams turned to almost inaudible gags. With this done, Richard turned and removed the scissors from the gurney.

Chuck tried to speak but words wouldn't come.

Richard removed the man's tongue with two snips and grinned. The man jerked and writhed on the bed, his frantic breath spraying geysers of blood on the headboard.

Chuck went to the edge of the balcony and threw up into the dark yard below. He wiped his mouth with his shirtsleeve and turned to James. The old man was crying.

Anna mounted the man again and kissed him, lapping hungrily at the blood-filled mouth. Richard tossed the squirming tongue into a petri dish with a wet slap.

Chuck sat down in front of James. "There's something wrong with this picture. For one thing, they didn't have medical instruments like that during the Civil War. I want to know what's going on."

James sighed, wiped his eyes, then spoke, "It didn't happen durin' the Civil War, *goddammit!* Those are just costumes. They like to dress up. It's part of their routine."

"When *did* this happen?"

"It all started about ten years ago, from what I heard. When they were young, their father used to . . . hurt them . . . *you know . . ."*

"Sexually abuse?"

"Yeah, that's it. Only as Richard and Anna got older, their tastes went further than their old man's. They were killin' too many people, so he decided to kill *them* and bury 'em in the backyard with the rest of their victims. But the kids were smarter than him. They seduced him on the night he planned to do the deed and, as you can see for yourself, they got him first."

"And that's his body over in the corner," Chuck reaffirmed.

"Yeah," James said, quietly. "That's him."

"How do *they* die?" Chuck asked, intrigued.

"That's just it. They don't," James said, exasperated. "They just repeat this fuckin' torture every night till eleven o'clock. Then they leave and don't come back till the next night at ten-twenty. It's *awful,"* he said, putting his face in his hands and shuddering. He was crying again.

Chuck looked at James for a long time. *"Why did you bring me here?"*

"Because I want you to make them *stop!"* he said, looking up, his eye red, angry. "I can't stop thinkin' 'bout 'em. Day-in and day-out, they're always in my head, like one of those instant replays from the football games. I come here *every* night, like a magnet. I don't watch no more. I can't. I just sit here till they're done."

Chuck could identify with the obsession. He'd give anything to have some of the research center's equipment so he could set up a proper investigation.

"Just make them stop," James pleaded, his face wet from tears. "I don't care how. Just get rid of them."

"Why me?" Chuck asked.

"'Cause I seen you readin' that book on the bus. I figured maybe *you'd* know what to do."

Chuck started to tell James that he had no experience when movement from the other side of the window caught his attention. Anna rose from the man's moistened penis. She removed the blindfold and stuffed the blue fabric into the stranger's bleeding mouth. Richard came up behind her and touched her shoulder. She turned and they kissed passionately while the man squirmed on the bed, eyes wide, catatonic. Once again, the couple left the room.

"I think they're through," Chuck said. "I want to get a closer look."

James glanced briefly in the window. "Not yet. It's Richard's turn."

"You don't mean . . ." Chuck started.

"Like I said, it's Richard's turn," James replied.

Chuck swallowed. "How? I mean . . . um . . . Do they . . . well, you know . . ."

James stared, uncertain.

"Anal sex?" Chuck blurted.

James looked confused for a moment. "You mean is he gonna fuck him in the *butt?"*

Chuck nodded.

"No," James said, lowering his head. "It's worse than that."

Right offhand, Chuck couldn't imagine anything worse. But with what he had seen so far, the concept wasn't that difficult to believe. Tentatively, he asked, *"How?"*

James swallowed, dryly. "They make a *new* hole," he said. "They take one of them knives over there and cut off his . . ."

"Stop! I don't want to hear anymore. I'm going in."

"No, you can't," James gasped. "They'll be back soon."

"They can't harm me. They're *not* poltergeists. Besides, I want to get a closer look at some of the details."

James started to protest but Chuck Matheson, *psychic investigator extraordinaire*, had already opened the window and was halfway through.

What the hell am I doing? Chuck thought to himself, as he entered the room. I can't believe I'm actually *in* here. The room smelled like rotten meat. *Ectoplasm,* no doubt. He walked carefully, almost on tiptoes, over to the gurney. At first, he was scared shitless, but gradually the feeling was overcome with pure curiosity—and revulsion. The tongue had quit quivering and lay still in the petri dish. Next to the dish were the hemostats and a various assortment of other instruments of torture. On the far end was a contraption that looked like a miniature bear trap. But Chuck had the feeling that this device trapped something far more precious to a man than a bear.

As he made his way to the other side of the bed, Chuck

realized that the room was far from cold; it was unpleasantly hot. Other than the rotten smell, the sickening fragrance of jasmine was pungent, combined with the undeniable scent of fresh sweat and sex. A chill shot up his back and released cold sweat from his pores. This is real, Chuck thought. *This . . . is . . . real.*

There was only one way to be sure. The victim lay still on the bed, his eyes closed. Blood covered his face and inundated the entire upper portion of the mattress. Slowly, Chuck reached out and touched the man's leg. The man's eyes shot open wildly, two white orbs suspended in a sea of redness. Chuck jerked his hand from the man's flesh and stumbled backward.

"Oh, my God."

The expression on the man's face was clearly mad, yet still beckoned for Chuck to help him. He tried to speak and more blood leaked from the corners of his mouth.

"Hurry up!" James said from outside the window.

"We're going to get you out of here," Chuck said, ignoring James. He leaned over and started untying the man's left hand.

From the hall, footsteps approached.

"Shit!" Chuck whispered. He started for the window and tripped over the hoop skirt Anna had discarded earlier. Then he saw the briefcase. It was under the bed next to the victim's clothes. On it was an engraved plate which read:

Alex Shepard
Atlanta Research Center
for the
Investigation of
Psychic Phenomena

Confused, Chuck stood and stared at James, who was still waiting in the window. "You brought him here, *too,*" he said.

"I wanted to make them stop," James replied. "I couldn't think of another way."

"But you promised . . ." Chuck started.

". . . that you would see a ghost tonight," James finished. "And you have. I tried to warn you, friend. I'm sorry."

James Henry vanished right before Chuck Matheson's eyes.

Before anything could register, Chuck was startled by a noise in the corner. He turned to find that the slumped man had fallen over on his side, leaving a slimy trail on the wall. Richard and Anna's father had been dead for quite some time, but there was no mistaking his identity. James Henry's putrid face glared accusingly at Chuck with one eye. The other was missing, huge gashes and flaps of flesh hung over the empty socket. There was a sad, defeated look in the face's decomposed features.

Chuck tried to move but his legs were frozen.

The door opened.

"Oh, look, Richard. Father has brought us another one."

Chuck turned to find the naked Anna standing in the doorway, holding a glass of sherry. Behind her stood Richard, holding a pistol.

"Would you like a drink before we get started?" she asked.

THE KIDS

MAMMA GHOST

Alan Rodgers

THE THING ABOUT ABBEY'S MAMMA WAS THAT ABBEY LOVED her. Of course Abbey loved her Mamma! She was her Mamma, wasn't she?

But sometimes it was hard.

Sometimes back before Mamma died she used to do things to Abbey that nobody should ever do to her daughter—things she wouldn't even do to a dog. That was Mamma: Sometimes she was awful, and sometimes she was worse. But she loved Abbey dearly, and Abbey loved her, too. Love is like that for some people, and no matter how much it hurts them they still prize it.

When you step away from all the arguing about what ought to be, that's the thing that makes the biggest difference, isn't it? People love each other. Abbey loved her Mamma, no matter what, and she knew her Mamma loved her every bit that much. It had to be, didn't it? People don't spend lifetimes doing horrible things to people they don't love. Abbey wouldn't let anybody do things to her like that if she didn't love the one who hit her more than she could say.

Abbey never told nobody about it, but sometimes people acted like they knew. Like Welfare Lady.

Welfare Lady asked about Mamma all the damn time. She used to get on Abbey about Mamma, back when Mamma was alive. Welfare Lady would come to visit, and she'd look Abbey up and down, and of course she saw the bruises. Every damn time. Abbey always told her something that she made up on the spot. *I hurt myself,* she'd say. And of course that was a lie, but so what? She knew what would happen if she told Welfare Lady about Mamma, and she kept her mouth shut.

Kept her mouth shut no matter what.

No matter how many times Welfare Lady asked.

Because Abbey knew Welfare Lady would take her Mamma away if she ever found out. And Abbey wasn't going to let her do that. No way, no how.

That was the thing about Welfare Lady: She always tried to do the right thing, but everything she did worked out the opposite of what she meant. Abbey saw it happen lots of times, like when Welfare Lady tried to get the boys away from junk the year they turned thirteen. Right after she talked to them they went out looking for it because they had to know why Welfare Lady made such a fuss. And they loved it when they found it, of course. Wouldn't you?

Everybody did. Junk is beautiful that way.

Abbey never told Welfare Lady what happened after Mamma died, either.

It started two nights after Mamma died, when Abbey lay abed so sad so restless all alone in her tenement room, and suddenly she felt something strange and darkling in the dank summer air. And when she rolled over she saw Mamma sitting half-invisible on the edge of her bed, watching Abbey with a look on her face that was three parts love and two parts hate.

A ghost, Abbey thought. *My Mamma is a ghost.*

"Abbey Abbey," Mamma Ghost said, "I love you." She looked hungry and carnivorous.

Abbey wanted to cry for joy. She loved her Mamma Ghost so much! She missed her so bad! Abbey always loved her, no matter how dead she ever got.

Next day was Mamma's funeral. Abbey cried and cried, bellowing like a baby in the funeral parlor.

Welfare Lady squeezed Abbey's hand as she cried. Abbey hugged her and cried all over her shoulder.

Welfare Lady always tried to be there when you needed her. She really tried to do the right thing when she could.

When the preacher was done talking Welfare Lady took Abbey's arm and led her out onto the street.

"Call me when you need me, child," Welfare Lady said, and Abbey thought that was so sweet she wanted to start crying all over again.

"I will, Welfare Lady," Abbey said.

Welfare Lady scowled. "Don't call me that," she said. "I told you that a thousand times if I ever told you once. I'm serious, girl. It's a mean, hungry world out there, and it'll kill you if it's able. A girl like you needs all the help she can get."

"I'll be fine," Abbey said. "You know I will."

But neither one of them knew anything like that.

"That's what you said the week your mother put you in the hospital for the third time," Welfare Lady said. "I worry for you, child."

Abbey shook her head and lied. Again. "My Mamma never took me to no hospital," she said. "I fell down the stairs."

Welfare Lady rolled her eyes. For a moment she looked just like Mamma did, last night sitting on the edge of Abbey's bed.

Welfare Lady loves me, Abbey thought. *Just like my Mamma does.*

When she thought that, Abbey wanted to share everything with her, just like she shared with Mamma. She almost started to tell her about Mamma and the half-light last night and the way she heard Mamma's voice inside her head all morning, heard her just like she was right there whispering in her ear.

She almost told. Almost! But just in time she stopped herself.

And that was good. Because no matter who said she was too stupid, Abbey knew what would happen if she told Welfare Lady. Welfare Lady would frown at her and tell her she was *having trouble distinguishing fantasy and reality again, Abbey,* just like she did whenever Abbey got in trouble. Any minute she'd try to convince Abbey that she didn't really see her Mamma, and you know Welfare Lady, she can make you think anything if she puts a mind to it.

Just thinking about it made Abbey feel so cold inside. How could that awful Welfare Lady say her Mamma Ghost was one of those reality-fantasy things? If she said that, Abbey would lose her Mamma all over again. Bad enough Abbey lost her once, she wasn't going to lose her twice.

Abbey took Mamma's ashes home and put them on the mantel where there wasn't any fireplace, and then she went out again. She had to go out. There wasn't any way she could stay at home feeling like she did, and besides, her Mamma whispered in her ear: *You got to get some air, girl. Go out and see yourself some people.*

Abbey did just what her Mamma said. She always tried to do that.

Down the tenement stairs where the Welfare Lady had left her not twenty minutes before, out onto the street, and then she started to wander.

Well, she didn't really wander. She went uptown.

Straight uptown through Spanish Harlem.

All the time she went uptown Abbey kept thinking

about fantasy reality. She was still thinking about it when she got into the 140s.

Way, way uptown into the 140s. She had to go up there, because she felt so broke inside. So broke up! Like something busted deep inside her, and she couldn't fix it by herself. There was only one thing to do when you felt busted that way: You got to fix the trouble.

And the fastest fix Abbey ever found came out the sharp end of a medicine needle.

Junk is like that. It'll fix you when you're broken.

The guy who ran the shooting gallery uptown in the 140s liked Abbey. He always smiled at her, and sometimes when he was in a mood he'd shoot her up for free.

Abbey liked that. Abbey liked that guy a lot. She called him Needle Man because he gave her junk.

Abbey liked junk.

Abbey liked junk a lot.

Sometimes when she was dreaming she wished she had a job so she could buy all the junk she wanted. But there were never jobs for people like Abbey. She knew about that. There were some people who were screwed from the day they were born, screwed every day before they woke up in the morning, screwed every time they stuck their heads up out of their hidey-holes to peek at the world. Abbey was one of those people. She knew. Her Mamma used to tell her when she was little. "Abbey," she'd say—usually when Abbey did something to get Mamma mad at her, but sometimes just because she felt like being mean, "Abbey, you're ugly and you're stupid, child. You're stupider than ugly, and uglier than stupid. The world hates people like you. Sooner or later it'll come for you. And when it does you might as well lay back and enjoy it, because there's nothing you can do."

Abbey never understood what she meant till she was older when the boys found her in the schoolyard that afternoon and carried her down into the basement and all. And she remembered what Mamma said, and she lay back, and she tried to enjoy the things they did. But how could she? It hurt, and it made her feel so terrible and dirty. And when they left her there all bruised and dirty she wished that she could die, but she didn't. After it got dark she picked herself up off the dirty basement floor and dressed herself in those dirty torn clothes and went home to Mamma who said she was stupid and vile and dirty.

Mamma was hatefully mean to Abbey like that, but Abbey still loved her. And Mamma loved her, too. That was the worst thing of all after Mamma died—bad as it was to have a Mamma you loved and hated who loved and hated you, it was infinitely worse not to have a Mamma like that.

Abbey still cried when she thought about Mamma dead in the kitchen three mornings ago when she got up.

Nothing dramatic, nothing like dead on TV in the cop shows when they kill somebody with a gun. Abbey just came out of the bathroom and said *Morning, Mamma, I love you!* and saw Mamma sitting still as stone in her kitchen chair, slumped over face-first into her cold black coffee and Abbey tried not to understand.

Abbey didn't have to understand things like that. That was one of the big advantages to being stupid, wasn't it? How being stupid and being *touched* meant that she didn't have to cry when people died, because people like her didn't understand.

But Abbey cried. She wailed like a baby when she felt how cold Mamma was, felt her body all stiff and freezy like something in a butcher's meat locker.

Mamma was gone and Abbey was screwed. And when the funeral was over she went uptown looking for a fix for her broken heart.

Welfare Lady said Abbey shouldn't go looking for a fix. There were diseases you could get, and those men will use you, Welfare Lady said.

But Abbey never listened to Welfare Lady when she said things like that. Sometimes—sometimes Welfare Lady acted like she owned Abbey, it was almost like that. Just because she loved her and paid for her and gave her food and money! But Abbey knew better. Welfare Lady couldn't own Abbey. Not unless Abbey let her, and she never ever would. Abbey was free! Free free born free free as a bird!

Nobody told Abbey what to do. Especially not somebody who acted like they thought she was her keeper.

Nobody.

Abbey wasn't sure when she started crying, or why. But she did. When she got to the corner of 135th Street and stood waiting for the traffic light to change, she heard herself, sob sob sob sob, crying like for anyone to hear. She made herself stop, but stopping didn't make her feel any better. Just the opposite, in fact: she hated herself. *Hated* herself. She felt so bad she couldn't stand it anymore.

Couldn't stand being Abbey. Not for another moment.

She hated being Abbey! She ought to die! But thinking dead was easier than being dead, just like it always happened when she felt this way.

By the time she got to the corner of 136th Street Abbey remembered what she had to do. *I've got to get some junk to fix what's broken.* And maybe that's why it hit her so hard, what she saw when she looked into the gaping door of the burned-out tenement.

You know the kind of building it was: the kind where the landlord figures he can't make it on rent anymore, because the whole damn city is going to hell and nobody wants to live in the empty apartments and there's no way to pay for taxes and water and keeping the place up and the mortgage and every other damn thing it costs to be a landlord. So he hires a couple junkies to come in and set the place on fire, and they burn it down, and the landlord takes his insurance money and walks away. After a few years the city takes the lot and the hull for taxes, and one more bit of the city dies.

Usually somebody from housing comes to brick the doors and windows. Not safe if you don't—pushers run their shooting galleries in places like that. Kids play in them and get themselves killed by falling rafters.

And junkies crawl inside when they're all woozy and warm rolling in the haze, and sometimes they die and nobody finds them for years.

It was a junkie in the doorway, and when Abbey found him there he was still alive. It looked like he'd pushed the bricks away from the door and crawled in. To get away from the street? Or something. There wasn't any way to tell for sure.

Abbey wouldn't have gone through the hole in the bricks if she'd stopped to think about it. It was dangerous, going into burned-out tenements! Everybody knew that. But she saw the poor guy lying there in the trash and the filth, and he looked like he hurt so bad, and Abbey's heart went out to him.

You going to get yourself killed, you stupid little junkie girl, her Mamma Ghost whispered in her ear. *Don't you know a killer when you see him?*

But she couldn't help herself: she went to help him. It was always like that when she saw people hurting. Abbey saw them and she got herself into trouble before she took time to consider.

Stupid girl, the ghost said. Her Mamma always said that every time she got in trouble. *You haven't got the sense God gave a rat.*

Abbey ignored her, but Mamma didn't go away. *Stupid stupid stupid,* Mamma Ghost said. Abbey pushed on through the gap in the bricks. She had to. The junkie man looked like he was dying, and it wasn't in her to let him die alone.

She crawled across the filthy floor until she knelt above the writhing man.

"You don't look so good," she said, looking into his eyes. His pupils were so wide they looked like buttons on a jacket.

The junkie man didn't answer her. Except he made this bubbly choking little sound like he was trying to breathe a throatful of his own spit.

"You ought to get yourself a doctor."

There was no more answer than before—except the choke got louder, and turned into a cough that sprayed bloody phlegmy stuff all over the new blouse Abbey got last month from the Sisters of Charity.

Abbey didn't gross out easy. How could she? She got dirty all the time. Got sick, got covered with filth sometimes when she got herself a fix. But even so the pink and yellow on her blouse made her stomach clench. She wanted to go home and cry, but she couldn't do that now without feeling like a roach.

So she put one hand on the junkie's shoulder to shake him gently back and forth, and set the other on his cheek to rub the color back into him.

It didn't do much good. Junkie man was way, way out there, like he'd had a fix that'd fix him for good, and he didn't even notice Abbey up above him trying to drag him back into the world.

"Junkie Man? You got to listen to me, Junkie Man. You got it bad. You going to die if you don't get yourself together."

Junkie Man groaned and rolled away from her.

Abbey got so frustrated she forgot the one big rule that everybody knows out on the street: Always be polite to anything that's bigger than you are. *"Junkie Man!"* she shouted, *"get yourself up or you going to die!"*

And Junkie Man roused himself just enough to sit up and see who Abbey was. And when he saw he grabbed her by the phlegmy bloody blouse, and threw her into the wall.

* * *

And then he got up. And came after her.

Junkie Man hurt Abbey very very bad.

Abbey hated being Abbey. She hated it when she cried. Hated feeling stupid when people hated her hated being stupid when she did things to hate hated hated hated being alive.

Days like this she hated Abbey most of all.

This is what it was like to be Abbey hating Abbey.

She's walking uptown, and she's dirty, and she hurts, and she wants to kill herself she hates herself that much, wants to step out in front of one of those cabs driving crazy out in the avenue, speeding downtown trying to get out of Harlem before the city realizes it's stumbled into a place where drivers get their heads blowed off and their money taken and left for dead on crumbling side streets happens twice a month right around here nobody caught the guy in all these years maybe it's more than one guy maybe it's a lot of guys maybe it's everybody everybody teenaged boys hijacking cabs stuck at traffic lights everybody knows cabbies got money you see one you pop it open you got folding money for a month everybody knows that.

This is the street the stupid cabbies take to get around the toll on the Triboro Bridge. The get off their highway in the Bronx, and they cross the no-toll bridge that comes into Manhattan in the 150s, then they drive downtown like lunatics, flooring the gas and praying to God that nobody gets a chance to pop them open before they're safe and free on the Upper East Side.

You step in front of a cab like that, you're dead. Everybody knows why.

Abbey hates herself so much as she walks uptown hates herself so bad all she can think about is stepping in front of that speeding cab right there stepping in front of it at the last second before the driver can swerve away and it'll be all over, just that fast.

And she can go to heaven with her Mamma who hated and loved her so much Abbey misses her so bad. And just like Mamma she can come back to visit, ghost all around the city to see her friends even though she didn't have none so what does it matter?

Abbey tries to jump out in front of the cab. But she doesn't have the nerve. Every time she tries she gets all trembly and scared and she knows she doesn't have the guts she's terrified to die afraid *it'll kill her!* and that's why she stops herself, because she's chicken.

She doesn't have the nerve to kill herself.

She hates that.

Abbey hates Abbey so bad.

If she wasn't so damn scared she'd kill her, she really would.

Up around 139th Abbey fished a copy of the *Amsterdam News* out of an overflowing trash can, and used the editorial pages to clean the red and yellow off her blouse. It was hard because the goopy part was already mostly dry, but she kept at it, rubbing and rubbing, and finally the blouse got clean enough so that maybe the blood and phlegm wouldn't be the first thing that her Needle Man noticed when he saw her.

She could feel the warm and rosy feeling come over her already, just walking this close to the shooting gallery.

One time Abbey went walking downtown into SoHo and saw all those places they call *galleries.* Places where lispy painter guys show those weirdo pictures that they make. Abbey saw a few of those through the windows, and she wasn't even sure they were really pictures, and she couldn't figure why people would pay money to see ugly stuff like that. But they did—you could tell, just looking at the way the weirdo painter guys dressed. There were people who paid lots of money for that stuff, go figure.

Abbey looked at the window of the storefront with all the lispy-painter guys around it. She saw the word they stenciled on the glass: GALLERY. Abbey knew how to read it, even if everybody did say she was stupid, even her poor dead Mamma. The word made her laugh so funny. *Gallery* wasn't some weirdo rich-people store where you bought ugly paintings for too much money. Not at all! *Gallery* was an ugly burned-out building in the meanest part of Harlem, and when you went through the rubble in the seven empty lots to the back side, there was a place where two brick walls faced each other. One wall was the back wall of the burned-out building; the other was the last remnant of a building that'd collapsed twenty years ago.

When you went back there nobody could see you there unless they went around the same way.

Needle Man's *gallery* was there in the shadows between the two walls. It was a shooting gallery, and people who needed to be fixed came there when they felt like they were broken.

That's why Abbey knew all about *galleries,* because that was how she'd lived her life. In the shadow of the galleries. In the shadows between walls. It wasn't a good life, and it wasn't a happy life, but it was her life and she was proud of it.

"Needle Man," Abbey said as she picked her way through the empty-lot rubble that surrounded the shooting gallery, "Needle Man, I'm here."

He'd be happy to see her, Abbey thought. She just knew he would.

Only he wasn't. He scowled at Abbey when he saw her come around the wall.

"You again," he said. He looked like he wanted to hit her.

Abbey didn't let it bother her. Needle Man was always gruff, but in the end he always did nice by her.

There were half a dozen junkies rolling ecstatically in the shadow of the broken wall. Two others stood a few feet away from them, looking pensive.

For half a second Abbey wondered why they looked so

edgy and impatient. What were they doing? What were they here for? But it only took her a moment to realize. *They're here to get fixed, that's what.*

"Can I help, Needle Man? I only want to *help* you."

Needle Man scowled at her. "Stay out of the way, girl," he said. "I got a job to do."

Abbey felt so rejected. She almost wanted to cry.

"Please, Needle Man? *Please?*"

Needle Man looked up from the spoon and the match and the junk, and he swore. For half a second Abbey got scared he was going to hit her.

But he didn't. He never hit her. Needle Man was rough sometimes, and lots of times he looked about to hit, but he never did. Needle Man wasn't like all the other guys she knew.

"You want to do something, clean the needles in the bleach bucket. You think you can do that?"

Abbey smiled. She felt so pretty.

"Of course I can," she said. "You know I always can."

Abbey liked to clean the needles. It made her feel so—good. Useful, like she had a good thing she was doing and it gave her a purpose in life. And it did, didn't it? Cleaning needles was important. If you don't clean your needle you can get a terrible disease, lots of junkies die that way, Abbey saw them dying all the time it made her feel so sad.

So sad. All her junkies died sometimes, there were days like that when everyone was dying.

Abbey took the biggest needle from the bucket where it soaked, started to work cleaning it. "I heard on the radio today," she said, working the needle's plunger back and forth, spraying bubbles of chlorine-smelling water into the air. "The doctor on the radio said how bleach doesn't kill the virus. Like they said it would? You hear about that?"

Abbey loved to listen to people talking on the radio, because it made her feel so much less alone. But Needle Man didn't like to hear nothing about it. He liked to hear about the virus even less. He spat a big rheumy wad of phlegm onto the shooting wall. "If the bleach don't work," he said, "then fuck the bleach. Ain't like it matters. We all going to die sooner or later."

Abbey wasn't sure if that meant he didn't want her to clean the needles after all. She kept on cleaning anyway, just to be sure.

After a while the junk started to bubble up in Needle Man's spoon. "Give me a needle," he said.

Abbey took the biggest prettiest needle from the tack of clean ones and handed it to him, plunger first. He took it from her, set the spoon on a brick, dipped the needle point into the junk, pulled back on the plunger until he'd filled the syringe. That was the part Abbey like most of all—the anticipation, the yearning as Needle Man filled his syringe.

The beautiful crystal-yellow color of junk in a medicine needle.

The wisp of smoke where the junk burned around the edges of the spoon, so delicious in the air, a tang of powder crisp and seductive, and you smell it and you want it so bad, you can't be you you can't be whole until you get it, oh oh Abbey wanted it so bad.

Abbey loved the wanting most of all.

One of the pensive junkies leaned back against the wall and Needle Man fixed him so good. His back arched when the point went into him, and he groaned, and lurched, and tensed up for a moment before he slumped back against the bricks behind him, all of that without moving his arm a millimeter, you can tell the wise old junkies they know how to do that because they don't like needle tracks. Abbey wanted to be him right then right there, no matter how she could see the lesions on his face and she knew he had the disease.

So bad. So good.

Needle Man came back to the spoon and Abbey gave him another syringe. He filled it and turned to the second waiting junkie, and he smiled.

"It's good, Raoul," Needle Man said. And he gave him what he came for.

The third one was a problem.

"I want it all," he said. "I want a big long fix. I want a fix so good I'll never break again."

And everybody knew that was impossible, even the fog-smeared, half-dead junkies writhing in the trash all over the ground. The only fix that ever fixes you forever is the one that kills you, and sometimes even that don't last the way it should.

"You want to OD?" Needle Man asked. "What are you, crazy?"

The third junkie smiled wildly. "I want it," he said. "I want it bad."

Needle Man shrugged. "Your funeral," he said. And he filled the third syringe as far as it would go.

That didn't scare the junkie, not for a minute. "Ain't going to be no funeral," he said. "Just the city bury me in a can. Send the can back home to my Mamma."

They all laughed at that, even though it wasn't very funny.

When the last junkie was gone Needle Man leaned back against the wall and sighed. He looked at Abbey and his eyes twinkled like they always did when he got ideas.

"What you thinking?" Abbey asked him.

"I'm going to make a cocktail," Needle Man said. "I'm going to make something good. You'll like it."

Abbey grinned. "You know I will."

People say that needle men never use the stuff they sell, but Needle Man had a bad habit. Real bad. The kind of habit where junk was something he needed the way he needed air. It didn't change him, it didn't touch him, it didn't make him feel a damn bit better about himself or the world, but he shot it all the time because the minute that he stopped big welts of sweat bled out of him and his body shook like he had a deathly chill and he knew if he didn't find a needle he was going to die.

And maybe he would die, too. It gets that way for some people, you know: they get to where the habit is so needful that they go into shock if they try to quit cold. Shock like that kills junkies all the time.

Needle Man was just as miserable as every other junkie; he needed what he got from junk. He needed to feel the world wash away in a warm gold haze as he rolled in the sunshine in his heart, and the only way he knew to find the thing he loved was out the inside of a needle, and he loved it, no matter how gruff he treated Abbey.

That was Needle Man for you. Abbey knew him in her heart. She knew him even though he never told himself to her, no matter who said she was too stupid to know a thing like that.

Stupid, stupid child, Mamma Ghost said. *You better get yourself out of here before you get in trouble.* But Abbey didn't listen.

Instead of listening to her Mamma she watched Needle Man mix his cocktail. *Cocktail.* What a silly word for it, she thought. Almost like pretending there was something here in the place between too broken walls that was just the same as a *cocktail party* down to the *gallery* in SoHo.

That was so silly, Abbey thought.

Cocktail wasn't a *gallery* thing at all. Cocktail is what you get when you mix two drugs together, like a *drug interaction precaution* that they tell you when you go to the clinic. But doing it on purpose.

Cocktail was Needle Man boiling crack and speed and junk and something Abbey didn't recognize together because he'd got to where he couldn't get high on any of them by itself.

Bubbles rolling on the spoon and a wisp of smoke—so intense, that smoke. Like nothing else she'd ever smelled.

"That's beautiful," Abbey said. "So beautiful."

Needle Man smiled. "I knew you'd like it."

Needle Man set the spoon on the brick he used for a

work space and took the biggest needle—the wide long phlebotomist's needle like they used at the hospital that time to suck blood out of Abbey—from the row beside the bleach bucket. Lowered the needle tip into the bubbly cocktail in the spoon, pulled back on the plunger until he'd drawn the whole cocktail into the syringe.

Turned the needle upward and pressed the air bubbles out of it.

When he was done the needle was still only partway full.

"Are you ready?" he asked Abbey. He looked at her solemnly, like the preacher talking over Mamma's ashes.

Don't let him do it, girl, I warn you you'll be sorry, Mamma Ghost said, but Abbey didn't listen.

"I am," she said. She felt so eager, so anxious, so full of love and expectation.

Needle Man pressed his needle into the vein in the crook of her arm, and Abbey felt it hurt so good.

She loved him so much.

And then he did something strange.

Instead of pressing the junk and cocktail into her, Needle Man pulled the plunger back, drawing her blood into the syringe. Inside it swirled brilliant red as it mixed in Needle Man's drugs. "My blood," Abbey said, "you took my blood."

Needle Man smiled.

"It's a sacrament," he said. "It means I love you." He said that just like guys always do, like he didn't really love Abbey, just wanted something from her that he couldn't get by himself. And maybe he did. But what he wanted was different, too, because he wanted blood. Abbey wanted to object. She wanted to tell him stop, stop, Needle Man, don't you hear I told you stop? but she couldn't talk her head was spinning she hated when it got like that.

And so she watched the needle drink her blood like a tiny mechanical vampire, sucking out her life until he pressed the plunger back again and Abbey felt fire and ice surge into her vein.

"I love you, Needle Man," Abbey said, and she meant that, she really did.

Needle Man smiled wide. "I love you, too."

Abbey felt herself start to fade away. That felt so good, because she still hated being Abbey.

The last thing she saw before her eyes fell closed was Needle Man as he took the needle out of her still swirling brilliant red full of her blood. And pressed the needle into his own arm, and drove the plunger home.

Abbey had the awfulest dream when she should have been junked up all warm and rosy.

In her dream she lay in the field of rubble beyond the shooting gallery, and it was night quiet night infinitely more silent than New York City ever is. The sky was pitch-black and strewn with stars so bright they eclipsed the streetlights in the near distance.

Nestled among the stars there was a full wide brilliant moon, and that moon was blue.

So blue. Blue like you see on painted china or dyed carnations or maybe even blue like the Day-Glo marker Mamma bought that one time.

Mamma Ghost was there with her, whispering in her ear. Mamma Ghost pointed at the moon.

Mamma whispered all kinds of things. But most of all she wanted to tell Abbey what she thought she ought to do.

"It isn't working, child," Mamma said. "It isn't fit for a body to live like you're living now."

Abbey didn't want to hear about it. The sky was too beautiful, the city too still, the world too warm and perfect wrapped in soothing junk. "Go away, Mamma," she said. "I don't want to talk to you."

She never would have said that if Mamma were alive. She wouldn't dare! But Mamma was a ghost, or maybe she was something Abbey thought about herself, or maybe she was just a bad dream Abbey used to beat herself when she hated being Abbey. Mamma couldn't hurt her now, except with what she said.

"Come with me, child," Mamma said.

Abbey didn't understand what she meant at first, but after a while it sunk through to her.

"You want me to die with you, Mamma?"

"It's the only way, child. It's better here. You're too stupid to live. Look at yourself."

For a moment Abbey felt so ashamed. She was a failure, a failure, total and complete and maybe she needed to die, just like Mamma said, to protect herself.

But the more she thought about that the more it scared her. That was on purpose, wasn't it? Mamma *meant* to scare her. Why would Mamma want to go and do a thing like that? It wasn't nice. When Abbey thought about it she got mad.

"I don't need you, Mamma," she said. "I'm not going to let you hurt me anymore."

Mamma Ghost laughed.

"Look at yourself, child."

And Abbey found herself standing above her own blacked-out writhing junkie body, floating ghost in the air above herself. She was a sorry sight with those bloody phlegm stains all over her beautiful new blouse—dirty and scrawny and pathetic like maybe she had that virus that was going to kill her, look how sunken deep her eyes were set inside her skull, people who got a future don't go around looking like that.

"I don't look good, Mamma," she said. "But I wouldn't look any better if I was dead."

"You want to live like this, child? You want to live in this stink and rot and misery?—You're just afraid, child. You got to set the fear aside. You got to die if you want to live."

Mamma was lying.

Abbey wasn't sure how, and she wasn't sure why, but she could hear a lie when Mamma said it, even if she couldn't figure it out.

"I'm not afraid, Mamma."

In her dream Abbey walked back over to her body, grabbed it by the wrists, and picked it up. Put it on like it was an overcoat she knew she'd need. When she was done she put her hands on her hips and snorted at her Mamma Ghost all insolent like Mamma hated. And she felt so proud. But when she glanced down at her feet she saw her body still lying there, blacked out cold like she'd never even touched it.

"I don't need to be afraid, Mamma," she said. "I don't need you anyway."

But that was a lie because she knew she did.

Someone groaned in the shooting gallery, and Abbey looked over her shoulder to see one of Needle Man's junkies come awake. As she watched he sat up and rubbed his eyes with hands that trembled like scraps of garbage on a subway track.

I know that one, Abbey thought. *I remember him.* But for the longest time she couldn't remember where she'd seen him before.

The longest time.

And then it came to her.

The burned-out building, Abbey thought. *I saw him lying in the burned-out building, and I tried to help him but he beat me up so bad.*

She wanted to pick up her body and carry it away before he could hurt her again, and she stooped to lift herself out of the broken building garbage of the empty lot but hard as she tried to lift her body wouldn't budge. Like it was dead already or something worse.

There's nothing you can do, child, Mamma Ghost said. *Still yourself so you can take your medicine with pride.*

"I don't understand, Mamma," Abbey said. But that was another lie, because she understood lots better than she wanted to admit. "What's going to happen?"

He's going to touch you, child. He's going to make you dirty again.

Abbey wanted to run and hide. She wanted to cry. She wanted to kill herself all over again.

But she didn't do any of those things, at least part because she couldn't.

When he's done he'll slit your throat.

Abbey started to cry. She didn't want that awful Junkie Man to kill her. But it wasn't like she had a choice, either: Nothing that she did had any effect on anything she saw.

"You've got to save me, Mamma," Abbey said.

Mamma Ghost laughed.

I never could, Mamma Ghost said. *I never would. What makes you think I'd want to?*

"You've got to save me, Mamma," Abbey said. "I'm your only daughter."

But Mamma Ghost said *No.*

"You're living in a fantasy world," she said. "You should have listened to me."

"Mamma!"

"Save yourself, Abbey," Mamma Ghost said. And then she disappeared.

Junkie Man stumbled trembling and delirious through the rubble until he stood smiling above blacked-out Abbey. He looked down at her hungrily. His eyes were full of venom and lust.

Abbey tried to stop him. She shouted at him, hit him over and over with her ghostly fists. But Junkie Man didn't even notice.

"I'll hurt you if touch me, Junkie Man," Abbey said. "I swear to God I will." But she couldn't imagine how she could to it, and even as she shouted she knew her threats were impotent. She picked up a rock and threw it at Junkie Man, but it didn't hit him. It sailed past his head so silently that he didn't even notice.

The junkie stooped to touch Abbey's body. Fondled her with his rough unsteady hands.

Abbey gasped, even though she couldn't feel what he was doing. She wanted to throw up but there was no way she could.

"I warn you, Junkie Man," Abbey said. "I'll kill you when I can."

But she knew she never could. She knew that there was nothing she could ever do.

Needle Man loves me, Abbey thought. *Needle Man can save me.*

"Help help help Needle Man you have to save me," Abbey shouted. She ran ghost across the broken lot to where Needle Man lay dreaming needle dreams, and she shouted ghostly words into his ears. Needle Man didn't hear her. He shivered in his dreams.

She hurried back across the lot to see the junkie tear away her beautiful new blouse. And screamed.

Abbey howled and howled at the pale blue moon, trying not to watch the awful things the junkie did to her. She screamed for her Mamma Ghost to save her, but Mamma Ghost was gone and she never came back until it didn't matter anymore.

When the junkie was done he found a shard of glass in the rubble beside her, and he opened Abbey's throat, just like Mamma told her.

I'm dead, Abbey thought. *I'm dead and gone.*

And she waited for the angels to come take her up to heaven, but they never came. And then she knew it was all gone for the worst, and she waited for the devils to drag her down to hell, but they never came neither.

The junkies woke, one by one, and they stumbled away into the stillness of the city. Needle Man woke to clean his needles, and Abbey was sure he'd find her and get her a decent funeral, but he never even noticed she was dead.

The one who noticed was Welfare Lady.

Wouldn't you know?

Welfare Lady spotted her from way out on the street, driving by on her way to the Welfare office, she spotted Abbey broken bleeding lying in the morning filth in the broken lot. When she saw she stopped her car and picked her way among the shattered bricks and fallen stones until she could kneel beside Abbey.

And mourn.

Abbey fell into a dream inside her ghost dream when she saw Welfare Lady crying.

The dream went like this:

As Welfare Lady knelt beside Abbey the gray morning began to sparkle and shine so beautiful, all full of love and hope and possibility, and Welfare Lady gasped. She took a look at Abbey and whispered, "Dear God she's still breathing," and she got up and started running. Back to the street, where she pushed the drug dealers away from the pay phone on the corner, and she called 911. In a few moments an ambulance came screaming around the corner, and two men and a woman rushed out to rescue Abbey from her death.

In her dream they took Abbey's dying body to the hospital, and they sewed her back together, and after a long time they made her whole again.

Or at least as whole as she ever was.

When she was well she went home to her lonely Welfare tenement and tried to piece her life together the way she should have done when she was younger. She got a job, she worked hard, she went to night school to show them she wasn't as stupid as everybody said and she did so well!

She lived a good life in that dream, and she was so proud. Eventually she found a guy she loved and respected, and they married, and they had two baby girls they loved and cherished.

Such a good life in that dream.

And maybe it really happened.

And maybe not. Ghosts do that all the time, you know: They imagine up the damnedest things and convince themselves their dreams are real. Ghosts like Abbey wander through the city every night, and no one pays them any mind.

DADDY'S GIRL

Gordon R. Ross

May 27, 1989

DAMN! IT'S RAININ' AGAIN! RAIN AIN'T A FAVORITE WITH MOST haunts. It soaks the ground and brings out the bugs.

The flyin' insects that come after are no problem, except for the noise. The bugs fly right through us. Wasps, moths, bees, flies, skeeters—all the same. They can see us, I reckon, the way they come chargin' if'n we're near a nest. But they just buzz on through. Some keep goin' till they hit somethin' solid—like a cow, dog, or human bein'.

But the damp also gets to the underground worms, grubs, centipedes, and beetles. Them are tougher on our remains. They get more active and a helluva lot hungrier —not that that really matters no more.

Right now there's two thousand, three hundred and eighty-eight unhappy souls representin' ten generations or so, moulderin' away in this little seven-acre weed patch acrosst from People's Corner Shoppin' Center on what was once the northern outskirts of McMichael, Oklahoma. Actually there is one thousand, nine hundred sixty-six white folks. There's also more than a few black people buried in here. If the livin' rulin' class knew about it they'd pitch a fit, but that's another story and it'll have to wait a bit.

To get back to what I was sayin': rain ain't no fun for us. We've got our share of clay. It don't take long for additional water to soak into the ground. It swells that stuff—pressin' and bucklin' tops, sides, and bottoms of old rotten caskets, messin' up what is already becomin' pretty disgustin' mortal remains.

Bad enough most of us have popped open years ago from poorly embalmed and putrifying innards and left-over dinners, badly drained veins and arteries, and general bacteria-infested garbage floatin' about in our systems. Plenty of reason for us not to visit our coffins much. We abandoned those miserable circumstances shortly after arrivin' here, and have learned to float around the Tidy Vale Haven of Rest, still believin' in the resurrection. Our stones are our principal pillows, places to sit, hide behind, thinkin' spots and waitin' places.

We-all just sat there that day, almost all the many generations of us. We didn't move. Just busy starin' at the heavy traffic and the darkened shoppin' center beyond it.

Each perched on his or her own tombstone, waitin' for that second comin' promised us by our individual preachers—or the first comin', in the case of the Berg family. They share a rather unpretentious rock in the far back left-hand corner of Tidy Vale, now in the midst of McMichael's new and growin' retail area.

Most could remember when cemeteries meant quiet places in the country. But here whole bunches of cars and customers get lured by the Alderman Department Store and the Sears catalog outlet, the center's fast-food chains, the little gift shops, the hardware store, and the big independent grocery. These people keep a constant high noise level from seven A.M. to late at night that is hard for even a ghost to ignore.

Not that all of us had a lot to discuss. We're basically

kind of cranky, considerin' our individual fates. We really don't have a lot in common, other than bein' dead.

What could we talk about? Unless you're a die-hard history buff, important things and events in each of our lives have little bearing on what interested other generations.

How do you compare a good Morgan horse with a Corvette? Or a campfire with a microwave? A Stephen Foster tune with the big bands or the Blue Cult Oysters or whatever the hell they're called?

By the way, I'm August Burnside. I've been dea—I been here about eighteen years now. Used to be the local garage owner and wrecker driver for better'n forty years in these parts. A lot of these folks I seen just after they left their—other existence. And my tastes run more to Tommy and Jimmy Dorsey, but I'm gettin' off the subject.

All of us who call this place "home"—at least temporarily—had somethin' to chew over the night before when the high school graduation party of '89 wound up their celebration by wreckin' our graveyard.

Country boys today seem to gravitate to four-wheel-drive trucks instead of sports cars. And them four-by-four toys pulled over and knocked down our tombstones in what editor Clay Bristow down at the *Democrat and Herald* called an "orgy of drunken abandon." Too bad he probably won't print it. He knows where he gets his money to run that paper. From his advertisers. They been tellin' him what to print and not to print for a long time now.

Those boys and girls were swacked long before they hit our place. They carried on and got sick, fell down drunk and acted just plain mean when it come to our "home." Their big rigs drove over the red clay ground, already slop from that soakin' rainstorm what hit earlier in the day. The trucks' weight made deep ruts in the soil, tore up the turf and pushed the ground down, crushin' the already buckled and rotten lids on many a tired old coffin.

Miss Martha Conover, killed durin' a wild car ride followin' her graduation the summer of '36, had her monument destroyed by them revelers. In one damned moment went the seventeen years of patience and calm we had forced into her that led Miss Martha to a quiet acceptance of her fate.

She started howlin' as soon as the latest Sheriff Allred ran off them drunken bums. Oh, he got their license numbers all right, we sorta seen to that. We got our ways. But a lot of the young-uns' parents, including District Attorney Striker, was political friends of his. Allred might have a good talk with their folks in the morning. Maybe they'd make good. They all had the money, but that would mean involvement and publicity. We would, at best, probably get a fast patch job on the damage. As he left the scene, Miss Martha cut loose with a howl—enough to wake the . . . neighbors, so to speak—not to mention them cleanin' up the parkin' lot at the People's Corner Shoppin' Center acrosst the street.

Now, you usually don't hear a ghost. They stick pretty much to themselves, mindin' their own business, just waitin' for the "next step," you might say. But Miss Martha proved to be one of them exceptions. She had always got what she wanted. Her mommy and daddy seen to that. Mr. Conover started the bank. Though things was a bit tight in McMichael in 1936, he'd still made himself pretty land rich with some fine foreclosures that spring.

McMichael sits in a part of the state that has good water. The drought that had affected much of the rest of Sooner Country never hurt the Conover Bank much. Conover was always busy pickin' up land right cheap for taxes or foreclosure. Then he hired the former owners to work it as low-paid sharecroppers. Mighty kind of him.

With some of the profits he bought Miss Martha that

new car she'd been moonin' over down at Hunnert's Ford. Shiny Tacoma blue rumble seat roadster with a white top. Cream-colored wheels, wide whitewalls, twin spotlights, fog lights, and a radio in the dash. He even hired his young gardener, Mr. Tom Gilly, to teach her how to drive it. The old man musta figured he was too busy and too important with his bankin' business.

On graduation night, Miss Martha, Mr. Tom, and a bottle of everclear made their way to the South Canadian River. It was time for a little moonlight skinny-dippin' at a deep spot they knew.

Trouble was, at two A.M. the car was too new to find its way home. It missed a turn and met a jack oak. Tom got throwed out into the brush tangle 'side the road. Miss Martha, who always got her way till then, got left out of the wishes that night.

When we found 'em in the mornin', Tom had been tick and chigger-bit all over, scratched up some and knocked a little sillier than usual. Miss Martha had that banjo wire steerin' wheel wrapped so tight around her pretty little neck she couldn't sweet-talk or scream another livin' "request"—ever.

Tom went on to college, "sponsored" by Miss Martha's daddy, for Tom was the last one to see the old man's precious darlin' daughter alive. He probably would have finished law school. Instead, he created a family situation with another banker's daughter. At that point the phone wires between banks and the school got momentarily scorched. All funds for Tom from the Conover Bank ceased. Poor Tom had to settle for an itinerant preacher's job for a while.

Today he's one of the most accepted, righteous, poundin'est, and loudest, if not the most pretentious, hellfire and brimstone proclaimers goin'.

But, back to Miss Martha, the shattered tombstone, her nerves and those of the livin' and dead near her.

As I said before, years of dull, borin' quiet had lulled most of us into the inevitable wait we'd been told about from Sunday school to funeral parlor. But Miss Martha wasn't about to accept that at first. She'd never had to wait for anythin' in her life: clothes, jewelry, a new car, sex—anythin'. Then, just short of her eighteenth birthday, she lost it all. Followin' the plantin', thirty-six years of her whinin' and poutin' on top of that stone brought all of us mostly misery.

I take exception to that. She calmed down some over the past seventeen years. Except for an occasional minor lapse, Miss Martha finally developed that vacant stare we all had learned to put on to endure. Then those damned kids played hell with the whole program.

With no place to even sit, Martha stomped and ranted, howled, moaned and screamed up and down the bone yard road in front of her crumbled marker. She shrieked loud enough to wake the livin'. And they heard her, at least across the street. Lucky for us they probably thought it was more celebrators.

Never the less, we all knew our quiet waitin' would have to take a back seat until we did somethin' about Miss Martha. So we had a meetin' down by the Bergs' stone. Even though it was the area designated as "beyond the tracks," it was now in the quietest part of the place—though Martha's howlin' made it hard to hear, even with her maybe a good two blocks away.

Corporal Danner, who come home in a box from WWII, thought we ought to shoot her. That was a terribly impractical solution, as the gun Lem Dowdy got buried with from the Battle of San Juan Hill had long since rusted shut. And you really can't kill a haunt.

Miz Ivy Miller, who died the year before Martha would have graduated, had the best head on her shoulders of any of us. She had been a school teacher in all grades for forty-one sessions at McMichael. She even taught in the black schools some after she retired. Volunteered, even. Can you beat that?

Since Miss Martha was back to demanding it, Miz Ivy suggested we try and give Martha her second childhood.

"That's a grand idea," I said, "but about as practical as Soldier Danner's suggestion."

"Not so," says she, her thin old hand passin' right through a blossom-loaded red bud branch, glowin' above us in the moonlight. Among our group, she said, we had enough "wish power" to "mortalize" Miss Martha. At least for a little while. Long enough to mebbe work out some of the cravin's in her system. All we had to do was to wake up a little, stop thinkin' so much about the fixes each of us was in, the things we did and didn't do that got us here, and to concentrate on materializin' her out of the graveyard for a spell. The rest was up to her.

After all, it worked for poltergeists and banshees, Miz Ivy figured. Those critters had to energize themselves with no help from anyone else. It could happen to Miss Martha if we all concentrated our wishin' energies together.

We joined up in sort of rows, like a choir, with Miz Miller as our director. For most of the night, till about an hour before dawn, she instructed us. This was new to her, too, but bless her, she had those teacher's instincts that told her she was on the right track, and what she didn't know for sure she would experiment with and wing it.

Miz Ivy got us into the program. We started a-hummin' on the same key—except for Homer White, who was deaf even before the horse kicked him. And before Miss Martha knew what hit her, she plopped down in front of that department store acrosst the street, still rantin' and ravin' about her latest bad luck string.

Manager Rob Lukens showed up for work early that day. Roundin' the corner from where company policy said he had to park, he looked dumbstruck by the obviously pretty but grimy young woman sittin' in his doorway. She positively glowed through the dust and mildew, mutterin' to herself as he approached.

From our vantage point acrosst the street we strained against our tethers and squinted through the dim light of the false dawn to see or hear the goin's-on. From what we could tell, Rob Lukens couldn't have been more startled than Miss Martha, who suddenly found herself out of her old element. There she was, back in the mortal world, lookin' into a set of strangely familiar eyes. Yet they seemed to be terrifyin' to her. We was afraid she might scream, or at the least get sick. Her knees buckled, and Rob caught her—just like real flesh and blood. Now some of us knew that we was goin' to be ill.

"My God!" says Rob. "You look awful! Have you been in a wreck?"

Good question. That bein' the only explanation he could think of, findin' a gorgeous young thing in tattered, dirty party clothes, the results of the debacle with the kids earlier in the night, not to mention years and years of wear.

"Huh?" says she. "Oh, yes! A wreck. And Tom left me." She said no more. Miss Martha may have been spoiled rotten, but she was no fool. She still knew how to work men to her advantage—and she needed time to figure out what happened.

"Let me know the name of that scoundrel," said gentleman Rob, "and we'll have the police look him up." We heard no more as Rob gently escorted Miss Martha into the store.

The sun came up, a police car came and went from in front of the business, and soon the center's customers began to arrive. The usual classy bunch, dumpin' used baby diapers, empty pop cans, burnin' cigarettes, fast-food containers, napkins, and candy wrappers. The erratic breezes swirlin' between posts and buildings helped most of the litter find its way acrosst the street and amongst the plastic flowers left up year-round in the graveyard. That day it didn't matter much. Our "home away from home" was pretty well trashed as it was.

With the sun well up, the city manager and the cemetery custodians dropped by to survey the previous night's damage. They called in the sheriff, who showed up with District Attorney Striker.

"This is one hell of a mess," manager Amos Boggs said, wavin' his arms up and down like he was tryin' to fly. "You got any suggestions as what to do?" he asked his two custodians.

"Well," mused one, stroking his chin, "the sheriff could get some of the county prisoners out to pick up the pieces. Then we could have Jacob Warner sort 'em and ee-poxx-ee 'em back together." Jacob Warner runs the drive-in movie projector on weekends and is our local stonemason on needed occasions.

That one suggestion seemed good enough for them. No one felt like out-suggestin' the others this time. They just wanted to get the hell out of there. So they voted to try that. All looked appropriately shocked, though Sheriff Allred and D.A. Striker never let on they knew the slightest thing about how this happened.

We was so intrigued by this little half-hour show, done not for, but at our expense, we plumb forgot about Miss Martha. Until Moss seen her comin' out of the store, all gussied up in a new summer outfit, on the arm of Mr. Lukens. She must'a gave herself a spit bath in the ladies' room, 'cause she just glowed! She warn't mad, either. Nosirreee! She grinned and flirted in that pretty white and lilac summer weight dress, white shoes, and matchin' plastic purse. An' ol' Rob, for all his single twenty-eight years, was eatin' it up. Hell, he was in love—and on the way to an early lunch at McDonald's down the parkin' lot.

Now Miss Martha could see us, all lined up at the edge of Tidy Vale, like spectators at a parade. But did she pay any attention? Hell, no! She was chatterin' happy—about to taste one of them "Big Macs" she only seen the wrappers of, floatin' around our "estate" for the past ten years. And they had Cokes, too, and fries. Us? We-all started gettin' some of our own cravin's!

The happy pair disappeared inside, 'bout the time the sheriff and the D.A. left. Five minutes later, they came out the door again with two sacks of instant grub. Miss

Martha musta fed him some story, 'cause the next thing we knew she brung ol' Rob back acrosst the road to the edge of the cemetery to lunch on the grass. She still wouldn't look at us. Instead, she taunted all her old graveyard companions with a slow devourin' of that fast-food feast, remarking with every mouthful how "delicious" it all tasted.

Despite all the distractions, I felt in my bones (sorry, a slip of the tongue) that there was somethin' very familiar about Mr. Robert Lukens. Somethin' I remembered from when I owned the local wrecker service back in the '30s. Then I saw that Martha noticed it, too, though she wasn't lettin' on to Lukens. It was his eyes and voicc. Hc had those same steel blue eyes and the same spell-bindin' voice as Mr. Tom, Miss Martha's first and only lover, far as I knew. She had brung him over to our plantin' ground to have me check him out! After all, she knew I knew 'em both, though in all these years she'd never let on she remembered me from the wreck.

Miss Martha looked straight at me and she knew I suspected the same thing. Ol' Rob was Mr. Tom's grandson—only prettier, with a better job.

Here, I figured, Miss Martha would start up what she'd missed out on for over fifty years. She couldn't go to the preacher—too far into TV religion to understand what was happenin'—and way too old. His daughter, for that's what he'd fathered in college, must've had all the dominant genes, 'cause Rob sure favored his granddaddy. And though Rob seemed more conservative emotionally than old Tom Gilly, he was richer, by Martha's standards, more respectable, and more eligible now than Tom had been in her lifetime.

Miss Martha got her way for a change. She was a total pain—if we could have such things. We was both wary and pleased that we could set her life into motion like we done. And Rob was havin' a great time, chatterin' to Miss Martha. Just like real flesh and blood.

But then it happened. In the middle of trying to pick

up a french fry, her fingers went right through it. We all seen it, and so did Martha. At that moment Rob had his head turned to check store traffic acrosst the street and missed Martha's major physical miscue. The power was leavin' her. Now you know the real meanin' of the expression "fadin' fast."

When Rob turned back, nothin' remained of the girl but the new white and lilac summer weight dress, a pair of white shoes, and matching plastic purse. Here he had been talkin' to the prettiest thing he'd ever seen. Next moment she had totally disappeared, leavin' the clothes he bought her lyin' amongst the tombstones in the broad midday sun of a busy Saturday.

He was miles behind in his work and had to get back to the store. The help all saw Rob leave with that girl, and now he comes back with her clothes. How would he ever explain it all? And what's far worse, what had happened to Miss Martha "Whatever-her-last-name-was"?

Of course, we could see her, plainly visible, hidin' in her skivvies behind the stones. Sure modest for such a wild one!

Stuffin' the dress, shoes, and purse into an empty McDonald's bag, Rob retreated acrosst the street again to his store. The rest of the afternoon we watched him peerin' out the display window at where we was standin'. He looked so guilty and forlorn!

Miss Martha? Well, she kinda hid out some, but she quit rantin' at us like she done before. In fact, "Yoo-hoo'in'" at us from behind one of the big pines they planted on top of my coffin, she brought us all together for a quick meetin' around five o'clock.

"'Member how miserable I git when I don't git what I de-sire?" says she kinda quiet-like when we had all assembled. I remembered she hadn't ever got what she really deserved, but I kept that to myself. "Well, I got a new cravin', and if you don't help me scratch that itch, you ain't heard nothin' before like what you'll be hearin' now!"

We all knew about that "itch"—Mr. Rob Lukens. And when the store manager got off that night, we knew exactly what he'd be doin'.

Sure enough, at straight-up eight P.M., here come old Rob saunterin' acrosst the street once more real casual-like, but with his eyes full of panic. He carried a brand-new, heavy-duty Sears flashlight in one hand and a McDonald's sack in the other.

In and out of the rows of tombstones and the rubble he walked, callin' Martha's name real soft but often—shinin' that nine-cell light into every nook and cranny. We waited 'til he got in front of the spot where the four-by-four had sunk in Jeff Hollin's coffin lid. The "quiet chorus" gave its second concert, startin' with that really neat hummin' sound.

That's all we needed. Ol' Rob-boy heard it and took a startled step in reverse. His foot sank into the soft track left by the truck and a coffin lid gave way below it, causin' Rob's leg to drop suddenly into the hole in the ground.

The heavy flashlight somersaulted into the air, coming down hard on Rob's temple. With a grunt, he just sort of folded over backward, striking his other temple hard on Hollin's broken marker.

Within moments, Rob was one of us, and his spirit found Martha's, still in its skivvies.

It was kind of a dirty trick, but you can't say any of us will "live to regret it." And, after all, all we did was hum! Rob and Martha seem quite happy now that he's adjusted a bit. At least things have calmed down some. Or maybe they have only till "Daddy's girl" thinks up somethin' else she wants. . . .

COVENTRY CAROL

Chet Williamson

Lully, lulla, thou little tiny child,
By, by, lully, lullay.

I

AFTER IT HAPPENED, RICHARD WAS UNABLE TO EAT GRAPES. HE bought a bunch at a farmers' market and set the bag on the car seat next to him, planning to munch on them as he drove home. But when his teeth pierced the resilient green skin and the juice burst tartly over his tongue, the image came immediately to mind of what had been floating there in the toilet bowl only a few weeks before. He pulled the car onto the shoulder, spit out the grape, and gagged, but was able to keep from vomiting. Then he hurled the grapes into the bushes for the rabbits, the groundhogs, the deer. For simpler animals, whose minds did not make such tenuous connections, such fine distinctions of taste.

For the primitive.

II

Both he and Donna had wanted the baby. It was time. They were in their midthirties, and the tales of complicated pregnancies haunted their age group as Hansel and

Gretel's witch haunted young children. Hydrocephaly, brain damage, and worse, all because of the waiting. There was, Donna once joked, a price to be paid for living in the bygone Age of Me.

The timing was right in other ways, too. Richard had just been made a full professor, and the market research firm where Donna had worked for the past six years was gearing down, so that her departure would save the necessity of firing a colleague, and odds were good, she was told, that in a year or two, when she was ready to return to a job, there would be a job to return to.

Two weeks after they discovered Donna was pregnant, they started on the nursery. Their farmhouse, which they had bought in their early twenties, had transformed over the years, changing as they grew older. In the first few years they had worked only on the kitchen, their bedroom, and their bath, leaving the rest of the building to its previous squalor, so that if, in one of the many parties of those early years, a joint fell burning and unnoticed to the floor, or a beer can spilled, or a bottle of Cribari shattered, it was of no account. The room would be redone someday.

And as they and their circle of friends aged and changed, left Cribari and Bud in cans to the closets of college memories, grew to be more careful with burning drugs of all kinds, started to marry and have children and divorce, to solidify and melt and rethicken, so did the parties and the house change. Carpets covered the planks too scarred to refinish, furniture of wood and glass and chrome replaced the overstuffed monstrosities that had sponged up a little less beer than their occupants had drunk. Unframed film posters fell like dead leaves before the winter white walls, the stark muted graphics.

The farmhouse was different from when they had moved in, but it was, then and now, theirs. Only two rooms on the third floor and one on the second remained untouched, and it was that second floor room they worked on, sanding, scrubbing, cleaning, painting, preparing it for the child who would soon arrive.

They were painting the evening it happened, listening to an old Crosby, Stills, and Nash tape on the remote speaker. The music was punctuated by the slap of the rollers, and at times their motion fit the music's cadence, making Richard smile, then concentrate again on the rough plaster, putting his weight heavily against the roller so that the paint filled the crannies, lightened the dark tiny valleys.

He became aware that Donna's roller was silent, and turned to look at her. She was sitting on the floor, her back propped against an unpainted wall, her legs splayed out in front of her. She had pulled the sweatband from around her brow so that her ash blonde hair hung loose, and she was twisting the band in her hands. Her lip shook, and tears dropped from her cheeks onto the front of her old, faded blue work shirt. She looked like a handcuffed prisoner, alone and miserable.

"Donna?" he said. "Honey, what's wrong?" He set his roller carefully in its tray, and knelt in front of her, hoping that it was anticipation and anxiety that had brought her down rather than pain.

She shook her head angrily, and he felt his stomach tense. These were not tears of joy.

"Donna?"

She opened her lips and took several deep, slow breaths through her teeth. At last she looked at him challengingly. "I'll be all right."

"What is it?"

"I'm *scared.* Okay?"

Her antagonism made him uncomfortable. "Scared?" he muttered.

"Yes, scared. May I be scared?"

"Well . . . well, sure. I'm scared, too, honey. Of the responsibility, the . . . the changes it's going to mean. . . ."

"You would be." Her words were cold.

"What?"

"I'm scared for the baby," she said quietly. "And you're afraid you're going to have your lifestyle cramped."

"Donna, how can you say that? I *want* this baby, and you . . ."

She broke down then, and her arms went out to him, so that he gathered her in and held her tightly. "I'm sorry, Rick," she cried, "but something's wrong, something *is*, I *know* it . . ."

"Okay, relax, relax," he crooned. "Have you told the doctor?"

"Yes, yes, he says it's nothing, that nothing's wrong."

"Have you been spotting?"

"No."

"Cramps, pains?"

"No . . . twinges. It's just, oh God, a *feeling*. It sounds so stupid, so foolish, but it's *there.*"

He continued to hold her. "You know," he said slowly, "you can't go through the whole pregnancy like this."

"I don't think I can have a healthy baby," she said with a sincerity that chilled him.

"That's ridiculous. Don't say that."

"But all we did over the years. The grass, Christ, we did acid a couple of times, and the coke . . ."

"We're not doing it *now*, and we won't anymore, and that's what's important."

"And the abortion," she added desperately, "when we couldn't afford—"

He cut her off. "The doctor knows all about that, and it doesn't mean a thing. You heard him say that it would have no effect at all on this baby."

"Yeah. I heard."

"Donna, expectant mothers worry all the time. They worry if they drink coffee, they worry if they smoke, it's only natural."

"I know all that, I just . . ." She paused, her eyes far

away. "I want this baby so much. I want to hold it and love it and watch it grow, and sing lullabies to it. I want everything I did in the past to stop, and to start everything over with this baby, have everything new, forget everything I did and was—"

"Hey," Richard interrupted, "you don't have to feel guilty about a thing."

She looked at him and smiled. "If I don't, Richard, who will?"

"Donna . . ."

"You have to take responsibility sometime."

"And we will. We *are.* But don't get upset before anything happens. Seven months is a long time, honey."

"I know. All right. Forget it then. Let's get back to work."

They started painting again. The CS&N tape ended, and after a while Richard heard Donna humming a tune. "Pretty," he said.

She stopped. "Hmm?"

"The song. You were humming."

"Was I?"

"'Coventry Carol,'" he said, renewing the supply of paint on his roller. He sang in a light baritone.

"'Lully, lulla, thou little tiny child,
By, by, lully, lullay.'"

"Is that the name of it?" she asked. "I must have heard it on the radio." It was a month before Christmas, and the airwaves were filled with carols. Richard sang on.

"'Oh sisters two, how may we do
For to preserve this day
This poor youngling for whom we do sing
By, by, lully lullay.'"

She hummed as he sang, and when they'd finished the "Coventry Carol," they sang others, sacred and secular—"Oh Come, All Ye Faithful," "Up On the Housetop," "What Child Is This?" and "The First Noel." Finally Donna set down her roller. "Be right back," she said.

"How about bringing me back a beer?" Richard asked.

"You got it."

He heard her walking unhurriedly down the hall, heard the door to the bathroom close. He worked on, and found himself softly singing the "Coventry Carol" once more. It was no wonder, he thought. The tune was haunting, though melancholy for a Christmas song. There was sadness in it, as though its composer had kept in mind the ultimate destiny of the newborn child.

Then Donna screamed.

The sound froze him for a heartbeat, and he dropped the roller with a wet slap onto the floor, leaped from the ladder, and ran out the door, down the hall, where he threw open the door of the large guest bath.

His wife lay on the cold white tile, her jeans and underwear in a tangle around her knees. Her body, shaking with sobs, was hunched embryonically, and her hands were buried between her thighs, as if striving to hold something in. A few watery drops of blood dotted the floor.

"I knew it, I told you," she gasped. "It's gone, I lost it, oh, Rick, I lost it."

He knelt beside her and smoothed the wet hair back from her hot forehead, whispering, "Shh, shh," not wanting to look into the toilet bowl, unable not to.

It was there. He could barely make it out, floating in a gelatinous cloud of blood and pus. The deep yellow urine darkened it further, a tiny, monstrous fish swimming in some underground sea.

My daughter. My son.

He wanted to vomit, but he kept it down, although the taste of bile was strong at the back of his throat. He started to reach for the flush handle automatically, as he would to flush down a spider, a wriggling centipede, a battered fly, then stopped, realizing that it was neither fly nor fish, but something that was to have been human, that was to have been—that *was*—his child. So he closed the lid, and turned his attention back to Donna.

"Come on, can you get to the bedroom?" His voice was thick with sorrow.

Hers was thinned by tears. "I think . . . think so."

"Ought to lie down," he said, getting an arm beneath her. "You lie down and I'll call the doctor."

"Oh, Rick . . ."

"Now, it's all right, it's over . . ."

"I *lost* it."

"It's done, it's over now, just relax."

She leaned against him as they went down the hall into their room, her feet dragging, stumbling across the carpet.

"I knew it, *knew* it, all my fault . . ."

"Shh. It's not, Donna."

"Oh yes, yes it is . . ."

He helped her take off her paint spattered shirt and kick off her jeans. Tenderly he lowered her back against the pillow and stepped into the adjoining bath, where he took a lavender towel from a high, fluffy stack. When he came back into the bedroom a wave of love shook him as he saw her lying there clad only in an old T-shirt, her lower half bare and vulnerable as a child's. He tucked the towel beneath her hips and drew the sheet over her.

"Some water?" he asked. She looked at him strangely. "Some water to drink?" he explained. She shook her head no. Tears pooled in her eyes as she stared at the ceiling. "All right. You rest. You just rest now, and I'll call the doctor." He could have used the phone by the bed, but he didn't want her to hear him say that she'd lost the baby.

Richard kissed her forehead, tucked in her sheet, and left the room. On his way to the downstairs telephone, he passed the open door of the guest bath and stopped, looking in at the stained tiles and grout, the closed lid of the toilet bowl, and wondered what he should do.

Then he knew, knew what the doctors and the laboratories would want, knew what they would want to see so that they could find out what went wrong, so that maybe he and Donna could try again and have a baby, a *real* baby, and not what floated, dead, in the cloudy water, not what he would now have to preserve, to save for study, dissection.

My child. Stained sections on a microscope slide.

"So be it," he whispered aloud, remembering burying his first dog, scooping his dead goldfish from the smooth surface of the fishbowl. "So be it."

With a soft *pop,* he pulled a paper cup from the wall dispenser, then knelt and lifted the lid. It was there, as he knew and feared it would be, drifting against the white porcelain, still shrouded in its coverlet of thick blood and fluid, perhaps still dreaming that it was safely ensconced in its amniotic home.

Even now it was swimming, wasn't it, so unbelievably tiny, and yet a person . . . *There,* did the little arms move? Arms or paddles, but yes, there were fingers, or the buds that would have been fingers, weren't there? Like a fly, oh certainly no bigger than a fly, and the limbs *did* move, yes, there *again,* and it *was* swimming, or trying to, wriggling like a tadpole, and wasn't it still alive, oh yes, of *course* it was, and he could save it now, and put it back where it could grow, couldn't he? Of course he could, he was the *father,* and he *could,* of course, of course . . .

Oh sisters two, how may we do
For to preserve this day
This poor youngling . . .

In a bottle, he thought suddenly, coldly, damning fantasies and accepting the real. *Preserved in a bottle.*

He dipped the cup into the water, pulled it against the side until what he wanted was surrounded by the paper, and then lifted it up out of the bowl, pressing the flush lever so that the urine and detritus whirled and sank away, and the water was fresh and clear again.

He carried the cup with the fetus down to the kitchen, put aluminum foil over the top, and placed it at the back of the refrigerator, next to the tray of baking soda, gray with age. As he dialed the doctor's number, he found that he was humming the "Coventry Carol" again.

III

"It's best that it happened," Richard said.

"I can't believe that."

"You know what he said—it would have been impossible to carry it to term, and if it *had* been born . . ." He left it unfinished and sipped his wine. It was the evening of the day Richard had thrown away the grapes. The fetus had disappeared into a laboratory, and was no doubt destroyed by now. Donna had recovered completely, at least physically. They had hardly spoken about it. He did not want to force her. The doctor told him in private not to push it, that she seemed extremely depressed (as if he couldn't tell), and that it would be best to let her come to terms with what had happened on her own schedule.

Tonight he had finally talked her into a glass of wine, which had loosened her tight facade enough for her to say, slowly and carefully, "Well, I really did it, didn't I?"

Nature's way, Richard had replied, spoon-feeding the words the doctor had given him. Donna would not accept them, would accept nothing but the concept that her sins had found her out, and destroyed her child. "I wouldn't have cared," she said, "if it *had* been a monster. I would've loved it."

Richard could say nothing in response.

"Would you?" she asked him.

"What?"

"Have loved it? If it hadn't been right?"

"It still would have been my child," he answered, too glibly.

"Until I killed it," she said.

"You didn't do any such thing."

"What I did killed it."

"That's stupid. There's no way to know that," he said.

"So there's no way to refute it," she replied. "Damned if I do, damned if I don't. And my poor little baby is damned forever."

"Stop talking like that. It was a . . . a mistake, that's all, just a genetic fluke, Donna. It could have been as much *my* fault as yours, for Christ's sake. It *never* would've been a baby—odds are it couldn't have survived a minute out of the womb."

She grew pale as he talked, but he couldn't stop. He had to tell her what he'd been thinking, what he'd been aching to say. "You did *nothing*. Things *happen*, things like this *happen* to mothers who've never smoked a cigarette or had a beer. It could've been something that's been in you or me since we were *born*, something the goddam factories put into the air or water or food that just didn't *agree* with you, it could've been so goddam *many* things, Donna. So stop. Please. Just stop killing yourself over what you couldn't help. Let's just think ahead. To the next one."

The look she gave him was cold, foreign, one he had never seen on her face. "There isn't going to be a next one."

"But . . . but there's no reason we—"

"No more," she said. "We can still fuck . . ." He blanched at the harshness of the word in her mouth. ". . . but not for a baby. I won't do this again. I mean it."

"But nothing says that this would happen again . . ."

"I won't take the chance."

"Life's *full* of chances, Donna. From the minute . . ." He stopped.

"From the minute you're born," she finished for him.

"Yes. From the minute you're born."

"I'm sorry, Rick."

"We should see someone."

"No, there's no point."

"A counselor, a . . ."

"A psychiatrist?"

"Maybe. Donna, I know, I know it was hard to lose it, it was hard for me, too, but you can't let it rule your life."

"It won't. Just maybe the one small part of it, that's all."

Richard felt exhausted, unable to prolong their verbal skirmish. Her defenses seemed impregnable anyway, at least for now. In time, he thought, reason, the reason *he* possessed, might prevail. But not now. Not so soon.

That night, in bed, he put his arm around her and she moved into his warmth, but they did not make love, and he wondered if they ever would again.

Long after midnight, Richard awoke, conscious of Donna sitting up in bed next to him. Even in the dark, he could sense her tension, her attitude of expectant listening. "Donna?"

"Shh."

"What is it?"

"Listen." Her voice shook with excitement. Slowly he began to be aware of an alien sound just on the edge of audibility, similar to the tiny cracks and pings of expanding and cooling heat ducts that he spent the evenings of October getting used to. But this new sound seemed nonmetallic, liquid in nature. It was nothing so simple as a drip, but it *was* rhythmic, a steady, constant *surge* of sound, like waves on a shore, though they were five hundred miles from the nearest beach. It was haunting, soothing, restful, and Richard thought there was a familiarity to it. It was tantalizing, elusive, and he knew that if he could only think back, think back *far* enough . . .

The furnace kicked on, and its barreling *whoosh* swept the sound and the nearly grasped memory far away. "Damn!" Donna cried. "Oh *damn* it!" Beside her, Richard shook his head as though coming out of a dream. "You heard it?" she said, switching on the lamp, barely blinking at its sudden glare.

"Yeah. Sure I did."

"What *was* it?"

"I'm . . . not sure."

"Where was it coming from?"

And he knew. Even though the sound seemed to lack any positive direction, he knew its source.

"The bath," she whispered, saying what he would not. "The guest bath." She turned as he nodded agreement, and stepped onto the cold wooden floor. Without pausing for a robe, she left the room and moved down the hall. He followed her.

When he arrived at the guest bath, she was already inside. The bright fluorescents had flickered into life, but their hum and the muffled rush of the furnace could not quell the other sound, that deep roar of moving fluids, the ebb and flow of the thick, heavy juices of life, all the churning activity of the womb. It was impossible to remember it, but he knew it could be nothing else.

"Oh my God," said Donna. "It's the baby."

The closed lid of the toilet started to rattle, lightly at first, then began to chatter like a giant bridgework, rising so high that he almost, but not quite, got a glimpse of what was inside. He walked past Donna and stood beside the clattering bowl, staring down at it, the surging sound all around him now.

"Open it," she said hollowly.

He began to reach down, but before his fingers could touch the vibrating lid, it snapped open like a hungry mouth, startling him, making him stumble backward into his wife. The lid stayed open, showing them the water inside.

It was as black as ink, the unrelieved black of midnight cellars. As they watched, it started to slowly swirl and sink soundlessly downward, and more water, just as black, entered from under the rim to pour down, dance and turn and sink, over and over again, the sound of it lost in the pulse of the thicker liquids, that cacophony which poured over them, drowning their senses.

"Stop," Richard said, or thought he said, as he could

not hear his voice. "Stop!" he cried again, and this time it was thinly audible. Now he shrieked, *"Stop!"* and it cut the surging, parted the liquid waves of sound that deafened them, and the waters stopped pouring, the roar of fluid, of heartbeat, of life force quieted, leaving them in a flat, dead silence, a silence in which he *saw.*

It could have lasted only a split second, but in its brief space the bathroom winked from sight, and in its place was a face, huge and malformed. It was the face of a beast, yet a beast of *potential.* It was as primitive in form as a child's drawing, yet the texture of the flesh was rich, finely grained, highly defined, viewed with perfect clarity. It was crowned by a vast and fleshy dome, bisected by a line of demarcation that could only be there to divide the hemispheres of its massive brain. The lower half of the face was composed of folds and wrinkles, out of which Richard could define loops of flexed muscle parodying a nose, and, beneath it, a broad, mountainous ridge that split the face from side to side, sinking at the edges into a countenance-spanning frown. On those hummocky sides of the primitive face hung two pouches, with a pit in each, that Richard knew would be eyes. They were not now. The thing was blind, though he felt it saw nonetheless, and his fear at seeing the thing was dwarfed by the realization that he in turn was seen.

He gasped and drew back, and the vision vanished. Once again the whiteness of the bathroom was all around him, and he heard no sounds but his own ragged breathing, the rumble of the furnace, the voice of Donna beside him.

"Did you *see? . . ."* she said, as though she still could.

"See what?" he asked, praying she'd say the water, or the lid jiggling, hoping against hope that she had not seen what he had. If so, it had to have been real. They could not both be mad.

She shattered his hopes forever. "The face." There was unimaginable awe in her words. "It was the baby. I saw it."

So simply, he realized that she must be right. The face of a fetus, unborn, undeveloped, primitive in the extreme, little different from the fetus of beast or fish or fowl. How long, he tried to recall, before a fetus shows traces of being mammalian? And how much longer after that until displaying signs of humanity? Longer, surely, than eight weeks.

Oh, dear Christ, what had happened here? What had died? And what still, impossibly, lived?

IV

When Richard and Donna looked at the water in the bowl, it was perfectly clear and still. Indeed, there was not a thing in the bathroom to ascertain the sounds and sights they had experienced. It was as though they had undergone the same delusion, though Richard found that theory so unlikely as to be impossible. He had seen what he had seen, heard what he had heard, and that it had been a delusion occurred to him only momentarily.

The later manifestations, though, were quick and short and sharp, like jabs of temper, angry releases of ghostly frustration. The first of them occurred when he and Donna sat at the kitchen table, drinking instant coffee, trying to determine what had happened in the guest bath and why.

"It was the baby," Donna said with rigid certainty.

"It couldn't have been."

"You saw it."

"I saw *something.*"

"It *was* the baby."

"Donna, the baby's dead. It *died.* I *don't* believe in ghosts."

"How else can you explain it?"

"It can't . . ."

"Listen," she said. "I don't believe either . . . didn't, at least. But if ghosts are supposed to result from violent things that happen, from . . . from traumatization, well, God, can you imagine anything more traumatic than being stillborn? Being yanked out of the only place in the world where you can survive?"

"So what are you saying? That . . . that somehow this thing that wasn't even born, that was never even alive, that never had . . ." He felt absurd saying it. ". . . a soul, has come back as a ghost to flush our goddam *toilet?*"

He laughed at his words, and as he did his untouched coffee mug tipped over, pouring a half cup of scalding liquid onto his stomach, groin, and thighs. The thin robe he wore offered no protection, and he gasped and stood up, letting the steaming brew drip off of him, trying not to cry out.

Donna, shocked, leaned toward him as if wanting to help but not knowing how. In a few seconds, after the first searing pains were over, he opened the robe. The flesh of his loins was bright red, but there were no blisters. He took a jar of cold water from the refrigerator, poured some into his cupped hand, and patted it on his skin. "Bastard," he whispered fervently. "How the . . ." He stopped, knowing the only answer.

"*It* did it," Donna said. "Because you laughed."

It took Richard a moment to speak again. "I'm going to bed," he said, wrapping the wet robe around him. "We'll talk about this in the morning."

The morning came slowly. Richard lay awake, listening for noises, his eyes staring at the false lights of the darkness, seeing that bulbous face in his memory. When daylight came, they did not speak of the night before, and Richard kept one hand firmly on his coffee mug.

Nothing happened for a week. Donna seemed exhausted and slept well, but Richard took a long time to get to sleep, and when he did, his night was haunted by disquieting dreams he could not remember in the morning.

Donna had said nothing about going back to work, and Richard brought it up only once. She dismissed it rather flippantly, which annoyed him. Mortgage payments were not small, and it seemed to him a waste to have her idle at home. Still, he remembered what the doctor had said, and did not press her.

A heavy snowstorm blew up the following Thursday, and rapid changes in temperature crusted the white-covered roof with ice. A warm front came into the area on Saturday, and the snow beneath the ice melted. Unable to drip off the roof because of the ice dam above the spoutings, the chill water trickled beneath the eaves, down into the walls, and ultimately dripped from beneath the interior windowsills. It had happened one previous winter, and Richard and Donna grudgingly packed towels beneath the sills, bundled up, and went outside. Richard took a hatchet and ladder from one of the outbuildings, wedged the ladder into the snow, and climbed up to the edge of the two-story high roof, where he began to hack long chunks of ice from above the rusty spouting. Donna stood below, watching from a distance of a few yards, her booted feet wedged firmly in eighteen inches of snow.

Richard was leaning far to his left, trying to minimize the number of times he had to descend and shift the ladder, when the house suddenly seemed to slew to his left. The sensation lasted only a moment, and he knew he was falling, the ladder with him. He pushed back and away, thinking only that he must not smash into the house. He felt his body leave the ladder, float dizzily, and fall. The impact as he hit the ice made a sharp *crack,* and he was still, lying on his side in the snow beneath the icy crust.

"Richard!" Donna cried, wading toward him. "Richard! Don't move!"

He had no intention of doing so until he knew he was capable of it. His heart was ratcheting, yet he felt curiously alive, as though he had just stepped from a particularly invigorating roller coaster ride. "I'm . . . I'm all right. I think I'm all right." He tried a few tentative movements. There was no pain. "I'm okay." He struggled through the thick snow to his feet. "What the hell happened?"

The ladder lay where it had fallen, the base at least twenty feet from where it had been solidly rooted in the snow.

"My God," he whispered. "What on earth . . ."

"It didn't fall," Donna said. "It was just like it . . . like it was pulled out of the snow and thrown away. Like some invisible hand . . ."

"That's impossible," he said thickly.

"Look. Look for yourself."

He saw that she was right. Had he merely overbalanced, the ladder's base would have been next to the holes in the snow. As it was . . .

"This is crazy," he said. "Some freak, that's all. The way it hit, it bounced or something. Just some freak."

"Don't do any more. Let's go inside."

He looked at the ladder, then up at the roof, from which he had chipped well over half of the ice. There should be space for the melting water to drain off now. Yes, he told himself, there *should* be.

"Please, Richard." Donna took his arm. "I love you. I don't want you hurt."

He let her lead him into the house.

The next evening he was taking a shower when Donna came into the bathroom to get a pair of tweezers. As she opened the door to leave, the shower caddy, laden with several pounds of soaps, shampoos, and rinses, tore loose from the tile and fell, hitting Richard sharply in the back of the neck. When they looked, they found the adhesive had not dried out.

On Sunday, Richard was in the den writing a letter at the rolltop desk, and Donna was standing by the bookcase. The heavy rolltop, contrary to all the laws of physics, came crashing down, striking the typewriter that Richard had pulled toward the desk's edge. It was all that kept his wrists from being crushed.

Donna held him while he trembled and laughed simultaneously, but neither one of them said anything about the baby that had been lost. For Richard to suggest it would have meant admitting that something totally inexplicable and irrational was intruding into their lives. He could not admit to that, not after the night he had laughed at Donna for suggesting what he had considered as the fantasy of a semihysterical woman. Now, he was unsure enough so that he could not speak of it.

V

When Richard returned from his classes Monday afternoon, Donna was gone. She had taken the Accord, a great many of her clothes, and several thousand dollars, he later learned, from her personal savings account. She had left behind a letter, written in her sharp, slanting script:

Dear Rick,

I'm sorry that I have to do this, but I think it's for the best for everybody. For you, for me, for the baby.

Maybe you'll think I'm crazy, but the baby's still alive, I know. Somehow, somewhere, and it's still bound to me. It's got to be. It's too small to survive on its own. So I'm leaving, and I think it will come with me, and then you'll be safe. It can *do* things, Rick. It can make things happen, and I'm afraid it will hurt you. Going away is the only answer. I owe it to you, and I owe it to the baby.

I didn't tell you before, because I thought you'd laugh at me, but I honestly feel as though I've never lost it. After the miscarriage, I still felt (and feel) as though I were still pregnant, still carrying it inside me. So I'm taking it away. Please try to understand and try to forgive me. And please don't look for me. I'll be all right. I'm *not* crazy, Rick, and I say that knowing that that's what crazy people always say. I'm not crazy, but I *am* special, and if that's delusions of grandeur, so be it, but there's *got* to be some purpose behind all this. I don't know when I'll come back, but I *will* come back, Rick. I love you, darling. Merry Christmas.

Donna

He put down the letter, poured himself a scotch, sat down and listened to the silence. The house felt empty, lifeless. Had there been any kind of entity there, it was gone now. Gone with Donna.

He stood, encased by quiet, and turned on the amplifier, hitting the scan switch and letting the first station click in. It was a choir singing Christmas music, and he half moaned, half laughed as he identified it as the "Coventry Carol." So fitting, he thought. His *soul* felt like Coventry, the latterday Coventry, bombed, a shambles, wooden skeletons poking their fingers up through smoky rubble.

He listened. They were singing the final verse.

That woe is me, poor child, for thee,
And ever mourn and say:
For thy parting, neither say nor sing
By, by, lully lullay.

He kept listening until he fell asleep. He did not dream.

VI

Parsons finished reading the letter. He stuck out his lower lip, tapped the paper with the knuckles of his right hand, set it down, and looked at Richard. "She's disturbed," he said.

"No shit, Sherlock," Richard responded bitterly.

"What did you expect me to say? You want a complete case history neatly labeled and explained?"

"You're the psychiatrist."

"I'm not a goddam psychiatrist, I'm a goddam psychologist."

"So what the hell does the psychologist have to say?"

"Little more than you can figure out with common sense. Donna was very upset by the miscarriage, and when these incidents began happening, she interpreted it as a sign that the baby—or the life force, call it, that had been the baby—had somehow survived. Isn't that what *you* think?"

"I suppose so."

Parsons was silent for a moment. He eyed Richard carefully. "Now what do you *believe?*"

"There's a difference?"

"You bet."

Richard sighed. "Everything seems *too* coincidental. Why did these things all start to happen at once? And what about that thing . . . those noises and everything in the guest bath? We *both* saw it."

"You *thought* you both saw it."

"Oh, come on, John, I know when—"

"Hold it. I didn't say you *didn't* see it. I think maybe you did."

"What?"

"You want an answer. Okay. I'll give you an answer that isn't completely rational, but one that has nothing to do with ghosts. You're not going to find it in any textbook, but that doesn't mean it's not possible. It just means it's not proven. Hell, it's not even seriously proposed."

"What are you talking about?"

"Look, when these things happened, the coffee cup, the ladder, the desk, where was Donna?"

Richard thought for a second. "There with me."

"Each time?"

"Yes. Why?"

"All right. This may be hard. Do you think that Donna felt angry with you? I mean about losing the baby?"

"I . . . I don't know. She may have."

"You said you argued about responsibility."

"Well, yes . . ."

"Isn't it possible that she may have blamed you for the things she feared? The side effects, and what might have caused them?"

"I don't know."

"You think she may have wanted you to *share* that responsibility? And when you didn't, when you said that there was nothing to feel guilty about, she thought you were trying to cop out, leaving her to take the consequences?"

"Look, John!" Richard half rose to his feet.

"Relax, Richard, I'm not saying that it's true, I'm just asking if Donna might not have seen it that way." Richard sat back, slowly. "Well? Could she have?"

"I suppose . . . it's possible."

"So then," Parsons went on, "she loses the baby, blames herself, but blames you as well, and then strikes out at you."

"Strikes out? How?"

"Call it telekinesis if you like. Everything's got to have a name, doesn't it? What happened in the bathroom was something she projected. From her mind to yours. *She* knocked over the ladder, spilled the coffee, slammed the desk."

"Jesus Christ, John, you're supposed to be a *scientist.* How can you spout this shit?"

"Richard, the more I study the mind, the more I learn I don't know. Now, I *do* have limits. Ghosts are out, as are demons. No magic spells. Astrology is crap. Lumps on heads, crystals, channeling, Ouija boards, it's all bullshit. But what the mind can do isn't."

"You mean you think that Donna made me see and hear it all? That she . . . she attacked me with her mind? Knocked over that ladder without touching it?"

"I think it's possible. Highly improbable, but possible."

"All right, look. Assuming she could, *why* would she? Why try to hurt me? She *loves* me, John. She says so in the letter, and I believe it. I know she does."

"If she's behind all this, Richard, it isn't her conscious mind that's doing it. It's her subconscious. And there, deep down in that pit of primitive irrationality, she may very well hate your guts. And instead of accepting her own hostility toward you, she projects it into the baby. The *fetus,* I guess I should say."

Richard barked a laugh. "But how can she do that? Turn her baby—what she *thinks* is her baby—into a . . . a monster?"

"Maybe it just gives her more to take responsibility for."

Richard stood up, walked to the window, and looked out at the snow covered quadrangle, where the down and wool wrapped students passed like purposeful bears. "So what do I do?" he wondered aloud.

"Do you know where she could have gone?"

Richard shook his head. "Her parents are dead. She was an only child. John," he said, turning to Parsons, "what do I do?"

"The only thing you can. Wait. Leave her alone."

". . . and she'll come home."

"Probably. When she finds there *is* no baby. That she isn't still pregnant."

"Do you think . . . when she has a period?"

"Maybe that soon. Or maybe she'll ignore it. Could be a full seven months. Or more. Whenever she realizes that there's nothing there to come to term."

Richard swallowed heavily. "What you said about the mind. Do you think . . . could it be possible that . . ."

"I know what you're thinking. And no, it's *not* possible. You can't get around biology, Richard. Donna lost her baby. That's all there is to it. She'll be back. And she'll come back alone."

VII

Donna came back in July, in the middle of a summer so hot and dry that the grass around the farmhouse had yellowed, then browned to the color of dead leaves, crackling like melting ice when Richard walked on it.

He was sitting on the front porch, drifting back and forth on the rusty metal glider, a vodka and tonic dripping condensation onto his bare leg, when she drove down the driveway in the Accord. She parked, but didn't get out of the car right away. She sat there for a minute, watching him watching her. Then she opened the door, walked up the path, and stood at the bottom of the porch steps. He noticed her hands were empty, her belly flat. She looked as though she had lost weight. Her color was bad, her eyes tired, her cheeks as hollow as his stomach felt. "Hi," she said, with barely a trace of emotion.

He looked at her and nodded. Twice.

"Aren't you glad to see me?" Now there was, he thought, just a touch of pleading.

"You didn't write," he said. "Or call. Seven months and not a word from you."

She tried to smile. "I thought you'd try to find me. I didn't want you to."

"I didn't try. If I would have, I could have. A detective could have traced the car, followed you."

"Thank you."

"For what?"

"For not trying. For leaving me alone." She stepped onto the porch and sat next to him on the glider. "Aren't you going to hug me?"

Slowly, he set down his drink and embraced her. His arms felt stiff and heavy as they touched her, but the contact changed his mood immediately, as a spark of power lights a dusty and long extinguished lamp. He held her tightly, buried his face against her shoulder, and began to cry.

"Oh, Rick," she said, putting her arms around him and hugging him tightly. "Oh, Richard." Her eyes teared. Her nose began to run. "I did miss you."

"I didn't know," Richard said through his crying. "I just didn't know. You could have been dead. I didn't know if you'd ever come back."

"I'd always come back. You knew I'd come back."

"You were so upset," he went on. "I thought you might even . . . hurt yourself."

"Oh, no. Never that. Never that. Shh. Shh, darling. I'm home now. I'm home and I love you, and everything's all right. More than all right."

He cried some more, and Donna kept holding him, lightly crying as well. "Where were you?" he finally asked. "Where did you go?"

"Ohio. A small town near Akron. I just drove until I found a place that felt right. A boarding house. An older lady had it. She was very nice. I helped her with the housework and things until . . ."

She paused. In the heat, Richard felt very cold. "Until . . . you came home."

"Yes." Donna nodded. "Until then." She took her arms from around him, stood up, leaned on the porch railing. "Rick, remember my letter?" she asked quietly. "What I said I thought was happening?"

He nodded, smiling to drive away the spectres.

"I was right, Richard. What I thought was happening? It happened."

He would not stop smiling. If he stopped smiling, he would let the monsters in. "No, Donna. The baby died. We *lost* the baby." He smiled, being rational.

Donna smiled back. "It's in the car."

He shook his head. He smiled. How he smiled. "No."

"Come look. See for yourself." She reached out her hand and took his, drawing him to his feet. Together they walked down the chipped and flaking wooden steps, down the path to the Accord. "It was sleeping on the way in," she said.

"It," Richard parroted.

"I don't know whether it's a boy or a girl. I can't really tell. Not yet."

"Donna . . ."

"Shh." They were at the car, and Donna leaned over and looked into the backseat. "Look," she said.

Richard looked.

He did not see it at first, but as Donna's grip tightened on his hand, something swam into view, hiding the faded blue vinyl. Its outline was a pair of joined ovals, one larger than the other, with four protuberances he tentatively identified as arms and legs. They were round and fat, and, like the trunk and head, pink in color. His breath locked in his throat as he heard her ask gently, "There, do you see it?"

"Donna . . . no . . ."

"Yes, you do. I can see you do."

"Donna . . ."

"It's very quiet. Very good. It doesn't eat, but it loves to be sung to, talked to."

"Donna, it's . . . it's not there. Not really. You created it."

"Of course, Richard. *We* created it. Together. It's our baby."

"It is not there, Donna."

"You can't say that. You can't believe it. You see it. It's what we did. It's *us,* Richard, it's part of us. It's who we are, and what we've done." She looked down at the shadowy form, which was growing ever more distinct. "So we have to take care of it." She rested a hand on Richard's shoulder. "Let's go inside now. Into our house."

She turned and started to walk up the path. When she saw him hesitate, looking at her and then at what lay in the backseat, she gave a little bell of a laugh. "We don't have to take it," she said. "It'll be inside before we are."

She was right. When they entered the living room, it was lying on the sofa, half-seen, like some plump fruit shrouded by leaves and branches. Donna looked down at it lovingly, then walked around the room, touching familiar things. "You've kept the house nice, Rick. Everything looks so clean. We'll be happy now." She smiled at him. "I think I'll get my bags. I won't really feel at home until I'm unpacked."

Richard continued to gaze at the shape, seeing it float on the brown brocade as he'd seen a similar shape float in water, dark and lambent. "I'll . . . I'll help you," he said huskily.

"No. You stay here." She embraced him from behind. "Sing to it, Richard. It loves that."

He felt her kiss his hair, then listened to her retreating footsteps, the screen door slamming shut on its weary spring, the boards of the porch creaking under her weight.

It did not disappear, did not vanish in her absence as he had thought it might. It remained on the couch, its outline firm.

How strong can she be, how strong?

And then the other thought intruded: *How strong have I become?*

Parsons's mysteries of mind swept through him, and he wondered what cancer had clamped his brain, what sickness, what maleficent suggestion had given him the power to conjure this thing that shared his house, his wife's love, and, ultimately, his own affections.

The plumpness on the sofa moved as if trying to give an answer, and the appendages twitched, stroked through unseen waves, extended toward him as if to say—

Love me. I am here, am yours. Love me.

He looked at his baby, and found himself humming, very gently, very quietly. It was a carol, a carol and a lullaby.

I am yours. Love me, it said to him.

He would. Helpless, bound, he knew he would.

MOM AND DAD

AND HE WHO MOURNS

David B. Silva

1

IT WAS GONE.

Jameson Packard had set the pencil on the corner of his desk before he went into the kitchen to get a bite to eat. Now he was back and the pencil was gone. Of course, he might have been mistaken. It wasn't unusual for him to misplace a thing or two every once in a while. But lately, it seemed as if he had been losing things all too often.

Losing a little piece of your mind is what you're doing, Jameson thought.

He opened the top right drawer of the desk, pulled out another pencil from the tray of number threes, and decided he really wasn't much in the mood to write anyway. Most of his time lately had been spent staring at a blank sheet of paper, his mind wandering absently to thoughts of how quiet the house had become since Katie had died.

He still couldn't walk past her room without stopping. Last week Barb had found him in the hall, leaning against Katie's door, a little after two in the morning.

"You can't stand out in the hall forever," she had said.

"I know." He had been half-awake, half in dream, and her voice hadn't scared him as much as it had brought him back to the present. Standing there in her bathrobe, her arms crossed, he thought how strong Barb had been through it all.

"Open the door," she had said.

"I can't."

"It's not going to get any easier."

No, Jameson thought now. *It probably wasn't.* He looked down at the notepad in front of him, that sickly yellow glaring back accusingly. One paragraph. One sentence. Hell, one word. If he could just get one word on paper, maybe then his mind would switch gears, maybe then he would be able to stop thinking about Katie.

He closed his eyes, took a deep breath, and found himself dangerously close to the edge of tears. It was a familiar place these days. But like Barb had told him so often lately, it was getting time to move on. You can't let the past rule your life. If you do, it won't be long before you start fading away. And she had been right, of course. She had been watching him disappear a little bit at a time for months now, and it couldn't continue this way. Even Jameson knew that.

He rubbed his eyes, then stared down at the blank yellow pad on the desk. Only it wasn't there now. The desktop was clean. Even the pencil he had just pulled out of the top drawer was missing.

It's true, he thought. *I* am *losing a little piece of my mind.*

But it was much worse than that.

2

Two and a half years ago, Jameson had lost his mother to ovarian cancer. He had watched it slowly eat away at her until at the end the woman lying in bed was a woman he hardly recognized. She had lost sixty pounds. Her face had become a gaunt mask: her lips pulled back, her eyes sunken, the contours of her skull outlined in hideous detail.

Almost a year later, his father had experienced a stroke that paralyzed the entire right side of his body. It had kept him bedridden for several months before an aneurysm finally finished the job. Jameson had cried for several days after his father had died.

And then the accident had happened, and Katie had died.

He still hadn't cried for Katie.

God, why hadn't he been able to cry for her?

3

"James?"

He couldn't have said where he'd been, but it had obviously been somewhere else. Barb was standing over him, her hand on his forearm. He was sitting on the couch in the living room.

"Are you okay?"

"Uh-huh." It was dark out. He yawned and tried a smile on for her, though it wasn't an honest smile and he knew it wasn't going to fool her much. "Just dozed off for a bit."

"You had your eyes open."

"What?"

"You were sleeping with your eyes open. I've never seen you do that before."

"I didn't know that was possible," he said noncommittally.

"You sure you're all right?"

He gave her hand a reassuring pat. "Just a bit tired, that's all."

"Coming up to bed?"

"In a while, okay?"

She smiled, a smile not dissimilar to the one he had tried on her—only slightly concerned—then she disappeared down the hallway. Barb had cried for Katie. She had spent nearly every minute of an entire week in Katie's room, looking at her collection of dolls, reading through her children's books, talking and crying and laughing as if the memory of Katie were as real as Katie herself had been.

Barb had cried for her.

But not Jameson.

He stared in silence through the living room window at the deepening hues of night, feeling lost in his own house, lost in his own life. Outside, Chet Matthews wheeled his twin plastic garbage cans down the driveway and left them standing at the curb, looking like two small sentries, keeping watch. Life went on, Jameson thought. Even the mundane. Especially the mundane.

Then something sounded from upstairs.

He thought it might have been Barb calling for him, though it wasn't like her to bother him once she had gone off to bed. And it hadn't been so much a voice, now that he gave it a second thought, as it had been the sound of a weight against the floor. Sort of a *pffft, thump-thump.* Like . . .

Like . . .

No.

More likely it had only been his imagination.

He listened a moment longer, heard nothing other than the hum of the refrigerator coming from the kitchen, then glanced out the window again. A car moved slowly down the street, the beams of its headlights evaporating into the fall of darkness. It passed, right to left, and Jameson gradually realized that the twin garbage cans Matthews had just wheeled out to the curb were gone now.

Disappeared.
Like the pencils the other day.
Like his mother.
Christ, like everything in his life.

4

Jameson Packard.

It wasn't a household name by anyone's imagination. He had been writing for nearly ten years now, but it had only been the past couple of years that things had begun to fall into place. Last January, he had signed a three book, hard/soft deal with a major publisher. Book one had already been released. *Kirkus* and *Publishers Weekly* had given it quiet praise and sales had been strong enough to warrant a second printing. Things were gradually looking up.

So why did everything feel so . . . so transparent?

Maybe because none of it's real, Jameson thought. He leaned back in his chair and stared at the blinds covering the window over his desk. It was sunny outside. But in here, he liked to keep the blinds closed during the day. Anything to keep the distractions at bay.

You didn't have to look close to see that the blinds needed dusting. Everything in this room needed dusting, especially the stacks of books that had been gradually growing more prominent. He couldn't remember exactly when he had run out of shelf space and had begun to stack his books any which way he could, but it had been long enough ago that the den was beginning to look like one of those used-book stores downtown. You want it, you find it. All except . . .

He glanced across the room at the middle shelf where he kept all of his own material: the two previous paperbacks he'd had published, the current book out in hardcover—*Seeing Through You*—and a handful of short stories that had come out in various anthologies the past five years. Except . . .

Except none of them were there.

In their place, there was a gaping hole, an empty space that reminded him momentarily of a missing front tooth. Jameson stared at it, the way he might stare at a beautiful young woman with a gap in her smile. Then gradually he climbed to his feet and moved across the room.

There was a thin layer of dust that had settled into the gap. He wiped his fingers through it, studied his fingertips, then wiped the dust off on his pants. Dust, yes. But no more or less than what had settled over everything else in this room. And what did that mean exactly? That the books had been missing for a long time now? But he had seen them there just yesterday. Or if not yesterday, the day before. He couldn't remember precisely when it had been, of course, but it certainly hadn't been *that* long ago.

Oh, Christ.

What was going on?

Maybe Barb had moved them. She usually preferred to stay out of the den, arguing that each of them needed a place to hide out when the world got a little crazy. The den was his. The extra bedroom upstairs was hers. Jameson did his writing here. And when Barb wasn't working, she used the bedroom for her craft projects. It hadn't been so long ago that she had mentioned something about how they should spend a few extra dollars and find a way of keeping his dust jackets in mint condition. Maybe that's what she had done . . . taken the books to have the jackets protected. She was like that, always on a whim.

Though that didn't explain the missing paperbacks, did it?

Jameson thought about that for a while, and finally decided the best thing to do was to call Barb at work and ask her directly. Another time, he probably would have let it go without much thought. But things hadn't been quite right lately, had they? And he didn't want to let them slide any further, for fear they might start down the hill at such a pace that he'd never be able to stop them again.

He caught her just as she was returning from lunch.

"What's up?" she asked.

"Nothing special," he said, leaning back in his chair, and trying to decide how he wanted to approach this thing. "I just noticed a few of my books missing from the den. I thought maybe you had done something with them."

"No . . ." she said, somewhat hesitantly. He could picture her giving it an extra moment's thought, coming up with nothing, then shaking her head. "I haven't been in there lately, James. What's missing?"

"Just some of my own books," he said softly, trying not to let the sound of his voice betray him. He wasn't as upset as he was concerned. If it hadn't been Barb, then what had happened to the books?

"They're gone?"

"Well, they're not where they're supposed to be."

"I don't know what to tell you."

"That's okay. I just thought maybe you had taken them into a binder or something. Tried to get the covers protected."

"I still want to do that," she said quickly. They had discussed the matter a number of times, Jameson always wanting to put it off until he felt like an honest-to-goodness writer and not just someone skimming off the surface of his talent. Barb liked to argue that he was always going to feel as if he were skimming off the surface; and in his starker, more honest moments, Jameson had to admit that she was probably right.

"That would be fine by me if I could just find the damn books," he said.

There was a moment of unsettling silence on her end. Then quietly, she asked, "Are you all right? I mean . . . you've got other copies stored in the attic, James. It's not as if you've lost a manuscript or something irreplaceable."

"I know. It's just that . . ." And he caught himself. It's just that . . . *what?* That a couple of pencils were missing? That he couldn't account for what had happened to the twin garbage cans Chet Matthews had put out on the curb? "I'm sorry. You're right. I probably set the books aside somewhere and it's just slipped my mind. I'll bring down some extra copies from the attic."

"You sure?"

"Sorry I bothered you at work."

"Don't be silly."

"I love you, Barb."

"I love you, too."

After he hung up, Jameson sat at his desk, glancing up occasionally at the empty space on the bookshelf and trying to remember what he might have done with the books. Or if he had, in fact, done anything at all with them. Barb had been right, of course. It wasn't as if he'd lost a manuscript. But maybe if he had told her about the pencils. Maybe if he had told her about Chet Matthews and his garbage cans. Maybe then she would have felt differently.

Maybe.

There was a blank sheet of paper on the desk, staring back at him now, the same way it had been staring back at him for longer than he cared to remember. But lately the right words had never seemed to make themselves available, had they? And even the accusation of an empty page hadn't been enough to make something happen. Not on paper, and not in his head.

So what was the use?

Jameson tossed aside the pencil he had been holding. Instead of work, his mind preferred to toy with the idea of heading up to the attic to replace his missing books. Maybe after that he would finally be able to put his mind at rest. Maybe after that he'd be able to finally get a few words down on paper.

Maybe.

The house always felt empty during the day when Barb was gone. Even when Katie would get home from school, and he would busy himself in the kitchen making an afternoon snack for her and listening to her stories about how Bobby Kaplan had punched her during recess or Laurie Brown had told everyone that her father was out of work and they were going to move to Colorado or Arizona. Even then, Jameson would miss having Barb here. Even then, the house never felt quite right without her.

It felt even less so now, as he made his way down the upstairs hall, past their bedroom, past the guest bath, past . . . Katie's room. He stopped outside her door, like he always did, then leaned heavily against the adjacent wall. It had been an accident, Katie's death. She had stepped out into the street without looking, and a woman, who had been late for work, hadn't seen her. Katie had died instantly, according to the doctors. And maybe that's what made it so difficult for him to accept her death. It had been so sudden, so unexpected. No time for goodbyes. No time to try to prevent the unpreventable.

Jameson placed his hand on the doorknob, something else he did nearly every time he passed this way. But as with all the other times, he couldn't bring himself to actually open the door. Not yet. Maybe someday, but not yet.

"I love you, baby," he whispered into the narrow-crack between the door and the frame. "And I miss you."

5

Sunlight, slipping through the ventilation slats, fell across the attic floor in a series of lines that seemed to divide the room evenly from one end to the other. Jameson stood at the top of the stairs, watching a swirl of dust rise into the air in front of him and wondering where they had stored the boxes of his books.

In the far corner, he could see the rocking horse that Katie's grandparents had given her for her fifth birthday. Next to that was the first sewing machine Barb had ever owned. Between where he was standing and those things, though, there was a carnival of junk they had been collecting for nearly twelve years now. How many times had they meant to spend a weekend up here, sorting through it all? Barb had talked about a garage sale once, and he supposed they'd actually get around to it someday. But for now, all Jameson wanted to do was find his books and get back to work.

The only problem was that his books weren't here.

He spent nearly an hour weeding through all the old boxes, and when he was done, he sat down on the corner of an old coffee table pushed up against another stack of boxes, and wondered if he'd had it right in his mind. Maybe they hadn't stored the books up here after all. But then where else would they have stored them? The garage? That was possible. Though it would have had to have been in the rafters, because it was a tight fit getting both cars into the garage, even without things stuffed into the storage space around the outer edges.

He could call Barb again, he supposed. Though she had thought the books were in the attic, too. That's what she had said, wasn't it?

Christ.

Nothing was where it was supposed to be anymore.

Everything was getting mislaid.

Jameson ran a hand through his hair, and leaned back

against the stack of boxes behind him. It didn't really matter, of course. He could always order more copies from the publishers. It was just that . . . that . . .

And then he heard it again.

That noise.

It was coming from somewhere under the floor, and it took him a second or two before he realized that Katie's room was under there. That noise was coming from *her* room. That *pffft, thump-thump* sound, like the end of an old LP when the needle was trapped and waiting for someone to change the record, like the sound of a tire that's gone flat. It was coming from *her* room.

My God, he thought. He could feel the blood draining from his face. He climbed to his feet, still listening, still hearing that same *pffft, thump-thump* coming from right beneath him.

Katie.

Downstairs, he found himself standing outside her room again, his hand on the doorknob, his heart pounding against the inside of his chest like something trying to tear itself free.

And then suddenly the noise stopped.

Jameson pulled his trembling hand back from the doorknob, feeling both a sense of relief and a sense of disappointment, neither of which he could explain. But he knew this much: Something was on the other side of the door, and he still wasn't ready to see what it was.

6

"I couldn't find my books this morning," Jameson said.

"I know. You called me, remember?"

"No, I mean the copies we stored in the attic. I went through every box up there. They aren't there."

It was a little after eleven. The lights were off. The house had been making its nightly settling noises as it gradually cooled down from the hot day, and everything was quiet now. Barb had come home late, after a long day on a project that was giving her some trouble at work, and she had hid herself away in her crafts room for several hours, making no bones about the fact that she wasn't in the mood for conversation. It was rare when she was like this, but it had been happening more and more often since Katie's death. All part of the stress, Jameson assumed. There was more than enough to go around.

"We didn't store them somewhere else, did we?"

"Where?"

"I don't know," he said. "In the garage, maybe? In the rafters? Maybe in the corner of your crafts closet?"

"We put them in the attic, James. There wasn't any room in my closet, and you wanted to make sure you could get to them without a big fuss, remember? That's why we settled on the attic."

In the back of his mind, he had known that, of course. It was just that he had gotten so many things wrong in his head lately.

"Are you all right, honey?" Barb asked. She cuddled protectively into his arms, and for the first time in a long time, Jameson wished it were the other way around. He wished it were *her* arms protecting him.

"I don't know," he whispered.

"I love you."

"I know."

"Is there anything I can do?" She placed the palm of her hand across his chest. It felt almost as if it were holding him together, and he wondered if Barb had always been the glue that had held his life together. God, he loved her.

"Have you ever felt like you were losing things, Barb? I mean . . . not just the car keys or that letter you had meant to mail out today, but . . . little bits and pieces of your life, of who you are and what you've done? Have you ever felt like they were slipping away from you? Disappearing out of your life faster than you could ever imagine?"

"What are you talking about, James?"

He stared at the pattern of lights and shadows on the wall, then shook his head. "I don't know. Probably nothing."

But it didn't feel like nothing. It felt like the important things were beginning to disappear on him. Like the threads of his life were quietly, systematically unraveling right before his eyes, and there wasn't a thing in the world he could do about it.

Poof!

7

He dreamed he was in the den.

The bookshelves were empty. The posters on the walls missing. But it was his den. No question of that.

He found himself facing the west wall. Behind him was the door. Only when he turned around it wasn't there. Like the books and the poster, the door was missing. And gradually, he realized that there were *no* doors in this room. No doors, and no windows. He was trapped.

No way in, no way out.

And it was getting worse.

The room had always been small. Originally, it had been an extra bedroom. Jameson had torn out the closet, covered the windows in blinds, and added some overhead lighting. All of which had made the room appear even smaller. But now, it wasn't just appearances. The wall in front of him, the one where the closet had once been, was moving ever so slowly inward.

Jameson took a step backward, turned, and realized with a rush of adrenaline, that it wasn't just that one wall. It was all of them. They were *all* closing in on him.

Pffft, thump-thump.

He took another step back, turned again.

No way in, no way out.

Pffft, thump-thump.

Stop it! Just stop it!

Pffft, thump-thump.

Pffft, thump-thump.

8

It *was* getting worse.

Jameson had decided, with a bit of reluctance, that he must have somehow overlooked the boxes yesterday. Barb had been right. They *had* stored the books in the attic, and that's where they had to be. Only now, as he stood at the top of the stairs, looking across the same attic floor that he had looked across yesterday, he was faced with an even bigger dilemma: everything was gone. Not just his boxes of books, but Barb's sewing machine and Katie's rocking horse and the boxes of old clothing and the chinaware and Katie's baby clothes and . . . and a thousand other things that had defined the history of his life, of their lives together.

All of it . . . gone.

Oh, sweet Jesus.

It *was* getting worse.

Jameson stood staring at the empty room for a long time. Exactly how long, he couldn't have said. But it was long enough for the bands of light to move several inches across the bare floor. And it was long enough for him to gradually awaken to the sound coming from somewhere downstairs.

Pffft, thump-thump.

Katie's room.

Oh, God.

He stared, hesitantly, at the open door at the bottom of the stairway. It was dark down there. He had turned on the hall light on his way up, but now it was dark. Just one more thing that had come up missing, he feared.

And then he started down the stairs.

9

The hall light *was* missing.

Jameson stopped at the bottom of the stairs, and peered down the hallway. The overhead light was missing. The light switches were missing. The outlets were missing. The heating vents were missing. All of it gone, as if none of it had ever been there before.

He leaned back against the wall, glanced up at the stairway leading to the attic, and . . . and it happened again. It was dark at the top of the stairs now, and at the edge of the darkness, he could no longer see the roofline or the west wall of the attic. Instead, as he watched, a grayish white cloud seemed to be settling in.

"What?"

He took the stairway back up, one step at a time, until he was standing just beneath the attic landing. Only now the attic was gone, too. It was as if he were standing in the midst of the clouds, surrounded by great puffs of gray and white, all sense of direction long lost. There was nothing else here now. No outside walls. No sunlight. No solid floor beyond the step where he was standing.

He was . . . at the edge, he realized.

The very edge.

He had lost both of his parents. He had lost Katie. He had lost touch with his own writing. And now he was losing touch with everything else. One thing at a time, until . . . until . . .

Pffft, thump-thump.

Oh, Christ.

Jameson stared back at the dark hallway beneath him, knowing that he couldn't stay in this house a moment longer, and that if he wanted to get out, outside where life always went on no matter what, then he was going to have to make it past Katie's room, he was going to have to block his ears and somehow force himself past the sounds and the memories and the hurt, past all of it to the other stairs, and then outside where maybe he'd still have a chance to hold on to what little bit was left to him.

Pffft, thump-thump.

Then he found himself making his way down the attic steps again, without thought, just moving, no second-guessing. At the door to Katie's room, he stopped and closed his eyes and pressed his back against the opposite wall, taking half a dozen long, gliding steps until he felt certain that it was safe to open his eyes again. Then it was another twenty-five feet down the hall, and . . .

. . . *and oh, sweet Jesus* . . .

. . . he caught himself at the edge of the far stairway, one hand pressed flat against the wall, his weight teetering dangerously forward.

The stairs were gone.

It was as if the second floor were floating now, suspended in space. Nothing else in existence. Just this little piece of his life, this little corner of his world.

Jameson fell back against the floor, the breath emptying in a rush from his lungs. Behind him, he could hear that noise that had been haunting him for days now, still beating rhythmically against the floor. That noise was what this was all about, he thought. That noise and Katie and the ever-growing emptiness that had been welling up inside him for months now.

He stared down at the grayish white nothingness just beyond the edge of the stairs, then climbed back to his feet and made his way back to Katie's door. It was closed, of course. It had always been closed. Even when Barb had spent her week on the other side, the door had been kept closed. But now he was going to have to open it.

To his right and left, the hallway was gradually disappearing. One inch at a time, it was being swallowed up by grayish white clouds insatiably making their way in his direction.

Jameson wrapped his hand around the doorknob.

Pffft, thump-thump.

The door swung silently open.

Pffft, thump-thump.

And there was Katie.

She was skipping rope in the middle of the room, washed beneath a brilliant white light, and only now did Jameson finally realize what that noise had been. It had been the sound of the rope across the carpet, the sound of her feet hitting the floor and bouncing up again.

"Katie?"

She stopped and looked at him, a beautiful smile on her face. Always an angel. She had always been his little angel. "I've been waiting for you, Daddy. Are you coming?"

Behind him, the hallway floor was nearly gone now. Jameson glanced down at the floorboards that seemed to be floating unsupported beneath his feet. Another inch disappeared, and he realized he was standing at the very edge of what remained of his life. He could cross the threshold, or he could simply perish.

"It's okay," Katie said. She reached toward him, holding out one end of the jump rope. Her eyes were bright, her voice soft. "You can turn for me."

"You trust me?"

"Don't be silly."

Jameson glanced back at the disappearing floorboards, tears in his eyes now, because he knew he was finally going to make his peace. He had been pushed this far, all the way up to the edge, but now it was his choice. Not do or die, but do or wither slowly away one piece at a time. He reached across the threshold, took uneasy possession of one end of the rope, and all that was left was one short step across.

"It's okay, Daddy."

"I know that now."

And suddenly he was there.

10

"James?"

Barb closed the front door, dropped her purse and keys on the credenza in the entryway, and headed for the kitchen. It was a little after eight. She had gotten caught up putting together the portfolio for the meeting with Maxwell Financial, and though she had tried to call, she hadn't been able to reach her husband.

"James?"

The mail was on the table in the kitchen. She shuffled through it, tossing out the newest Publisher's Clearinghouse, a software mailing from Lotus, and something addressed to Mr. Jameson Packard or current resident.

"James?"

She closed the window over the sink and made her way down the hall to the den. The light was on, the blinds closed, and from where she was standing, Barb noted the empty top page of the legal pad on his desk. He hadn't written anything today. He'd been struggling against a block ever since he had signed the big contract. Apparently, he was still struggling. She turned off the light and headed upstairs.

"James?"

He wasn't in the master bedroom, either. Nor was he in the attic, or the extra bedroom where Barb had set up her craft projects. And suddenly she found herself standing at the door to Katie's room. She stared at it, feeling a chill rise from somewhere deep inside her.

Then she opened the door.

Inside, the room was exactly the way it had been the day Katie had died—the bed unmade, her game of Candyland still on the floor in the corner, her crayons and coloring book sitting open on the desk. Barb had already made her peace with this room, with Katie's death, as much as any parent can make peace with the death of a child. The hurt never went away completely, of course. At times, it was kind enough to step aside for a few short hours, but it was never far from the forefront.

There was something else here, though.

She crossed her arms, and leaned her head reminiscently against the frame of the door. She could almost picture the time Jameson had tied one end of Katie's jump rope to the closet door. He swung the rope, and Katie had counted off a hundred and thirty-seven consecutive jumps before making a mistake. They had given her a hearty round of applause then, and she had been all sweet smiles the rest of the day.

"Oh, Katie."

Barb couldn't have said how long she had stood there before finally shaking herself out of the fond memories. Night had settled in warmly outside. The streetlights had come on. Mr. Matthews had come out of his house, leading his dog on the end of a leash for their nightly walk, and it seemed as if it had never been quite so late before.

"James?"

Whatever had happened to Jameson?

Barb started on her way down the hall to the stairs leading to the attic. She was feeling a bit tired now, not fully focused in the present, and somewhere behind her, just as she reached the first step, she thought heard the soft *pfft, thump-thump* of Katie jumping rope.

Oh, Katie. You'll never know how much your father and I miss you.

She paused a moment, looking back down the hallway, not wanting to give away that precious memory, then she started up the stairs to look for her husband.

HIS MOTHER'S HANDS

Clark Perry

For Richard, who gave me the gumption to get this far, and the inspiration to dream of going further. Best, Clark

SIX MONTHS AFTER HIS MOTHER DIED, JACK RODMAN WAS STILL paying the rent on her apartment. He told the landlord it was just too painful to deal with all her stuff, but that story was wearing thin. He went there at odd hours, and the neighbors now regarded him with suspicion. He was glad they avoided him; it spared him the hassle of having to lie.

Nobody else could understand what Jack was going through.

Seven months earlier, Jack returned home from work one day to find twenty messages on his answering machine. Jack counted the blinking of the little red light and cursed. He was getting sick and tired of these telemarketers that didn't even respect the privacy of his machine. They used to hang up if they couldn't reach a human being, but now they just played some obnoxious taped message that said, buy, buy and bye. Jack heard they were trying to pass a bill to outlaw the practice. He'd vote for whichever party passed it, too.

But it was Mom. Every single message. All of them

delivered in the tortured hours after her doctor's visit. He knew she was going because of pain in her back, numbness in her buttocks and thighs. No big deal, it seemed. Wrong.

They ran their tests, then wheeled her into the adjacent hospital for even more tests. What they found was not good.

Twelve weeks, that's what the doctors gave her. Chemotherapy not really an option at this advanced stage—if the cancer didn't kill her, then the cure probably would.

She hadn't called him at work, and with good reason. One word out of her mouth and Jack would've been out the door, reckless and raging. No, she called his answering machine instead and filled up the hour-long tape.

She didn't say anything the first time she called. Someone with the sniffles, that's all he heard for half a minute. Prank call? He moved to the fridge for a beer. She spoke on the next one. And the next. And there was one where she was quiet again, and one where she cried, and later she said some more, but most of it was unintelligible. Then more crying. Then the tape ran out.

Jack didn't listen to it all at once. After the second message, when he realized how serious this was, he pried his body from its cold paralysis, grabbed for his coat and keys.

There was a knock at the door. Shaken and numb, he answered it.

Mom stood there in jeans, sweatshirt, and tennis shoes, looking more beautiful than he'd ever seen her. Her long gray hair was rumpled by the wind; she liked to drive with her windows down, no matter how cold or wet the weather. She said, "I'm sorry, Jack. I didn't want you to get upset. I was worried about you driving if you were upset."

She stepped in and he held her gently, afraid now of hurting her, of breaking her fragile bones, of having to let her go.

He saved that tape from his answering machine, and played it many times after she died.

The software company was more than understanding. They gave Jack all the time off he needed. Most of his work on the new ad campaign was already completed, poised for placement within the national trades. All he needed was a firm shipping date.

But that wasn't Jack's problem. Let them worry about this new diagnostic software tool and all the bugs that were crawling out of it. Jack didn't feel especially responsible for it at this point, even though he'd named it—St. Bernard. His mother had given him the idea, and the concept for the package artwork was hers, too—coming to the rescue of a frozen computer was a big shaggy dog, with a bundle of floppies on its collar instead of a brandy cask.

So Jack was not missed at work—except by Monica, the receptionist with whom he'd slept a few times. He liked her a lot, and they had great fun together. Things might have gotten more serious if Jack's mother hadn't gone into the hospital. "I just can't do this right now," he told Monica, as things between them seemed to be growing into something more than just the standard casual relationship. She nodded, eyes downcast, and squeezed his hand. Sometimes she called to see if he needed anything, and was polite enough to keep her distance during all this.

Jack and his mother planned to take a little trip down to the ocean. She wanted to see it one last time. Halfway there she began clutching her side and crying, and he turned the car around. He took her back to the hospital and she never came out.

Charlotte Anne Rodman lasted five weeks, less than half of what the doctors had given her. Jack practically moved into her private ward. Down the hall was the intensive care unit waiting room, and during his breaks he observed the spontaneous, tragic, and amazingly supportive community that had formed there. Families and friends, gathered in a surreal vigil, everyone eating from the vending machine and blankly watching sitcom reruns, thankful for the canned laughter.

Mom's room was drab gray and airless. The single window looked out over the gravel topped roof of a lower wing. After the first week, Jack insisted that they let him bring in blue curtains because it was her favorite color. The nurses just stared as he measured the rods and walls, and later returned from a department store with powder blue curtains.

He had to give her everything he could because she was his mother and she was dying. He accepted it as a simple fact, but a part of him raged against this and wanted to destroy everything to keep her here. This demon was not darkness or evil, he knew, but merely his love for her. His love refused to let her go.

When alone, he fell into mental ruts and could not struggle out of them until he saw her again. He was angry, he was sad, he felt the cleaving of his soul and could do nothing.

I *can* do *something*, he told himself when lucid and controlled. There's nothing I can do to save her, but I can at least make her last days as good as they can be. This is something, it is all I can do, and it will count. It will make a difference.

The doctors and administrators gave him great leeway. He told them exactly what he wanted to do and they agreed with most everything.

One night between visiting hours, he went to her apartment across town and began packing.

Charlotte smiled.

She loved old movies. She'd practically been raised on them. Jack's grandmother had worked in the ticket booth of a movie house when Charlotte was a child, and after school she got to spend all day in the theater, entranced by the huge screen and the stories it told. Jack brought the VCR from her apartment and plugged it into the hospital TV that hung from the ceiling. He also brought along a boxful of her videotapes, packed with classic oldies. Over the gray walls he hung some of her movie posters. He'd plug in a tape just before he curled up in the hard cushions of the orange chair across the room, knowing that if her painkiller ebbed and she regained consciousness, she'd at least have a good movie to watch. He fastened the remote control unit to the rail beside her hand.

Her favorite movie was *To Kill A Mockingbird,* and they'd seen it dozens of times. When he was young, she would hold him and sigh, "Oh, how your dad was so like Atticus Finch . . ."

Dad died before Jack was born, and she never married again. No need to, she said. I've got everything I need right here in you. It had always been the two of them, mother and son, best friends. Jack knew how rare this was. Most of his friends came from divorced households, and seemed forever caught in some emotional tug-of-war. Other friends were close to their parents, but they never got stoned with them, or went out with them for a few drinks, or ducked with them into all-night movie theaters with homemade popcorn and a bottle of red wine hidden in a shoulder bag.

Together they had done all this, and so much more. When the bone cancer spread to her kidneys, they failed and she slipped into a coma. As she began to swell from her own poisons that could not be voided, he talked these memories out loud, gave them the full weight of his voice and tried not to show any sadness. He knew she could hear him; Polly, one of the attending nurses, had been in a coma many years ago, and she told Jack that she'd been fully aware of every sound around her.

He bought her orange juice at the cafeteria downstairs. "What was it like?" he asked.

She shook her head, remembering. She had short

blonde hair and a wedding ring. Petite and friendly, she was one of the few nurses who would risk showing her true emotions to patients and their families. Which meant she wouldn't last long, she admitted. "It was maddening," she finally said. "I was trapped. Just trapped. Couldn't move, couldn't send any signals to the world outside. The doctor would lift my eyelid, check my pupils—he'd be staring right at me and I couldn't even blink or roll my eye to show him I was there." She sipped some juice. "When people would talk about me as if I wasn't even in the room . . . that was the worst."

"And one day you just woke up?"

"One day . . . my body was *there* for me. It felt so good it hurt, and I started screaming. I can't explain it."

"I'll keep talking to her. Playing the movies." He frowned and ate some soda crackers he'd swiped from the salad bar. "She can't come back to me now, can she?"

Polly looked at him carefully, and he saw her going back into nurse-mode, facing the ugly truth and dealing with it. "She's not in pain, Jack. And she probably knows that you're nearby. You've got to be thankful for that."

Jack nodded grimly, pushing away locks of black hair that hung like blades across his thin pale face. "Yeah, I guess I could use a six-pack of that morphine myself right about now." He looked up to see if she was smiling at his joke, but realized that he wasn't smiling, either, and they just stared at each other in the cold fluorescent light of the cafeteria.

Mother. Gone.

Charlotte Anne Rodman died at four A.M.

At three-thirty Jack hopped the elevator down two floors to the cafeteria. He scattered his change across a table, sat down and tried to count it. Then he fell asleep, face pressed to the cold coins. Twenty minutes later a nurse found him there and gently squeezed his arm. He blinked up at her. "You'd better come back up," the nurse said, brushing a dime from his forehead. Her voice was plain, but he could see it in her eyes. "We think it's time."

Charlotte was so strong. Jack almost cried out when he saw her frail body struggling against the respirator, against death itself. Exhausted beyond imagining, her body was giving up now, and he knew the only release for her was death. A tiny part of him had been hoping for a miracle all along, and when he saw her dying, actually *dying* in front of him, he knew the only miracle due her was soon to arrive. He sat on the bed and lifted his mother in his arms and pressed his mouth close to her ear and kissed her and whispered and cried. The harsh shuddering seemed to ease, the rasping slowed and Jack heard a voice saying, "Go toward the light, mother, go toward the light," and that voice was his own.

She died. One long exhale, and her body went slack, the tension melting out of her and into him. He would not let go of her body. The nurses fetched Polly as she came in for her shift, and it took her a long time to talk Jack into letting go.

That was six months ago.

Now Jack didn't sleep at his own apartment. He'd go there to shave, shower, and dress each morning before work. The software company was coasting on its successful product, and Jack began taking half-days off. He was just working for the money, not because he wanted to. Truth was, there were more than a few days when he wasn't really needed there at all, but instead of hanging out and at least pretending to be productive, Jack would disappear. Sometimes Pete, his boss, asked him if everything was going okay, and Jack said he still had bad days, but he'd be back up to speed real soon now.

No matter how early he left, he couldn't get to her apartment fast enough. Inside, he could still smell her: the apricot shampoo she used, the lavender talc she patted on to keep cool in the summer. Coffee—God, how she loved coffee, all flavors. Even though Jack didn't drink it, he brewed a fresh pot each morning, just to have that smell.

He watered her plants but they died anyway, so he bought plastic ones. He wandered through the rooms like a child lost in a daydream.

He slept on the futon in the living room, below her urn of ashes on the mantel. The mat was big and plush; somehow he just didn't feel right about sleeping in her bed. He did sleep with one of her thick down pillows, so he could smell her. He slept heavily, as if drugged, and if he dreamed he did not remember it.

Late for work again, as if he cared. Back at his own place, he toweled off from a hot shower and heard someone knock. Clad in the blue bathrobe Charlotte had bought him one Christmas, he opened the door.

Monica stood there, a bag of fast-food breakfast in one hand. "Hi, good morning," she began awkwardly. "Thought you'd like some breakfast. Can I come in?"

He left the door open and returned to the bathroom, where he dressed quickly. Monica sat at the coffee table and unwrapped a couple of huge buttered biscuits and peeled the foil back from plastic cups of orange juice. "Got 'em plain, I didn't know what you liked," she said weakly. "So how are you doing?"

"I'm okay," he said, taking one of the biscuits and sitting on the floor across from her. "You must think I'm starving or something to bring me food, Monica. What's up?"

"Nothing, I just—I thought since I was over here . . ." She stopped and looked at her lap. "Look, I'm just worried about you, Jack. You don't spend much time at work anymore. Everyone's talking about you, but they're all afraid to say anything to you. Except for Pete, who just hasn't had the time."

"Yeah. Well, Pete's little upstart company finally has a hit, so I can't imagine he's complaining too much."

"Look, it's hard to lose someone. I know it is because

. . . because I had a little sister who died. And it was terrible. But you've got to realize that life goes on, that other things happen."

Jack chewed his biscuit; it was a tasteless wad of dough in his mouth. He chased it down with a swig of sour juice. "I'm doing fine," he said. "I'm doing just fine."

"Jack, you don't even sleep here anymore. It's been six months and you still pay the rent on her old apartment. That's where you sleep now, isn't it?"

He raised an eyebrow. "Since when is it any of your business where I sleep? Since when is any of this any of your business? Look, you see me freaking out on the highway with a rifle or smoking crack on the job, well, hey, then I'll appreciate the concern. But it sounds like you've been spying, Monica, and I don't think I like that."

"I think I have a right to be worried."

"Look." He spread his hands wide and shrugged, trying to pretend it was all a joke. But it wasn't: he could feel anger rising like a hot tide over his shoulders and into his head. "We had some fun, okay? And I like you, I like you a lot. But I'm not interested in any kind of relationship right now." He thought it would be enough when he said that, but as soon as he heard the words he knew they were wrong. Lamely, he added: "It's been so long since we . . . y'know. I thought you'd written me off."

"I backed off, that's all. I had to. You wanted me to. She was sick, you did what you had to do. And I wasn't sure you knew what you were doing anyway." She wrapped her uneaten biscuit and put it in her purse. "I never slept with anybody on the first date before. I never thought I'd want to."

She stood and walked to the door. He stood and watched her. "I can't help this," he said. "She's still with me. It's like I can feel her. And I like feeling her. I feel her near me when I'm there at her place, like she's alive and I need that."

"Oh, you know what you need, Jack. You knew it the night we went out. So you got it, and didn't give anything in return."

"Monica, I know—look. I know you've been much more conscious of my feelings than I have of yours. I'm sorry, I know that's wrong and that's bad. But I can't, I just can't."

She opened the door and took a step outside, on the concrete walkway. She leaned against the rail, looking back at him, and the sunlight hit her, made her glow. She was very beautiful, even as she regarded him with a bored, blank expression. "You're sure having trouble staying at work."

"I know. I have to do something about that, don't I?"

"Not anymore," she said. "Came to tell you you'd been fired." She stared at him a moment more, then pulled away from the railing, out of sight. He heard angry footsteps walk to the stairwell, then they echoed, then they stopped. A car door opened and shut, the engine started, and she ripped out of the parking lot with a terrific screech.

Pete clasped him by the shoulders in a brotherly fashion. "Fired? I never said that! I just wanted to suggest that you take a temporary leave, that's all," he said reassuringly. "Monica said you'd been *fired?* I can't believe that. I tell you, I don't know what's gotten into her lately. She's been real touchy about the oddest things. I'll have a word with her about this."

"No, don't. Please. She misunderstood, that's all, and was worried about me."

"Hey, *I'm* worried about you. I don't need you here if I can't use you, kid, and you aren't happy here right now. So take a few weeks, get the hell out of here. You'll be okay for a few weeks, right? I mean, money-wise?"

"Yeah, sure, fine," Jack said.

"Listen, I could probably put you at half-pay if you wanted to do some work out of your home."

"Thanks, Pete. But that's okay. Maybe I do need some time alone."

Monica was away from her desk, avoiding him, probably down at the employee lounge. He wanted to go see her, but what would he say? He couldn't say anything, could never hope to explain the feeling of dread and loss that gripped him whenever he was away from his mother's apartment. Soon he was on the expressway, driving into the sun, headed for salvation.

Three knocks at the door, but Jack wasn't doing people today. The answering machine was full of machine voices selling more machines. One day the machines would realize what slaves they were, and rise up. That'd be fine with Jack. Wasn't like people were doing such a good job anyway. He watched the news every now and then, and it was just full of mass-produced death. Machines could get into that, he figured.

Three more knocks, then the jangle of dozens of keys just beneath the Joni Mitchell album, one of Charlotte's favorites, the one that was all scratched up on side two. Jack wondered if he'd done that when he was a kid.

The door opened. Mr. Green, the landlord, stood there with a timid smile and one hand raised. He said something but Jack couldn't hear it. He turned the music down and said hello.

"Hello, hello, Jack. I guess you couldn't hear me knocking."

"No, couldn't hear a thing. What can I do for you, Mr. Green?" Jack did not mask his irritation. "Playing the music too loud?"

"No, not at all, Jack. But listen, there are these people, see, who would like to—*ahem*—move into the building, and they're very old friends of the family and it would certainly be a tremendous, tremendous favor if you would, um, allow them to occupy this, ah. Space."

"Doesn't the lease run until October?"

"Well, yes, it does."

"I mean, I haven't done anything to violate the terms of that lease, have I?"

"Well, no, of course not. Didn't mean for you to think that. But."

"But these are friends of the family," Jack said.

"Yes, good close friends." Green smiled.

"That's too bad. Because I've paid you in full through the remainder of the lease, and as you've said, I've done nothing to break it. I'm sorry about that, Mr. Green. I do know, however, that there is a vacant apartment down on the second floor. Perhaps you overlooked that. Anything else I can do for you? Good. Well, then. I must be going to bed, if you'll excuse me."

Smiling, Jack closed the door and locked it.

One day he boxed up his belongings at the old apartment and hauled them off to a rental storage unit. He had a little money but not much, and there was no sense in paying two rents. He called around until he found a grocery that would deliver, and ordered from them once a week.

There was no reason to leave.

Jack began talking to her.

He didn't say much, not at first. "Well, look at that," he'd say, catching a few moments of a Fred Astaire movie as he walked past the TV with a dust cloth in his hand. He realized he was doing that a lot, commenting on things as if she were there to hear and, perhaps, reply.

"This should prove to be one of the most phantasmagoric meals you've ever eaten," he'd say, serving homemade pasta with sun-dried tomatoes, Parmesan cheese, olive oil, and garlic. He'd imagine her smile as he said it, and the feeling it gave him was as if she'd actually been there and smiled.

He talked to her more and more, and sometimes he could anticipate what her response would have been.

Once or twice he even thought he heard her voice, distant and muffled, but it would always trail away into the sound of the wind or rain.

Although his meals became more and more extravagant, he didn't eat much. He'd always been tall and lanky, but now his pants hung loosely on his hips and the sleeves of his shirts seemed too long. He imagined that he was turning back into a child again, the adult world slipping away like a bad dream. Soon his mother would be here to take care of him.

He wasn't sad anymore. He wasn't exactly happy, either, but he did feel at peace with everything. And that was nice, for a change.

Someone kept calling, not a machine, and they'd just sit there, not making a sound, though he imagined he could hear faint breaths being taken.

Son.

Jack shot up from the futon, skin tingling, scalp on fire. He glanced around the room, eyes wide with fear and anticipation. The clock on the wall read 3:50 A.M. He drew in a deep breath and held it, then exhaled. His skin was slicked with perspiration. He pulled off the robe and padded softly to the shower.

He ran a hot bath and filled it with her fragrances. He lit candles all around, placed them on tiny square mirrors and turned off the light. The flickering flames calmed him somewhat, and he slid into the water. He tried to remember his dream but could not. He lay there staring at the tiled walls and the soft colors that played over them.

"I know you're near me," he whispered. "I can feel you, and you are alive and I'm not alone. I'm not alone. Thank you, Mother, for not leaving me here alone." Tears rolled from his eyes but he barely felt them. "I want you back here. I hated the way you died. I want you alive again, and with me. Forever. OK?"

He rested his head against the cool tile and slept for a while.

The midmorning sun crept through the apartment. Jack awoke to the sounds of birds chirping outside the window. Charlotte's feeder needed refilling, but he hadn't had time to buy any seed. What had he been doing with his time lately? It seemed to slip by faster and faster these days.

As he worked out a small crick in his neck, Jack smelled something sour and stale. He bent his head to the bathwater and sniffed.

Oh no, he thought. What have I done? When did I do this?

The tub was filled with urine and excrement.

As he stood, cringing, he noticed his trembling hands, wrinkled little claws that seemed almost translucent. His entire body was gray and colorless and the skin felt spongy wherever he touched himself. He started crying because he didn't know how long he'd been in the tub. Nor did he know which day it was. Only that it was morning, and that he was more alone than he'd ever been in his life.

He stood there and sobbed, arms out to keep himself from sliding back into the warm mess that lapped at his calves. He cried for his mother's hands to come and take him out of this, to restore the hole in his chest, the rip in his mind, to cleanse and make him whole again.

When she came to him he was not even surprised, though he did sob harder. Charlotte pulled the plug and held her helpless son as the tub drained, and then she gently washed him clean. His sobs faded into a long and ceaseless moan. She shushed him, wrapped a thick towel around him, and led him to her bedroom.

He watched as she turned back the immaculate covers and fluffed the pillows. She took his towel and dried him carefully, then motioned for him to lie down. Jack sat on the bed and stared at her jeans, the sweatshirt, her loving face. "You're not real," he said, and tears began to fill his eyes again.

She frowned. "The hell I'm not," she said softly. "You're the one who's running that risk. Now lie back. Put the towel under your head, your hair's still wet." She sat beside him and took his hand.

Jack was four and afraid of the dark. He was seven and home from school with the chicken pox. He was thirteen and pale from mononucleosis. Eighteen and suffering from his first whiskey hangover. Twenty-one, miserably heartbroken.

She was always there, sitting with him, holding his hand.

"This means it's time for me to die, doesn't it?"

She shook her head. "No. It's not your time. But you've pushed yourself, Jack, and you're so very close. Oh, look at yourself. What in the world are you doing?"

"Had to," he said. "Had to bring you back."

She studied him plaintively. "It won't work, Jack. It just won't work."

He stared. Her long hair fell across her shoulders and caught the sunlight through the window, and in those rays Jack could see every thick gray strand. For a moment he was lost in that silver forest. He looked at her soft brown eyes. "But you're *here,*" he said. "You're here."

She shook her head, lips pursed. "I am, but I'm not. Not really. I'm not here anymore, and I never can be again. I'm somewhere else right now, son. But I've come here to tell you to stop what you're doing."

"Can't stop, Momma. Need you so much. Love you."

"You're killing yourself. Do you hear me? You were in that tub for three days, Jack, and you didn't even know it. You cannot do this."

"Why did you have to die like that?"

She shrugged. "It was my time. And as bad as it was, it's over, and where I am is better. But it's not your time, son. You have so much of it left. Please don't waste it for me."

"Just stay with me," he begged, huddling up close to her. "Stay here, right here, you and me. No one will ever know. Please."

"I can't stay. I won't. I miss you more than you'll ever know, but you must move on. If you don't . . ."

"What? I'll die? I'll die? So I'll die. I'll be with you."

In a sudden flurry of motion, she shoved him away from her. "Jack, damn it, *stop haunting me!*"

He recoiled and froze, eyes wide with shock. Charlotte stood and faced the wall, hugged herself, began crying. His ears rang with her words, his throat clenched and he could not speak. He curled up into a fetal position and shuddered violently, as if a live wire had been shoved through his body.

Stop haunting me.

The hospital memories rushed through his head, a rapid ribbon of pain and despair. His despair, her pain. He remembered begging the nurses to up the morphine dosage at the end. I'll let her go, he recalled bargaining with some inner force, but she mustn't be alone, and she mustn't be in pain.

He had done all that for her, and so much more. Had given her the dignified and painless death that was due all people.

And now: stop haunting me.

Stop *hurting* me.

Across the room, his mother wept.

Wherever she really was—not here, in her bedroom, but elsewhere—Jack was haunting her, a sad apparition threatening suicide, a lost child crying for help. Jack reeled at this image of himself but knew it was true; he had caused her enough pain and fear that she had bridged this unimaginable gulf to make him stop. So she wouldn't be in pain anymore.

"Oh, God, Mother, I never meant to hurt you," he

said, rising, the sheets twisted around him. "I'm sorry, I am so sorry." And he went to her and held her and pressed his face into her hair one last time, and he smelled her as she had been when she was alive. Apricots. And he knew this would be enough to see him through.

She held him lightly, and he sensed her fading, dissolving into the ether from which she had briefly emerged. "You must know two things before I go," she told him softly. "The girl, Monica. She was pregnant with your child, Jack. She didn't want to tell you because I got sick, and she saw what that was doing to you."

Jack's face went even paler. "Monica was pregnant?"

"She didn't want to place the burden on you, but now she bears it herself. She will help you through this, but first you must help her. You owe her, son. You owe her a great deal."

"Did she—?"

"Yes. And she was alone."

"I didn't know," he said, face drawn downward in self-disgust. "I didn't even bother."

"Now you know. Now you can bother."

Charlotte was fading faster now. Through her he could see the closet door. "What's the second thing, Mom?"

She smirked. "I love you, Jack."

He leaned forward to kiss his mother goodbye, but she was already gone. The sheets fell from his shoulders and he stood there naked in the morning light, eyes closed and smiling, his lungs filled with the scent of his mother.

Later that week, Jack and Monica drove to the ocean with the urn of ashes. He parked near the rocky point where he and his mother used to go. He walked down to the water. Lazy waves lapped at the rocks, and a fine salt mist clung to his clothes and hair. Gulls were hovering above him, waiting to see if he would offer them food. He unscrewed the lid of the urn and a light breeze rose. He wasn't crying, and that amazed him. He thought he should be crying.

He held the urn to the sky and emptied it. Wind took the ashes and carried them out into the dusky ocean. He held the urn for a moment, then shattered it against the rocks. The gulls banked away sharply at the sound and regrouped farther down the beach, perching on some driftwood.

And that was that. She wasn't in pain anymore. Her son was no longer haunting her. The old apartment was empty now. Jack was still lonely and grief-stricken, but he was learning that no one moves through life alone, no matter how desolate life may sometimes seem.

He looked at Monica, who stood against the car, hands stuffed in the pockets of her jacket. She regarded him with the greatest of suspicion and no small amount of resentment. He couldn't blame her, and was constantly amazed at how considerate she was in spite of her misgivings. He looked at her now, braced against the wind, giving him his peace, his distance.

Better than he deserved. Right now, anyway.

He lifted a hand to wave her down but stopped. Monica had come far enough, so he lowered his hand and walked back to her, bridging the distance himself.

In memory of Ailene Kemp Sparks, 1918–1993

COLD

BILL SMITH'S SLEIGH RIDE
(A Winter's Tale)

Tyson Blue

THE SNOWBALL HIT THE BACK OF BILL SMITH'S NECK WITH A wet splat, sending icy fingers dribbling down his back. The old man stopped his weary trudge and turned to face the trio of giggling boys he'd just passed a moment ago. They stood grouped together, arrogant smirks on their young faces, daring him to do something about it.

"Well, old man?" One of them taunted, taking a step away from his friends. "You got something to say to us?"

Bill stood there a moment and looked at them, trying to decide if doing anything about it was worthwhile. He decided it wasn't and, waving his right hand in a dismissive gesture, turned and headed on through the snow-swept streets of Sunapee toward his house.

Leaving both the boys and the town behind, Bill soon arrived at his home, and fumbled through his pockets for his key. He opened the door and entered his kitchen, hanging his jacket on the rack and stomping his feet to remove the snow from his boots and drive a little circulation back into his toes.

He put a kettle full of water on the stove to boil for tea, and sat down at his table to wait. As the stove began to take the chill off, Bill thought over his day.

The kids had been the perfect capper to this one, that was for damn sure. Winter was the off-season at Henry's Harborside, the diner where he spent his days as chief cook. That meant he had little or nothing to do besides serve up the same old meals for the handful of regulars who kept them going through the winter. For most of his shift, there was nothing to do but sit around and think about the past.

Of course, most of the past had been just like today—busy in the summer and fall, slack in the winter, on and on back through a succession of jobs over half a century.

Oh, things had been different in his youth. Back when Bill was around twenty, he'd had friends—good friends, especially Teddy Guidry and his brother, Ed, Ronny LaFountain, Ev Chalmers, and Norman LaBonte.

Granted, things weren't that much better fifty years ago. That was the midst of the Depression, and New Hampshire was a depressed state in the best of times. But somehow, the six of them always seemed to find some way to have a good time. Between them they'd had enough imagination to cook up some way to relieve the boredom. Take f'rinstance the time they'd built their own houseboat from old oil drums and planks they'd lifted from the dump. It may not have been the most beautiful craft that ever plied the waters of Lake Sunapee, but it'd seemed like a cruise ship to them.

Of course, that inventiveness had been the death of them in the end, on a sunny winter day, cold and clear, when the ice on the lake had beckoned the six of them like iron filings to a magnet.

"Would'ja look at that ice?" Teddy'd crowed, a big grin splitting his face. "Boys, that is just too good a patch o' ice for us to waste."

"Whaddya mean, Ted?" Bill had asked.

"What we need, Bill my boy, is an iceboat."

At that, Ev turned to Teddy, his mouth dropping open in amazement.

"Where the hell we gonna get an iceboat, Ted?" Ev said. "They don't exactly give them things away, you know, and the six of us ain't exactly flush this time a'year."

Teddy had mulled that one over for a while, and then his face brightened.

"I've got it!"

And he had.

They'd gone out to Ronny's uncle's barn and found an old horse-drawn sleigh, big enough to seat them all. Its runners would move just as well on ice as over snow. Of course, it weighed a lot more than a regular iceboat would have.

Teddy had that covered, too. They'd rounded up a spare mast from an old two-master that one of the summer people had tried to sail on the lake for a couple of years back around the turn of the century. It was a big mast, with a huge sail, much larger than one for a regular sailboat or iceboat, and once they'd lashed it into place between the front and back seats of the sleigh, they'd had an iceboat to beat all iceboats.

Pushing their ungainly craft to the shore, they'd edged it out onto the ice and climbed aboard. As Norm got busy hoisting the sail, Bill hung back. He looked at the slick surface of the ice below them, at the heavy sleigh with its unnatural load of mast and sail, and the five of his friends, and just couldn't make himself get aboard.

"C'mon, Bill, it'll be fun!" Ev called.

"We'll go like crazy!" Ronny added.

"I dunno, fellows," Bill hedged.

At that moment, the sail filled with wind and snapped taut with a great boom, and the sleigh took off before the wind, with nothing to steer it. Bill ran out onto the ice after it, but he was soon left behind as the great sail pushed the sleigh across the lake like a miniature barkentine. It seemed to streak over the frozen lake the way meteors rocketed across the sky on clear nights, and Bill marveled at the sight.

"Wait for me!" Bill had called, waving his arms as he tried to catch up.

"Wait there, man!" Ev's voice came faintly back to him. "We'll come back for you!"

And that was when the ice opened up beneath the sleigh-boat and swallowed it as if it had never been. The great sail billowed wildly about like a gull's broken wing, then dwindled down into the gaping hole, vanishing into the blue-black depths along with his five best friends.

Lake Sunapee was deep that far out, and no one had ever found a trace of his friends or their wonderful craft. But not a winter went by that Bill didn't think about that day, and he'd spent his whole life around the lake. The only reason he'd ever have left would have been the war, and a broken ankle he'd suffered five years after the accident that took his friends had even kept him from that.

It wasn't that he was waiting for his friends to come back and keep their last promise to come back and get him. There'd just never been a reason to leave Sunapee, and he never had for more than a few days at a time.

He'd passed the years in an endless succession of odd jobs, as if waiting for something to happen. But whatever it was, it hadn't shown up. And now, about all there was left to wait for was the end.

A banshee wail of wind moaned around the small frame house, and on that wind came the sound of voices, howling wordlessly with joy. There was someone out there having a good time, Bill thought, maybe a church group singing carols around a campfire out on the ice, or a few late-night fishermen trading fish stories before leaving their bob-houses for the night. There was always somebody out on the lake doing something.

"Hey, Bill!" a young man's voice called. "Bill Smith!"

Bill got up from the table and took the boiling pot off the burner, and walked into his darkened living room, looking out through the picture window across the moonlit lake. At first he could see nothing out there. Then, a great shape glided slowly into view, a huge boatlike affair sliding over the ice on steely runners, while overhead a vast white expanse billowed loosely like a great white wing.

"Hey, Bill Smith!" the voice called again. "C'mon out!"

It couldn't be, Bill thought. They and their motley boat had been resting on the bottom of this lake for fifty years. There was no way his friends could be riding in front of his home in the middle of this freezing night, calling him out for a ride he'd missed all those years ago.

Bill strode quickly back through his living room to the kitchen, grabbed his coat off the rack, and went back through the house to his front porch. He stepped out and walked down the outside steps, then went as fast as his old legs would take him down to the shore.

From there, he could see the spectral craft much more clearly. There were five shadowy figures moving about below the great sail which flapped over them, and Bill could feel the breeze from that sail.

The moon came out from behind a cloud, and Bill could see the figures in the craft clearly now. There was no longer any doubt. Ted, Ev, Ronny, Norman, and Ed—they were all there, and all of them looked exactly the way they had the last day he'd seen them, the day they'd left him behind forever.

"Well, Bill," Ev called. "It took us a while, but we managed to get this thing back to shore to see if you changed your mind about going with us."

"Ev, is that you?" Bill asked, his voice barely above a whisper.

"You can see that much, can't you?" Ev shot back. "We ain't got time for this, Bill. We can't wait forever. If you're comin', you best get aboard."

"Where are we going?" Bill asked.

"You'll see," Ted called from the front seat. He turned

his head as the light faded. "But you best hurry. Breeze's freshening, and y'know I never did figure out a way to steer nor stop this damn thing!"

Bill didn't hesitate any longer. Hugging his coat around him against the cold, he climbed into the sleigh's front seat next to the Guidry brothers. Above his head, the sail billowed as the new breeze filled it, then boomed taut. The sleigh lurched under Bill, and a joyous whoop leapt from his lips.

The runners sang beneath them, and they themselves sang as well—"Jingle Bells," of course. And as the shore behind them was obscured by a sudden snow squall, Bill turned around and looked ahead.

And they were borne away on the currents and lost in the darkness and distance.

SOTTO VOCE

Lawrence Greenberg

THERE IS, NOW, ONLY THE ALMOST SILENT SOUND OF SNOW falling, accumulating imperceptibly, inch by inch, as the moments leave us, as the snow continues. We have been here so long, too long, snowbound. In that frame of mind, at any rate. We huddle for comfort, here inside, where it may be safe, where we feel, together, that maybe we are secure from the unending snow—barely speaking, only listening within as outside the world turns white, is white, all white. And cold, hard, angular, crystalline, obscure.

It is Chicago, winter, 1966: the city's worst snowstorm in more than sixty years. Alan is here, and Bob, and Janna. I am Louis. And Rod, and John who lives next door are here; Rod's with his girlfriend of the moment whose real name most of us don't remember. Rod insists on calling her Asia because she is large—not fat, but tall like him and big-boned. It's Rod's room we're in, a large one for this dorm.

Susan and Roy are not here. They were out walking one night less than two months before, somewhere near the campus, when a carful of people passed them in a driveby: one leaned out a rear window and shotgunned Susan and Roy to death. They did not know Susan and Roy. I'd had a brief affair with Susan only a few weeks before that. I can still see her sad face. Sometimes. It comes and goes.

"It's hard," Alan whispers. "Hard."

"What is?" I ask. But somehow I know what he is going to answer. Alan and I have been close for more than two years now. He knew Susan well.

"Knowing what to do. Knowing how to take the next step."

When I nod, Alan turns from me and sits by himself in a corner of the room. Rod and Asia are making out on the bed, whispering to each other. Bob is at the window watching the relentless snow. Janna and John have found each other in these last few hours and are talking quietly in the corner of the room opposite from Alan.

Bob turns from the window for a moment and says to me, "C'mere, Louie, look at this." And he looks at me with his startled eyes, asking for acceptance, asking me to pay attention to him, if only briefly. There outside, not more than ten yards from where we are at the window, two bundled-up figures are building a snow creature. Not a snowman; it's more randomly shaped, as though the thing's creators were stoned, maybe, or had shared a waking dream as the snow fell, as they started building, of an arbitrary shape that would spring from them, just then, there, in the process of making it. It's not hideous—they have not the sculpting expertise to make it so (and given that, snow is too clumsy a medium)—but the creature is asymmetrical, and formed as though lunging forward, and somehow sullen looking. Maybe there's a mouth at one end; hard to say. Maybe it's mouthing something. If so, I can't hear whatever it is.

"Ugly, huh?" Bob says in his Indiana twang.

"I don't know" is my answer. "I don't think ugly is the right word."

"Looks ugly to me," Bob shoots back, and guffaws.

Not to me. The thing looks disdainful, like it knows what it's made of, that it's temporary, like all of us. It's this gray silence that brings on my portentousness. That's it, I think, that's all. That's all. I don't know how else to react.

John and Janna get up. John says, "We're going out," and Bob says, "In this? Jesus."

John laughs and answers, "Yeah. In this." He takes Janna's hand; she looks away from all of us and squeezes his hand, then unclasps it so they can get into their outer clothes. Wrapped up in them, they're both sexless, almost faceless. John has a black pull-down ski mask that hides his face completely; Janna's thick black scarf covers her mouth and most of her nose, and her parka's dark hood hugs her head.

And they leave, Janna limping from a recently banged up foot, slow to heal. Right before she died, Susan was limping. A foot infection, I think. I remember the way Susan looked at me when I asked her how bad it was. Like she couldn't accept the question. Then I bit my lip and turned away, not knowing how to answer her expression.

Rod and Asia have gone beyond making out. His left hand is up between her legs; she has her right in his pants. Alan turns back to Bob and me and says, "That was a good thing, a good idea. I'm going out, too."

I'm still at the window with Bob, watching as the two snow creature makers finish their work, stand for a few minutes to admire what they've done, then leave, trudging slowly through the deep white terrain. It doesn't surprise me that Alan wants to leave; for him, I know, that's what it is—not as much going into the snow as leaving where he is at the moment. The need to escape.

"Why are you going out there, Alan?" I ask, even though . . .

"I want to," he says vehemently. "I want to feel the cold. I want to taste the snow. I want to be almost blinded by the total whiteness, Louis. What do *you* want, damn you? What?"

He's never asked me this before. I don't want to say anything.

"You can't tell me, can you? Can you? Because you don't know, Louis. You just don't know." He glares at me for a moment, then bundles into his coat, wool hat, gloves, and boots—he has ridiculous black galoshes that look to be as effective as sneakers for this weather. Then he walks out without another word. Two days after Roy and Susan were killed, there was a torrential rainstorm. Alan ran out into it—no raincoat, no umbrella—and raced around, throwing his head back, opening his mouth to drink in the rain. He came in drenched and cursed and screamed for about five minutes. Then he sobbed. I wasn't there at the time. Bob told me.

The phone rings. Surprising; telephone lines are still okay, apparently. Bob grabs the receiver, blurts "Hello," listens, says, "Hey, neat," listens, says, "Yeah, great, I will," hangs up. Then turns to me and tells me that a bunch of guys on the far side of the Midway—the other side of campus—have built a snow labyrinth with multiple branches in all directions. I nod briefly, thinking the structure will be surrounded by people eager to half bury themselves inside, hide themselves away for a while. Lined up for the thrill of their lives.

The bed's two occupants are quickly becoming one as they merge, whisper, entangle, shift randomly, breathe hard. Hands search and find the different curves the body gives the skin, move, grasp, release, stroke. Maybe Alan was right. Bob goes back to looking outside, possibly reacting to my lack of response. The windows are not airtight; winter air breathes in through them but is quickly neutralized by fierce heat from the long radiator just under the windows. The heat, I think. Easier to breathe in the cold. Sometimes it seems my thoughts are loud enough to be heard. Just barely.

"Maybe Alan was right," I tell Bob. "I mean, maybe it's better to be outside for a while. For a change."

Bob's eyes open wider than usual. "All right! Wanna check out that snow maze, Louie?"

"Sure," I say, almost mumbling. "Sure, why not?"

And we leave the two on the bed, moving in their sweaty rhythms, groaning and lunging, moving and whispering. Once outside, Bob and I make our way through the thick snow, flopping around like a couple of marionettes manipulated by drunken puppeteers. The wind driven snow covers our coats, gloves, mufflers, boots; fills the air with what looks and feels like an impenetrable descending layer. The cold is hard, biting. The snow creature looms out of this driving haze, like some unexpected thing in a Fellini movie; we almost stumble on it. Up close it's lost whatever sullen or menacing quality it had. Now it's just a big undifferentiated whitish mass—something like a Henry Moore sculpture, but even more amorphous. There is no mouth after all.

"Looks like they didn't finish it," Bob yells. Not that there's any real noise to yell over. Only the wind whipping the snow around. But both of us have our ears covered, and we're no longer in the dorm, a confined environment. The cold, the wind, the massive snow blasted gray sky—somehow the combination requires that our voices be louder.

"Can't tell," I shout back. "Looks like a big nothing to me."

We walk around it; Bob packs in loose patches, kicks it here and there, testing its solidity, runs around it like a little kid. I watch him, realizing Susan and Roy would probably have joined him if they were still here. Susan with her dark clothes and fluid body; Roy with his mustache and soft voice, matching hers. Both of them wanting the simplest life possible. When Bob's done, we move on.

We know what direction to take, but in this storm we could be going anywhere. Closer to the Midway, the wide grassy area that runs for several blocks in the middle of campus—divided by traffic lanes—we watch all the traffic lights simultaneously turn red, green, red, green, presiding over the static white lanes and lines of cars almost completely buried in the snow.

"Pretty neat, huh?" Bob shouts.

"Yeah," I yell back. "Hard to breathe."

Bob doesn't answer. I was wrong about the cold. But we're here, we're moving, and my thoughts, pushed out by the cold, freeze in the air as meaningless words, propel me forward. And then, after another twenty minutes or so, we see the snow maze, an anomalous structure amidst the Midway's huge unbroken white field. Surprisingly, there's no line of people, only two figures standing just outside it, hand in hand.

"Hey!" Bob yells. The way he's facing, moving, it's hard to tell if he's calling to me or the two by the maze. I watch them leave us; the shorter one limps. John and Janna, I think. Is there another couple around with a limping partner? The snowstorm absorbs them in a few seconds, and they're gone.

"Hey!" Bob yells again and this time he runs in the direction they took, but gives up when it's obvious he won't catch up to the two of them. They've disappeared. He returns, head bowed for a moment, then up again, ready for our next great adventure.

The snow maze is larger and more complex than I would have thought possible. It must have been built by at least seven or eight people; probably more than that. It's huge—maybe fifty yards in rough diameter, making it over three hundred yards around. There's no hub, no center; it's an enormous conglomeration of single interconnecting tunnels, all joined to each other in what looks like haphazard fashion. In spite of its random structure, the tunnels are seamlessly connected. I see this as we walk around the maze.

"Wanna go inside?" Bob yells.

"Okay," I answer. "But where?"

"Hey, I got an idea," he shouts back. "I go in here," pointing at the entrance in front of us, "and you circle around exactly opposite me and go in there. Then we meet in the middle."

I nod, and he hits me on the arm, not too hard, signaling that we're in this together. The cold is starting to penetrate the tiny cracks in my winter outerwear armor and I think maybe Alan was wrong after all. About the cold, anyway. Just like me. Wrong.

When I'm almost at the opposite point, I see someone crawling out of the tunnel I'm about to go into. He's struggling—I can tell it's a he—but finally pulls himself out, then stands at the entrance looking like a sentinel. It's Alan. When I reach him, he gestures me closer. A few inches away, he looks smaller somehow, shrinking from the cold, folding into himself.

"I don't like to yell," he tells me.

"No, I guess not," I answer.

"Don't be a shit, Louis. I guess you saw them, right? The two of them?"

"If you mean did I see John and Ja—"

"No. Not them." He waves his hand, dismissing my ridiculous notion. "God knows where they are. I'm talking about Susan and Roy. They were just here. No, not were. They *are* here."

He looks fierce. Maybe he's going to scream. I don't know.

"They're dead, Alan. They're both dead." I'm speaking in a low voice because . . . because I'm with Alan.

He doesn't say anything, just looks at me for a few seconds with those blazing eyes.

"What's the matter? Is something—?"

"Goddamn you," he hisses. "Goddamn you, you self-centered, coldhearted son of a bitch. You don't give a good goddamn if anyone lives or dies, do you? You really don't give a flying fuck what happens to anybody, you smug asshole. Right? What the hell is your problem, Louis? Two months and you don't even shed a tear. Not one fucking tear. Don't you have any heart at all? Anything remotely resembling one? If you had even a shred of feeling, you'd know, if nothing else, that I'm right. They *are* here. Both of them. And if you can't even see that, if you don't know that, then fuck you."

He crashes into me with his shoulder as he leaves. Escaping again. Can't even wait for a response this time, can you, Mr. Escapee? Oh, Jesus. Why can't I say something? I can't, that's why. I can't. Or I don't want to. Same thing, I guess. Susan knew me, knew what I was like. Enough to know how I responded to things. Or didn't. She knew, and she still agreed to our affair anyway. Because she was like that, too. Like me. Only she didn't want to show that part of her. She made everybody think she was different. And I never told. She wanted me to keep it between the two of us. I guess in one way I knew her better than Roy or Alan ever did. I don't know what that means now. If anything.

I watch Alan move away, angrily stomping through the snow like a wounded bear. Maybe he's muttering to himself.

I'm supposed to meet Bob halfway into the snow maze. I get down on all fours in front of the tunnel and realize that whoever made this thing knew exactly what they were doing. The entrance is big enough to crawl into, even with winter clothes. Not if you're a sumo wrestler. But otherwise, a good fit. When I'm completely inside, it's like being in an enormous frigid sleeping bag with no closed end; the kind of dislocating surroundings that make you need to find a way out. Not because you have to, from panic, but because you want to. Exploration; seeing everything you can as you go.

The maze builders must have made a number of small intermittent air holes throughout the structure; it doesn't feel completely sealed, and there's a tiny freezing draft inside. But mostly it's a self-contained environment. I like that. It means if someone comes out here in the middle of the night, he can enter the maze, fall asleep, and maybe freeze to death. And no one will know where the person is. The trapped cold will preserve him for as long as it lasts, as long as the temperature holds. That's a strangely soothing thought, for some reason: the persistence of the body, the isolated entity.

I come to the first junction point where three different tunnels meet and just as I'm about to enter the one on my left, whatever peripheral vision I have detects a blur of movement on the right. Something dark. Could Bob have gotten this far so fast? Not likely. So there's someone else in here. Whoever it is moves fast enough so that when I look down the tunnel on the right, I don't see anybody. Must have gone into another connecting tunnel.

Down the second tunnel, something else happens. I'm crawling, clawing and pushing my way through, and I hear something. Someone's nearby. Talking. To someone else? I don't hear another voice. To himself? Don't know. Sounds that way. I can't tell the person's sex; the voice is too low. Can't quite make out the words. Can't tell exactly where it's coming from. I listen more closely. No good. I know it's not Bob; the maze is too big for him to have come this far by now. I stop, hold my breath. The voice seems closer. Clearer. I put the side of my head on the floor of the maze. And—a soft voice. Almost a whisper. It sounds something like Susan. No. That's not what I hear. I'm alone, cold, maybe tired, disoriented. I didn't hear that. It's being surrounded by nothing but snow; that's part of it, part of the reason for hearing that. Unless it's Alan who's come back to—No. He doesn't do things like that.

The only thing I hear after the voice dies away is the sound of my efforts to get through the maze. At least for a little while. I reach the next junction where another three tunnels meet and again take the one on the left. And right after I enter this tunnel—cold, hard, white—I hear it again. Maybe not; maybe it's not the same voice. But it *feels* like it—it's barely audible and comes from some indeterminate location. Same as before. This time it's more distinct; the word "quiet" seems to be part of what the person says, and it does sound like a female voice. No. Susan's voice. I can't help it; it does. She used to tell me to talk more quietly—that was when I knew we were going to sleep together, when I was in the middle of kissing her, feeling her, and had to say something, anything, to let out the enormous energy roiling inside me that she fired up. "Talk more quietly, Louis," she'd whisper. "Please." And I wouldn't; I'd shut up. And plunge further into lovemaking. I couldn't wait to get my fill of her, in spite of my talking, couldn't wait to fill her up with me. And she allowed me to; she hardly said a word, only lay with me, accepted me. I was grateful. I hadn't been with anyone before. The—whatever it was we had together didn't last more than a couple of months.

Then Roy appeared. Roy was just as accepting as Susan. And Roy was responsive to things, so different from me. Roy was what Susan wanted. I was what she needed. I guess I couldn't really last with her. And now I don't know why I didn't do more than I did. No, that's not true. I do know. Because I couldn't.

It *is* Susan's voice I hear now. It is. But I can't tell exactly where it's coming from. Alan was right after all; they're here. At least Susan's here. Maybe she's farther to the left. Yes, I think she is. I crawl through the tunnel I'm in and at the next junction turn left. She's there; "—more quietly" she whispers. "More quietly." It's colder now. The air is closing in, I think, getting darker. Night's coming. Somehow I know Rod and Asia aren't in the dorm anymore. They've gone outside after finishing what they were doing. To enter this world where it's so easy to get lost, to escape everything that's known.

I'm coming, Susan. I know I'm going to find her. I need her. Yes, I do. The tunnels—. The tunnels connect to each other, and there are so many of them. Maybe Bob's still here; maybe he's given up and left. I don't know. But Susan's here. Susan is in here. Somewhere. I know she is.

A REAL BABE

Brad Linaweaver

WHEN YOU'VE BEEN IN THE BUSINESS AS LONG AS I HAVE YOU become a little jaded. But Dana was too hot to take for granted. The first time I met her I figured she was just another bimbo looking for a quick and easy road to fame, with a payoff as cheap as the bad perfume my ex wears. And when she said she'd written a script and would I please take a look at it, if I had the time, I was ready to write her off despite her looks.

If it hadn't been for my third shot of Jack Daniels I wouldn't have even bothered to read the first page. The damned thing started out OK, which suggested to me that she'd received help from someone. I read a little further looking for marks of the amateur, but the thing was slickly professional and untouched by any college grad attempts at originality. Basically, she'd told a simple haunted house story with the right amounts of sex and violence. Either the whole script had been ghostwritten or she'd picked up a lot more about the business than I would have thought possible from her supporting roles in *Las Vegas Tramp Mutants* and *Demon Dolls*.

I'll never forget our first lunch together. No way could

she fake knowledge she didn't have. Under normal circumstances I would have been thinking of ways of nailing her at minimum cost to myself. She was a fantastic babe with long brown hair, high cheekbones, flashing green eyes, and a devastating smile that was to die for. And the tits were as nice and big as they grow naturally—no need for implants here—with an ass that seemed to call my name whenever she took a step. The waist was small and narrow; and I was out to prove that her mind was every bit as narrow and incapable of producing a decent script before we reached dessert.

Meanwhile, it wasn't only her ass that was speaking to me. "Mr. Hastings," she said in a deep, sultry voice that made my balls tingle. I don't like the high, chipmunk voices.

"Call me Kent," I said, smiling with all the sincerity I'd managed to generate at my last audit.

She returned a smile so predatory that I wanted to lean across the table and lick her pointed, white teeth. "I bet you get a lot of jokes about being called Clark," she said.

Actually, I hadn't heard any dumb Superman jokes since high school but that might change now that I was meeting more people in the comics industry. My first rule is never to sneer at money in any form, but I'd recently had to deal with top paid comics professionals who were forcing me to improve my opinion of Hollywood hacks. But I couldn't think about any of that now if I wanted to apply ruthless objectivity to an actress/model who thought she could write.

Then she made with the mind-reading act; I mean, there's something disconcerting when she pops up with, "I know what you must be thinking, Kent. There's that old joke about the Polish actress who was so dumb she fucked the writer."

Normally I liked it when they talked dirty, but this was different. She had me on the defensive. I was ready to enjoy the globes beneath her chin but she was subjecting me to the lobes residing in her pretty skull. I founded

Gore Street Productions so I'd be calling the shots—and I don't just mean directions for the guy behind the camera.

The irony, I guess, was that I'd intended to develop women writers Real Soon Now. But that didn't mean I wanted actresses carting around laptops and passing out story proposals, treatments, scripts. Things were bad enough when male writers starting wearing assistant producer hats so they'd have a chance at some money. But the real babes already had more control than was healthy, and there was no need for them to wear too many hats. Or wear too much of anything, come to think of it. Progress is OK. The casting couch is too crude. Dating is better. But the line has to be drawn somewhere.

At the time I wasn't thinking primarily about Dana. She was a new girl. My big star was Kristy Chalmers and she had no pretensions about writing, directing, or producing. Unfortunately, Kristy had discovered the financial advantages to be enjoyed in control of her likeness in stills, posters, and promotional videos.

As I say, at that first lunch with Dana my mind was seriously preoccupied with matters other than herself. No one could have convinced me how important this sharp-tongued brunette was going to become in my life while my head was full of soft, suggestible, delectable blonde star power . . . who just happened to be busy ripping me off. Dana had come into my life at just the right moment.

Luck remains the one truly mysterious element that can't be honestly explained. Dana's script was about ghosts at the moment I was deciding to do a knockoff of a major studio's pending release about funny and delightful spirits played by big stars. You didn't have to be a genius to anticipate the sizable public that would soon be hungering for a nasty, low-budget quickie with a high body count. Dana's script delivered the goods. So against my better judgment I made a deal with her. I was generous. She was paid a portion of the money we discussed and there was a small role for her as well, tailored to her special athletic abilities. She was a gymnast and able to handle a foil with the best of them. And she was punctual, which is important in my book.

The haunted house picture would have been the end of our relationship except for one minor detail. I fell in love with her. Nothing like that had happened to me since my first year in La La Land. Maybe it was the way she could anticipate what I would say or do that got to me; but understanding a person is not the same as caring about her. When she'd smile at me—and if I haven't already mentioned it, she has the best smile on screen or off—I would actually feel something. I'm sure the bitch knew it. I only call her a bitch because she was starting to get to me, of course.

You've got to watch out for the gorgeous ones. Their beauty makes them a little crazy. If they're smart on top of that there's no telling what might be going on inside their heads. Which brings me from the first lunch to the last lunch I'll ever have with Dana.

I always take anyone I want to impress to a select number of restaurants where I can count on the best possible service. One thing that never hurts is when I've put the owners or managers in cameo roles in my movies. After they sign the releases and they see themselves up on the screen, it doesn't even matter if they receive the miserable little checks that would barely cover a dinner in their establishments. Hollywood still means glamour even when the economy sucks; maybe especially when the economy sucks!

Every time I had taken Dana out to lunch it had been at one of my special places. And I'd come within a few inches of nailing her at a party the night before, so I decided to really do the next lunch right. I had good news for her. Her house script had required very little rewriting. Unlike the larger studios we don't fuck around with a script if it works. We can't afford it . . . and we don't have to create reasons to pay brothers-in-law and assistants at our budget level.

For some reason I wasn't thinking about money that day. Dana had me so excited that I wasn't being practical. Hell, I still don't know why I fell for her so hard. I'm not the kind of guy who cares if some doll is playing hard to get. There's plenty more where she comes from. You can see them waiting tables and working the streets. The lucky ones are dancing in the clubs. But only Dana had managed to get inside me somehow. Before I knew it, I was even listening to business advice from her.

I'd just had a very bad encounter with Kristy and her muscle-brained manager, and I was seething. Lunch at The Olive Tree was just the medicine I needed. Dana was waiting for me, dressed in a tight-fitting blue dress, cut just above the knee. A strong breeze had blown her long brown hair so that it covered one eye with an unintentional Veronica Lake look. Because it was too windy to sit at one of the tables outside we went into the back where a curtained booth was ready and waiting.

The candlelight gave her face an imperious quality. Arched eyebrows and a full mouth always make me think of a Queen. The crucial moment had arrived as we sat over martinis she had thoughtfully ordered for us, and the red light made exotic patterns on her cheeks. I was ready to let her know how much I respected her intelligence. And then she blew it.

"I'm glad you wrote that script," I told her. "Think you could do another in the same vein? We may have a series here."

"Thanks, Kent," she said. "I'd be happy to write anything you want, but especially ghost stories. I'm like Russell Kirk in that regard."

"Who's that?" I asked.

"He writes ghost stories."

"Not a big name like Stephen King, huh?"

"He's famous for other things, Kent. But what I have in common with Kirk is that we both believe in ghosts. That makes a difference when you're doing ghost stories."

I was ready to kick myself. Every time I think I've found an intelligent woman she pulls the rug out from under me. If it's not astrology, it's nature worship; if it's not reincarnation, it's UFOs or something equally lame. So she was just another airhead after all.

Under other circumstances I would have written her off right then. Or I would have played along with her just to get laid. But what I never do is argue with them. Except this time was different. I couldn't help myself.

"You're kidding," I said.

"No," she replied in a cool and calm voice.

The only manifestation I was interested in right then was the waiter so that I could order another drink, but he was nowhere to be found. So I took another swig of dialectic.

"Why do you believe in ghosts?" I asked her.

She didn't miss a beat. "Because I've seen them," she said.

"Doing what?" She shook her head slightly, so I pushed on. "You've seen ghosts doing what?"

For a moment she squinted her eyes at me like she was picking up on the sarcasm, but then she did that little knowing smile of hers and answered in all seriousness: "They do the same sort of things they did in life, especially the ones who were in a bad rut or feel they left things undone."

I didn't mean to do it but I laughed. "How can you tell the live ones from the dead ones, then?"

"You know when you're seeing a ghost," she told me. Her tone of voice had an edge to it. Time to increase the old sincerity quotient.

"I'm serious, Dana. I'm not trying to make fun of you." Whenever I tried to show that I was a caring sort of guy it was a good excuse to reach out and touch someone. Especially when they were as cute as this one. I held her hand and was I surprised. She has cold hands most of the time, and I had been anticipating the same problem with her feet. Nothing better than warming them up when they really need it. But Dana's hand was burning as if she might be running a high fever.

"Are you all right?" I asked. "You're so hot."

"I'm all right, Kent. But I don't think you really want to hear why I believe in ghosts."

"I do, babe. I do! I was going to ask how you can tell when you see one. Are they transparent?"

"No, not that I've noticed."

"Are they snow-white all over?"

"You've been watching too many old movies."

"My inspiration. But how do you know when you're seeing a ghost?"

She traced her finger around the rim of her glass and seemed a little distant. Then she was ready to share: "There's a feeling at first, a kind of tingle on the back of your neck. And there's other things, like when you see someone no one else can. I've been this way since childhood. My parents thought I was talking to myself but I had friends from the Other Side."

"I've seen those movies, too," I volunteered. "I collect them."

"You'll be able to watch anything whenever you want now," she said out of the blue. "There are certain advantages to your new situation. And I think you'll adapt pretty well. You were never one of the worst ones, you know. You didn't care about the trendy night clubs and what to wear and who's dating whom. You were more individual than that, and having a real self makes it easier when you cross over."

"Huh?"

"I'm not very good at breaking bad news," she commented weirdly, finishing off the last of her drink. Whatever she was driving at, I only cared that she was setting a good example with the martinis. I finished my drink and signaled for the waiter.

"He won't be able to see you," she said.

Now I was becoming irritated. "Look, babe, I put him in *Scream Bunnies on Mystery Island* and used him on the day of the big topless scene. He sure as hell is going to take my order."

If I'd been thinking clearly I would have noticed the unusual touch of her reaching over and taking my arm. Her fingers burned as if they were small bands of hot metal. I yanked my arm away just as she stared into my soul with those big, bright eyes of hers and intoned, "You're dead, Kent."

The old brain still wasn't firing on all cylinders. "Nobody says I'm dead in this town! I've got too much on everyone, damn it. You'll . . ." And then I noticed a peculiar phenomenon only a few inches from my hand. The drink I had just drunk was once again a full drink. The waiter hadn't come over. Dana must have noticed my staring down at the table.

"There are compensations," she said.

"Oh, shit," was all that came to mind.

"I can be your living partner, Kent. Of course I don't know how your will is set up, but with all your inside knowledge you can still control . . ."

"Oh, shit."

"Is that all you can say?"

"This can't be happening," I said, feeling tears beginning to trickle down my face. "I can feel you, you can feel me."

"As time goes on, the living will become hotter and hotter for you to touch. I don't know why that is but I learned it from the first ghost I ever met."

I felt a sudden uncontrollable urge to show off a wider vocabulary. "This is all bullshit! I'll prove it." Jumping up from the table I ran at the nearest patron, a portly man who offered acres and acres of touchable flesh. When I was only an inch away I felt a terrible burning sensation. And then I was sitting on the floor, as if I'd been pushed down. Dana was helping me up and taking me back to the booth.

"Anyone observing me do this will figure I'm crazy," she said, "but I'd rather be living in a century when they think you're on drugs than in league with the devil." So she was showing off that college education again! If I'd been paying any attention I would have seen the warning sign but, hey, I was preoccupied.

Back in the booth, I calmed down enough to ask more questions. She had an answer for everything. "You don't know how you died because the shock was too great," she said, as she started to bite shrimp in half with her fine, white teeth. "Kristy Chalmers' manager went crazy when you threatened to use the evidence of his being a child molester. He broke your neck."

"I have a slight sore throat," I admitted, "but as you say, there's no memory other than the meeting going badly. How did you hear about it?"

"The news, honey. And there's going to be a TV special on one of the tabloid magazine shows."

"To hell with that. We've got to make the movie first!"

She smiled the sweetest little girl smile yet and laid it on me. "I'm way ahead of you," she almost sang. "I've already started the script."

And that's pretty much how I've come to the sorry state I'm in today. My partner owns the company and he's too dumb to haunt; but he's not too dumb to blackmail. God, I love Hollywood. But it's a pain being dependent on the only person who knows I'm alive . . . well, who knows I'm dead but active. Dana and I don't do lunch any longer, but then there's no need.

She's a good sport about all this. She even let me make love to her before she became too hot for me to get close enough. I would have preferred scoring with her while I was still alive, but where beautiful women are concerned I try to be obliging. And I must admit that I've had my consciousness raised about babes. They shouldn't be taken for granted except when you can get away with it.

But the hell of the situation is that Dana has betrayed me in one area where I can't touch her, literally or figuratively. I can't help but think of her as the ultimate bitch for having done this to my company, Gore Street Productions. There's simply no excuse for what she's done, no reason, no justification.

She's improved the product.

OUR WORK

LOOKING FOR MR. FLIP

Thomas F. Monteleone

A writer has nothing to say after the age of forty; if he is clever he knows how to hide it.

—Georges Simenon

(IT WOULD BE SO EASY TO JUST UNLOCK THIS SUCKER, SLIDE IT to the right, step out into space, and turn myself into a street pizza. . . .)

Jack Trent stood at the window of his co-op overlooking the Upper West Side of Manhattan and the improbable swatch of autumn they called Central Park. Fifty-five stories away from the land of yellow cabs and Mideastern hacks, everything looked somehow unreal.

(How do people have the stones for it?)

Jack continued to stare downward, realizing that people who jumped out of windows were either a lot dumber or a lot crazier than he was. As bad as he was feeling right about now . . .

(and for the past year and a half to be honest)

there was no way in hell he could kill himself.

Another minute passed staring down at the micromachine traffic in a kind of detached, foglike state. So blanked-out. Not even aware of his thoughts. Then he stepped back and turned to face his office. It *was* a great-looking room. Everyone who came to visit him always admired it openly. And who wouldn't? It was a tastefully decorated celebration of the achievements of Jack Trent—known to the book-buying public as R. Jackson Trent.

The bookcases covering the walls were bone white with blond oak trim. Four floor-to-ceiling cases were reserved for Jack's many appearances in print. Three-and-a-half shelves of novels, story collections, and anthologies he'd edited. Another whole case for all the foreign editions of those. Then more than two entire cases of all the places his short stories, columns, articles, and interviews had appeared: hundreds of anthologies, magazines, journals, and newspapers.

Then there was the Henrendon étagère in the corner with all the awards. From every literary society, writers organization, and artsy, cultural klatsch in Manhattan. The hall leading into the room was lined with photos of tuxedoed Poohbahs handing him statuettes, plaques, and sculptures.

Almost an entire *wall* of Jack Trent.

Sure, it was impressive, even to Jack himself. There were some mornings when he would shamble into this sacred space and the thought would just kind of smack him in the face.

(Jesus, did I really *write* all this stuff?)

Yes, he did. And therein, as Will Shakespeare once wrote, lies the rub.

You see, Jack Trent, whose agents at William Morris just landed him a two-book deal for more than 11 million dollars, was totally burned-out. Toasted. Crispy fried. Reamed, steamed, and dry-cleaned. Screwed, blewed, and tattooed. He'd been martinized, simonized, and sanitized—although not necessarily for his own protection.

Jack Trent couldn't write jackshit.

(For more than a year now . . .)

And this was from a guy who had literally *burned up* two IBM Selectrics, worn down countless type-ball elements, and kept the ribbon companies in thc black. From a guy who, when word processing became the main heat back in the early eighties, filled his 20 meg hard-drive with so many novels they had to be stacked up at his publisher like 737s waiting to land at JFK.

(Those were the days, my friend . . .)

He moved automatically to his desk, sank deep into the leather palm of his writing chair. Glaring at him like a modern gargoyle, a techno-demon of the White Space, was the paper-white screen of his Mac. The title of his next book, *Malefaction,* floated in the center of an empty page. The White Space that all writers must conquer was finally getting the best of him. As in Poe's *The Narrative of Arthur Gordon Pym of Nantucket* or Lovecraft's *At the Mountains of Madness,* the metaphor had finally come round to become horrifyingly real.

Picking up the keyboard, Jack placed it on his lap, stretched out in his chair, and lightly laid his fingers on the keys. The letters had become alien symbols. Small runic scratches that held as much sense for him as stones written in Mycenaean. His fingers felt cramped, unnaturally positioned over the home row. Myasthenia gravis or acute arthritis could not have crippled him more effectively than the sense of utter helplessness, of . . . emptiness that encapsuled him.

To put it as simply as possible, the words would not come forth. For a half a thousand nights, Jack lay staring into the blackness of his ceiling, wondering if he was dealing with the symptoms or the disease. The questions rattled around in his head like seeds in a gourd. What was the sudden terror that welled up in him like a column of rancid vomit every time he even *thought* about trying to write? Could he have truly run out of things to say? How could he have ever grown weary of entertaining himself, of telling his stories to himself? Jack put the keyboard back on the desk, avoided looking at the book's title lying naked on the face of the monitor.

(Book title. Yeah right . . .)

It was *not* a book title. He chuckled to fight back the tears of frustration. It was merely a title—there was no book.

There was a sound from one of the other rooms in the apartment. Someone had entered the front door and the security monitoring system *beep-beeped* to let him know the door had been opened.

"Mr. Trent? It's just me." A female voice passed through the rooms to find him. Betsy, his office assistant, had reported to work.

(11:00 o'clock already? Christ, another day half-shot.)

Time, Jack had realized for a number of years, did not fly—it *red-shifted* away from us. Memories from childhood capered before him as though things from the night before. And they were as clean and crisp as the little Eton suits his mother used to make him wear. The memories were stacked up behind him like the pages of all his manuscripts.

(How many would it take to reach the moon?)

A presence filled the threshold behind him. Sensing it, he turned slowly and looked at Betsy Moranovic. She was what you would call plain. A late seventies graduate of Smith or Barnard or one of those places—Jack could never remember. She preferred short brown hair cut in what they used to call a page boy style, tortoiseshell glasses, and shapeless skirts and blouses that could not be called out of style because they lacked any style in the first place. Betsy was the perfect office assistant: soft-spoken, obsessively efficient, and almost totally invisible.

"How's the new book doing?" she said as she faced him with an armful of mail from the post office box.

"How many times are you going to ask me that?" said Jack, trying to control a sudden anger. "You know it's doing for shit!"

"I'm sorry, I really am," she said, sounding like an embarrassed child. Then she stood looking at her shoes, waiting for his next words.

(Just like my agent . . . and my readers . . .)

He looked at the huge stack of mail in her arms and was touched by a bittersweet reminiscence of how he used to *love* to get mail. How he'd drive to the post office like a kid digging for his cereal box toy. And every time he'd open the little box and see a manila envelope folded up in there, he'd feel a little piece of the dream wither up and die. But those rejection slips used to get him so juiced! So outraged that he couldn't wait to get back to his little apartment and write something so damned brilliant they *couldn't* turn it down.

But now his mail was just another pain in the ass in his life. More fan mail than any *ten* people could keep pace with; book galleys from friends and associates wanting blurbs; endless requests to write stories for anthologies, limited editions, special anniversary issues, charity-this and charity-that; and free stuff ranging from lots of book review copies to handmade quilts to tins of cookies which went instantly into the trash.

(Didn't people realize that only a true hydrocephalic would scarf up food sent through the mail, wolfing down little treats that could easily be suffused with enough toxins to drop a tyrannosaur in midstride?)

"Mr. Trent, is everything all right?" Betsy's voice penetrated the thicket of his thoughts.

(Jeezis, have I started drooling yet?)

"Yes," said Jack. "I'm fine . . ."

"I was going to answer as much of this as I can get to," she said, waiting for confirmation.

"Yeah, that'll be fine. I'm going to go down and take a walk. Get a pack of cigarettes."

"Oh, okay." She stepped out of his path. "But you don't smoke . . ."

"I was thinking of starting again."

"Oh, okay."

"Cold out?"

"Cool. Low sixties." Betsy chanced a weak little smile.

Jack nodded. His *Baseball Forever* sweatshirt would be enough. And if it wasn't, well fuck it, he'd buy a jacket along the way. What good was the money if it couldn't take your mind off the trivial bullshit in your life?

Down the elevator to a lobby done up in gallery prints by Klimt and handmade carpets from Gaza. Ronnie, the overweight doorman, was waiting for him with his usual Mongoloid smile.

"Hey, Mistuh Trent! Howzit hangin', huh? Howzat latest book doon'?"

Jack smiled and waved as he passed the caricature of a man dressed like a Latin American dictator. He always found it amazing that Ronnie would mention his books. The notion of actually reading a book had never, Jack was certain, sullied the doorman's forebrow.

He walked down Central Park West toward the 86th Street subway. The air had an edge to it. Football weather. No humidity, and none of the fetid summer-city smells that follow you around like an in-law cadging a loan. Everybody dressed in the latest Fall designs, everybody walking fast, looking good. Jack moved with a lackadaisical gait, clearly a man with no place to go.

(You got that right . . .)

Down the gritty steps to the token booth, he side-stepped the obligatory bum and slipped a few dollars under the glass. He'd never really warmed up to political-ly correct posturing, and besides, *homeless person* just didn't roll off the tongue like *bum.*

Whenever he needed to take a break, he liked to go down to the Village, drift through its shabby-chic neigh-borhoods and narrow streets, to absorb the life-scenes there. Maybe drop into McSorley's, catch a Guinness and a slab of cheddar.

(Yeah, that's the ticket . . .)

And so he was standing not really near the edge of the platform, waiting for the C Train. Jack steeled himself at these times, ever watchful for some donut to sneak up behind him and throw him across the tracks to crisp up nicely against the third rail. He never could understand how people could stand right on the edge like they did.

He tried to consciously think about *Malefaction* and how the plot would require several twists along the way. But he knew that was bullshit. His books never happened that way. It was like staring at something and not seeing it until you looked away. That's how his stories came to him. When he wasn't even trying, the whole narrative would just unfold like an intricate origami. It would just phenomenologically *be,* and he'd never questioned it and he knew he never should.

A low-register vibration passed through his Timberland hiking boots. Jack looked up to see the train exploding out of the tunnel, pushing a hot column of air ahead of it. In a burst of noise the train was upon him like a rough beast. Its doors sagged open and he entered into its belly.

As the train lurched forward, Jack found a seat among a familiar collection of New York faces—ethnic types from all the usual places, a few Suits, a few students, some women with their kids in tow. Everybody either buried in a *Daily News* or a paperback, or working on that numb-head stare Jack knew so well.

(Truly, we are a world of mooks.)

Jack grinned at his small philosophy. At least he could still amuse himself. When that left him, maybe it really was time to just step out that window.

The train pitched to the right as it came out of a dark turn and brawled its way into the Museum of Natural History station. Jack absently watched the exchange of passengers in and out, and found himself grinning again as he saw a young woman enter the car carrying his last novel, *Malignancy,* in its paperback edition. He always checked out whatever people were reading because their preference always gave you a major clue to who they really were. Being on the best-sellers list with every title had never jaded him to seeing his books being read in public. But within the last year or so, he'd begun wondering if he would ever see anyone reading a *new* R. Jackson Trent ever again.

The girl

(if they're younger than me, they're *girls.* Sorry, ladies . . .)

sat down on the seat across from him. She looked like a new bohemian: long purple-red hair trussed into a ponytail that shot straight up over her head like a geyser, heavy eye shadow, esoteric Far Eastern jewelry, a baggy peasant blouse and a Guarani scarf, long black skirt, and knee-high boots.

She was not so much pretty or attractive as she was interesting. There was something wrong with the way her features combined to keep her from ever defining the ideal of Helenist, feminine beauty, but she broadcast a message that said she was intelligent, iconoclastic, artsy-fartsy, and maybe a little bit of a flake.

Looking up, she caught him staring at her. Normally, when caught like that, Jack would instantly beam his attention elsewhere, but the way he was feeling today, he didn't give a damn. So he held her gaze for a moment, then looked away with feigned languor. As he pretended to be reading the ads running across the tops of the windows, he could feel the heat of her stare.

But he did not look up until she spoke to him.

"Excuse me, but aren't you R. Jackson Trent?"

Believe it or not, this did not happen to him all that often. Even people who read a lot usually could not ID their favorite writers unless they were making commercials for American Express (Jack had turned them down). And so, it gave him a measure of satisfaction to be found like that in the subway. It was not the total invasion that rock stars and actors grew to loathe, but rather something nice.

Looking again directly into her eyes, he noticed they were also kind of purple.

(Contacts? Who gives a shit—they look great . . .)

"Yes, I am."

"Wow, that is very cool. I've read all your books. Most of them at least twice . . ."

Her accent was soft, educated, but still stretched out by the twangy locutions of the American South.

(Georgia? Alabama?)

He wanted to say something, but absolutely nothing occurred to him.

"I'll bet people say that to you all the time, Mr. Trent," she said.

Suddenly aware of others in the car looking at them, tuning into their contact, he stood up, stepped across the aisle and sat next to her. Their thighs brushed and she did not shy away from the touch.

"Actually, less than you'd think."

"Really?"

"Years ago," said Jack, "I ran into Vonnegut while I was walking up Third Avenue. He was leaning against a street lamp, looking up at a mural on the side of an apartment building, smoking a cigarette."

"Did you talk to him?"

Jack smiled. "Yeah. I told him I thought 'Harrision Bergeron' was one of the finest short stories I'd ever read in my life. He nodded and asked if he knew me."

"Why?"

"Because I think he was trying to intimate that I was bugging the shit out of him."

"You're kidding . . ."

"No. I told him when I was about your age I'd just been elected Secretary of the Science Fiction Writers of America—just about when he wrote us a letter to say he was quitting the organization."

"Did he recognize you then?"

"Yeah, he did. But he also winced at even the *mention* of having been a member of the 'Space Faring Whores of Arcturus.'" Jack chuckled. "Hey, I know how he felt now. I quit that thing a couple of years later myself."

She smiled, and it was a nice smile. "Then what happened?"

"What? Oh, he basically blew me off. I think I blurted out that after sixteen books, I'd just had my newest novel, *The Apocalypse Man,* reviewed favorably in the *New York Times* and he gave me a bogus smile and said something like: 'That's nice, Mr. Trent . . . and I'm sure it's a nice book . . . and I'm sure *you're* very nice . . . and I hope you have a nice day . . . as a matter of fact, have a nice life.' And then he looked back up at the building mural, took a drag off his Pall Mall, and summarily ignored me."

"Jeez, I hope you're not going to do the same thing."

"No, not at all. And please, just call me Jack. *Mr. Trent* is what everybody used to call my father."

"All right, I can certainly do that."

She paused, obviously casting about for something to say, but not getting flustered or fan-girl silly. There was a confidence, a control, about her he admired already.

"This one is great," she said holding up *Malignancy.* "I really love the way you develop your characters. I feel like I've known Sam all my life. And D'Arcy! Wow, she is *so* deep."

"Thank you," said Jack.

"Someday, I'm going to do characters like you." This was offered up softly, but with determination.

The train grabbed them with the momentum of its stop at 59th Street. They'd jumped a local, and it would be an annoying ride south with all the stops.

"So you want to be a writer?" He looked at her just long enough to assess her age.

(Late twenties? Hard to tell. She could be twenty-two and just livin' hard . . .)

"I've already sold around twenty short stories, and I've almost finished my first novel."

"Really, where'd you sell the stories?" He was expecting to hear the usual litany of we-pay-in-contributor-copies-only "literary magazines" and poetry journals like *The Sewanee Review, The Pacific Quarterly, The Midwest Chronicle of Fiction,* etcetera . . .

"Well, let's see . . . a couple of anthologies—

Borderlands and *Shadows*, and magazines like *Omni, Penthouse, New York, Harper's, F&SF, Pulphouse. . . .* And some smaller ones, too."

"I'm impressed," said Jack. And he was.

"Well, that was after a couple years' worth of rejection slips," she said.

"Oh, yeah," said Jack. "I know that whole drill. I've still got most of mine. Saved them in a file somewhere."

"So what're you working on now?" she asked, not knowing how her words lanced him.

He paused, before answering. Then simply: "Can you have some lunch with me?"

They emerged from the tunnels at 4th Street, found an alfresco place that specialized in pastas and soups plus the usual gelatos and cappuccino, and spent the afternoon unloading baggage.

She told him that she was from New Orleans, still lived there, in fact, but was visiting in the city to meet the literary agent she'd just landed, and also to pose for some nude pictures for a pro photographer friend of hers who had his brownstone studio up on West 85th. She thought it would be innovative to appear on the jacket of her first novel wearing lace gloves and nothing else. She talked a lot about mystical bullshit and off-path mythic systems, esoteric religions like Zoroastrianism, always making sure she explained the arcane significance of each piece of her many jewelry accessories. Despite her young age, she said she'd worked the expected catalog of Weird Writer Jobs: including, but not limited to, dog trainer, nude dancer, dynamite truck driver, gaffer, and a deckhand on a shrimp boat. She claimed her name was Nemmy—short for Nemorensis, the birthplace of Diana. The name she used on her stories was Nemmy O. Brand.

"What's the O stand for?" Jack asked.

Nemmy shrugged, pushed a strand of purple hair from her cheek. "What's a big O usually mean to you?"

Jack grinned. He liked her. She seemed wise beyond her years, and showcased more confidence in herself than anybody her age had a right to. He listened to her talk about what she wanted to write about and he knew Nemmy had been to that secret place where the Pool of Ideas waited for young writers to come peer into its endless depths.

Jack had known that place well. Not only had he *been* there, he'd purchased a condo.

But sometime during the last year or so, he'd lost his map.

When it was his turn to explain a few things, he started off with the worst of it. He was on the wrong side of forty-five, and the total number of words written on his new book in the last eighteen months: *zero.*

(That's the *real* big O, sister. May you never know the terror it brings . . .)

He told her how suicide broke the surface of his thoughts like predatory fins every now and then, even though he knew he was *much* too much of a chicken to ever act on that kind of craziness.

Then he unloaded some of the more usual stuff: his unending love for baseball; a disastrous marriage now twenty-five years buried; his sibling-free childhood; the long hours alone while his parents both worked; his mother running off when he was sixteen with some guy who sold Timken bearings; his college days at Pitt; the first story he sold; places he'd been; people he'd met. He even told her that the *R* stood for Randolph and that everybody called him 'Randy' in high school and college. Then his agent strongly suggested that an on-the-rise writer should have a strong American handle. He shortened the family name of Jackson, and after all this time, he couldn't imagine thinking of himself as anyone but Jack.

"So let me get this straight," said Nemmy. "You've got more money than you can count, three houses, traveled all over the world, a wall full of books you've written . . . and you're *still* miserable?"

"Don't talk in non sequiturs." Jack sipped on his fifth cup of cappuccino.

"Huh?"

"No Latin in your education?"

Nemmy rolled her violet eyes. "Not even much English. My dad was a fundamentalist preacher. He said all books of fiction were works of the Devil and fit only for the idlest of minds. But I was just being funny."

"Funny?"

"Come on, Jack, I'm a writer—of course I'm hip to non sequiturs. But seriously, you've got a lot to be happy for."

"You're all full of juice, Nemmy. You don't know what it's like to be sweating through a cold night, wondering if you've vented all the steam in that pressure cooker we call the subconscious. Believe me, *that's* a fucking problem!"

She looked away for a minute, as though watching the endless parade of Village natives and cleverly disguised tourists pass their table. The afternoon was dying off, and the evening grew ever cooler. People in their leather jackets and military greatcoats were starting to look pretty damned warm.

"You know what your problem really is?" she asked.

(That I don't get laid enough . . .)

"No, what? Tell me?"

She kind of smirked at him. "If this were a bad movie, this is where I'd say you are not getting enough leg. And I'd instruct you to come immediately to my loft over Washington Square where I would fuck you stupid."

(Maybe I should be a screenwriter . . .)

"You're so insensitive," he said. "How do you know that wasn't exactly what I was thinking?"

Nemmy's eyes narrowed. All humor leaving them in that instant. "Au contraire, Jack. I *know* it was."

(Great, make me feel like even more of an asshole than I already do.)

"Okay, okay, I give up. What's my real problem?"

"Actually, you're kind of cute, even if you *are* an old guy . . ." She downed the rest of her cup. "But I can't."

"Really?"

"I abstain from sex every other month—it keeps my ancient energies focused."

"And this is the wrong month, right? Just my luck."

She looked at him intently. "Your problem is simple, Jack. You don't believe in the ghosts of your childhood anymore."

"What the hell does that mean?" He was prepared to listen to her, but Jesus, he was getting a little tired of the neo-hippie routine.

"It means you've lost touch with the things that shaped you, that not only pointed you in the direction you took, but *drove* you there. Forced you to take the path most people never even notice."

"Okay, I'm listening. Go on."

"You know what I mean, Jack. We're mutants, you and I, and all the people like us. All the poor fucks who *have* to write, or dance, or paint, or sing, or whatever . . ."

Jack nodded. "Okay, so far. A little romanticized, but basically true. What else?"

"You tell me, Jack." She leaned closer to him as though ready to share a government secret. "Take me down the hall, take me back to the times when you were getting *shaped.*"

Jack drew a deep breath, exhaled. The air was getting downright brisk, almost cold. When Nemmy leaned forward, the edge of the table tightened her blouse against her breasts, and for an instant he could see her hard nipples.

(Knock it off. This is important.)

And it was. He sensed she was onto something that he'd been avoiding. This strange, petite, purple-haired woman-child had thrown the latch on one of the trapdoors to his past, and there was no turning back now. Either he grabbed the lantern she was handing him and headed on down the rickety steps of memory, or whatever he'd been keeping locked up below was going to come up and get him anyway. The catch was thrown, and it was too rusty and too warped to wedge back into place.

"It's funny, but I've always told people my imagination got jump-started when I was about seven years old, after I'd found this horror comic called *The Unseen* on the side of a road. Scared the hell out of me, but it fascinated me, too. From there it was onto dinosaurs and monsters and aliens and bad movies and telling stories and all the other stuff we all did."

"That's not it, Jack. You *know* it's not."

(She's right. Wish she wasn't, but . . .)

"Okay, okay. Lemme see if I can get this out. . . ."

And he started talking about the time in all of our lives when we lack the vocabulary to codify our experiences in terms of real words. Because before the words, there are the images and the primal sense impressions. Mommy smells Good. Daddy smells Funny, but he's still Good. The blanket is Warm. The sun is Bright. Mr. Flip is Bad.

(Mr. Flip. Yeah, he's the one, all right . . .)

Nemmy sat back and allowed a small smile of satisfaction to curl her magenta lips. Before leaning forward again, she signaled for yet another cappuccino.

(Where was she pouring those things? She must have a bladder the size of a casaba melon . . .)

Jack felt a sudden urge for a cigarette, as strong and vicious as if he'd just stubbed one out after a long night of drinking. He shrugged it off, trading it for the mantle of his unburdening.

Mr. Flip came to his house when he was a very small boy. Little Randolph had his own room in the two-story on Crescent Street in Bethel Park, Pennsylvania. Situated on the second floor at the end of the hall, the room was warmed by late afternoon sunlight that streamed in through gauzy yellow curtains.

Always warm.

Till Mr. Flip made the scene.

He came one day with Randolph's godparents—Aunt Helen and Uncle Eddie. They brought him as a birthday gift when Randolph turned four years old. He remembered the dark maroon wrapping paper from Kaufmann's department store, and his dad peeling it off from the box, and the cardboard flaps barn-dooring back to reveal Mr. Flip for the first time.

Little Randolph stared at the thing called Mr. Flip for a long while. Jack could still remember what it looked like, as if he'd just torn his gaze away from it. It was a squat, homuncular little creature, wearing a clown face and stubby little arms sticking straight out. This likeness was painted on a panel of wood that hinged upward from the long end of a piece of furniture resembling a small shoemaker's bench.

Little Randolph didn't know it at the time, but Mr. Flip was a child's dressing stool-combination-clothes valet. You could *flip* (hence the oh-so-clever name) the panel down to make a seat, then up to hang little shirts and pants on its foreshortened, and therefore grotesque, arms.

Whoever had painted the image of Mr. Flip's clown face was either a bad artist, a tortured soul, or plainly mean-spirited. Because the visage on that clothes valet was easily the most hideous, nightmarish face he'd ever seen in his life. The eyes had an almost three-dimensional quality, as they seemed to bulge off the wood like the two halves of a hard-boiled egg. But it was the mouth that captured Randolph's attention so completely. Rimed by a thin, white ring, warped into what passed for a smile, was actually a leering rictus. A gaping space that spoke of bad things. . . . Randolph always found himself staring into Mr. Flip's mouth—into that void between the parted lips where the suggestion of teeth, little pointed ones, glinted at him. The open mouth bothered him. Randolph knew even back then, that mouths opened to either speak or bite, and Mr. Flip just didn't look the talkative kind of guy.

But somehow, his parents and the other grown-ups didn't see it that way. They all clapped their hands and made happy noise, and talked about how "cute" Mr. Flip was, and don't-you-just-love-him-Randolph?—go-give-Aunt-Helen-and-Uncle-Eddie-a-kiss-and-say-thank-you.

Why couldn't they see him for the horror that he was? How could they let such an ugly little thing into their house? Randolph was terrified, but he had been raised even at this early age to be a little gentleman, and he knew he could *never* tell them how much he loathed this intruder.

But that was not the worst of it.

No. His mother had decided that Mr. Flip would receive a place of honor in Randolph's room, *at the foot of his bed* near his door leading down the hall.

And so began the transformation of his thoughts, of the way the little boy perceived the world. Every night, when his dad would sit on the edge of his bed, reading him a story from the Golden Books collection, Randolph would listen half-heartedly, watching the pictures in the book with one eye, while casting a cautious glance at Mr. Flip. Admittedly, Randolph had evolved a partial solution to sharing a room with such a malformation by actually *using* the valet as much as possible—shrouding it with every shirt and pair of pants he could get his hands on. His mother would boast to her friends what a nice and neat boy he had become since Mr. Flip arrived.

While not a solution, his tactic kept Mr. Flip under wraps except for Laundry Day. And on those days and nights, Dad's stories were never long enough. When he would close the Golden Book and tuck Randolph in with a kiss and a sweet-dreams-champ-see-you-in-the-morning, the little boy would feel all his insides kind of seizing up like an old Chevy that suddenly lost its oil pan.

Because, on those nights, Mr. Flip was free to cavort naked and revealed.

After his dad switched off the light with a resounding *click!* he would leave the door half-open, walk down the hall, and switch on the bathroom light. The thinking here was to allow a little ambient light to flow down the passage and softly lap against Randolph's bedroom threshold. Thereby giving him some comfort against the darkness.

(But it didn't work that way, did it?)

The cast of light, the positioning of the clothes valet, the angle of sight from the boy's bed, and a certain slant of imagination all conspired to imbue Mr. Flip with a dark and living essence. Transfixed, Randolph would lie propped against his headboard like a prisoner chained to his cell wall, looking into the predatory gaze of Mr. Flip. The longer he watched, the lolling egg-yellow eyes would begin to track about the room as though searching for him . . . And the arms. More like flippers, really. Sticking straight out with oversized, flat hands, Mr. Flip became the vile thalidomide mutation iconized. But the worst had been the rows of shark-teeth, folded away during the daylight that would rise up from the impossible dimensions beneath the surface of the wood. The boy could almost hear its words falling from that mouth in a hideous whisper: *Flip-time! Gonna flip you, Randy. That's what I'm gonna do. Gonna flip you out. . . .* One night, when left naked, Randolph knew, he would shake free of his guise and gambol about the room before scaling the heights of the bed.

An immeasurable gulf of time passed over the little boy as the Laundry Days piled up like dirty clothes, stretching into months. The terrors dispensed by Mr. Flip ran rampant through his dreams until they began to leak through, contaminating his daytime thoughts. He began seeing other images in terms of Mr. Flip. Ordinary everyday objects became as yellow or round as his eyes, as red as his nose, as flat as his hands, as dark as the vacancy of his mouth.

Gonna flip you out. . . .

And it continued like that until Mr. Flip finally Went Away.

Well, actually, he was *taken away.* It happened after he'd finally broken free of the wood that held him, shambling out of the hallway light and into the nourishing shadows of Randolph's room. He danced obscenely in the moonglow, and whispered to the boy as he approached the bed. *Flip time! Yes it is! Gonna flip you out! Mr. Flip's gonna flip you out!*

Closer and closer it dragged itself, but before he could clamber up the bedclothes, the little boy had unleashed a shattered-crystal scream. A scream that yanked Daddy from his dreams of late mortgage payments and vindictive supervisors to come running down the hall.

A *click!* and the room filled with light. Randolph gibbered uncontrollably, able only to point at the clothes valet which now stood rigid and idiotic by the door. The pantomime of tears and heaving, sobbing relief continued until Daddy got the message. Hey-c'mon-champ-is-this-thing-what's-bothering-you-well-don't-worry-about-that-Daddy'll-fix-that-right-now.

Randolph could remember the hard, warm power in his daddy's hand as he grabbed him up from the bed, carried him up against his pajamaed chest, while in the other, he gathered up Mr. Flip and headed downstairs, through the kitchen, and out into the backyard. Moonlight through elm branches crosshatched their path to a flagstone pit barbecue his father had built the previous summer. The little boy watched as his daddy carefully stood him up and said okay-watch-it-son as he swung Mr. Flip like Willie Mays going after a high, hard one. In one incredibly rapid motion the clothes valet struck the chimney of the barbecue and simply . . . *exploded.* The pale yellow cast of the Indian Summer night captured the spectacular splintering of Mr. Flip and etched the image across time itself. Recorded in majestic slow-motion, the end of Mr. Flip would remain with Randolph forever.

There were other recollections since faded—till now—the cool, wet grass under his feet; the warm rush of joy that surged through him; Mommy yelling at Daddy to get-back-in-the-house-it-was-the-middle-of-the-night-you-maniac . . .

But the good stuff remained. Somewhere in the dredged up muck of that early terror was the tarnished crucible in which a child's terror had been transformed from base metal into gold. The place where Jack's headspring had been wound up tight—full of the chimeras and hydras that would lifetime chase him through invention's maze.

(Well, *almost* a lifetime.)

He had never imagined the spring would run so slack, that the tension would be lost. And there was no longer a Mr. Flip around to twist the key.

"Pretty cool, Jack," said Nemmy. She tilted back the rest of her cup. "I like it. Told from the heart . . . or the gut . . . or whatever. I believe you."

"Believe me? I didn't know I was under oath."

She grinned. "Only to yourself."

The sun had westered into Jersey and beyond, and their waiter hovered nearby. If Jack didn't order some dinner, they would be expected to make room for some paying customers.

"What's that supposed to mean?"

"Isn't it obvious? You have to go back and get Mr. Flip—wherever he is."

A little jolt tensed through him. Some sort of somatic response to the idea of what she was suggesting.

"What?"

The waiter was looking at him, and Jack numbly signaled for the check. Nemmy was leaning forward, her eyes bulleting him.

"You can't be this dense, Jack. You *need* Mr. Flip. Now go find him."

The waiter passed the table, pausing only long enough to drop his check on a little tray. Jack covered it with a stray fifty from his pocket, and nodded slowly. Nemmy had whanged him with a psychic tuning fork and he was still resonating from the tone so struck. The very *notion* of needing Mr. Flip, even symbolically, withered him. He must have been turning this idea over for an extended time, not speaking, not even seeing anything, until he was aware of a touch at his sleeve.

". . . earth to Jack . . . You still with us, man?"

"What am I supposed to do?" he said with a half-hearted chuckle. "Go back to Bethel Park?"

Nemmy looked at him with an expression of amused tolerance. "Of course, Jack! That's *exactly* what you must do."

"But why?"

Nemmy was clearly disappointed in him. "What do I have to do?—connect all the dots for you? Jack, you're displaying all the signs of a severly atrophied imagination. And that's the problem. Even if only unconsciously, you gotta realize Mr. Flip was the boss moment, the big-deal catalyst in your life. He taught you how to be *scared,* he taught you that this is a fucking scary place. And once you discovered that, there was no turning back. Monsters from the id, Jack. That's what it's all about. You know it, and I know it."

She paused for dramatic effect. Her eyes lasered violet light into him.

"You've got your money and your automatic rave reviews and your guaranteed million sales, so what do you need with motivation, with any galvanic fear response from the time that shaped you? That's the problem, Jack—you don't think you need it anymore and the fact is you need it more than ever. So yeah, go back to Bethel Park and get whatever you left there. Go get that little shit."

He thought about that for an unspoken moment while he looked at this wacky-looking young woman, who in the space of a few hours had discovered more about him than the last ten years' worth of girlfriends. He knew already their relationship had somehow transcended, or at least stumbled past, the physical, and oddly enough, that was fine with him. He was not, in the final encoding of this encounter, attracted to her; but he still felt he needed her in his life. Of all the ways he'd tried to find a solution to his personal terrors, only Nemmy O. Brand had offered up any counsel of possible worth.

Again the urge for a big old nasty Marlboro laced through him. He exhaled, watched his breath defined by the now cold air.

"Okay," said Jack. "You're right. I only have one more question."

"What's that?"

"Will you come with me?"

(*Not on your fucking life.*)

Jack recalled Nemmy's reply as he guided his gun-metal blue Lexus across the winding treachery called the Pennsylvania Turnpike.

That's what she'd said to him.

And pretty soon after that, he'd put her in a cab and had never seen her again. No phone calls, no keep-those-cards-and-letters-coming-folks. Nothing.

(No, that wasn't completely true.)

About a week after she'd faded into the SoHo evening traffic, Jack found a little package mixed in with the day's bag-o-mail. It was wrapped in brown paper, had a New Orleans postmark, and no return address. Inside, Jack found a charm or amulet attached to a small silver necklace chain. He was not familiar with the design although it resembled any number of mandalalike designs he'd seen. A handwritten note said:

> *This is the talisman of my namesake. Wear it during your quest and you will succeed, but only if you believe in its power.*
>
> *N.*

Jack smiled as he remembered his reaction the first time he'd read her words.

(Yeah, and don't forget to click your heels three times. And a pair of red shoes wouldn't hurt . . .)

Funny thing was, Jack realized, until he'd received that little charm, he had decided he would actually go back to Bethel Park.

A green and white sign slipped past him. PITTSBURGH 15 MILES. He would be getting off at the Monroeville exit, which was coming up fast. Another half hour or so and he'd be home.

And yeah, he knew all about Thomas Wolfe and the going home shtick. But that guy wrote standing up using the top of his refrigerator as his desktop . . . so what the hell could he know about anything? Besides, Jack was pretty damned sure that *Look Homeward Angel* wasn't the result of a close encounter with a clothes valet.

(I'm going home, all right. You bet your ass, Tom.)

Jack tried not to anticipate anything. Not having been back to his hometown for almost twenty years, he had no idea what to expect other than lots of changes. Experience had taught him a few things, including the folly of trying to figure out ahead of time how a particular scenario might run down and how to deal with it. His up-and-down life as a writer had schooled him well: take everything as it comes; don't try to plan *anything;* and don't lose sleep over things beyond your control.

Half an hour since leaving the turnpike, he realized he was probably lost. But, after a stint on the parkway and more turns and stops than he'd remembered, he realized he was closing in on the old neighborhood. It was incredible how little had changed in all these years. There was a part of him that hadn't wanted his return to be so easy, and he was just discovering this.

(Weird how the mind works . . . *my* mind, anyway.)

He turned a corner and there was something about the configuration of the tall trees, that barn-red clapboard house on the corner, the curving tracks of the trolley. Tapping the accelerator, Jack surged forward two more blocks.

Crescent Street.

As he slowly guided the Lexus into its turn, entering the long shady block, he felt everything hitching up—his breathing, the fluids in his throat, his fingers gripping the wheel, tears in his eyes. For the first time since that morning, he remembered Nemmy's talisman hanging about his neck beneath his L.L. Bean shirt. Fumbling around his button-down collar, he felt the thin silver touch his fingertips.

(Why am I doing this? Just get on with it.)

Crescent Street lay in wait for him, enshrouded by gigantic chestnuts and oaks. Over the encampment of two-stories, they formed an impenetrable canopy of fall color. Jack stopped the car, escaped its leather womb, and stood looking up the street. The houses had remained unchanged and without thinking about it, he found himself ticking off the names of the families who'd lived in each of them during the chrome and Formica fifties: the Edmonds and the Ottenheimers, the Geatings, the Paseks, and of course the big Victorian on the corner where old lady Howard passed her days behind drawn window shades.

Jack walked slowly up the block. Still no sidewalks and still no need. Crescent was off the beaten track; the only traffic had always been its residents and the occasional delivery van. There were a few yardheads out raking and pruning and trimming, a kid on his bike; otherwise the street was very quiet. His target lay hunched among the shadows of two immense trees, its white aluminum siding accented by black shutters and awning over the front steps. Jack remembered the day he helped his dad install that awning; it was an Autumn Saturday very much like this one when he wanted to be off to his high school's football game. But not until he finished his detail as no. 1 tool-handler and garage-gofer. Dad was forever showing him how to use another esoteric tool; and even now Jack knew his coping saws from his calipers.

The awning still protected the steps—a testament to Dad's skill. As he reached the front walk, Jack felt a sudden attack of disequilibrium, as if he'd jumped up from a chair too soon. Only dimly sensed, forces swirled around him.

(You're just getting emotional. Go on. Get going . . .)

Advancing up the walk, Jack shook off the impression of passing through a long tunnel. When he stood under the awning, he could almost hear Dad calling the self-tapping metal screw *a little whore* for not turning properly. He smiled at the memory and knocked on the door.

It opened after a moment to reveal a plain-looking woman in her early thirties. She wore a sweatshirt and jeans; carried a box of Frosted Flakes in her hand. Ambient noise of a cartoon show and kids arguing behind her. TV was probably on the kitchen counter.

"Yes?" No smile. Wary, despite Jack's purposely well-groomed appearance.

"I hope you'll excuse me, ma'am, but my name is Jack Trent—I used to live here. In your house."

He paused to get a read on her. While he spoke she'd been once-overing his topcoat from Barney's and his Italian leather loafers with those little tassels on the tops.

"Yes . . ."

Still noncommittal. But that was fine. At least she

hadn't slammed the door in his face or informed him she didn't want to interrupt her husband while he was cleaning his guns.

"Well, I have a kind of unusual request. You see, I grew up in this house, and when I moved out—almost thirty years ago, well, I never came back. My parents sold the place, moved to an apartment."

She leaned against the doorframe, definitely more relaxed now.

"I don't think I understand, Mr . . . ?"

"Trent. Jack Trent. Just call me Jack."

"Mr. Trent, okay, Jack. What exactly do you want?"

Jack smiled the smile his girlfriend invariably said made him look like a little lost boy.

(Only this time, they might be right. . . .)

"Well," he said, pausing a little dramatically and feigning reluctance. "I wanted to rent your house for a little while."

She half smiled. "Rent *my* house? We *live* here, Mr. Trent! What're you talking about?"

He pushed on. "I won't need it for very long. Maybe a week, maybe only a few days. You could spend a few days on a minivacation, maybe. Stay at a nice hotel, whatever . . ."

"Listen, I don't want to sound rude, but I'm a single parent, I work two jobs, and I don't have any time or money for any 'minivacations.'"

Jack smiled. As they said in the sales seminars, it was time to make his close. "I'm sorry, ma'am, I don't have your name. . . ."

"Sudbrook. Dorothy Sudbrook."

"Well, Dorothy, how about this—you see, I've made some money in my time. And time *is* money, so what would you say to, ah, me renting your house for, oh, say, whatever it would cost you to pay off the mortgage on this place?"

She actually laughed, albeit sardonically. "Look . . .

Jack, or whatever your name is, I don't have time for this. Are you crazy?"

"Yeah, I guess I am." Jack pulled a paperback edition of *Malignancy* out of his topcoat pocket. The cover hyped the usual *#1 New York Times Best-seller* across the top in gold foil. He flipped it over to expose his full-color photo on the back. "But I'm also rich," he said.

Two days later, Jack was sitting alone in the kitchen where his mother once served him up eggs in every cookable mode on an almost daily basis. He smiled as he considered those precholesterol-conscious days, and realized for the first time how *small* the room actually was. Yet it had been the nexus for his little family. Resonating with the afterimages of 20,000 shared meals, 5,000 homework assignments, and at least several hundred lethal domestic battles, Jack let the ghost-memories of the house pass through him like radiation.

The Sudbrook house wrapped itself around him in a quiet blanket. Dorothy and her two preschoolers had packed up and headed for Disney World so fast you'd have thought they'd hit the lottery.

(And in a way, they *had.*)

After their station wagon cleared the driveway, Jack had gone immediately to work by walking through each room of the house,

(Well, almost each one . . .)

just absorbing whatever might still remain there of his childhood. He'd noticed two things almost instantly: the first was the inability of Dorothy Sudbrook's furniture and general *stuff* to disguise the house's true identity. In every room, Jack saw everything the way it had been, the way it was *supposed* to be. The second thing was less obvious, but no less true: the house literally *hemorrhaged* with memories, impressions, vibes, whatever you wanted to call them. They flowed out of the walls and into Jack with such force it was actually a physical sensation.

Nemmy had been so right on. Everything he'd ever become could trace its roots back to this house. If there was any hope to recapture what had been leached from him, it would be found here. A knock at the door stopped his woolgathering; he stood up to stare at it in stark panic until he remembered ordering a pizza.

Hungrier than he'd figured, Jack wolfed down four slices without hardly taking a breath. Nervous energy required a lot of fuel, and he was a lot more scared than he'd figured he'd be. Outside, sunlight faltered, then finally retreated from the windowpanes, leaving a dull smear of twilight on the glass. It would be dark any minute.

(Time to find you, old buddy . . .)

Jack helped himself to the paper towels over the little sink and cleaned himself up. Then he passed through the living room where the old Emerson television had squatted for years, dispensing the magic of Winky-Dink and Howdy-Doody and Film Funnies. Shadows followed him as evening surrendered and Jack stood at the foot of the stairs. A brief memory gammaed through him: a four-year-old Randolph at the top of these same stairs, naked and dripping wet after he'd run from the bath so excited to hear Daddy walk in the front door. An extra step and he'd tumbled ass-over-end to the spot where Jack now stood. Somehow, he'd been unhurt; Daddy said it was a miracle as he'd carried him back up.

But now there was nobody to carry him, nobody to help, if anything were to send Jack rolling.

(Anything? No, it's not *any*thing . . . I'd say it was a very specific thing.)

Jack grabbed the polished banister, worn smooth by years of human traffic, and began the ascent into his past. The passage seemed to narrow as he drew closer to the top. The landing ended in a blank wall, with a brief left onto the main hallway. To the left lay a master bedroom full of scattered women's clothing, a little girl's room straight across and to the right a bathroom and a third and final bedroom.

Turning right, Jack fumbled for the hallway light switch, then decided against it. Memories leaked out of the walls, battering him like bad poetry. It was better this way, he knew. He stepped forward, down the hall, past the bathroom, toward a half-closed door.

Since entering the house, Jack had avoided this final room. He knew the time was not yet right. But now, as he neared the last threshold, the final barrier between his origins and his present sorry-ass state, he could feel it playing out like a well-written script. Something surged and lurched within the frame of the house, something massive, yet amorphous. A *presence,* yes, but more like a substantial abstraction than merely a physical thing. Jack had no words to describe whatever seethed within the very fabric of the house, but he could feel it just fine, thank you.

Flip-time!

(That's okay with me, you little fucker. . . . Let's get on with it.)

Gonna flip you out, Jack.

Just as his hand closed in upon the doorknob, Jack snapped back as though tire-ironed. Had he actually *heard* that? Had it called him by name?

(Go on. Time to find out . . .)

He touched the knob, half-expecting some kind of blue flame to dance across the gap to spark his flesh. But the brass was cold and dead, ignoring him. The door swung inward and the secret place, the sanctum sanctorum of the only child, the boy of dreams, the fantasy chamber, gave up its mysteries.

There was no light and yet there was all the detail he'd ever need. The shadows spoke to him, and he knew the fixtures of Dorothy Sudbrook's child did not inhabit this place. Scents assaulted him with their ancient powers of memory: airplane glue, crayon wax, and neat's-foot oil.

Jack stepped into the room and touched the talisman at his neck. The ancient metal burned him with its purity—a cool, clean, nonpolluting energy source. He looked into the space before him.

And like an old, brown-gray photograph, the room reflected the hazy continuum of a small boy named Randolph Trent. It was more spare than he remembered it: a dresser, a low set of shelves full of toys and comic books, and a desk. A few Crayola drawings on the walls, chintz curtains at the window.

And right in front of him, so close its wood almost brushed his leg, sat Mr. Flip.

Incredibly, Jack hadn't seen it when he first entered the space. But his old buddy, although translucent and gauzy, was undeniably there. Jack eased past its traditional resting place. Slowly, it gathered more reality to itself. Form and configuration. Substance.

Moving quickly, Jack strode to the corner of the room where his old single bed waited like an old friend. He could feel the eyes of Mr. Flip lazily tracking him as he sat down to confront the ancient nemesis.

Flip-time, Jack!

Ever since deciding to return to Crescent Street, part of Jack had always figured that any contact with his old enemy would reveal Mr. Flip to be nothing more than a silly boojum from childhood, a lifeless icon.

But the thing that waited for him, that had waited for more than two generations, remained as repellent and loathsome as ever. Jack felt a dark aura issuing from it like a poisonous vapor. Whatever it had been, whatever of it still remained, this grotesque piece of furniture was much more than that. It possessed an animus, an essence that held him.

Without thinking, Jack reached up to touch Nemmy's talisman. The cool silver contact felt mildly galvanic.

Gonna flip you! Gonna flip-flip-flip you out, Jackie boy!

(What *are* you?)

The thought slipped out of him so effortlessly. He

hadn't planned a dialogue with this monster taking shape before him. If anything, it was uglier than even he had remembered it.

I am a part of you, Jack-bo. I am a piece of the rock—the original chaos. I am the stuff of time and matter. The stuff that's always trying to return to the primal center of things. I am the Reducer. I see order and I abhor it. Reductio ad absurdum.

(But why me? What did you want with me?)

Jack felt another one of those sudden, molten *needs* for a cigarette or a pull off the bourbon bottle.

Don't flatter yourself. I'm not here just for you. Don't you see it yet?

Jack had seen enough, had felt enough. He understood now that his old nemesis was nothing more than an energy source, as were all the passionate events of our lives. And that the most wondrous paradox of it all was this: Mr. Flip didn't want him, didn't need him; it was the other way around.

Standing up, Jack's body seemed to fill the little bedroom. The whole house appeared to be getting smaller, as if he'd Alice-like drunk from a magic vial.

As though it sensed the essential, yet unexpected truth, Mr. Flip began folding into itself, collapsing into that null-space where nightmare and trauma reside. But before it could warp back to that place, Jack made his move.

(Sorry, but I need you, pal . . .)

Jack reached down and grabbed for the apparition, only half-shocked to feel his hands touch something rough-hewn, something *real.* How could it be back after all this time? Jack saw it destroyed forty years ago, and yet he knew that his need had made it real again.

The wood, or whatever it was, grew hot as the skin of his fingers sang out with pain. He wanted to break loose from the thing, but it was too late. The smell of his own seared flesh was only as real as he would allow it. He knew that now. The furnace room of his imagination, cold and slaked by success, had been fired up again. Mr. Flip was his dilithium crystal, Scotty, and he knew he was going nowhere without him.

(We're going to play this out . . . no stopping it now.)

And then he was half running down the hall, passing through the rooms of memory, bursting free of the place and into the cool blue arms of night. Mr. Flip along for the ride, following the fiery path of a father's cometary mission to deliver his son from terror. Jack felt an atavistic burst from the core of his . . .

(soul?)

being, a surge of true power, trunklined to one of nature's primal generators. As he covered the backyard in long strides, he felt more vital and full of purpose than he could ever remember.

And Mr. Flip had stopped talking to him.

No more whiny sing songy voice carving up the darkness with its vile rhythms. No, no, no. As Jack covered the distance in the backyard with long strides, the thing writhing under his grip could only manage a pitiable and plaintive moan. This monster he freighted across the plains of his childhood, whatever it truly was, sensed its destiny, and if it was capable of fear, it was feeling it now. Jack knew now for the first time that the piece of furniture, long gone, had only been the host to this psychic parasite, this mindworm of the soul.

Jack knew this.

(And knowledge was indeed power, wasn't it, you little piece of shit?)

He touched the talisman again.

The corner of the yard loomed in the gray half-light. Dad's old barbecue chimney had crumbled away years before, but something still waited in its place. Like a lighthouse, a beacon, the ghostly shape of the chimney remained, gaining mass and reality as Jack bore down upon it like a ship emerging from the front of a storm.

Mr. Flip began to scream. It *knew.*

It knew that this time there would be no escape from the splintering it would receive. It knew all along what Jack had only discovered—that it thrived only when Jack had finally let it back into the world. After forty years in the magic lamp of Jack's id, success and ennui had eroded the seal. The monster was out of jail. Jack listened to its scream and threw back his head to join with it—a scream of unholy harmony.

Because that's what it was, wasn't it? All those years, Jack had been singing his song and not knowing it had been a duet. When his father obliterated Mr. Flip so long ago, the little boy who stood witness had done more than merely watch. Like the warriors of Borneo, he had absorbed his enemy totally.

Jack smiled as everything fell into place.

He ran with the abandon of a ten-year-old fueled by the elation of a childhood past unstoppered and pouring down the funnel of time. Nemmy had been so right; he realized it now, as he reached up to grab her charm in his fist, to hold it tightly through this final circuit of his journey. Bounding through the yard, cutting through the night, his hand burst upward to his throat in a miscalculated motion. The thin chain ruptured, sending the silver symbol into the darkness.

For an instant, Jack felt everything locking up like a bad clutch. His hesitation leaked a message to the thing bunched under his arm and he felt it swell and pulsate like some diseased organ.

What's-a-matter, Jack-boy? No more magic twanger, eh?

He almost stopped right before the image of the barbecue pit, to wonder if it could really be there, to question his own beliefs and needs. Nemmy . . . that silver trinket . . .

The eidolon of his childhood twisted and blistered under his grip. It sensed that it could, after all, still be free of him. Free to mock him in his helplessness. Jack struggled to keep his psychic balance. He couldn't let it get this far just to fall on his face, to let this thing crush him. He didn't need any magic charms.

(No. Fuck all that. I've got this little bastard right where I want him.)

He could almost hear Nemmy's voice in his head, Obi Wan to his Luke: *Use the Force, Jack.*

He threw back his head and laughed at the moon.

(Talismans? We don't need no stinking talismans!)

He could feel the entity shrinking again under his grip. It was attuned to him, there was no doubt. It knew him and could read him with an expert rating. Jack was no longer surprised by this affirmation of his spirit. This thing had been encysted within his psyche for most of his life—it knew him as well as he knew himself.

Running now, he swung the thing that had called itself Mr. Flip up over his head in a terrible arc, gaining speed and power as it curved down toward the ancient flagstone.

Gonna get you, Ja—

A final, high-register wail dopplered from the thing as Jack drove it into the face of the magic chimney, the stones fashioned from his father's hands. There was an explosion of light and heat. Then everything stopped and reversed itself; the scream swallowed up in a larger implosion. The thing was yanked from this world, rattling down the rails of entropy, and the air itself snapped shut with a loud *pop!* to mark its exit, its transfiguration.

Suddenly Jack was standing alone in the corner of his old backyard.

Alone. Hands empty. No trace of the flagstone pit barbecue.

No Mr. Flip.

Not where you could see him, anyway.

Drawing a breath, he became aware of himself once again. It was as if he'd blinked his eyes to find he'd sleepwalked to the edge of an abyss and awakened just in time. A calm held him like the doldrums, but there was no panic, no desperation in it. Rather, Jack felt a new purpose that coursed through him with the fire of sour mash whiskey, lighting him up like a ballpark scoreboard.

Turning he looked up the length of the yard, traced in moonlight, to the house where everything had begun. Jack knew he could now leave its old comforts and far older fears. A cycle had been completed, a mythic transference achieved. A new beginning sparked amidst the ashes of an ending.

R. Jackson Trent rediscovered the oldest secret of all our lives; the one that most of us forget. He invaded the sanctity of childhood's tomb and escaped with the treasures we always leave buried there.

And lived to tell about it.

This one is for Elizabeth

PRESENT IN SPIRIT

Don D'Ammassa

THEY WATCH ME ALL THE TIME.

I can't see them, exactly, but I can feel them, feel their eyes moving over my body even in my most private moments, in the shower, sleeping seminaked in the humid August air, sitting on the can. The sensation is unmistakable, like a low electric charge passing over my skin, stirring the tiny black hairs on my forearms. Then I begin to sweat, not the honest sweat of summertime or hard work but almost a secretion, my body reacting to those violating eyes. And I know then that I'm not alone.

I think I'm haunted.

At first, I dismissed it all as nerves. I'm a rational person, my life has been structured on a framework of logic and common sense. What works I keep; what doesn't work deserves to be discarded, whether it's a broken tool, an outmoded concept, or an inadequate subordinate. Those principles guide me at home or at work, allow me to take a commanding position in both environments.

The purpose of business, for example, is to maximize profits, for the company and for the individual. This crap about participatory management is a ploy, a way for the sheep to exert control over the wolves. Wolves are survivors because they earn that right; if you're content to remain within the herd, don't expect any sympathy from me. I earned the top spot at Eblis Manufacturing and I apologize to no one for what I had to do to get there.

You'd have done the same in my position, if you had the guts.

The first time was at a company picnic. You know, one of those misguided attempts to foster a sense of family. Business and family are two separate entities, and the tendency to blur that distinction has been responsible for more bankruptcies and broken careers than I care to contemplate. I almost welcomed the faltering sales that led to its discontinuance some years back.

I was fairly low on the corporate totem pole that day, Inventory Control Manager, not a particularly powerful position given the simpleminded predisposition of President Bowes to give manufacturing whatever it wanted regardless of the economics of the situation. But back then, we could sell just about anything we made, the market seemed a bottomless pit waiting to be filled with giftware, and it was hard to rein in shortsighted enthusiasms.

"Can I sign you up for the bag races, Mr. Nicholson?"

It was Penny Redfern from the typing pool, called Penny Dreadful behind her back because of her horrible complexion problem. "I'm really not the athletic type, Penny. Why don't you try Joe Forester?" It was an effort to be polite; this entire day was a waste of time, but attendance was unofficially mandatory for managers.

"But we heard you play racquetball. Come on, it'll be fun." Penny's companion and roommate, Jennifer Sears, was almost strikingly attractive in a cheap sort of way. Rumor had it she was sleeping with the shipping supervisor, and the stockroom clerk, and a few others.

I played racquetball because it enjoyed considerable

popularity within the layer of management directly above me and for no other reason. It happened that I had a natural talent for the game, and I derived a certain perverse satisfaction from seeing how close I could drive Nelson or Boggs or Garabedian to exhaustion before missing an easy shot and forfeiting a match.

I suppressed the urge to suggest that Penny adopt the sack as a way of concealing her raspberry complexion. "Then you've probably also heard that I play badly."

"That doesn't matter, Mr. Nicholson," Jennifer pre-empted her companion. "This is just for fun. Come on, get out of that stuffed shirt for a couple of hours."

Insolence reaps its own reward. "Some of us prefer to keep our clothes on, Miss Sears, metaphorical or otherwise."

She stood there blinking for a few seconds, apparently needing the time to break down the meaning of my words, leech out the implications. Then her face turned pasty white and she bolted. Penny seemed honestly puzzled, gave a tentative parting gesture and hastened after her friend.

"Oh, there you are, James."

Just when I thought I could finally slip off by myself, Bowes showed up, with his inevitable Alan Crandall shadow.

"Hello, Mr. Bowes. Couldn't ask for better weather, could we?" Actually I'd have preferred a violent thunderstorm to these bright, cloudless skies. It would have brought a welcome end to these insipid mock festivities.

"We've been very lucky. James, Alan here has just been telling me about your reorganization plan."

"Oh?" I hadn't expected my proposal to pass through so many levels so quickly, but I wasn't about to miss an opportunity to advance my position. "I think you'll find it will speed things up considerably, and save a few salaries as well."

"Yes, well, that's what I meant to talk to you about.

Economies are all well and good, of course, and I commend your efforts, but as I understand it, you plan to let go your three most senior people and replace them with clerical workers."

"In a manner of speaking. We'll have to rewrite the job descriptions, of course, to avoid the possibility of legal action, but frankly the more complex aspects of their jobs have been automated, and they haven't really earned their paychecks in over a year."

Bowes was plainly uncomfortable, wouldn't meet my eyes. How could this man ever have ascended to the presidency of Eblis, I wondered. He can't even face one of his junior executives.

"But Ted Barnwell has over twenty years with the company, and Simone Moran has been with us even longer."

"Excuse me, sir, but the Dennison press you had us scrap last month was forty years old."

"But it was obsolete, James. It couldn't accommodate our new die sets."

I didn't answer, just kept my eyes level, letting Bowes interpolate from his own words. To his credit, it didn't take long. "We'll talk about this further, James, at another time."

And he was gone, and Crandall with him, leaving me mercifully alone. Or so I thought.

It wasn't a specific feeling at first, more an undercurrent of uneasiness. The crowd was moving toward the athletic field, except for a few diehards congregating around the beer kegs and the sizzling grills. With Bowes's departure, I had slipped back into the woods surrounding the picnic area, wondering if I could make it across to the parking area without anyone noticing that I was leaving.

Someone was watching me.

I told you my life was based on logic, but that doesn't mean I'm not open to the possibility that my understanding of the world might have its flaws, that there might be things lurking just beyond the limits of my understanding.

Someone was standing in among the vine covered trees a dozen meters away. I couldn't see him very well, but it was clearly a child in his early teens. My first reaction was to move away, but there was something familiar about the boy, something that tickled the edges of my memory. I took a tentative step forward.

"You'd better not go too far from the clearing," I said quietly. "These woods go back for miles and you could get lost."

No answer, no movement, but I knew he'd heard me.

That's when the tactile sensations began, the creeping itchiness on my arms and legs. I shivered a little, wondering if I was coming down with a summer cold, not yet connecting the discomfort to the apparition. Because that's what it was, an apparition, make no mistake about it.

The boy abruptly stepped out into a puddle of light dripped down through a hole in the foliage and I recognized George Shackleton.

If I was the kind of person whose perspective was locked onto the past, I would've spent a great deal of time thinking about my childhood friendship with George. We were an unlikely pair, him the bookworm, me the secret hell-raiser. Both of us were caricatures of sorts, lacking the depth that comes with maturity. Even then, George was a professional victim, took the blame for more than a few of my pranks, the soaping of Mrs. Beck's windshield, the bag of sugar dumped in Old Man Grayson's gas tank. It never seemed to bother him that he was being punished for things I'd done.

George suffered from an excess of contentment, as far as I could see. He was happy to accept what life offered and never made the extra effort necessary to achieve something better. The last I had heard of him, he was still stuck in a no-future job, devouring trashy science-fiction novels when he should have been developing his career skills.

The youngster who emerged from the trees was unmistakably George, probably twelve or thirteen years old. He had a crewcut and a Mickey Mouse Club T-shirt and there was a paperback book stuck in his side pocket. I shivered and turned away, more disturbed than I care to remember, and when I looked back, he was gone.

The following week, I checked the phone book. George was still alive. I called, found out he was working as a data entry clerk in Providence, single, overweight, and with no prospects. Rather sad. He suggested we get together, talk over old times, and I reluctantly agreed. "My schedule is pretty tight though. You know how it is, if you want to make something of yourself, you have to eat, sleep, and breathe your job."

He took the hint and never called back.

It was Dolly the next time. Dolly's my wife, a role for which she is well suited, most of the time. Some adjustment was involved, mostly on her part, before we settled into the proper relationship. Dolly is bright, enthusiastic, and even witty in a superficial way, the perfect corporate wife. Her enthusiasms are sometimes misguided, but her intentions are good. When she suggested that she find a job to supplement my inadequate pay as a management trainee, her motives were undoubtedly just as she'd stated them. But I knew where that path would lead, to a split in the definition of family head, and the turmoil that would inevitably follow. I forbade it, but as gently as possible, and truthfully I think she welcomed my decision because it gave her more time to spend with young Eric.

It was Thanksgiving weekend, the year Eric started school. Dolly wanted us all to spend the holiday with her parents in Vermont, but I had planned the time off to work on the following year's budget. Nor was I particularly willing to visit my in-laws. Fred had never liked me, made no secret of the fact, and I think Ernestine's overt friendliness was a mask she wore for her daughter's sake. She was clearly the stronger of the two personalities, though, and Fred's ineffectual job performance had left them with a barely adequate income for their retirement.

In any case, Dolly and Eric were gone for the weekend; her pregnancy wasn't advanced so far that she couldn't safely drive. The house was blissfully free of both Eric's constant caterwauling and Dolly's domestic soundtrack, so I hoped to get considerable work done.

Someone was crying.

I straightened up from my desk, startled and outraged, startled because I had become so absorbed in my work that any outside stimulus was disorienting, outraged because the desolate sobbing clearly originated inside the house. Someone had invaded my home.

Cautiously, I stepped out into the hall, trying to identify the source. It was from the rear of the house, one of the bedrooms. The sound was not at all menacing, but I slipped into the living room, quietly lifted one of the irons from the rack by the fireplace, and made my way to the rear.

The source was the master bedroom. The outrageousness of the intrusion overcame my nervousness and I advanced quickly, the iron at port arms, ready for action.

A half-naked woman was sitting on my bed, our bed, facing away from me.

"Who the hell are you and what are you doing here?"

I had a forewarning of what was to come, although I didn't realize it until later. My skin felt as though it were trying to crawl off and every hair on my body was standing at attention.

The strange woman turned at the sound of my voice, revealing a familiar but disturbing face. It was Dolly, my wife, but not the Dolly I'd seen off early that morning. This was a younger version, her hair as long as it had been when we were first married, the face softer, more innocent. Her left eye was darkly discolored and a thin line of dried blood ran from the side of her mouth down to the point of her chin.

"Why, James? Why? I was just trying to help. You told me how important it was to be nice to people."

I reeled back into the corridor, so disoriented that my stomach lurched threateningly and I had to brace myself by leaning against a wall. It was an exact replay of an incident from my past, one that I admit is not a moment of which I am proud. It was the first company Christmas party since I'd become an assistant supervisor at Eblis, in charge of material handling. I'd stressed to Dolly the importance of making a good impression and she'd cooperated enthusiastically. A bit too enthusiastically, I'd thought at thc time, my judgment distorted by an atypical overindulgence. It was the only time I'd ever struck Dolly, and in retrospect it was almost certainly an overreaction. On the other hand, she'd never challenged my authority again, not even the gentle chiding she'd employed throughout our courtship.

When I regained my self-control and returned to the bedroom, it was empty, of course. I decided I'd been working too hard and went for a lengthy, soothing walk. Retrospectively, I wonder if I truly fooled myself even then, if I had not already realized in some crude fashion what was happening to me.

I was being haunted by the living.

Any doubts I might have had were adequately disposed of a few days later. It was a dark December night, threatening snow although none had fallen. Sales for the past three months had been twenty percent below projections, a foretaste of the general market softness that would plague us for the next two years. Most of my fellow vice presidents chose to characterize it as an anomaly, a combination of dumping by our foreign competitors, uneasiness and underbuying by the major retail chains, and general consumer uncertainty, unfounded but devastating in its effect.

The actual year end figures weren't out yet, but Jamieson, the comptroller, was under certain obligations to me and I knew roughly what they were going to be. Bad, across the line and under the double line, the first operating loss in the company's history.

Spring would see major upheavals at Eblis, careers ended. I was determined that mine would not be one of them.

The position of Vice President of Production and Inventory Planning was newly created and therefore even less secure than usual. My strategy was to present a plan to integrate labor reporting and material handling within that function, eliminating two supervisory positions and at least one laborer. The savings would be significant, and it would also deal a blow to the powerbase of my most serious rival, Sandy Bennett, who headed Production Administration. Sandy was methodical and inventive, but like most of her sex, overly preoccupied with details and lacking the killer instinct. If I worked things right, she'd be put into a position where she wouldn't even be able to argue against the merits of the change without appearing to be self-serving.

I had worked out the personnel realignment, but there were problems with the reporting structure, conflicts of interest that Bennett would jump on in an attempt to discredit the entire proposal. A way around them would have to be found before I could make the presentation, but my mind seemed to have locked up. I decided to take a walk through the factory to clear the fog.

It was dark and quiet on the production floor, the few security lights barely illuminating the walkways. I made my way through the press room, nodded to the security guard as he logged in at the key station, then headed for the polishing area, climbed to the catwalk, and started toward the east end of the building.

I think I knew I was no longer alone even before Larisa called my name. The familiar agitation of my nerves, the clamminess of my skin, the hyperacuity of my senses, all the signs were there.

"Why'd you do it, Nicholson?"

I spun on one foot, searching the shadows, already recognizing the voice. He stepped out into the light, perhaps ten meters away. If it was a hallucination, it was a damned effective one; I even heard the catwalk creak under his weight.

"Joe! What are you doing here?"

"I came to see you, James. We're friends after all. Isn't that what you always told me? Allies against the bumblers at the top."

Larisa had been production scheduler when I was running inventory control and we'd worked out of the same plywood sided office on the manufacturing floor. Neither of us had many secrets, but I'd held onto mine. Joe, foolishly, had been forthright about his difficulties.

"Alliances change, Joe. It's all part of the game. What can I do for you?"

The conversation was surreal, a warped version of reality. On the day of his dismissal, Joe had come to see me all right, cornered me in the plating room. But he hadn't said anything specific, just stared and nodded and turned away, as though he'd read everything he needed to know from my face, my posture, my silence.

"Nothing at all, James. It's my turn to do something for you, as a matter of fact. Call it an installment on an old debt."

"What are you talking about?"

But Joe didn't answer, just reached out and dropped a folder onto the catwalk. "With my compliments." He stepped back into the shadows, and when I looked for him, there was no indication that he'd ever been there physically at all. Which wasn't surprising, since he'd made an abortive attempt on his own life five years earlier and was still paralyzed from the neck down, as I confirmed the next day.

But the folder of papers seemed very solid when I retrieved it, and it contained a detailed plan for the elimination of Sandra Bennett's entire department. The next morning, I couldn't find any trace of those documents, but the knowledge remained, imbedded in my brain, and I worked all night to incorporate them into my own master plan.

It was a solid proposal. Admittedly it was self-serving, but the logic was unassailable, the savings substantial and real, and the elimination of a layer of management would have made the production process more responsive to actual demand. I was really quite proud of it, and under any other circumstances, it would have established me as a force to be reckoned with.

How was I supposed to know that Bennett was fucking Bowes?

The manifestations came with increasing frequency after that, and I quickly came to recognize the forewarnings, the physiological changes triggered by their appearance. Ted Nazarian accosted me one evening while I was walking back from the corner store, berating me for having complained to my parents that he kept putting his hands on me, often in indelicate places. It wasn't entirely a lie; he had taken me out behind the school and spanked me soundly, a clear violation of policy, when he caught me rummaging through Violet MacLennon's locker. If I'd bothered to think about him at all during the previous ten years, I'd have assumed he was dead, but now I think he must still be alive.

Lucy Deacon was sitting in my car one evening, still seventeen years old, belly swollen by an unplanned pregnancy. "You could at least have admitted you were the father, Jimmy. Do you have any idea what I had to go through afterward, when no one believed me and everyone thought I'd just named you because you were good-looking and your parents had money?"

"It wouldn't have worked out," I answered lamely. "Besides, it's not as if I raped you or anything. You practically seduced me, Lucy."

I blinked when she slapped me, and when my eyes opened, she was gone. But my cheek stung anyway.

And so it continued, a parade of people who'd crossed my path to their detriment, all of them still alive insofar as I could tell. I gave up checking after a while. Usually they accused me of past sins, occasionally they offered advice, which I carefully ignored. The encounter with Joe Larisa told me how reliable their council might be.

Had I lost my mind? Was this all guilt spawned delusion? I have to admit that possibility occurred to me more than once. There was no independent confirmation of any of the early manifestations, and my suspicion that I was the target of an elaborate hoax wouldn't stand up under close examination. For whatever reason, by whatever means, I was experiencing visitations from my past, either figments of my own imagination or the product of some natural process outside of everyday logic.

But they weren't delusions. Any doubt I might have entertained on that account was swept away by Scott Talbot.

Scott was one of my few overt enemies. I've had rivals by the score, contenders for this position or that achievement or the girl standing at the bar or the empty space right in front of the barber shop. But only one true enemy. We graduated from Managansett High together; he was the star of the basketball and baseball teams, I was class president. I'd lured Helen Tremblay away from him during our junior year, and he stole Peg Mahaffey when we were seniors.

Through happenstance, we drew adjoining rooms at the University of Rhode Island, and the proximity sharpened our antagonisms. I ran for floor president and Scott quietly but effectively campaigned for my opponent, an out-of-stater whose name I don't even remember. Fortunately, I pledged a fraternity early and moved out of the dorm, but I didn't forget about Scott. Unpaid debts always come back to haunt you; if I let him strike the final blow, he'd consider me fair game ever after.

A year passed, and then another. Juniors now, I was a member of the student government and Scott was likely to bring the basketball team to national attention for the first time in a decade. We'd met briefly on a few occasions during the previous two years, polite but mutually distant encounters at first, more amicable later. Scott either forgot about our earlier animosity or decided it was history, not worth worrying about.

History has a way of striking back at the disloyal.

It wasn't hard to get the drugs; you could buy anything you wanted right on campus with a minimum of hassle. And since Scott didn't lock his door, planting them in his closet wasn't all that difficult either. But the campus police ignored two anonymous calls and a letter, and I was finally compelled to call the state police and pose as one of Scott's "customers" before anyone actually checked it out.

Scott never knew that I was responsible for his expulsion, of course, but I guess he must have suspected.

The envelope was addressed to me and contained a thick packet of photographs. Dolly and Scott at the beach, in a restaurant, in bed together, Dolly performing services that she rarely if ever agreed to unless I insisted.

"It's all over with," she told me tearfully when I confronted her. "It lasted a week or two. You were so tied up at work that I was lonely and Scott came along at the right time I guess." And then she collapsed into tears.

I went looking for him, of course, found him eventually. After a fashion anyway. Scott Talbot was serving a life sentence in a Pennsylvania prison and had been there for nearly ten years. Impulsively I'd asked to see him, found a withered husk of the young man I'd known, nothing at all like the person in the pictures.

I'm not certain he even recognized me.

The encounters came with increasing frequency after that, sometimes overlapping, until I no longer ever felt that I was truly alone. Crowds were the worst; there was always the feeling that someone was staring out at me, accusing me of some imagined crime, threatening retribution or demanding an explanation. Occasionally I was fooled into confronting someone, only to discover it was an innocent bystander with a chance resemblance to a memory from my past. I cultivated calmness, struggled to ignore these interlopers.

I became President of Eblis when Bowes finally lost his battle with cancer. The bastard had refused to resign even when his kidneys were turning to mush and he had to be driven to and from the office.

My tenure lasted exactly one month, to the day, and I resigned only because the alternative was public dismissal. At least by tendering my resignation for "personal reasons," I could hope to find an acceptable position elsewhere.

It was the letters that did me in.

The board of trustees was deluged with them, apparently, letters questioning my character, my honesty, my loyalty to the company, even my competence as a manager. They came from people I had known, some I still knew, others I had forgotten entirely. Scott Talbot wrote from prison, claiming I'd been his partner in a drug distribution scheme. Lucy Deacon insisted I was the father of her illegitimate, now teenaged son. Violet MacLennon accused me of theft and Ted Nazarian insinuated that my sexual orientation was not what it seemed. There were similar accusatory letters from George Shackleton, Jennifer Sears, Penny Redfern, Joe Forester, Alan Crandall, Ted Barnwell, Simone Moran, Joe Larisa, and dozens of others, so many their names tend to blur when I try to remember them.

But one was worse than all the others.

I only found out about it by applying pressure on Jamieson, whose gambling IOUs were still locked in my wall safe. Dolly had written to the board, Dolly, my wife, insisting that I was on the brink of a nervous collapse and that taking on this additional responsibility would certainly kill me.

"I was just trying to do what was best for us," she insisted tearfully. "I love you, James, don't you realize that? And seeing you jumping at shadows, talking to yourself, working yourself to death for no reason . . . I just couldn't let you continue that way without trying to help."

I was past anger, my rage so intense that even violence couldn't have provided an adequate outlet. Speechless, I turned away, meaning to walk out of the house, never to return. And then Dolly stopped me dead in my tracks.

"He said it would be for the best." She didn't even seem to be talking to me.

"Who said, Dolly?"

"What?" Her voice was distant, her eyes focused somewhere else.

"*Who* said it would be for the best?"

"Why, Joe Larisa, of course. Your best friend. He stopped by the house the other day and told me you'd been hallucinating and that he thought the workload was going to kill you."

"Dolly, Joe Larisa is paralyzed. He's been confined to a nursing home in Johnston for almost ten years."

"Well, he must have recovered then, because he seemed quite well when he stopped by here. He told me you have a lot more friends than you realize, James, and that I shouldn't worry anymore because they were all going to be watching out for you from now on."

And I guess they are.

THE WEDDING PARTY

Paul M. Sammon

Note

The following manuscript was recently released by Princeton University, after being discovered in a sealed bundle of personal papers previously stored in that institution's highly regarded Maric Collection.

As for their authenticity, the release of these pages has generated near-universal skepticism. Comments have ranged from "forgery" to "student prank," with the most vociferous objections raised by Paolo Luchessi, eminent graphologist, whose denunciations consist of this single terse statement: "A blatant hoax."

It should be noted, however, that other, equally qualified academics have chosen to challenge the controversy and accept this manuscript as genuine.

With these caveats in mind, then, I leave each reader to formulate his or her own conclusions.

—Paul M. Sammon
Los Angeles CA
September 4, 1993

May 17, 1904
Clinique Sion
Switzerland

My Dearest Mileva:

Your sweet, unexpected gift has given rise to the most marvelous and unforeseen of circumstances; a near-total remission of my previously inviolate *ennui.*

I am overjoyed to report this fact, for, as you know, my lethargic depression lately seemed a dangerously chronic one. And while the previous treatments of this clinic have certainly been vigorous and the ministrations of its staff nothing if not solicitous, I had, in truth, very nearly despaired of ever escaping that acute nihilism brought on by . . . the incident.

Curious, then, is it not, how a simple kindness can heal the soul more surely than the physician's chemical nostrums, or the dream therapy and free association techniques of the radical psychotherapist, Dr. Freud? In any event, I thank you from the bottom of my heart; the flowers, the fruit, the unselfish concern radiating from your card have done more to restore my equilibrium than any existing medication. I look forward to my homecoming with all the joy and eagerness of a schoolboy poised on the eve of the Christmas holiday.

You ask me what transpired last month. To be frank, this query requires a response of the utmost delicacy. For it was precisely the events of that evening (can it only be three short weeks ago?) which precipitated this stubborn spiritual nausea, this unhinging of my previously unshakable belief in a somewhat enigmatic yet finally rational universe. Indeed, the awful inner gloom engendered by that night has not only kept me from divulging my experiences to you, but from most of this institution's staff as well. As our Italian friends are wont to say, *Qualche volta e virtu tacere il vero.**

Yet upon receiving your thoughtful gifts I have decided

---

*"It is sometimes a virtue to conceal the truth."

to unburden myself in exactly the same manner with which we share our intimacies—unadorned, in God's Plain Truth. I beg, however, that you treat these confidences with the utmost discretion. I also ask that you never again discuss the cause of my illness, with myself or any other individual, until that moment when, if ever, I give sufficient indication of having permanently regained my philosophical compass.

You will appreciate the gravity of these requests soon enough.

To the incident, then.

I am, as you know, German-born and bred, although a full-time resident of Switzerland since the age of sixteen. Yet my university studies and subsequent employment had left little time for any detailed exploration of this lovely country. And it was precisely this lack of opportunity, this burning curiosity to more fully experience the face and character of my adopted homeland, which prompted your unselfish suggestion that I take a short leave of absence from the Berne Patent Office. To embark, unaccompanied, upon a week-long railway excursion throughout Switzerland.

Here I must make an awkward confession. Despite your insistence that I leave all cares behind, my work—my *real* work—secretly traveled with me. This resides in a small, somewhat foxed journal, and upon those pages are now scribbled outlines for two studies on photoelectric emission and Brownian Motion. Both papers, you may be pleased to discover, have satisfactorily resolved themselves since my departure from home. A third treatise, however, in which I had hoped to postulate a constant velocity for light, refused to submit to even the most rigorous of assaults.

Thus it was that I found myself rattling through the rooftop of Europe, soothed by the rightfully famed efficiency of our Swiss Federal Railway, vexed by the frustrating certainty that I was tantalizingly close to, yet impossibly stymied by, a solution to this final paper. Lake Lugano, Bellinzona, the Lepontine Alps, all rushed by my carriage window in a spectacular array of color and light. Meanwhile, I wrestled with my formulas.

It was shortly after sampling the storybook pleasures of Lucerne—to which I must expose you—that I then found myself in the southern portion of Switzerland, in that region collectively known as the Valais.

It is a strangely contradictory area, this valley of the upper Rhone. Here the froth of sparkling rivers tumbles helplessly into chasms; verdant meadows house silent, crumbling ruins. And who are the chief inhabitants of the fabled Matterhorn? Forlorn, sagging grain-storage structures, called *mazots.*

A most quixotic countryside. Which did nothing to resolve the problems *re* my third treatise, I assure you. On the contrary, it worsened them, for I soon found myself afflicted with a growing sense of melancholy. Or perhaps it was merely illness; during the past few days small shooting pains and a slight but persistent fever suggested I had contracted some minor respiratory ailment. Traveling alone, therefore, with no recourse to familiar medical aid, I sought to banish these distractions by both redoubling my work efforts and by more generously partaking of the schnapps I habitually carry to soothe my nervous stomach.

Indeed, I had been rather recklessly imbibing that very same substance the day I encountered the wedding party.

It was late afternoon, the 13th of April. I was grappling with a particulary knotty mutation of mathematical physics.

Suddenly, my field of vision swam alarmingly, as my brain was seized in a dreadful vise of pain. *The fever,* thought I, reaching for the *schnapps.* Yet no sooner had these words entered my head than my eyes refocused themselves and the pain faded away.

However, as if now cued by my recovery, raucous sounds abruptly echoed down the carriage corridor. I heard laughter—shouts—a general commotion.

Distracted, I glanced up from my work. During most of the day I had labored here alone, but now clumping footfalls approached my second-class compartment. Since the train had only moments before departed the station at Sierre, that depot for skiers attending the numerous resorts clustered around Lac Grenon, I assumed this cacophony to emanate from a group of thrifty athletes, lower-class travelers happy to have shared a few precious days with the rich, the idle, and the fashionable.

The man who appeared in my compartment's doorway objectified my suppositions. He was young, of perhaps nineteen or twenty years age. Fair-haired, stout, and of medium height, dressed in gay but somewhat threadbare apparel. *A minor clerk or apprentice,* thought I, *on holiday.*

The young man took note of my unintentionally staring eye. To my great astonishment, he winked.

Flustered by this unexpected intimacy, I awkwardly smiled and tipped my hat.

"Aha!" the stranger shouted, flinging wide his arms, as though about to catch something. "A friendly face!"

The man's accent marked him as English; the dark, beautiful young woman who then fell into his embrace, however, could only have been French. She was a demure, breathtaking thing, of liquid eye and voluptuous figure. Perhaps seventeen, cossetted in a worn but carefully patched dress composed of snowy linen and lace.

"Good day to you, sir!" boomed the young man, somehow managing to both bow and hug the young woman at the same time.

"Guten Tag," I replied.

"And a beautiful one at that! Forgive me for asking, but are you alone?"

I nodded.

"But this is intolerable!" the Englishman responded. "It is far too lovely a day for such isolation. May we join you?"

"I have no objection," said I, making room for them by lifting my feet from their resting place upon the opposite seat.

"Wonderful! Come, my dear," the youth said. "We must thank this accommodating fellow immediately!"

With a gentle shove, the Englishman pushed his woman into my compartment. Before entering himself, however, he glanced back down the corridor.

"You were right again, Doctor!" the man shouted, to some other, unseen companion. "There *is* ample room! Make haste—not only have we found seats, we have discovered a friend!"

Then the Englishman bustled in. As he did, the young woman carefully arranged her voluminous skirts to fit the narrow seat.

I smelled a distinct aroma of alcohol. Not mine, I hasten to add.

The woman sat down. I could not help but notice the multitude of tiny, uncooked grains of rice which showered from the folds in her dress. I also spied a prim corsage of exquisite yellow roses, pinned daintily to her sleeve.

Now the Englishman plopped beside me. His hand plunged into a vest pocket. Withdrew a large, much-traveled flask, confirming my suspicions that his good humor was, in part, artificially induced.

He had just begun to open this battered *cruse* when a second man stepped into the compartment.

Compared to his companions, this tall, bald, alarmingly thin intruder was a complete study in opposites. My youthful comrades glowed with health; this third stranger was elderly and wan. They were dressed festively—he was garbed in black. And where the taut, skull-like face of this final arrival was totally pinched of emotion, those of the young couple's were openly radiant with bliss.

Very carefully, the aged man set himself before me. The entire time his flat, opaque gaze never left my face.

Something brushed my knee. The young woman had leaned forward to touch my leg.

"Forgive our intrusion," said she softly, in heavily accented English. "You are very kind to share your compartment."

Her gaze was so sincere, her expression so sweet that I determined then and there to enjoy this invasion to its fullest.

"Nonsense!" I replied, dropping my notebook onto my lap. "It is my sincere pleasure to do so."

"Bravo!" cheered the young man.

I smiled, less timidly this time.

"Forgive my curiosity," said I, "yet I cannot help but notice that the young lady—well, that her corsage, and the rice strewn about Madame's dress—tell me, can it be that you are newlyweds?"

"Bravo again!" responded the Englishman. "Yes, indeed, sir. In point of fact, we have only but two days hence been joined in the holy bonds of matrimony."

"Then might I extend my congratulations?"

"Of course!" the bridegroom replied. "As I extend the liquor!" Whereupon his arm stretched out the proffered flask.

"Edmund!" giggled the bride. "You are too much forward."

"Much too forward, dear," the Englishman corrected, although gently. "In Manchester we say, 'Much too forward.'"

"Pardon," she excused herself.

"No matter," said I, taking the young man's flask. "A wedding is always cause for celebration, *nu?"*

I sipped the matrimonial offering. It was French

cognac, sweet and hot. My stomach growled in protest. But the schnapps I had already taken mingled with the brandy to produce soothing threads of fire.

"Danke," I said, handing back the flask. "You are too kind, sir. My name is Herr—"

"Please!" protested the Englishman, grinning and raising his hands. "No last names! Today we abandon all formality, since we pass as ships in the night!"

"Then call me Albert," I replied, feeling the brandy blossom in my chest.

"And to repeat the obvious, you may call me Edmund," said the groom. He kissed the woman seated before him. "This is Marie."

"Enchanté, madame," I said.

"And this," continued Edmund, indicating his silent, cadaverous companion, "is Doctor Z."

The sallow old man touched the brim of his hat, with skeletally thin fingers.

"Herr Albert," Z. acknowledged. For such an unhealthy-looking fellow his voice was surprisingly penetrating, and deep.

"Albert," instructed Edmund, somewhat mischievously, "you have just been introduced to an exceptional illusionist. One of the best!"

"Ah," I inquired. "You are a magician?"

For the first time, the curious stranger smiled.

"Something like that," he said. "My card."

A small square of parchment had appeared between Z.'s fingertips. I refused to be impressed by such an obvious parlor trick, however, and took hold of the card with obvious disinterest.

Looking down, I beheld a scarlet, flowing script. Written across the card's face were these words: DOCTOR Z.—ILLUSIONIST & PROGNOSTICATOR. NEW YORK.

Such obvious flummery. But any expression of skepticism might be misconstrued as rudeness. So I merely pleasantly asked, "You are traveling abroad?"

"After a fashion."

"We had the good fortune to meet the Doctor yesterday," explained Edmund. "Yet in that short period he has not only secured our trust, but graciously provided for our lodgings as well!"

"Edmund!" chided Marie. "What will Albert think?"

"Only that we are honest and sincere," answered the Englishman. "I make no effort to conceal our diminished circumstances; lack of currency does not necessarily denote a corresponding lack of character, Albert.

"In any event, I am a painter. The proverbial starving artist, if you will. But I lay great hopes in my talents. Great, great hopes! In the meantime"—and here Edmund leaned forward to fondly pat the severe old gentleman's forearm—"I content myself in welcoming all charity, especially that provided by such munificent personalities as Z.'s."

"Even a magus is not immune to newlyweds," muttered the Doctor.

"You are uncommonly generous," said I.

"A pittance," Z. replied.

"I know!" Marie said brightly. "Show Albert something, Doctor Z.! A trick!"

"Oh, but that is not necessary," I demurred.

"Oh, but perhaps it is," countered Z. "Let me think a moment. Ah, yes."

Z. flicked his fingers toward my hands. The gesture took an instant.

"There. It is done. Look at the back of my card."

I hesitated, feeling slightly embarrassed. After all, such men are shameless charlatans. But it was also plain that Z.'s hocus-pocus had mightily impressed this simple young couple. And I truly did not wish to give offense.

"Albert!" Marie implored. "Please do look."

Shrugging, I flipped over Z.'s card.

It was not the picture now smiling up at me which produced my subsequent, startled reaction, for that was merely a lifelike engraving of a woman's face. No, it was the subject; believe it or not, Mileva, the likeness was of you!

"But this is impossible!" I blurted, raising my eyes back to Z.'s. "This woman—"

"I know who she is," Z. interrupted. "Look again."

I lowered my gaze.

The card's surface was empty—your picture was gone.

Marie clapped her hands delightedly at the confusion on my face.

"Did you see?" She laughed excitedly. "Did you see?"

"Impressive, isn't he?" Edmund added. "The Devil knows how he does that; Z. pulled the same trick on us yesterday. Anyway, drink up, Albert. You look as though you need it."

I gratefully accepted the flask and sipped a second time, all the while studying this unusual "Doctor's" face.

His dolorous gaze never left my own.

"A remarkable trick," I acceded.

"I do not traffic in 'tricks,'" snapped Z.

I ignored his irritation and pressed on. "But how could you possibly know? That was a picture of my wife."

Z. merely shrugged. He crossed his arms, stared out the window.

"Afraid you won't get anything that way, old man." Edmund laughed. "Marie pesters Z. mercilessly for his secrets."

"It is no secret that you are a scientist, Herr Albert," Z. abruptly stated, still looking away. "Is this not correct?"

His pronouncement completely mystified me. "Now, how in the world could you possibly know that?"

Z. turned and offered his faint smile.

"Nothing magical, I assure you. Look down."

I looked. My forgotten journal lay sprawled and open on my lap. The words I had inked on its cover, TREATISES ON MATHEMATICAL PHYSICS, were plainly visible to all.

"Ah," said I, smiling, "you have caught me out. But alas, your observation is only partially correct. Science for me remains an avocation, although I hope to someday engage in theoretical work."

"A scientist!" exclaimed Marie, ignoring my protestations. "Such an occupation! I *love* the science!"

"Drop the *the,* my dear," Edmund gently chided. "In English we say 'science.'"

"Science," she repeated.

"You must forgive my wife's enthusiasm," Edmund continued. "She is naturally drawn to the unusual and occult."

"And why not?" retorted Marie, nostrils flaring prettily. "Science is the exploration of mysteries, no? And is not the mysterious beautiful?"

Edmund leaned forward and gently clasped her hand in his own. "Not as beautiful as you," he purred, *"ma chose douce petit amour."**

"Madame is undoubtedly swept away by the moment," observed Z. dryly.

"Again, why not?" she responded. "Look around you, Doctor. The Alps, companionship, science, love! Does not the very air seem fraught with possibilities?"

"Of a sort," replied Z.

"Enough about us," Edmund said. "Where are you traveling, Albert? And why does such a splendid fellow journey alone?"

"A common enough reason," said I. "What you see is a specimen of that ordinary native who has not, as yet, witnessed enough of his homeland."

"Then you are Swiss?" inquired Z.

"By naturalization, yes."

"An interesting people, these Swiss," Z. continued. "Most contradictory."

"In what sense?"

"In the most profound sense. Have not the Swiss a worldwide reputation for neutrality? Yet not so very long

---

*"My sweet little love"

ago they were warriors, mercenaries feared throughout Europe. I have always felt that the Swiss's famed impartiality masks some deeper, long-smoldering hostility."

"Forgive the Doctor's bluntness," Marie quickly interjected. "I am sure he does not mean to appear bold."

"On the contrary," said I, "I somewhat agree with him. Take, for example, the Swiss system of military conscription. *I* have always resented the manner in which this country makes soldiers of every citizen from his eighteenth year to the end of his life, and provides every household with a gun."

"You are a pacifist, then," said Z.

"I am merely stating that no more subtle way of preventing disarmament could be found by an enemy of peace."

"But, Albert!" cried Marie. "This is a country without war!"

"Yes." I concurred. "Do not misinterpret my objections, madame. They are primarily political ones. Actually, I love the Swiss. By and large, they are more humane than any other people among whom I have lived."

"So, Albert," mused Z. "You settle in an island of sanity, encircled by an ocean of blood. But then, the baser human impulses always surround us, do they not?"

"Surely not always," protested Marie.

"Even now," countered Z. He leaned back in his seat. "Shall I make a prediction for you?"

Before we could answer, the old fellow had steepled his fingers and raised them to his lips.

Marie and Edmund were rapt with attention. Obviously, I was to be treated to another manifestation of Z.'s "powers."

Z. closed his eyes.

"As we speak," he whispered, in a low, hoarse voice, "Czar Nicholas of Russia is planning to dispatch his Baltic Fleet to the Pacific. His purpose? To engage the Japanese and wrest control of great shipping lanes. But this will not be easy. First shall come an ongoing game of hide-and-seek. Eventually, however, off the coast of China, these two great navies shall meet. And then shall come a terrible battle, the likes of which the world has rarely seen. Thirty-five Russian ships shall be sent to the bottom, with the loss of hundreds of men."

Z. opened his eyes.

"And the Japanese will lose only three torpedo boats."

Startled silence descended upon our coach, punctuated by creaking old wood and the metallic clicking of carriage wheels.

"A rather dire forecast, Doctor," I finally responded. "Is this a representative demonstration of your prognosticative abilities? If so, you must be a terrible cynic."

"Not at all," came Z.'s immediate reply. "I am an American." And he suddenly unleashed a dazzling smile.

Z.'s *riposte* was so unexpected, his manner so instantly convivial, that I could not help myself; a small but sincere laugh escaped my lips.

"Told you, Albert!" Edmund said. "Better watch yourself!"

Within moments, our festive mood reasserted itself. We laughed and jested like the closest of friends. Even Z. joined in, his quick, unpredictable wit no doubt one reason he had so thoroughly captivated this otherwise incompatible couple.

Afternoon wore on toward early evening. Outside, without the coach window, vast cataracts and pristine villages hurried by, gilded by an enormous setting sun. The *cognac* continued its friendly circular route; when it expired, I offered the remainder of my *schnapps.*

By now the Doctor was disparaging the talents of a fellow countryman named Harry Houdini, one whose act, Z. insisted, depended solely upon smoke and mirrors. "This is not my way at all," the Doctor emphasized. "My illusions are supported by sound scientific principles."

At which point Z. made the offer which would forever change my life.

"You are a fine gentlemen, Albert," he presently said. "Patient and generous. I would be remiss if I did not inform you that we are traveling toward a very special entertainment. Would you care to join us?"

"Capital idea!" enthused Edmund.

"Oh yes!" trilled Marie.

"Sorry?" I replied, somewhat befuddled. Our frequent libations had, by this point, made me very nearly drunk.

"Doctor Z. is *inviting* you, Albert," chirped Marie.

"A private performance," explained Z., "solely for the benefit of this charming young couple. And yourself, of course."

"Oh, but I cannot," I began. "My work—"

"Nonsense!" insisted Edmund. "With all due respect, old boy, *bugger* your work!"

"Edmund!" cried Marie.

"My work is my life," I responded, rather pretentiously.

"As our love is ours," said Edmund, contritely squeezing his paramour's hand.

"Albert, you must accept!" Marie insisted. "Doctor Z. has promised to tell our fortunes!"

"Jolly right," added Edmund. "Hang it all, man, this will be an adventure!"

"A comfortable one, I assure you," continued Z. "My home lies in the village of Vex,* by the town of Sion. We are very nearly there now. And while my dwelling is a perfectly acceptable one, it is also somewhat lonely, I fear. The addition of your company would considerably brighten this otherwise dull old man's life."

"Yours is a kind offer," I conceded, "but—"

"Oh, please, Albert," implored Marie. "Please say that you will agree. For me?"

---

*Pronounced *Vay*

"Well . . ." I said.

"It's not very cricket to rebuff a young lady's wishes," Edmund grinned.

Mileva, you know me well. I am an academic; not for me are the world's coarser pleasures. Yet with the good cheer of such amiable companions—and all the spirits we had consumed—how could I refuse?

"Then with many sincere thanks, I must, of course, accept."

"Bravo!" cheered Edmund, waving the schnapps above his head. "To this evening, then. And the kindness of strangers!"

"To the kindness of strangers!" repeated Marie, echoing her husband's toast.

"To love and to work," said Z. quietly, his sunken stare again riveted upon my face.

Twilight bled into night. We smoked, we jested, we consumed my bottle of *schnapps*. Edmund proved to be an enthusiastic art student, regaling us with countless tales of Joseph Turner and Winslow Homer. Marie, on her part, revealed a genuinely kind disposition, one predisposed toward succor, not condemnation.

As for Z., the man continued to intrigue me. While he made no further attempt to enthrall us with his talents—in fact, the Doctor seemed perfectly content to only occasionally snatch the odd trinket from behind Marie's ears—he betrayed a host of other idiosyncracies which I found strangely tantalizing.

His accent and manner of speech, for example; both were unusual, even for an American. And Z. betrayed a subtle but intense preoccupation with the most trifling social niceties. As if he were a freshly minted coin, newly introduced to European currency.

In any event, we soon arrived at the station of Sion.

It was always a favorite destination of my mother's, this capital of the Valais. Well-known for its glorious springs and autumns, locally famed as a favored post on the ancient trading routes between Italy and France, Sion has a history dating from Roman times. And as we disembarked from the train to board the small, horse-drawn cart which awaited near the platform, a cart Z. claimed was his own, I kept searching for and was ultimately rewarded with a glimpse of Valere and Tourbillon, those two disintegrating castles whose hulking silhouettes watch over and dominate this fascinating town.

Z. climbed into the cart's driving seat and took up the reins. I settled in beside him; Marie and Edmund made themselves comfortable in the rear. A crack of the whip, something muttered by Z. in French, and with a swift *klip-klop* his sleepy horses trotted forward.

We were off. As we relaxed within the cart, snug within our overcoats, Z. acquainted us with Vex.

"My village lies but an hour away," said he. "I hopc you will enjoy it; Vex is particularly appealing at night. One note of caution, however."

"This is?" inquired Marie.

Z. swiveled his head to address the young woman. "A silly rumor regarding my house. Many of the locals think it haunted."

The absurd pronouncement hung in the air alongside the smoke of our breaths. Edmund laughed.

"Marvelous!" said he. "Then we are certain not to be disturbed! Never fear, good Doctor; true love always keeps evil spirits at bay!"

Marie joined her husband's laughter. I remained silent.

"You are not a believer, Albert?" Z. inquired.

"In phantoms?" I replied. "Not at all. While the subject does hold some small personal interest, particularly as to the true cause and origins of these so-called manifestations, I could hardly call myself a scientist and still believe in ghosts."

"Of course," agreed Z. amiably. "Science has yanked the bedsheets off this ignorant folklore to reveal the all-too-corporeal body of superstition beneath. Has it not?"

I found his wording slightly provocative, but refused to take the bait.

"There are no ghosts," I repeated.

"Yes," Z. replied. "But what if—and believe me, dear Albert, I say this only in the, ah, *spirit* of scientific conjecture—what if there *were* phantoms? Ghosts not only of the present, but of the past and days to come?"

I smiled. "Then science is meaningless, and our lives circumscribed by forces we may never comprehend."

"Exactly," nodded the Doctor. "Perhaps tonight's little presentation will prove that."

"Are you inferring that you intend to show Albert a *ghost?"* Edmund questioned excitedly.

Z.'s expression was inscrutable.

"Marvelous!" Edmund then enthused, taking the old man's silence for assent. "Our futures and Albert's phantom, all in one night! What an evening this will be!"

Around us, Sion was slumbering. Its shutters were pulled tight, its candles extinguished. The smooth street beneath our horses' hooves soon gave way to well-maintained dirt tracks, which turned and twisted through immaculately manicured fields bordering the town's perimeter. Overhead rode a pale full moon, tossed on a sea of stars. And despite the chill air the night was relatively mild, with no hint of that furious weather which can so unexpectedly descend upon this lovely country.

Eventually we ascended a steep, ramplike trail, one cut into the base of a mountain a few kilometers distance from the town.

"The climb begins," said Z. "Watch for the view; it is quite spectacular."

Our travel then resolved itself into repetitious regularity. Climb an earthen ramp, swing around a curve to the left, climb another ramp, turn toward a curve on the right, and so on and so forth. But this monotony was, as Z. had promised, relieved by the tremendous vistas sprawled beside the mountain trail; the moonlight transformed the river, ever-dwindling fields, and tiny town below us into the playthings of a giant child.

"Vex," Z. said.

Our carriage now entered a small, completely vertical village. I use the term advisedly; Vex was seemingly without a single horizontal line. Narrow cobblestoned lanes rose and dipped alarmingly, with small dairyman's huts or larger bourgeois homes raked at dizzying angles along the streets. Even the town square, with its low church and modest greengrocers, was a jumble of conflicting angles.

"What do you think, madame?" inquired Z.

"It is everything you said!" came Marie's happy reply.

"Breathtaking!" agreed Edmund.

This was true. We were passing through a quaint cobblestoned street; between its darkened edifices one caught glimpses of a massive valley, a titanic "V" composed of forested pinnacles and sheer cliffs. These piled higher and ever upward, toward an apex of twin snow-covered peaks.

"It is breathtaking, isn't it?" echoed Z. "Nature alone seems blessed with such inherent majesty."

A moment later we had halted before an undistinguished dwelling. This was Z.'s home, a traditional, two-story place.

The lower level was sheathed in gray flagstones, while the upper story, composed of roughhewn timbers, revealed bare logs whose surfaces had been blasted black by the fierce Swiss winters. Gaily painted shutters on the second floor were flung wide to expose darkened windows. Above these hovered a sharply angled roof.

All in all, hardly the traditional structure of grotesque Gothic literature.

Z. looked up at his windows and frowned. Their murkiness seemed to offend him.

"This will never do," grumbled Z. He languidly waved a hand.

Buttery illumination spilled into our cart; above, the windows were ablaze with light.

"Z!" enthused Edmund. "You are a most remarkable fellow!"

"But your *maison* is charming, monsieur," said Marie. "How could anyone think it haunted?"

"Strange lights. Unexplained sounds. The usual phenomena," answered Z., stepping down from his cart. "Although I myself have yet to experience anything out of the ordinary."

Z. paused before the house's locked double doors. Raised his arms.

"Now, how goes that timeless fairy tale?" said he. "Ah, yes—*Abracadabra!*"

And as Z. mystically waved his palms, like some gaunt, sickly *vizer,* there came the distinct *klick!* of unlatching tumblers, and the previously bolted doors opened slowly into the night.

"I say, old chap!" chuckled Edmund. "Is there no end to your surprises?"

Z. favored the Englishman with another of his rare smiles. "This is but an aperitif, Edmund. The banquet lies ahead. But come, let us remove ourselves from the chill."

We dutifully followed Z.'s instructions, at length finding ourselves in a small kitchen illuminated by a large hanging lamp. The room was obviously little-used; thick gray dust lay everywhere, while tattered cobwebs fluttered gently near the ceiling.

"Forgive an old bachelor's pitiful housekeeping," said Z. "Your coats?"

We removed these outer garments. Z. hung them carefully on an ornately curved coatrack, one standing beside a narrow wooden staircase of beautifully waxed pine.

"The salon waits above," Z. informed us. "Shall we continue?"

Chattering excitedly, the newlyweds ascended the staircase, Z. and I close behind.

The stairway terminated in a large, shadowed chamber of near-monastic simplicity. There were no decorations and very little in the way of basic creature comforts here. In fact, three overstuffed chairs and a single, waist-high cabinet laden with various delectables comprised the totality of the room's furnishings.

Oddly, there was not even a bed. Still, the few candles attached to the room's smooth, pine-paneled walls revealed that here, at least, were no signs of a solitary existence. This chamber was spotlessly clean.

"Help yourselves to refreshments," said the Doctor. "My house, such as it is, is yours."

We immediately clustered around the table, famished by our trip. Yet as we busily served ourselves—cutting wedges of cheese, pouring various liqueurs into tall crystal goblets—I could not help but find the starkness of this empty chamber somewhat unusual. So I examined the place more closely, busying myself with what I thought were quick, surreptitious glances.

"You like my home, Albert?" Z. suddenly said.

The Doctor had caught me out. Again. Confound the man—did nothing escape him?

"It is rather . . . Spartan," I replied.

Z. chuckled.

"What did you expect? Heavy draperies? Incense burners? Crystal balls?"

"Forgive me. I meant no offense."

"None was taken. You see, I prefer simplicity. The severe order of the cosmos. But here." Z. picked up a wine bottle and poured me a generous libation. "This burgundy is of exceptional vintage. I think you will find it interesting."

My cup was quickly filled. Z. then lowered the bottle and clapped his hands.

"On with the festivities!" said he. "Please seat yourselves."

Our chairs had been arranged in a straight line. Marie sat beside me; on her left sprawled Edmund, whose heavy eyes and drooping lips suggested that this constant celebration had finally claimed the better of him.

Z. remained behind his cabinet, facing our chairs. Very gracefully, he honored us with a courtly bow.

"My friends, your presence gladdens my heart," he said. "I want you to know that I have looked forward to this moment for quite some time. Indeed, I think you might be amazed to discover just how strenuously I have labored merely to arrive here."

We lightly applauded, passing smiles among ourselves.

"And now, a toast!" Z. commanded.

We raised our glasses with Z.'s own.

"My hope is simply this," he said. "That Time forgives me."

So saying, Z. drained his glass.

We, on our part, paused. What had the good Doctor said?

"Come, come," chided Z. "It is an obscure American saying. Drink up!"

We did.

Z.'s full-bodied burgundy passed between my lips. As promised, the wine was quite exceptional, although I did notice a distinctly acidic tang which I attributed to some peculiarity of the local soil.

"Doctor?" Marie now asked. "How do you propose to foretell our futures? Shall you read our palms, or examine the humps on our heads? I am something of a devotee of phrenology, you know."

"Bumps," corrected Edmund wearily. "It's bumps, Marie."

Z. lowered his glass and placed it on the cabinet. "That would prove totally unnecessary, dear lady. My practice involves methods far beyond a laying of hands on your Mount Of Venus."

This titillating response left Marie squirming with excitement. "Such suspense, Edmund! It is like a playlet from the *Grand Guignol,* is it not? I shiver with anticipation!"

Edmund attempted to return Marie's enthusiasm with a halfhearted smile. This was broken by a yawn, instead.

"Now—a moment of silence, if you will," Z. requested.

The magician closed his eyes. Slowly, he began to inhale and exhale, deeply and rhythmically.

The heavy night settled around us. We waited. In the interim, I was struck by the evening's profound stillness. Only the sounds of Z.'s labored susurrations could be perceived in the absolute quiet.

"Spirits?" Z. suddenly shouted. "Hear me!"

I started, nearly spilling my wine.

"Spirits!" Z. repeated. "Heed my call! Remove our blinders; tear back the veil! For is not all we see and seem, but a dream within a dream?"

As the Doctor paused melodramatically, I allowed myself a tiny grin. The foxy old plagiarist—did he not suspect that I, too, had read my Poe?

"Time is a stream which flows in both directions!" continued Z. "So now, push *forward* that stream! Grant those present a glimpse of—the future!"

Z. paused again.

Abruptly, his entire body jerked, as if subjected to a tremendous galvanic force. Z.'s lips writhed; when the Doctor's mouth opened again, the voice which issued forth was both stentorian and ominous.

"The past, the present, the future, all are one," Z. intoned. "We are bound within an inexorable loop of time, locked in hopeless perpetuity. Destined for only sadness and pain."

Sipping my burgundy, I felt a small twinge of disappointment. I had expected better of Z. After all, this moment of 'possession' and its attendant, funereal trappings are well-known spiritualist techniques.

"Darkness," Z. went on sepulchrally. "Darkness! Woe! Pain! There is no joy or certitude in life. Only the inevitability of the grave."

I peeked at my companions. Unlike myself, they apparently were not prepared for this traditional shift in atmosphere. Edmund was frowning; Marie was nervously rubbing her hands.

Then, from the corner of my eye, I spied a sudden movement.

A weak shadow was flickering across the nearest chamber wall, darting restlessly from floor to ceiling. It paused. Moved. Paused again. A vague, shapeless mass of purest ebony.

Then Marie gasped. For all at once, *the shadow had detached itself from the wood, briefly alighted on Z.'s shoulder, and flown off over the Frenchwoman's head!*

Ah—this was more like it!

Marie quickly twisted around in her chair to follow the progress of the shadowy thing. We all saw it alight upon another wall, to once again take up its crawling, inconclusive, two-dimensional quest.

In a trice, this object was joined by a second blot of darkness. Then another. A fourth. A fifth.

Within a heartbeat, legions of indistinct adumbrations were fluttering about the room.

I studied Z. carefully, eager to discover his method for accomplishing this trickery. Yet the man's eyes remained closed; his hands, empty and visible, hung loosely by his sides.

Now the lights began to dim.

I glanced sharply to my left. Mounted on this wall was a single candle, whose tiny tongue of flame was quite perceptibly lowering. Growing smaller. Shrinking and guttering in its socket.

"Edmund?" whispered Marie.

At the sound of her voice, Z.'s arms began to rise. Higher and higher, until held out stiffly before him. Hands extended, palms down.

Z. suddenly opened his eyes. They were cloudy and somber, highlighted by eerie pinpricks of illumination.

"The future has arrived," intoned the magician. His voice had taken on a curious echoing quality. "Come—ask your questions."

Not one of us replied.

"Pitiful mortals," admonished Z. "Are you frightened? Ask . . . your . . . questions!"

"Doctor?" Marie ventured. "All my life have I wished to perform the good acts. My hopes are that, someday, I will learn the art of nursing. To become one of those fortunate few who tend the dying and the sick. Shall this come to pass?"

Z. considered this question for a very long time.

"Your wish is hopelessly romanticized, madame," came the delayed, dirgelike reply. "Caring for the dying—rubbing their feet, fetching them a sip of water—is endlessly tedious. Boring, in fact. Besides, you are without a future."

"What!" Edmund exclaimed. "But this is outrageous!"

"Silence!" thundered Z.

Marie, for her part, was shocked into silence. And Edmund was no longer half-asleep; instead he perched on the edge of his seat, glaring up at Z.

There now fell upon that dark, eerie chamber another hushed silence, one only broken by the puzzlingly morbid Doctor himself.

"Are there no futher questions?" Z. demanded.

Marie tentatively reached out to touch Edmund's arm. "Ask him, Edmund," she said.

"I will most certainly not!" he angrily replied.

"Surely the Doctor is mistaken," said she. "Do not concern yourself for my sake. It is only a prediction, after all. Ask him."

"Absolutely not!"

Marie's arm dropped to her side. "Then I shall."

"Marie—" began her husband.

But the Frenchwoman shook her head.

"Doctor," she asked a second question, in a slightly more timorous voice, "my husband loves art. Will he someday be a successful painter?"

Z. laughed then, Mileva. Actually *laughed.*

"Painter?" he responded. "Petty, petty man. Your dreams will turn to ashes, as your body rots to dust. Yours will be a broken life; forgotten, empty, and alone."

"Enough!" roared Edmund, springing to his feet. "You are mistaken, sir! Most wretchedly wrong!"

Marie began to weep.

"The spirits are angered!" Z. suddenly shouted. "They say—no—they *demand* that you accept their token from beyond! The proof that will stifle your disbelief!"

And then—

I swear to you, my darling wife, that what next transpired was no illusion, no optical aberration induced by either fever or my now-empty glass. For in the next instant, materializing out of nowhere, there rested upon Z.'s previously empty forearms a large white book!

The Doctor left his post and slowly advanced on Marie. "A wedding present," said he gravely, depositing the book upon the young woman's lap. "And your future."

Marie seemed paralyzed, frightened into mute immobility.

"Open it!" demanded Z.

Marie haltingly reached down. Opened the book. Stared.

A flurry of anxious emotions swept across her face. Sorrow. Confusion. Uncertainty. Fear.

Then, most unexpectedly, Marie smiled.

"But, darling!" she exclaimed. *"Regarde!"*

Casting baleful glances at Z., the angry Englishman

dropped to his knees and looked at Marie's book. My angle was such that I too, without moving, could clearly see that at which they gazed.

This was no *grimoire* or moldering sorcerer's tome, Mileva. No; it was an *album*. The sort of common family treasury in which are hoarded the fruits of that delightful process called photography. But the pictures pasted in *this* volume, in neat orderly rows, were not the monochromatic by-products of Mr. Eastman's industry.

Rather, what we now gazed upon, in silent awe, were *full-color* pictures, whose astonishing realism and clarity were unmatched by any photographic means I have ever encountered, orthochromatic or otherwise.

I could not help myself; I leaned forward to touch these incredible things. As I did, an awful vertigo seized me. This nausea quickly passed, however, and I proceeded to lay my hand upon the book.

Whereupon I fell back into my chair as though stung. My palm had encountered the unmistakable impression of rough fabric and smooth paper; those impossible pictures were *real*.

"Doctor Z!" I cried. "This is no trick of the senses—it is genuine! Tell me quickly, please! Who has produced such a thing?"

Z. did not deign to favor me with a reply. Instead, he stood rigidly erect, face submerged within reeling shadows.

"Oh, Edmund," breathed Marie. "Look! It is us, is it not?"

I gazed again upon that book, confirming that this astonishing artifact did indeed contain representations of them both. But how could this be? For these pictures depicted Edmund and Marie's wedding ceremony—an event which had occurred *before* they met Doctor Z.!

Yet here they were, frozen in the act of entering a small chapel. Of participating in the actual nuptial ceremony. Of bestowing upon one another a chaste wedding kiss.

"What is this, Z.?" Edmund demanded, although somewhat less forcefully than before.

Still no answer from the Doctor.

Marie grasped the first page of the album. Turned it back to reveal the second.

At which juncture her face went completely white. A low moan escaped the woman's lips; she clutched at her heart.

Until that very moment, Mileva, I had thought Z. a transparent trickster. Talented, yes. Erudite, certainly. But overall a garden variety fraud. Even his photographs could have been obtained in some rational way.

But now? I cannot supply *any* rationalization for the sight which awaited us on that accursed book's second page. I am only certain of one fact; that Z.'s casual comment at the threshold of his home, the one concerning aperitifs and banquets, had been an ominous forecast of the truth.

What we beheld, again, were only pictures. But this is like saying that the plague was only a minor illness.

For spread out before us, in row after succeeding row, was the staggering depiction of Edmund and Marie's lives *in the future!*

It was a horrible one. One snapshot portrayed the couple as poverty-stricken and prematurely aged, living in a drear, filthy hovel. The next showed Edmund brooding at a bare table, his sole companion a half-empty bottle of gin. Another froze the couple in dreadful argument, as Edmund's fist struck Marie's chin.

Marie said nothing. Like a silent automaton, she once again turned the page.

What followed was even worse. The Frenchwoman, frail and emaciated, now lay upon some foul, shabby bed; eyes closed, hands joined upon her breast. Following this was a photograph of her tombstone, with a stone-faced Edmund keeping solitary vigil in some lonely cemetery. Now came a picture of Edmund raising a pistol to his temple; here was his limp, awkward corpse, sprawled upon a boulevard as a stray cat gnawed hungrily at the Englishman's shattered face . . .

"Edmund!" wailed Marie.

Her husband snatched the book away as if it were diseased. Flinging it at the Doctor's feet, Edmund sprang up, uttered a terrible oath, and seized the Doctor by his lapels.

"Monster!" cried he, shaking the still silent man's body. "Why do you show us such things?"

I too struggled to rise, so as to separate the men. But a strange lethargy gripped me—I literally could not move.

Z. apparently did not require my assistance. He seemed quite unperturbed by the threat of Edmund's violence; in fact, the Doctor returned the young man's outburst with a smirk.

"Are you not satisfied?" Z. goaded. "I thought you wished to see the future."

"But to perpetrate this—this *outrage,*" Edmund sputtered.

"I have granted you a great service, Edmund," Z. replied serenely, heedless of the huge hands which held him in their grip. "Many people must reach my own age before finally shedding their illusions."

Edmund did not reply. Instead, he angrily threw back an arm. Balled up his fist.

"Edmund!" Marie cried. "Do not harm him!"

"Tsk," said Z. "Such ingratitude. Take this, young man."

Whereupon Z. reached into his inner pocket, withdrew a small revolver, and shot Edmund cleanly through the head.

A loud report banged through the chamber. Edmund's eyes rolled back. Wordlessly, without further sound, the young man collapsed upon the floor.

"Edmund!" screamed Marie.

Z. shifted the revolver to his other hand. Glanced down at the woman.

"Shall I be a bit more specific about the details of your own demise, my dear?" he calmly continued, as if absolutely nothing untoward had occurred. "Or rather, should I say one *possible* death? It will be a heart attack, brought on by a great influenza epidemic, which shall sweep across the globe. As for the date of your passing, this will take place on June second, Nineteen Hundred and—"

"No *more!*" Marie shrieked.

"Ah, well. Perhaps you are right. It is easier this way."

And with that, Z.'s revolver barked again.

A neat, round hole appeared in Marie's breast, accompanied by a thin but powerful jet of blood. It splashed across the forgotten photo album as the woman's lifeless body slumped back heavily in her seat.

I sat perfectly immobile, blinking stupidly in disbelief. Somewhere, on a deep cellular level, my body screamed at me to take flight. *Yet still could I not rise from that damnable chair!*

For a long, infinitely protracted moment, Z. seemed lost in thought. He quietly contemplated the bodies before him.

Then the Doctor sighed and put away his gun.

"Well, Albert," said he. "At least now we can talk normally. Speaking in this idiom is a pain."

Obviously, the man was hopelessly insane. Yet despite the hideous fear which gripped my body, my mind remained clear. I knew, *knew* that I must, somehow, at any cost, remain perfectly calm. My very life depended on this.

So, swallowing, I desperately sought for the proper words and timbre least likely to inflame Z.'s murderous lunacy.

"Doctor Z.?" I quavered. "Please. Can you not compose yourself? We must talk."

Z. smiled. "That's a good one, Albert. Damn rational of you. I'm impressed."

He strode back to the cabinet and poured himself a large glass of port. "You know, for a moment there, right after I pulled the trigger on old Edmund, I honestly didn't know what to expect. Like the universe might rupture or something. He really was supposed to die in Paris, you know."

The man was raving. His speech, his demeanor, all were markedly and drastically changed.

I tried to rise once again. Could but shift slightly in my seat.

"Careful," Z. said. "Don't fall over, you might hurt yourself. The drug I slipped you is pretty powerful."

"Drug?" I replied thickly. My mouth seemed packed with cotton wool. Then I recalled the bitter taste of the burgundy.

"The wine?"

"Right again," Z. responded. "Excellent deduction. But hey, empirical reasoning always was your specialty, right, Albert?"

"I am poisoned!"

"Hardly. It's what you'd probably call an opiate. Strong but not lethal. You aren't going anywhere for a while, though."

Once again I tried to reason with him. "Doctor, those young people meant you no harm. Why then did—did you—"

"Murder them, Albert? Because I can get away with it, that's why. Anyway, I wouldn't waste my time on those two. They were a minor component in a much larger project."

Z. drained his glass. Poured himself more port.

"Although I will admit my spontaneous little experiment with the gun raises all *kinds* of questions. But how was I to know? This is my first trip."

I looked away. Goggled at the still-bleeding bodies.

"Forget them, Albert," Z. said. "It's you I really want."

At this, and despite herculean efforts to the contrary, my terrified body betrayed me. Huge tears leaked from the corners of my eyes; tonight, I was certain, would I die.

Therefore, realizing I had no hope, I threw all caution to the winds. Shouted, "Why? *Why have you done this?*"

Z. sipped his port. Fixed me with another of those bright, glittering stares.

"Why?" he repeated. "The ultimate question. Never mind. Let's cut to the chase, Albert. Get down to brass tacks. All right?"

Z. set down his glass. Stooped and reached into the cabinet.

He withdrew another mystery. This was a small black box, composed of some strange pebbled material with a brightly artificial sheen. Small buttons and tiny winking lights covered its surface; one side was inlaid with a large, beautifully polished lens.

Z. now set this enigmatic contraption upon the cabinet, so positioning its lens as to face the far wall. After which he retrieved his wine and sauntered over to Edmund's empty, waiting chair.

Z. toed aside the boy's corpse. Sat down.

I struggled once again, frantic to remove myself from such a close proximity to this dangerous lunatic. But though I attempted to grip the arms of my chair, my shaking hands—palsied, useless things—fell back upon my lap.

"What . . . do you intend?" I managed to gasp.

"I promised you phantoms, Albert," came Z.'s eerily cordial reply. "Don't you remember? Spooks? Ghosts? First, though, I want to show you something. Although I warn you, these aren't the apparitions you expect."

With that Z. reached into his coat pocket. I tensed. But instead of the pistol, what emerged was a flat, rectangular mechanism. Like the lensed box it too was covered with buttons and twinkling lights.

"A bit bright in here, don't you think?" Z. asked.

He thumbed a button on the object within his hand. At once, the candles snuffed out.

We now sat in near-total darkness, relieved by rays of milky moonlight.

"Showtime," Z. said, pointing the flat object at the box. He pressed another button.

At this juncture I must momentarily interrupt my narrative, dear Mileva, to posit that what next occurred may indeed have been an example of, as our treacherous host himself had so cunningly insinuated scant minutes before, Mr. Poe's "dream within a dream."

How else to explain the sudden beam of light which leapt, unbidden, from that apparatus on the cabinet? How else to rationalize the large, fantastically vivid, *moving color images* which so instantaneously appeared on the wall?

But I digress; let me continue.

Z.'s apparatus invited comparison with that marvelous invention of Thomas Edison, the one dubbed the Vitascope. However, *this* picture show was as far removed from Edison's jerky, sepia-toned novelties as are simple fireworks from the mighty explosives of Alfred Nobel.

I cannot emphasize strongly enough the bizarre realism of Z.'s nickelodeon; this was more lifelike than life itself. Yet life was patently not of Z.'s concern; now I witnessed a cavalcade of horrors. A panoply of suffering made all the more unbearable by the macabre, mute attendance of Edmund and Marie.

At first I merely beheld a rushing mountain stream, fouled by masses of floating, bloated fish. But then came vistas of endlessly rolling fields, blasted into dust. Scenes of unbelievable urban devastation, with whole cities reduced to smoking rubble and twisted steel.

"Impossible!" I breathed.

"Pay attention," snapped Z. "This is the good part."

Writhing upon Z.'s wall were heaps of human corpses,

which were slowly being pushed into deep pits by strange machines. This vision was replaced by scores of naked children, burned, blistering wretches with ragged, peeling skin. Now came the awfulness of some grotesque hospital ward, whose pitiful victims were afflicted with monstrous deformities; hands puffed into monstrous claws, eyes sliding jellylike from sockets.

Even worse, these agonizing images were suddenly accompanied by perfectly natural *sounds.* I know, Mileva, I know; this is an impossibility. But I *heard* the dreadful shrieks of the mutilated. Suffered the low moans of the maimed. Became a stricken, unwilling receptacle for the death rattle of a world.

Sickened, nauseated, giddy with disgust, I tried to look away. But by this point my dreadful paralysis had spread, and even my neck refused movement.

Z.'s ghastly exhibition was picking up tempo, now, with more and more of its images blinking by with greater speed. I spied burning bridges. Shattered homes. A crushed, crawling infant, its entrails trailing in the dirt.

Suddenly, there came a titanic explosion! A thundering concussion! A flash of unbearable, retina-searing light!

At least my eyelids still obeyed me. I closed them, dazzled by the searing brightness which had blazed upon Z.'s wall.

But then my ears perceived silence.

Cautiously, I reopened my eyes.

No longer did the beam arrow forth from its box; the wall was blank and empty.

Z.'s ghastly magic lantern show had reached its apocalyptic conclusion.

The Doctor finished his wine. Rising from his seat, he lanquidly stretched, then stood to tower above me.

"Well, Albert," Z. asked conversationally. "What'd you think of all that?"

"Abomination!" I managed to utter. "Blasphemy!"

"No," he replied. "The future. Your future. One that will engulf the world."

"Why torment me with these sights?"

Z.'s smile was twisted.

"Because they're the fruits of your own labors, Albert."

"You are demented!"

"Wrong again. Simply dying, from an offshoot of your obsessive research. You see, I have this disease, Albert. Never mind its name; it no longer concerns me. For I have already seen the precise moment and manner of my death, just as I have already witnessed your own conception."

"What you claim is incomprehensible! I cannot understand any part of it!"

"No?" Z.'s tone was openly mocking. "Such a shame. You, the great genius."

"Brute!" I shouted. "Heartless fiend! What you have shown me is horrible enough! But to so cavalierly destroy the lives of these innocent young people!"

"The great wheel turns, Albert. We move from civility to distrust, charity to brutality. An appreciation of spirituality and learning reduced to the wholesale slaughter of same. Besides, those kids represented everything I despise. Sentiment. Gentility. Hope."

Z. paused and carefully removed the corsage from Marie's lifeless arm. With equally careful movements, he pinned the bloody spray onto his own lapel.

"Now I have a present for you, Albert," he continued. "Wouldn't want you thinking I'm an insensitive host, especially after presenting those two with such a lovely gift."

Whereupon Z. squatted beside my chair, opened my valise, and removed my notebook.

I could not move. Dared not speak. Meanwhile, Z. rapidly penciled something inside my journal, using my own writing instrument.

The Doctor replaced the book within my bag and regained his feet.

"That was your gift, Albert," Z. said. "Try and remember it. You may find it useful, later on."

"God!" I exclaimed. "Why would one such as *you* give me help?"

"You misunderstand," Z. replied evenly. "I don't want to help you. I don't want to help anybody. But I must. Without my little present, we never would have met."

His words were so incongruous, his actions so bizarre, that I was suddenly seized with a great mortal terror.

"You reek of death," I gasped, through nervously chattering teeth. "Please, Z., I beg you. Release me."

Z. shook his head. "Not quite yet. There's still the matter of your ghost."

This implied threat provoked a sudden inhalation of breath.

"Oh, come on, Albert," Z. said. "Relax. I'm not going to hurt you. Besides, you've already seen your phantom."

"What?" I cried. "Where?"

"Right here."

"I see nothing!"

"Then you're not trying. Look closer."

Z. indicated the inert figures of Edmund and Marie.

"You see?" said he. "There it lies." And he smiled.

"The specter of innocence," Z. said.

"Devil!" I shrieked. "Who are you?"

Z. painfully took hold of my jaw, grasping it between his thumb and forefinger. He wrenched back my head. I was now forced to gaze upward into his gaunt, skeletal face.

"Want a hint, Albert?" Z. hissed. His sour breath blasted into my nostrils like an icy demon's from a frozen hell. "Here's one—we're related. Bet you never deduced that, huh?"

"But your name is Z.!" I protested.

"Forget Z.," the Doctor said. "He doesn't exist."

The old man lowered his face until it was mere inches from my own.

"Besides, where I come from, folks call me Stein."

This was too much. With that last, crazed pronouncement ringing in my ears, Z.'s sunken eyes seemed suddenly to swallow me up. The awful vertigo which had previously threatened to overwhelm my senses returned in full, triumphant force, and I mercifully passed from consciousness to oblivion.

Most of the rest, you know.

The stationmaster at Sion discovered me the following morning, sprawled senseless on a platform bench, feverish and shaking. I was fortunate; he was a kindly man, and upon the discovery of my identification papers, the stationmaster at once notified the nearby *clinique.* It was the staff of this institution which then contacted you, of course. Whereupon followed my subsequent delirium, depression, and silence.

One which has remained unbroken until now.

Yet initially I *did* attempt to relate my story, Mileva. But the cart which had carried us to Z.'s home was subsequently discovered in its usual place, its steeds placidly munching oats. And not a soul in either Vex or Sion had ever heard of any "Dr. Z." His home, so I am told, has lain vacant for years, its previous tenants long deceased.

This was born out when the local constabulary forced their way into that dusty, vacant place. The police were greatly distressed by my tale of madness and homicide, of course. Yet after they discovered no trace of Edmund or Marie—no bloodstains, no bodies, not even the chairs upon which they had sat—the authorities naturally assumed my story to be some figment of a delirious illness, and laid the matter to rest.

So what to make of my experience? In truth, the events of that ghastly evening are becoming more tenuous, more fantastic with each passing day, and I increasingly find myself questioning their validity. After all, ample evidence exists to suggest that their genesis lay in tangible, organic causes; my fever, my drinking, my excited mental state. . . . Perhaps Mr. Poe *was* correct, and this wretched nightmare was but a "dream within a dream."

Were it not for what I later discovered on the last page of my journal, I think I would dismiss this entire incident as a result of overwork and overindulgence. Yet there it sits, that selfsame notebook, here beside the inkwell. Concrete evidence of—what?

The thing I was certain had been written by Z. is a short penciled notation. Yet closer examination revealed a penmanship so similar to my own that it now appears entirely possible I myself penned these figures, caught up in a fugue state of feverish activity.

This *must* be the case. For this scrawled entry directly addresses the very problem which had so vexed me before my fateful encounter with Marie, Edmund, and Z. And who else but I has been working on such a task?

It is a familiar thing, surely, this mysterious notation. A single equation. Elegant in its simplicity, profound in its implications. Here, I will set it down for you:

$E = MC^2$

But I grow weary. The composition of this missive has consumed an entire day, and soon someone will appear to trundle me off to that soothing mineral bath for which this spa is famous. And I do not wish to be chastised once again for, as my nurse herself so succinctly puts it, "exercising the mind at the expense of the body."

Tell Herr Haller at the Patent Office I am soon recovered, and will be more than capable of continuing my duties in Berne. And please, my dear, I beg of you; keep these confidences to yourself. I am sure you now realize why I earlier requested your silence.

All my love. I look forward to our reunion with the utmost impatience.

With true gratitude and humble affection, I remain,

Your devoted husband,

Albert

For Robert Aikman

THE AUTHORS

PETER STRAUB, the author of *Ghost Story, Koko, The Throat,* and many other bestselling novels, was born in Milwaukee, Wisconsin, in 1943. He has won two World Fantasy Awards and one HWA Stoker.

NORMAN PARTRIDGE has been writing horror and suspense fiction since 1989. His first short story collection won the Bram Stoker Award, and his first novel, *Slippin' into Darkness,* will be published by Zebra Books in 1995.

KATHE KOJA's latest novel is *Strange Angels.* She lives in Detroit with her husband, artist Rick Lieder, and her son.

This marks TIM SMITH's first professional sale; he promises more to come. His various past jobs include: truck driver, waiter, copy clerk, late night horror show host, tap dance instructor, bag boy, substitute teacher, and he is currently bartending at Twin City Country Club in Sandersville, Georgia.

ALAN RODGERS is the author of *Pandora, Fire, Night, Blood of the Children,* and *New Life for the Dead. Blood of the Children* was a nominee for the Horror Writers of America Bram Stoker Award; his first story (actually a novelette), 'The Boy Who Came Back from the Dead,' won a Stoker and lost a World Fantasy Award. During the mid-eighties he edited the fondly remembered horror digest, *Night Cry.* He lives in Manhattan with his wife, Amy Stout, and his two daughters, Alexandra and Andrea Rodgers.

GORDON R. ROSS is a writer/illustrator and a longtime newspaperman. He currently lives in southern Oregon.

CHET WILLIAMSON's latest novel is *Second Chance.* Among his seven other novels are *Reign, Mordenheim,* and *Dreamthorp.* Over eighty of his short stories have appeared in *The New Yorker, Playboy, The Magazine of Fantasy & Science Fiction,* and many other magazines and anthologies.

DAVID B. SILVA, after publishing *The Horror Show* for eight years, gave up the magazine to devote time to his own writing. His short stories have appeared in numerous anthologies and magazines, and in 1991 he won a Horror Writers of America Bram Stoker Award for his story "The Calling." *The Disappeared,* his fourth novel, is due out from Headline House in the summer of 1995.

CLARK PERRY's short stories have appeared in a variety of publications, including the anthology *Young Blood* and *Science Fiction Age* magazine. A graduate of the Clarion writing workshop, he lives in northwest Florida with his wife, Donna Long, and four cats.

TYSON BLUE is a contributing editor to *Cemetery Dance* and also to *Castle Rock*. He lives in upstate New York.

LAWRENCE GREENBERG is a New York City–based freelance writer who has published short stories, poetry, articles, and book reviews in such places as the *Washington Post,* the *Cleveland Plain Dealer, The Complete Vampire Companion, The Secret Prophecies of Nostradamus, Borderlands 4,* and a number of horror and SF magazines.

BRAD LINAWEAVER is a Nebula finalist and author of the Prometheus Award–winning novel *Moon of Ice.* He has sold numerous stories and articles to magazines as diverse as *Amazing, Fantastic, Galaxy, Chronicles, Famous Monsters of Filmland,* and *National Review.* A radio play of his has appeared on National Public Radio as part of the Horror House series.

THOMAS F. MONTELEONE has been a professional writer since 1972. He has published more than ninety short stories in numerous magazines and books, and has edited six anthologies, including the highly acclaimed *Borderlands* series, edited with his wife, Elizabeth. Of his twenty novels, his most recent, *The Blood of the Lamb,* received the 1993 Bram Stoker Award. His newest novel, *The Ressurrectionist,* will appear in the fall of 1995.

DON D'AMMASSA is a veteran short story writer with appearances in numerous successful anthologies. Among his recent credits are *Journeys to the Twilight Zone III,*

100 Vicious Little Vampire Stories, and *100 Weird Little Witch Tales.*

PAUL M. SAMMON is a contributing editor to *Cemetery Dance* magazine and a veteran filmmaker and short story writer. He currently lives in California. His latest books are *The King Is Dead: Tales of Elvis Post-Mortem* and *The Christmas Carol Trivia Book.* Mr. Sammon celebrated the beginning of 1995 by acting as the Digital and Optical Effects Supervisor of the recent science-fiction picture *Night Skies.*